ORSTEP

Anne Bennett was born in a back-to-back house in the Horsefair district of Birmingham. The daughter of Roman Catholic, Irish immigrants, she grew up in a tight-knit community where she was taught to be proud of her heritage. She considers herself to be an Irish Brummie and feels therefore that she has a foot in both cultures. She has four children and five grandchildren. For many years she taught in schools to the north of Birmingham. An accident put paid to her teaching career and, after moving to North Wales, Anne turned to the other great love of her life and began to write seriously. In 2006, after 16 years in a wheelchair, she miraculously regained her ability to walk.

Visit www.annebennett.co.uk to find out more about Anne and her books.

By the same author

A Little Learning
Pack Up Your Troubles
Walking Back to Happiness
Till the Sun Shines Through
Danny Boy
Daughter of Mine
Mother's Only Child
To Have and to Hold
A Sister's Promise
A Daughter's Secret
A Mother's Spirit
The Child Left Behind
Keep the Home Fires Burning
Far From Home
If You Were the Only Girl
A Girl Can Dream
A Strong Hand to Hold
Love Me Tender
Another Man's Child
Forget-Me-Not Child

ANNE BENNETT

THE CHILD ON THE DOORSTEP

HarperCollins*Publishers*

HarperCollins*Publishers*
The News Building,
1 London Bridge Street,
London SE1 9GF

www.harpercollins.co.uk

A Paperback Original 2018
2

A catalogue record for this book
is available from the British Library

ISBN: 978-0-00-816233-7

Typeset in Sabon LT Std by
Palimpsest Book Production Ltd, Falkirk, Stirlingshire

Printed and bound by CPI Group (UK) Ltd, Croydon CR0 4YY

In loving memory of Denis Bennett

ONE

Angela took her coat from the hook at the back of the door and stepped out into the early morning. The day was a chilly one – it was early yet but Angela was glad the bite of winter seemed to be gone at last, though it was only early March 1926. In the children's verse March was supposed to begin like a lion and end like a lamb so she knew they weren't quite out of the woods yet. But they were on the way to spring and that morning a hazy sun was trying to break through the clouds. Funny how it cheered a body to see the sun.

But then her good mood was dispelled a little when, despite the early hour, she saw Tressa Lawson on the road before her, carrying a cushion and an army-issue blanket. As the eldest in the family it was her job to lead her father, Pete, by the hand for he had been blinded by mustard gas in 1915. He wore his great coat against the chill of the day and immense pity for the man rose up in Angela.

'Why does he go out so early?' she'd asked Tressa one time.

1

'He says he gets the best pitch then,' Tressa had said. 'He positions himself by the tram stop in Bristol Street.'

Angela had nodded; she knew he did, for she had seen him there herself and never passed without greeting him and dropping some money in the cap on the floor before him.

'He says he gets the people waiting for the tram and those getting off, as well as those walking into the city centre by foot.' Tressa had chewed on her bottom lip before going on, 'Sometimes though, for all he sits for hours, often chilled to the bone, especially in the winter, despite his cushion and blanket, he has collected precious little. I hate the look on his face then. He hates the thought that Mammy has to take in extra washing from the big houses in Edgbaston, that he can't provide adequately for his family. He often says he feels a failure.'

Angela's intake of breath had been audible and she had hissed to Tressa, 'Your father is no failure.'

'I know that,' Tressa had said, 'but it's what Daddy thinks.'

Angela remembered him marching away to war, so proud that he had the opportunity to serve his King and country. And when it was over, four gruelling years after it had begun, they called it the 'Great War'. Personally Angela thought there was actually not anything great about that war at all. It was supposed to be the war to end all wars and all the men fighting in it had been promised a land 'fit for heroes', but in fact those who returned had nothing but the dole queue and poverty awaiting them.

Somehow, Angela could never see the decent and respectable Pete Lawson without feeling a pang to her heart. That bloody 'Great War' had also taken away Angela's beloved husband and Connie's father Barry, and at the time Angela had thought she would never get over the tremendous loss she'd felt.

The lovely letter of commendation that she had received from his commanding officer, who had said how brave and courageous a soldier he was, hadn't helped the searing ache inside her. The letter had told her that Barry had eventually lost his life saving another. While her mind screamed 'Why?' she imagined in the heat of battle there was little time for logical thought and Barry would have acted instinctively. But that act was the culmination of this very brave soldier's career; the officer had said he was recommending him for an award and in due course she received the Military Medal.

Angela still thought it cold comfort and if her husband had been a little less brave he might have been one of the ones who had marched home again. His mother, Mary McClusky, on the other hand, had been 'over the moon' that her Barry had received a medal for gallantry and Angela thought Connie might like it as she grew. It would show her what a fine father she'd had, for she was too young to remember him at all, and Angela had put the medal away carefully to show her when she was older.

In the end, despite commendations and medals, she had learnt to cope with her profound loss because she had Connie to rear and Barry's mother Mary to care for too, for they lived together. Anyway, she was by no means the only widow and when the Armistice was signed and the men who had survived were demobbed, it was only too obvious how few men there were about.

As Angela made her way to the Swan public house where she cleaned, she reflected anew on all the changes brought about because so many men had not returned from the war.

She could well remember what George Maitland, her old employer, had said on a similar subject.

He had no children and this was a great regret for him, but when the war began and the casualty figures began appearing in the paper, he had said to Angela one day when she was collecting her groceries, 'You know I've never had chick nor child belonging to me and at times that has been a cross to bear, for I would have loved a family. But now I look at my customers and see the ones who have lost sons and wonder if it is worse for them who have given birth to a boy and reared him with such a powerful love that they would willingly give their life to save him. But they are unable to save him from war and when he dies for King and country, the loss must be an overwhelming one. I have had women in the shop crying broken-heartedly about their beloved sons who will never return and at times I am almost thankful I have no sons of my own to suffer the same fate.'

Angela had often thought about George's words as the war raged on and could understand his reasoning so very well, but then she often did. In her opinion he was a very wise man. She had worked in his shop for two years before her marriage and just after it and had become very fond of him, and he had thought a lot of her too. So much so that, after he died, she found he had left her his mother's jewellery, which he had lodged in the bank with authorisation saying it was for Angela alone. It was totally separate from the will, in which everything presumably was left to his wife, Matilda.

Angela had never taken to Matilda, mainly because of the way she had been with George. She was a cold woman, who never seemed to have a high regard for him, and in Angela's hearing had never ever thrown him even a kind word, and there was no place in her life for children, or sex either, so people whispered.

By now Angela had reached the pub and would have to settle her mind to the job in hand. She went in the side door and called out to the landlord, Paddy Larkin, as she did so. She was very grateful to Paddy for offering her this job after the war, for she couldn't in all honesty say either her father-in-law, Matt, or her husband, Barry, were regular visitors there. She was more than happy to have it though, because it eased the financial pressure, and with Constance at school and Mary to see to her in the holidays, it was perfect for them all.

Angela seldom saw the landlady Breda Larkin for she was usually getting herself ready upstairs. She often wouldn't come down before ten thirty or so to open the pub at eleven and Angela would usually be on her way back home by then. However, one morning when she had been at the cleaning for three years or so, Breda got up early. She greeted Angela pleasantly enough, but when she had left she turned to her husband and said, 'She's wasted on the cleaning, that Angela McClusky.'

'What do you mean?'

'Look at her, you numbskull,' Breda said impatiently. 'Despite everything she is still a beautiful woman, blonde, busty and pleasant. She has a smile for everyone and she will bring the punters in, especially on Friday and Saturday night.'

Paddy might have bristled at being called a numbskull by his wife but he had to acknowledge what she said made sense. Angela was not only a very good-looking woman, but she had something a little special, and though she was always agreeable, she was not flirty – too flirty a woman behind the bar could cause all manner of problems. And so he put the proposition to Angela the next day. She knew it would be extra hours and so extra money and she also knew she couldn't have considered it if she hadn't Mary at home, for she would not leave Constance alone for the hours she would be behind the bar. She told Paddy she would have to ask Mary, for she would be the one looking after Connie, but it was only more for courtesy.

As she'd anticipated, her mother-in-law had no objection.

'Why would I even think about objecting?' Mary said to Angela. 'It is only two nights a week you'll not be here and I shall do what I do every night: sit before the fire and do a bit of knitting and a bit of dozing. But surely to God you won't be doing the cleaning as well?'

'No, well, I'm going to put a proposal to Paddy,' Angela said. 'He wants me Friday and Saturday night and Sunday lunchtime. So I could do the cleaning on Monday to Thursday, and if he was agreeable ask Maggie to take over the cleaning over the weekends.'

'Oh you do right to think of her,' Mary said. 'That poor girl.'

Angela knew how Mary felt for her best friend, Maggie, who was also Connie's godmother. She had married Michael Malone after the war, having been sweet on him for years, even before the war began, and had written to him when he was in the army. A few of the men from their town had been part of a pals battalion and had fought alongside each other and Angela had found out later that the shell that had killed Barry while he'd been trying to save another had blown Michael's left leg clean off.

He had thought any future with Maggie was scuppered,

that she wouldn't want to saddle herself with a one-legged man, but Angela knew her friend was a bigger person than that. And Maggie had said that it made no difference to the way she felt about him and Angela knew she spoke the truth. She also knew if Barry had lost his leg, but came home to her, she would have rejoiced. Though getting Michael to understand that took Maggie some time.

A major slump after the war meant that, with strapping able-bodied men finding any sort of employment hard to come by, no one was prepared to even consider employing a one-legged man, and he felt bad that he couldn't provide for Maggie. Maggie had said she didn't need providing for, and besides, as he had been so disabled in the war, Michael had been awarded a pension of twenty-eight shillings a week. Angela was pleased for them both, but was a little confused that as a war widow she qualified for a pension of only eighteen shillings, with an extra shilling added for Connie.

'No understanding the way governments work,' Mary had said when this had been explained to her after the war.

Angela had quite a sizeable nest egg in the post office because of her well-paid war work in munitions making and delivering shells, as well as the money Barry was sending her. But savings didn't last for ever if you had to draw on them constantly and so when Paddy Larkin had offered her a job she hadn't even had to think about it. She knew Maggie too wouldn't hesitate, because any job was better than no job, and it would do her very well for now.

'It'll be money the government won't know about because Paddy pays you in hand,' Angela pointed out. 'Will Michael mind that it's you working and not him?'

'He may well mind,' Maggie said. 'But he is above all a

realist. And so he will not show any resentment to me or give me any sort of hard time.'

'He's a good man you have there, Maggie.'

'I know it,' Maggie said. 'But the war exacted a heavy price from us one way and the other. Oh, I know Michael survived and Barry and our Syd didn't so maybe I shouldn't moan, but I would like to take the look of failure from his face. He knows in the present climate he hasn't the chance of a sniff of any form of employment and I can't even give him a child.'

She caught sight of Angela's face and went on, 'I see you think it irresponsible to bring another life in the world just now when our financial position isn't great and not likely to improve very much. But, oh, Angela, how I long to hold my own child in my arms – a wee girl like Connie, or a boy the image of his father. I don't think it will ever happen, that's the point, and that's hard to bear.'

Angela was upset to see her friend so downhearted and the worst of it was everything she said was true; none of the girls she worked in the munitions with had become pregnant. This was such a phenomenon across the country that investigations had been made and it was found that the sulphur many of them worked with had made them infertile.

Angela had wished at the time she had become infertile too and then there might have been no repercussions from the terrible attack that day she had driven to the docks for the first time. She had been one of the first and only female delivery drivers, transporting munitions around the country. It had been on one of these trips that something terrible had happened, something she had tried to push out of her mind but which had come back to haunt her and caused her to make the most heart-breaking decision of her life.

One dreadful night she had been attacked and viciously raped when making a munitions delivery at night in a strange town. Her assault had left her scarred, but worse, it had left her with child. With no other course available, with a husband away fighting at war and nowhere to turn, Angela had been forced to leave the child, a young girl with fair hair and blue eyes like her own, on the workhouse steps. The shame and the pain of it had stayed with her and Angela had had to shut off the past to keep the pain at bay.

At least she had Connie, though, who she loved with all her heart and soul, while poor Maggie had nothing. Angela had pushed all the awful memories away. Better to focus on the present and Connie's future.

Maggie was grateful for the chance of employment at the Swan and took herself off to see Mr Larkin. They got on fine and the upshot was that she was to take on the weekend cleaning, while Angela worked behind the bar.

In fact Paddy felt it was scandalous that two women, one a widow and one with a disabled husband, should have to take on jobs like the ones he was offering to keep the wolf from the door.

'Those men fought for King and country, both of them,' he said to his wife one night as they prepared for bed. 'You'd think their relatives would be taken care of if they were killed like Barry McClusky, or crippled like Maggie's husband, or Pete Lawson, blinded, and so many more.'

'You've just said it though, haven't you?' Breda said. 'So many more. Think about it, there were thousand upon thousand killed and even more injured. I should think it takes a great deal of money to fight a war and so they haven't got the money to provide adequately for all the dependants.'

'And since when have the government cared about the likes of us anyway?' Paddy said morosely. 'Cannon fodder, the common people are.'

'That's about the shape of it,' Breda said. 'And people do what they can to survive. And now Maggie doesn't have to make a decision this winter whether to order another hundredweight of coal or buy the makings for a dinner, and neither does Angela, so at least we have made two of those dependants happier.'

'And that's all we can do, I suppose.'

'It is,' Breda said decidedly. 'Now come to bed and stop fretting about things you can do nothing to change.'

As Angela worked, whether it was pulling pints behind the bar or cleaning, she was always well aware of what she owed Mary, for without her stalwart help in caring for Connie, she knew their lives would have been financially harder. But she didn't just appreciate Mary for the help she gave but she was glad she was there with them. She had been part of her life since as far back as she could remember and she hadn't a clue how she was going to manage without her. And though Mary might have years to live yet, she somehow doubted it. The news of Barry's death had hit her for six, combined with the death of two of her other sons in 1912 as they had travelled to America on the *Titanic* to seek better prospects, and the grief had done much to hasten the death of her husband. The bad times were wearing her down and Mary hadn't the resilience of youth.

It wasn't all bad. Mary still thought a great deal about

her other two sons in America who had gone ahead some years before the *Titanic* disaster, and she was glad they were so happy in their new lives. She often wished she could see them again just the once, but she had known when she kissed them goodbye it was final. They wrote regularly though, and she was grateful for that, especially when they included dollar bills folded inside the letter. They wrote about things she could barely imagine, like the flashing neon lights in a place called Times Square and the trolley buses and the trains that run underground in the bowels of the earth and the motor cars they helped build that were now filling the wide straight roads of America.

And they wrote of their marriages – for Colm had followed his brother Finbarr and married a Roman Catholic girl – and sent pictures of their weddings. But Mary could barely recognise her sons and their wives, and the babies born later were like the photographs of strangers, names on a page, and sometimes she was heart-sore knowing that she would never hold her sons' children in her arms and take joy in them. Connie helped there, for she still had to be looked after, and Mary knew Connie loved her with a passion that eased the pain in her heart.

As Connie grew up, she became very good friends with a girl in her class called Sarah Maguire. Angela had no problem with her having Sarah as her special friend as she herself had been best friends with Maggie Malone, née Maguire, at a similar age. She was friendly with Sarah's mother Maeve and knew them to be a respectable family and was glad to see Connie making friends of her own. It wasn't as if she'd be all that far away in any case, for the Maguires lived just a wee bit down Bell Barn Road on the corner of Great Colmore Street.

The Maguire home was so different from Connie's – although cramped and noisy it was filled with a vibrancy and vitality often lacking in her own. She liked them all, even Sarah's parents. She saw little of Mr Maguire but what she saw she liked. He was called James and his eldest son, wee Jimmy, was named after him. He had big swollen muscles that often strained against the fabric of his shirts, which he usually wore folded up to the elbow so that his lower arms looked like giant hams, and led to large, red, gnarled hands. His face was equally red, with his nose sort of splashed against it and his wide, generous lips tilted upwards so it looked as if he was permanently smiling. He did smile a lot anyway and laugh, and a full-throated and very infectious laugh it was too. Added to this he had a fine head of brown hair which was sprinkled only lightly with grey.

Mrs Maguire, Maeve, had an equally dark head of hair though it was always tied away from her face in a bun of some sort. She wasn't as pretty as Connie's own mother – few people were – but Maeve Maguire's face had an almost serene look seldom seen on those with a houseful of children. Connie had never heard her raise her voice and Sarah said she almost never did. So her face had a contented look about it, with no lines pulling her mouth down, although there were creases around her eyes which were a strange grey-green colour.

'Do you mind me coming round so often?' Connie asked her once. 'My granny says I mustn't annoy you.'

Mrs Maguire gave an almost tinkling laugh. 'Child dear, you don't annoy me in the slightest,' she said. 'You are like a ray of sunshine. And anyway, when you have so many, one more makes little difference and there is more company for you here. The children's friends are always welcome and you help Sarah with the jobs she must do, so you must assure your granny you are no trouble.'

Maeve Maguire had hit the nail on the head, for Connie, though she loved her mother and grandmother dearly, was often lonely. There was something else too. Sometimes her mother seemed far away. She was there in person but when Connie spoke, she sometimes didn't answer, didn't seem to hear her and her eyes had a faraway look in them. She had asked her grandmother about it and Mary had said that her mother was still remembering her daddy, Barry.

'You said that when I asked you why she was sad at Christmas.'

'Yes. She's remembering then too.'

'But, Daddy didn't die at Christmas.'

'No, but Christmas is a time to remember loved ones, especially those you might not see again,' Mary had said and added, 'Don't you feel the same when you remember your daddy?'

Connie didn't; in fact, if she was absolutely honest, she didn't remember her daddy at all, just the things people had told her about him. But even though she was a child she had known her granny would not like her to share those thoughts and so she contented herself by saying, 'Mmm, I suppose.'

So she went for company to Sarah and the Maguire house. They sat together at school and met often on Saturdays and holiday times and on Sundays at Mass.

'Beats me how you don't run out of things to say,' Angela commented dryly as they sat down for an early meal before she went to serve behind the bar one Saturday evening.

It was funny but they never did. They often talked about

their families and one Saturday as they went along Bristol Street, fetching errands for Maeve and pushing the slumbering baby Maura in the pram, Connie suddenly said, 'Aren't your mammy's eyes an unusual colour?'

'I suppose,' Sarah said. 'Neither one thing or the other. Mine are the same. Look.'

'Oh, I never noticed,' Connie said.

'All us girls are the same,' Sarah said. 'Well, that is, Kathy and Siobhan are. Too early to tell with Maura yet and the boys both look like Daddy.'

'It must have been more noticeable with your mother because she has her hair pulled back from her face,' Connie said. 'But now I come to look closer you look very like your mother.'

'Oh, the shape of my face is the same and my mouth is and thank goodness my nose is like Mammy's too. I would hate to have a nose like my father's, which isn't really any shape at all. Looks like it's been broken and not fixed properly or something. I asked him once and he said that if it had been broken he hadn't been aware of it. Mammy said she grew up nearly beside him on the farm in Ireland and Daddy grew up with a rake of brothers, seven or eight of them with only a year between them all. There were girls too, cos there were thirteen altogether, and Mammy said near every time she saw the boys two or three of them would be scrapping on the ground like puppies. She said Daddy's nose could have been broken a number of times and their mother wouldn't have had time to blow her own nose, never mind notice that one of the tribe had theirs busted.'

The two girls burst out laughing. 'Why do boys do that, fight and things?'

Sarah shrugged. 'Who'd know the answer to that or care either? It's just what boys do.'

'Glad I'm a girl.'

'And I am,' Sarah said. 'And it's a blooming good job because there's nothing to be done about it if we were unhappy. And never mind the likenesses in my family, what about yours? You look just like your mother. I've never seen hair so blonde and your ringlets are natural, aren't they? I mean, you don't have to put rags in your hair or anything.'

Connie shook her head so the ringlets held away from her face with a band swung from side to side.

'No,' she said. 'They're natural all right, it's just that I can't ever wear my hair loose for school. Mammy insists I have it in plaits.'

'That's because of the risk of nits,' Sarah said. 'The same reason Mammy won't let me grow mine long. But still, you're luckier than me because when you're old enough you can wear your hair any way you like and you've got the most startling blue eyes.'

'I know, I seem to have taken all things from my mammy and none from my daddy at all.'

'D'you remember your daddy?'

Connie shook her head. 'Not him, the person. Sometimes I think I do because I've been told so much about him, but I know what he looks like because Mammy has a picture of him in a silver frame on the sideboard. Remember I showed you? I don't look like him at all.'

'That's how it is sometimes though, isn't it?' Sarah said.

'Oh yes,' Connie said as Sarah's words tugged at her memory. 'My mammy was born with golden locks and blue eyes like mine, my grandmother said, but she's not my

15

mammy's real mother. My mammy's real mother died in Ireland when she was a babby, like I told you before.'

'Yes,' Sarah said, 'she lost the rest of her Irish family and that's when she went to live with the McCluskys who came to England. Their son Barry was your daddy.'

Connie nodded and added, 'And my daddy was killed in the war.'

That wasn't uncommon and Sarah said, 'Yes, I think lots of daddies were. But maybe your daddy and your other granny are in heaven this minute looking down on us all?'

'I'd like to think it.'

'Don't say you have doubts,' Sarah said with mock horror. 'If you have, keep them to yourself, for if Father Brannigan hears you he will wash your mouth out with carbolic.'

Connie grinned at her friend and said, 'When I die I shall ask God if I can pop back and tell everyone it's true.'

Sarah laughed. 'You are a fool, Connie. You'll have to come back as a ghost and that will frighten everyone to death,' she said. 'Anyway, when were you thinking of dying?'

'Oh, not for ages yet.'

'Good,' Sarah said. 'In the meantime I think we better get on with Mammy's shopping or she'll think we've got lost. And it looks like Maura is waking up so our peace is probably gone anyway.'

TWO

Early in 1924, when Connie and Sarah were almost eleven, Sarah's eldest sister, Kathy had left school and gone to work in the Grand Hotel in Colmore Row, Birmingham. Though she worked long hours, she loved the job and enthused about it so much that Sarah's other elder sister, Siobhan, applied for a job there too two years later when she also left school.

Although her sisters taking live-in jobs meant that they were no longer all squashed on the one fairly small mattress in the attic, and there was more space generally and they couldn't boss her about any more, Sarah missed them a great deal. She also knew, now that Siobhan had joined Kathy, the carefree days of her childhood were at an end, for she was the eldest girl and so she would be the one now to help her mother. She had been cushioned by the presence of two older sisters but now it was time to step up as the eldest daughter and help her mother and take a hand with her younger siblings, particularly Maura who was no longer a cute baby but a spoilt toddler. Sarah was convinced that Maura's

17

screams when her wishes were thwarted could shatter glass and her tantrums had to be seen to be believed.

Connie too had begun to rethink her life. She was coming up to thirteen now and in the senior school, and couldn't miss the reports of the miners' General Strike.

Now that the coal exports had fallen since the Great War, the miners' wages were reduced from £6.00 to £3.90. The government also wanted them to work longer hours for that, and a phrase was coined that was printed in the papers:

Not a penny off the pay and not a minute on the day.

No buses, trams or trains ran anywhere, no newspapers were printed or goods unloaded from the docks, the drop forges and foundries grew silent, no coal was mined and, much to the delight of many children, schools were closed. The strike finished after nine days but little had changed and though the miners tried to hang on longer they were forced to capitulate in the end.

'It is so sad really,' Angela said, reading it out to her daughter from the newly printed newspaper. 'We should be thankful we are so much better off than many.'

'We could be better off still if you would let me leave school next year when I am fourteen and get a job like Sarah intends.'

'Connie, we have been through all this.'

'No, we haven't really done that at all,' Connie said. 'You've told me what you want me to do with my life, that's all.'

Angela frowned, for this wasn't the way her compliant daughter usually behaved.

'You know that going on to take your School Certificate and going on to college or university is what I've been saving for. What's got into you?'

'Nothing,' Connie said. 'It's just that . . . Look, Mammy,

if you hadn't me to look after you would have more money. You could stop worrying about money, wipe the frown from your brow.'

'If I've got a frown on my brow,' Angela said testily, 'it's because I cannot understand the ungratefulness of a girl being handed the chance of a better future on a plate, which many would give their eye teeth for, and rejecting it in that cavalier way and without a word of thanks for the sacrifices I've made for you.'

Connie felt immediately contrite.

'I'm sorry, Mammy,' she said. 'I do appreciate all you do for me and I am grateful, truly I am.'

'I sense a "but" coming.'

'It's just that if I go on to matriculate I won't fit in with the others, maybe even Sarah will think I am getting too big for my boots and . . .'

'Connie, this is what your father wanted,' Angela said and Connie knew she had lost. 'He paid the ultimate price and fought and died to make the world a safer place for you. He wanted the best for you in all things, including education. Are you going to let him down?'

How could Connie answer that? There was only one way.

'Of course not, Mammy. If it means so much to you and meant so much to my father, then I will do my level best to make you proud of me when I matriculate. Maybe Daddy will be looking down on me and be proud too.'

Angela gave Connie a kiss. 'I'm sure he is, my darling girl, and I'm glad you have seen sense and we won't have to speak of this again.'

Connie hid her sigh of exasperation and thought, as she wasn't going to be leaving school any time soon, it was about time she started making herself more useful. She decided she would take care of her grandmother, rather than the other way round, and help her mother around the house far more.

So the next morning she slipped out of the bed she shared with Mary in the attic and, while her mother set off for work, made a pan of porridge and a pot of tea and had them waiting for Mary when she had eased her creaking body from the bed, dressed with care and stumbled stiff-legged down the stairs. She also filled a bucket with water from the tap in the yard and the scuttle with coal from the cellar and told her grandmother she would do the same every morning.

And she did and Angela was pleased at her thoughtfulness. On Monday morning Connie began rising even earlier to try to be the first one to fill the copper in the brew house with water from the tap in the yard, light the gas under it and sprinkle the water with soap suds as it heated. Then she would carry all the whites down to boil up while Angela made porridge for them all before she left for work. By the time Connie had eaten breakfast and seen to her grandmother, the whites were boiling in the copper and she would ladle the washing out with the wooden tongs into one of the sinks and empty the copper for others to use. That was as much as she could manage on school days and her mother would deal with everything else after she had finished at the pub, for lateness at school was not tolerated and all latecomers were caned.

In the holidays Connie would help her mother pound the other clothes in the maiding tub with the poss stick, or rub at persistent dirt with soap and the wash board. Then whites were put in a sink with Beckit's Blue added, and sometimes another with starch, before everything was rinsed well, put through the mangle and pegged on lines lifted to the sky with long, long props to flap dry in the sooty air.

For all they were such a small household, it took most of the day to do the washing and most of Tuesday to do the ironing, unless of course it had rained on the Monday, in which case the damp washing would probably still be draped around the room on Tuesday, cutting off much of the heat from the fire and filling the air with steam. Connie never moaned about this because she knew it was far worse for many bigger families, like the Maguires for instance. She could only imagine the amount of clothes and bedding, towels and clothes they went through in a week, though Sarah said that was another thing that had become easier since her sisters had left home.

'I can't wait to do that myself either,' Sarah said.

'What?'

'Leave home,' said Sarah. 'Siobhan and Kathy are going to keep an eye out for a job at their place and as soon as I am fourteen I'm off.'

'Does your mother know that?'

'Course. Only what she expected,' Sarah said. Then she looked at Connie and said, 'Your mammy wants you to take your School Certificate exam and go to college, don't she?'

Angela nodded her head.

'Do you want to?' Sarah asked

'No,' Angela said. 'I want to get out and work. All my life Mammy has worked and provided for me and Granny and I want her to take life easy for a change. If I am earning she will be able to do that. But . . .' she gave a shrug, 'she has her heart set on it. She has been to see the teacher and she says I am one of the children that could really benefit from a secondary education and so that is what she is determined I will have.'

'How will she afford it?'

'I asked my granny that when she first said it and Granny said all through the war when Mammy was earning good money in the munitions, every spare penny was saved for that very purpose. She said there is a tidy sum in the post office now.'

'Is your granny for it too then?'

Angela shook her head. 'Granny thinks no good comes of stepping out of your class.'

'Yeah, my mother thinks that too,' Sarah said. 'I mean, we live here in a back-to-back house and when we marry it will likely be to someone from round here. And, as my mother says, where will your fine education get you then? And my father says there's little point in teaching girls any more than the basics because they only get married. He said they should spend less time at school and more with their mothers learning to keep house and cook and rear babies.'

'I can see that those things might be useful,' Connie said. 'But we sort of learn to do those things anyway, don't we? And I like school.'

'I know you do,' Sarah said. 'Everyone thinks you're crazy, especially the boys.'

'Huh, as if anyone gives a jot about what boys think or say.'

'One day we might care a great deal,' Sarah said, smiling broadly.

'Maybe we will, but we'll be older then and so will they, so it might make better sense,' Connie said. 'But for now I wouldn't give tuppence for their opinion.'

'All right but your opinion should matter,' Sarah said. 'Tell your mother how you feel.'

'I can't,' Connie said. 'She'd be so upset.'

She remembered how her grandmother told her how her mother would go to put more money in the post office.

'It was all she thought about. Granny said she was even worse when she found out about the death of Barry. Mammy said the physical loss of him was one thing but she would make sure his daughter did not suffer educationally. She said she owed it to Barry to give her the best start she could. What the teacher said cemented that feeling really.'

How then could Connie throw all the plans she had made in her face? Connie was well aware of the special place she had in her mother's heart and for that reason she couldn't bear to hurt her. She knew she had a special place in her grandmother's heart too and it pained her to see her growing frailer with every passing month.

'I really don't know what I'll do when she's not there any more,' she confided to Sarah one day as they walked home from school together.

It was mid-June and the days were becoming warmer and Sarah said, 'She is bound to rally a little now the summer is here. The winter was a long one and a bone-chilling one and, as my mother says, enough to put years on anyone.'

Connie smiled because Sarah's mother was a great one for her sayings.

'And she is oldish, isn't she?' Sarah put in.

Connie nodded. 'Sixty-five.'

'Well, that's a good age.'

'I know, but that doesn't help,' Connie lamented. 'She has

been here all my life and very near all Mammy's life too. The pair of us will be lost without her.'

'You'll have to help one another.'

'Mmm,' she said, knowing Sarah probably didn't understand the closeness between her and her granny because both her grandparents had died when she was just young. It wasn't just closeness either; she could tell her grandmother anything, more than she could share with her mother. She loved the special times they shared when her mother worked in the evening in the pub. Her granny liked nothing better than to talk about days gone by, which Connie sometimes called 'the olden days' to tease Mary, and Connie loved to hear about how life was years ago. It was the only way she got to know anything, for her mother seemed to have no interest in how things had been.

'What's past is past, Connie, and there is no point in raking it all up again,' Angela had said.

That was all very well, but now she was thirteen Connie wanted to know how it came about that Mary had brought her mother up from when she was a toddler. That bit of information she had gleaned. She knew her mother's mammy had died in Ireland, but didn't know when, or anything else really.

Mary knew why Angela didn't want to talk or even think about the past and the dreadful decision she had been forced to make. Connie didn't know that, however, and Mary thought she had a point when she said, 'Mammy thinks that what has passed isn't important because she has lived it and doesn't want to remember, but I haven't and I want to know.'

Mary thought that only natural. The child didn't need to know everything, but it was understandable that she wanted to know where she came from.

'I'll tell you, when we have some quiet time together, just

you and I,' Mary promised and she did, the following day, which was a Friday night. With Angela off to work and the dishes washed, Connie sat in front of the fire opposite her granny with her bedtime mug of cocoa and learned about the disease that killed every member of her mother's family. Angela had survived only because she had been taken to Mary McClusky before the disease had really taken hold.

'Your dear grandmother was distracted,' Mary said. 'She didn't want to leave Angela, but the first child with TB had contracted it at the school and your namesake, Connie, knew she had little chance of protecting the other children from it because they were all at school too. But Angela had a chance if she was sent away.'

'Did she know they were all going to die?'

'No, of course she didn't know, but she knew TB was a killer, still is a killer, we all knew. Angela's family, who were called Kennedy, were not the first family wiped out with the same thing.'

'And only my mammy survived,' Connie mused. 'Did you mind looking after her?'

'Lord bless you, love, of course I didn't,' Mary said. 'I would take in any child in similar circumstances, but Angela was the daughter of my dear friend and, as your grandfather, Matt, often said to me, the boot could have been on the other foot, for our children were at the same school. To tell you the truth, I was proper cut up about the death of your other grandparents and their wee weans, but looking after your mammy meant I had to take a grip on myself. I knew that by looking after Angela the best way I could I was doing what my friend would want and it was the only thing I could do to help her. It helped me cope, because I was low after

Maeve's death. She was followed by her husband who was too downhearted to fight the disease that he had seen take his wife and family one by one.'

'What part of Ireland was this?'

'It was Donegal,' Mary said. 'We came to England in 1900 when your mother was four. It wasn't really a choice because the farm had failed, the animals died and the crops took a blight, and with one thing and another we had to leave the farm.'

'So you came here?'

'Not just like that we didn't,' Mary said. 'We first had to sell the farm to get the money to come. Once here, we had nowhere to live, but luckily for us, our old neighbours in Ireland, the Dohertys, had come to England years before. You know Norah and Mick Doherty?'

'Yes, they live in Grant Street.'

'Well, they put us up till we could find this place,' Mary said. 'It was kind of them because it was a squash for all of us. In fact, there was so little space my four eldest had to sleep next door.'

'Next door?'

'Well, two doors down with a lovely man called Stan Bishop and his wife Kate who had an empty attic and the boys slept there.'

Connie wrinkled her nose and said, 'I don't know anyone called Bishop.'

'No one there of that name,' Mary said a little sadly. 'Stan's wife died and then he enlisted in the army and was killed like your daddy and many more besides,' Mary finished, deciding that Connie had no need to know about the existence of Stan's son. It would only complicate matters.

But though Connie hadn't recognised the name, she knew about the woman who had died after her baby was born, because though she'd only been a child, she had overheard adults talking of how sad it was. There had never been any sign of a baby and so she had presumed the baby had died too.

'You haven't got four elder sons any more, have you, Granny?' Connie said. 'Mammy said two died but wouldn't say how. She said how they died wasn't important.'

Mary sighed. 'I suppose she's right in a way,' she said. 'Knowing all the ins and outs of it will not make any difference to the fact that they are dead and gone. They died trying to join their brothers in New York, but they travelled on the *Titanic*.'

Connie gave a gasp and Mary said, 'Do you know about the *Titanic*?'

Connie nodded. 'We were told about it at school. They said it was the biggest ship ever and it was her maiden voyage and she sank and many people died.'

'Including my two sons, but there were whole families, men, women and children, even wee babies, lost.'

'I know,' Connie said. 'It must have been really awful to have to deal with that.'

'I didn't think I would ever recover,' Mary admitted. 'And your granddad was never the same after. Officially he died from a tumour in his stomach, but I know he really died from heartache. It wasn't just that the boys died, though that was hard enough to bear. It was the way they died too, for they would have suffered, they would have frozen to death. It said in the paper most steerage passengers – that's what they call the poorest travellers down in the bowels of the

27

ship – didn't even reach the deck before the ship sank and, even if they had, there were not enough lifeboats for the numbers on the ship.'

'I know,' Connie said. 'The teacher told us that. I thought it was stupid to build a ship with too few lifeboats for all the passengers.'

'And so did I, Connie,' Mary said. 'And now that's one mystery cleared up for you and it's time for bed. You finished that cocoa ages ago.'

'Yes, but—'

'Yes but nothing and don't forget your prayers.'

'Granny, there's loads more I want to know.'

'Maybe but that's all you're getting tonight,' Mary said. 'I'll tell you some more tomorrow night.'

'Promise?'

'Promise,' Mary agreed and then, as Connie opened the door to the stairs, she said, 'And Connie, while the things I have told you and may tell you yet are not exactly secrets, if your mother wants to keep the past hidden she'll not want all and sundry talking about it.'

'All right. I can tell Sarah though, can't I?'

And as Mary hesitated, Connie pleaded, 'Please, Granny, she's my best friend and she'll not tell another soul if I tell her not to.'

Mary remembered Angela and her best friend, Maggie, the pair of them thick as thieves and always sharing and swapping secrets. Connie and Sarah were the same and so she relented and said, 'All right, but just Sarah, mind.'

'I only go round with Sarah,' Connie said. 'I wouldn't share things with anyone else.'

Mary knew she wouldn't. Some children growing up had

a wide circle of friends, but with Angela and now Connie they had just one best friend.

Connie told Sarah the following afternoon after first extracting a promise that she wouldn't tell anyone else.

'It's like a story, isn't it?' she said to Connie.

Connie nodded happily. 'It's nice knowing about your family, even if bad things happened like my uncles drowning in the Atlantic Ocean when their ship went down. Anyway Granny said she'll tell me more tonight after Mammy's gone to work.'

'Chapter Two tomorrow then,' said Sarah.

That night Connie rushed through her jobs and had only just got settled before the fire when she said, 'Granny, did Mammy miss her own mammy?'

Mary shook her head. 'She was too young,' she said. 'I know sometimes as she was growing up she felt bad she couldn't remember her family. She used to study the picture – you know, the one on the sideboard.'

'The one of my grandparents on their wedding day,' Connie said. 'Mammy told me that much. They wore funny clothes.'

'It was the style then,' Mary said.

'It was a shame Mammy couldn't remember anything about either of them,' Connie said. 'I know a little bit of how that feels because I can't remember my daddy. I'm glad as well that I have a picture so I know what he looked like. But that's all, so it's good that Mammy at least knew what her parents looked like.'

'Yes, that's why she was so taken with the locket.' Mary stopped suddenly and Connie watched a crimson flush flood over her grandmother's face. She had never intended to mention the locket because it brought back that distressing time when Angela was forced to do that almost unforgivable thing. Maybe Angela was right and the past should be left in the past.

However, Connie didn't connect her grandmother's odd behaviour with anything she said, she thought rather that she was having some sort of seizure.

'Granny,' she said. 'Are you all right?'

And when Mary didn't answer she put her hand on her grandmother's shoulder and said again, 'Granny, is anything the matter?'

Connie's touch and anxious voice roused Mary, who knew that now she had mentioned the locket she had to give Connie some explanation. She looked at her beloved granddaughter and said, 'No, I'm fine. Sometimes memories crowd in my mind and just then I remembered how upset your mother was when she lost the locket, for it meant so much to her.'

'I've never heard of it before.'

'That would be why,' Mary said. 'It was beautiful and bought by your grandfather and given to your grandmother on their wedding day. Your grandmother gave it into my keeping when I took charge of Angela and said if anything happened to them I was to give it to Angela on her wedding day.'

'And you did.'

'Of course,' Mary said. 'Your mammy was moved to tears to be holding something in her hand that had once belonged to her mother.'

'And she lost it?'

'Yes,' Mary said. 'Maybe the clasp was faulty or something. But, however it happened, she lost it on the way home from the munitions one night.'

'Oh, I bet she was upset,' Connie said. 'Did she look for it, or inform the police or something?'

'Oh, I can't remember the details of what she did now,' Mary said somewhat vaguely. 'But I believe she tried all ways to recover it.'

Mary thought of the locket, left in the care of the tiny baby on the workhouse steps, the only reminder of the mother who gave her away.

'Ah, someone will have picked it up and pocketed it with no idea what it means to the person who lost it,' Connie said. 'Was there anything inside?'

'Oh yes,' said Mary. 'There was a miniature of the picture on the sideboard, your grandparents' wedding day, and in the other side some ringlets from your mammy's hair tied tight with a red ribbon, for she had perfect ringlets just as you do.'

'Oh, I wish she still had it.'

'It was supposed to come to you on your wedding day.'

'Oh,' said Connie, surprised at the disappointment she felt that this wouldn't happen now. It wasn't as if she remembered ever even seeing the locket.

'Don't ever mention the locket to your mother though,' Mary warned.

Connie shook her head. 'I wouldn't. She must have been upset when she lost it and it would just make her sad. What did she do in the munitions? I know she worked there. I remember that and you used to take me to the nursery and then to school, but she doesn't like talking about what she did.'

'She made shells,' Mary said. 'It was in a very hot, noisy, smelly factory. They couldn't wear anything metal that might

31

cause a spark as that could easily cause an explosion – everything metal, even hair grips, had to be removed. Your mammy used to leave her wedding ring and locket here in the end.'

It was on the tip of Connie's tongue to ask, if her mammy had left the locket at home, how had she managed to lose it coming home from the munitions. She actually opened her mouth to ask, but she was forestalled for Mary went on, 'I was on at her to leave there at first, get something not so dangerous, but she said, though she hated doing it, there was a desperate shortage of shells. In the end though, she was seldom in the factory for they taught her to drive and she used to drive the lorries all over the country.'

'Golly, did she?' Connie said and she thought of her mother who, despite the fact she pulled pints at the pub, and cleaned there too, was so essentially a housewife and a mother and yet she had this quite exciting past. She thought of her behind the wheel of some of the big trucks chugging along Bristol Street and somehow the image didn't seem to fit.

'I find it hard to think of Mammy doing that.'

'Oh she did,' Mary said. 'And at first I was pleased that she was out of the smelly factory, but then I thought that driving those shells all over the place was no safer than making them in the first place. Really, in a war of that magnitude, people, and not just soldiers, had to be prepared to take risks and do things they wouldn't dream of doing in peacetime. And of course it was very well paid and that was important for your mother.'

'Yes,' Connie said with a slight sigh. 'So she could save some of it for my secondary education.'

'Yes, but more than that, she's thinking of university.'

Connie could hardly believe her ears. 'But, Granny, people like me don't go to university.'

Mary nodded. 'I agree, but what stops them if they have the brains to pass the exams?'

'Cost, I suppose.'

'And what if your mother could afford to send you?'

'How? Just how big is this nest egg?'

'Not that big,' Mary said. 'But your mother has something else.'

'What?'

'Your mother left school at fourteen and went to work for a grocer, by the name of George Maitland,' Mary said. 'Angela loved serving in the shop and all and was so pleasant and hardworking George said she was a godsend and I think he felt quite paternal towards her. She was there before she married Barry and after, till just a few weeks before you were born. George paid good money, especially for a girl in those days, and sent home a big basket of groceries every week too. He was very good to us and Angela was quite fond of him. He died suddenly just after your father enlisted and, though his shop and all went to his wife, he left some of his mother's jewellery to Angela.'

'He gave some of his mother's jewellery to Mammy?' Connie almost squealed in excitement. 'Is it valuable?'

'I'd say it must be worth something for it to be lodged in the bank for safe-keeping. The bank manager was anxious for Angela to see it and give him instructions as to what she wanted to do with it. However, Angela couldn't get there in normal opening hours for she was by then working long hours in the munitions, so the bank manager opened the bank especially so she could see what George had left her.'

'You went into a bank?' Connie said incredulously.

'I did,' Mary said. 'I went to support Angela, for she didn't want to go on her own and no wonder. Going into the bank in the normal way of things would have been nerve-wracking enough, but as the bank was opened especially just for us we were the only ones in there. Tell you, our boots sounded very loud on those marble floors and the lofty domed ceilings seemed to be miles away, and all around us were gleaming high counters with grilles in front of them. It was all very grand and I don't know how your mammy felt, but I was very uncomfortable.'

'But you saw the jewellery?'

Mary nodded. 'The bank manager took us into a special room for that.'

'And so what did you think of it?'

'It was very fine.'

'Is that all you can say?' Connie said, disappointed.

'What d'you want me to say?' Mary said. 'I know nothing about jewellery and this was during the war nine or ten years ago and I have never set eyes on any of it since. Anyway, that's what the bank manager said when Angela asked him if any of it was valuable. He said he didn't know the absolute value of it, because he wasn't a jeweller, but he did say there were some fine pieces there. He offered to get them valued, but your mammy said not to bother, that she could make no decision till the war was over and your daddy was back home. Till then she was leaving them in the bank.'

'But he didn't come home.'

'No, he didn't,' said Mary with a sigh. 'But she had a plan for what to do with it anyway, for she told me. And if he had survived the war, Barry would have supported her, for all that pair thought about was you.'

'What was the plan?'

'To sell most of the jewellery to enable you to go as far as you were able in your education and save a couple of the prettiest pieces to give you on your wedding day in place of the locket. There,' said Mary. 'I probably wasn't meant to tell you that, but the damage is done now.'

'I'm glad I know,' Connie said. 'But I wish Mammy wasn't so set on this. I really don't think I am that brainy and, even if I was, I don't want all this money spent on me. It's her money, she's earned it, and I would rather she spent it on herself and wore the jewellery someone was kind enough to leave her in a will or whatever. I'm sure that's what this George Maitland intended. I bet he never imagined for one minute that she would plan to sell it all and give all the money made to someone else.'

'I agree with you,' Mary said. 'But I doubt you will ever get your mother to see things that way. Educating you seems to be her life's work.'

'I know,' Connie agreed gloomily. 'And I suppose I must accept it, unless of course at the end I turn out to be a real dumb cluck and she can see for herself that funding further education would be money wasted.'

'There is a saying that you can't make a silk purse out of a sow's ear,' Mary said.

'Of course you can't,' Connie said. 'And that's what Mammy is trying to do, make me out to be someone I'm not and someone I don't want to be either.'

However, they knew all the talking under the sun would not change Angela's opinion once her mind was made up.

THREE

A few weeks later it was almost time for the schools to break up for the summer. Connie was pleased, for it meant she would be able to help her mother more, especially in looking after her grandmother, whose health had had a little boost in the warm days they'd had of late.

Both Angela and Connie were surprised when the knock came to the door, for few people knocked in these streets except to collect debts. As Angela was in the cellar getting a scuttleful of coal, Connie went to open the door. She saw at once that the young man outside looking at her quizzically was not of these parts. He had no hat, but his brown hair was brushed sleek and she could tell that the navy suit he had on was of top quality. Beneath it his shirt was snow-white and the handkerchief in his top pocket matched the tie, which was fastened with a gold tie pin. Gold cufflinks glistened in the shirt sleeves just peeping out from beneath his jacket and he wore shoes, not boots, and they were black leather and polished so they shone.

Suits were familiar to Connie for most men wore them

for Mass unless their wives hadn't the money to get it from the pawn shop where most suits were taken on Monday morning. However, none of the suits she'd seen were like the one the young man had on, nor were they worn in the same way. Her neighbours often looked uncomfortable in their suits, encased some of them seemed, but this young man wore his suit as easily as if he wore one every day.

All this Connie took in in an instant, and the young man was fair dazzled by Connie's smile, which she bestowed on him as she said, 'Can I help you?'

The young man wasn't half as self-assured as he appeared. He wasn't at all sure he had got the right address and he said a little hesitantly, 'I need to speak to a Mrs Angela McClusky.'

That took the wind right out of Connie's sails, for it had been the last thing she had expected him to say, and she wondered what such a person would want with her mother.

The man, seeing her reaction, said, 'Have I come to the right place?'

'Oh yes, that's my mother,' Connie said.

'Who is it, Connie?' Mary asked from her chair by the fire.

'Someone to see Mammy,' Connie told her and to the young man she said, 'You'd best come in. My mother is in the cellar, I'll tell her you are here.'

The young man thanked her and stepped into the room. Connie made for the cellar steps as Mary swung round in her chair.

'Come nearer,' she said, for her eyes weren't as good as they once were. The man hesitated and then took a step forward. 'Closer than that,' Mary said. 'I can't see you from there.' And as the man took another step so Mary could see him clearly he started with shock when Mary burst out, 'Almighty God. You're Stan Bishop's son, aren't you?'

The man was a little shaken and he said, 'How . . . How do you know that?'

'Because you're the spit of him, lad,' Mary said. 'Your father was a fine-looking man and you look just like him. Angela will get a shock too. You'd better take a seat.'

He sat on the edge of the settee but when Angela came into the room a few minutes later he rose again and Mary was impressed he had been brought up with such good manners. The words dried up in Angela's mouth when she saw the young man in front of her. Memories of his father, Stan Bishop, came flooding back. He had been her husband's best friend and a friend to her too – she missed him almost as much as her husband. She was almost in shock at seeing the young man in front of her. When Connie had described the man, she presumed he was after money and she wondered how quickly she could get rid of him, but her heart gave a jolt for it was as if the years had fallen away and she were looking at Stan again.

'You're Daniel Swanage,' she said. 'Stan Bishop's son.' Realising he had stood up at her entrance, she sat down in the armchair and said, 'Please sit down. You are the last person on earth I expected to see.'

Daniel sat on the settee as before, as Connie followed her mother into the room. She had heard her mother's words and her first thought was that Stan Bishop was the name of the man her grandmother had told her about just a few weeks before and she said to her, 'Granny, you told me about a man called Stan Bishop, but you never said he had a son.'

'I didn't think you'd ever need to know.'

Connie ignored that and said to the man directly, 'And how can your name be Swanage if your father's name is Bishop?'

'Daniel was adopted after his mother died,' Angela said. 'His aunt and uncle adopted him and their names were Betty and Roger Swanage.'

'Yeah,' Daniel said, and the bitterness of his tone was at odds with the hurt Angela could see reflected in his grey eyes. 'Your grandmother was right,' he said to Connie. 'My real father never had a son because he gave me away and then forgot all about me.'

Angela's heart constricted in pity for the man who had presumably just found out about the existence of his father. She knew, though, that the hurt Daniel was feeling was nothing like the betrayal her own younger daughter would feel as she grew up, for Angela hadn't left her in the loving arms of an auntie, but completely alone on the workhouse steps. She had thought the guilt would ease as the years passed, but in fact it had increased as the child had grown older and Angela knew her daughter would now be aware of being a foundling that no one even cared about.

To cover her emotions, she got up and filled the kettle and put it over the fire, getting cups out of the cupboard in the cubby hole of a kitchen. Mary had been a little surprised by Angela's silence till she caught the preoccupied look in her eyes and knew she was thinking of the abandoned child. And so before the silence became uncomfortable, she said, 'Your father never forgot you, Daniel. He gave you up because he had to.'

Angela swallowed the lump in her own throat and pushed

her own sorrowful memories away because she felt it important to set the record straight as far as Daniel was concerned.

'Listen to me,' she said. 'I knew your father well and cared for him a great deal and what he did, signing away his rights to you, he did for your sake. Look around this area and think what your life would have been like if he hadn't have done that. Your home would be a house very like this and in this area. Your father had to work so you would probably have been left in the indifferent care of some slattern, who might have had no thought of you other than as a way to earn easy money.'

'Angela's right,' Mary said. 'It hurt Stan greatly to sign all rights to you away. I know because I was there. I was with your mother when she was in labour giving birth to you and a kinder, finer woman never walked this earth and your father loved the very bones of her. She was everything to him and when she died, your father was beside himself. He had no idea what to do. It was a tragedy a young woman should be taken like that and your father was grateful for Betty who came and cared for you from when you were a few hours old.'

'I think that's really sad,' Connie said. 'It must be awful to grow up without a mother.'

Connie's words were like a dagger in Angela's heart and yet she said to Daniel, 'Has Betty just told you all this?'

'She won't tell me anything,' Daniel said. 'Even now she won't. It was the man at the bank. See, I was twenty-one in April and the bank contacted me. Apparently my mythical father had left money in the bank for me to have when I was twenty-one if he didn't survive the war. As they hadn't heard from me – well they wouldn't, seeing as I knew nothing about it – they asked me what I wanted to do with it. Along with the money was a letter and in the letter it said he was my father and the money was mine to do with as I pleased.'

'That must have been a shock if you had not been told about the adoption.'

'I'd been told nothing,' Daniel said. 'And the letter was a far greater shock than the money, though there's over two hundred and fifty pounds he has left for me. What threw me completely was that he continued to add to the account until 1918, which must have been when he died. I could have written him. Hell, I could have seen him before he enlisted, got to know him a bit, but he obviously didn't want to do that.'

'Daniel, he did,' Angela said. 'Look at the money he put on one side for you, the letter he sent.'

'What's a letter?' Daniel said, disparagingly. 'Even money is easy enough to give if you have enough to spare and letters are just words on a page. It's guilt money as far as I'm concerned.'

For a moment Angela considered leaving Daniel thinking that. It was important that he still got on with his adoptive parents, for that's all he had, and their relationship already appeared to be somewhat strained. Whatever he thought of Stan couldn't hurt him now.

But she couldn't do it, she had to put Stan's side of the story. And so she said, 'Daniel, your parents Betty and Roger cannot have children of their own and that has been a great cross for them to bear. I believe she suffered multiple miscarriages, didn't she, Mammy?'

'She did,' Mary said. 'Your true mother, Kate, told me that herself. She said she was always the type of person who

41

wanted to be needed. She liked to care for people and she had been a great big sister to her when she was growing up. She longed for a child of her own and was quite jealous of Kate when she was expecting you. When Kate died she was undoubtedly upset. She was, after all, her little sister. Many were upset for she was well-liked, your mother, but your father was burdened down with grief. You were only hours old and when Betty suggested looking after you Stan was only too pleased. After the funeral she took you away to Sutton Coldfield.'

'That's not that far away,' Daniel said. 'He could have come to visit me if he'd cared enough.'

'Betty forbade him to,' Angela said. 'I think Betty wanted to pretend you were all hers and Roger's, their own child, and Stan popping up now and then would have spoilt that.'

'So he just left them to it. I call that spineless.'

'Betty said if he was going to keep a stake in your life then she would refuse to look after you and he would have to find someone else,' Angela said. 'My husband always said your father should have called her bluff. He said Betty loved you too much for that and he should have carried on visiting you and letting you know you had a father who cared.'

'But he didn't do that,' Daniel almost spat out. 'You can say what you like, but as far as I'm concerned he just bowed out of my life and let me think the only father I had was Roger Swanage. He didn't want me in his life and that's that.'

'Why are you here then?' Connie asked from the hearth where she was making tea for them all as the kettle had begun to sing. 'If you really don't care as much as you say you do, why did you come here asking questions about him?'

Daniel shook his head. 'D'you know, I'm not totally sure,'

he said to Connie and then asked, 'Did you ever meet my father?'

It was Angela who answered. 'Connie did, but won't remember. She was very young when he enlisted. And you too were just a child. I am sorry that you didn't get to know him, but regardless of how he seemed to neglect you, he was a good and honourable man. I think his insecurity with you stemmed from the time he took you home for the weekend.'

'When was this?'

'You were very young,' Angela said and she remembered the heartfelt story Stan had told them that Christmas Day years ago that he had spent with them all. 'Stan wanted to spend the weekend with you and collected you from Betty after booking the time off from work. But you loathed everything – his house, the area, him – and became so distressed he eventually took you back to the only home you knew. You said you hated him and didn't want to see him any more and that broke Stan's heart.'

'I don't even remember that.'

'Why would you?' Angela said. 'You were a small boy and you hadn't really got to know Stan. Stan didn't know you either and took the words you threw at him at face value for it was at a time when he was hurt and vulnerable. He told me he felt he had failed miserably as a father and then Betty issued the ultimatum to shut Stan out of your life in exchange for them adopting you. He had to sign to say he'd have no contact with you and he did it because he knew Betty and Roger loved you and you loved them. And added to that they had a fine house, where you would have your own room, and there were gardens back and front to play in. He knew you would never want for anything and your happiness and security mattered far more than his own. And so he signed away all rights to you.'

Connie handed around the tea and Daniel stared down at it while he stirred his spoon in his cup and it was the only sound in the room.

Eventually the silence went on so long Angela felt prompted to say, 'Daniel, I'm sorry if I have upset you by casting Betty in such a bad light. That was not my intention though – I believed you needed to learn the truth of what happened at the time. Having said that, Betty and Roger have done a good job raising you for you are a fine young man.'

'I'm not offended by anything you said,' Daniel said, raising his head at last. Though his voice was firm enough, his eyes were very bright. 'I know that you spoke the truth and perhaps it explains why my mother, especially, was the way she was.'

'In what way?'

'I grew up knowing I was somehow precious to my mother. She barely let the wind blow on me. I grew up only a short distance from Sutton Park. Have you ever been there?'

'Only once and it was in the winter,' Angela said. 'I was impressed even so and always intended going back when the weather might be more clement.'

'What a pity you didn't.'

'Circumstances dictated otherwise,' Angela said. 'Once war was declared the park wasn't the same. Some of the army training camps were there. I mean, certainly Barry and possibly your father did their basic training there and later a POW camp was set up there too. It meant much of the park was commandeered and out of bounds and Barry said it was ruined and we must wait for peacetime when we'd be

44

able to take Connie. I couldn't have taken Connie during the war anyway. I was working making shells six and a half days a week with no time off and on Sunday, the only day I was free, I was too tired to think of going on such a jaunt. And after the war I seldom thought of it, and now I work Friday and Saturday evenings and Sunday lunchtime at the Swan pub on the corner of the road. We should go up one Saturday though, Connie. As I don't work till the evening we could have the whole day. Sutton Park is well worth a visit.'

'Oh yeah,' Connie said enthusiastically.

Angela looked at Daniel and said, 'You were lucky growing up near a park like that. I bet you lived in there in the holidays.'

'That's just it,' Daniel said. 'I seldom went there and never without at least one of my parents, usually my mother. Other children from school would go, but I wasn't allowed.'

'Why ever not?'

'My mother seemed jealous a lot of the time, even of my friends,' Daniel said. 'My father brought me up to know that the very worst thing I could do in the world was upset my mother, so when she said she didn't want me running wild in Sutton Park with my friends, which was the one thing I wanted to do, I didn't go. Instead I would be taken on a sedate walk, where I was expected to talk of sensible things with my father in particular.'

'Ugh,' said Connie, for it was the worst thing she could think of. 'Didn't you mind?'

'Course I minded,' Daniel said. 'But I minded more being called namby pamby and a mummy's boy. I didn't have many friends. Most, I suppose, thought me a bit wet.'

Angela suddenly sorry for this young man, for she could

imagine how sterile his life had been, but he caught the look and said, 'I was better off than many, I know that. I never have known hunger and I always had shoes on my feet and a warm coat in the winter and gloves and a hat. The house was always warm and I had a fire lit in my bedroom through the winter months.'

Connie's mouth dropped open, for a fire in the bedroom was luxury indeed. The bedroom in the attic that she shared with her granny hadn't even a light except the candle balanced in a saucer.

'Lucky you.'

'I know,' Daniel agreed. 'That's why even now maybe I shouldn't complain so much. At the time I didn't really think my life narrow or strange because, though I hated the teasing, I accepted life the way it was. I knew my parents loved me and, if I had been in any doubt, my mother told me often and would hug and kiss me as long as I would stand it. They had no friends either. Their life was me and that too I was told often and so it was the three of us all the time.'

'No grandparents?' Connie asked.

Daniel shook his head. 'Both dead and after my real mother died there were no uncles or aunts either.'

'Well, we are a small household too,' Connie said.

'But I bet you all have friends.'

Connie thought about it and thought really they were friendly with all the street and certainly the yard – and some, like Nancy Webster, closer still. Her grandmother was liked by all, but her particular friend was Norah Doherty who had moved to Birmingham before the McCluskys and helped them so much when they were newly arrived. And her mother had a special friend she called Auntie Maggie who had married Michael Malone even though he only had one leg. And because she was a special friend of Sarah Maguire, her mother was friendly with her mother Maeve and at Mass they seemed surrounded by friends.

'Yes, I suppose we have,' she admitted. 'But surely your parents made friends at church?'

'They could have done if they'd wanted,' Daniel said. 'We went to Mass every Sunday certainly and they would greet people but that was all. They had a manner that wasn't exactly unfriendly but told people they definitely didn't want to take the conversation any further. So, in the end, people just greeted them then left them alone. I didn't find this odd at the time, it was later looking back on it that I thought it was a peculiar way to go on. But still, looking at the suffering others were enduring after the Great War and all the hardships many were enduring, these things were minor.'

'I see what you're saying,' Angela said. 'It's hard not to feel immense sympathy when some people can't heat their house or feed their barefoot children adequately. And yet to be friendless too is a lonely place to be, don't you think, Mammy?'

There was no answer, for Mary was fast asleep. Angela smiled sadly, for Mary was dropping off to sleep more and more of late. She knew it was more than likely that one day Mary would not wake from one of these naps; she would slip into the ultimate deep sleep and Angela dreaded that day.

Daniel, however, hadn't followed Angela's train of thought and shrugged as he said, 'University saved me.'

'Golly, you must be clever.'

Daniel smiled as he said, 'It's easier to work when you

47

have no friends to distract you and parents and a school that expect you to work hard. My parents did all they could to make study as pleasurable as possible. I was doing what they wanted so a desk and bookshelves were put in my bedroom. The shelves of the bookcase were filled with books recommended by the school and often a merry little fire burned in the grate.'

Connie said nothing, but she knew her life would be a lot harder than Daniel's if she took the route her mother wanted her to take. Between October and April she went into the attic only to sleep, for it was far too cold to linger in. And she had no desk or bookshelves, let alone recommended books to put on them.

'How do you mean, it saved you?' Angela was saying.

'I saw how other chaps lived,' Daniel said. 'I saw my upbringing was not the same as most of theirs and for the first time I made friends. My parents would not permit me to leave home to attend a university further afield so I got a place in Birmingham University.'

'Where's that?' Angela asked.

'Edgbaston.'

'Hardly easy to get to from Sutton Coldfield, I wouldn't have said.'

'It isn't,' Daniel agreed. 'I had to take a train to New Street Station, cross the city and get a bus out. It was hellishly difficult to get there in time for morning lectures, so one of the others would often put me up. I slept on a great many sofas, armchairs, even a bath a time or two, and some floors.'

'How did you get away with that?' Connie asked.

'Well, my parents didn't like it when I started staying out overnight, as you might imagine,' Daniel said. 'So I showed them my timetable and told them how many times I had been late for lectures initially. As they obviously didn't want me to be late, they could do little about it and let me share a house with some of the others. And being away from home I learnt that life isn't all about study, that normal students go to the pub, have parties, get drunk and generally enjoy themselves. I felt I was living for the first time. My parents knew nothing of my double life. I did enough to keep up in class, hand essays in on time and do well in my end-of-term exams.'

'What did you study?'

'Maths and Accountancy.'

'So, are you following Roger into the bank?'

Daniel made a face. 'He'd like me to.'

'And you're not keen?'

'It's not that, and not really about the job, it's just that I have tasted freedom now and I don't want to go back to the life I had. I am turned twenty-one now and my friends all said I should stick up for myself more, but it's hard when you have never done it. And then I got the letter from the solicitor chap and learnt about this man I'd never heard of leaving me all this money. The letter told me who he was – my father – and I realised all my life I had lived a lie. My parents have lied to me and they weren't my parents at all, so I don't have to consider them any more.'

'Yes you do, Daniel,' Angela said. 'They are not your birth parents but they adopted you legally and so they are your parents and they have done their best by you. Admittedly they have smothered you and you have to confront that and tell them there is to be no more of it, but I'd say you are their reason for living. Don't turn your back on them totally.'

'If only they'd told me,' Daniel said. 'My mother said if I wanted to find out about my father who had just abandoned me to their care I had to come here.'

'Your father didn't just abandon you, as I've explained,' Angela said. 'And I'm surprised Betty knew exactly where we lived.'

'I don't know whether she did or not,' Daniel said. 'The point is, my real father had left your address with the solicitor in case there were any problems. The stipulation of no contact was null and void when I was twenty-one so the solicitor had my address to write about the inheritance. So you see, even after I confronted her, my mother wasn't at all helpful.'

'She was probably in shock and perhaps a bit frightened.'

'I don't know why you are making excuses for her,' Daniel said. 'Doubt she'd do the same for you. And I don't know what she has to be frightened of. My father is dead and when I could have got to know him, my parents – principally my mother – prevented me.'

'She thinks you may hold it against her.'

'Well I do a bit now, if I'm honest,' Daniel said. 'And, like it or not, if I can't actually meet him, I think I'd like to know all there is to know about him.'

'Well, as a young man both before your birth and just after, Mary will know more than me because I was just a child. She will probably be able to tell you bits about your mother too. But I can fill in the gaps later, before he enlisted, and so you can have as complete a picture of your father as we can give you.'

And then Angela stopped and cried, 'Oh, I almost forgot. I have a photo of your father, the army took it. Here's Barry's, look. I put it in a silver frame.' And she took it from the sideboard and showed him. 'It was important for Connie to know what he looked like so she couldn't forget him.'

'I understand that,' Daniel said. 'I would so like to see what my father looked like too.'

'It's upstairs, won't be a minute.'

When Angela had gone, Daniel said to Connie, 'Could you remember more about your father when you saw his photograph?'

Connie shook her head. 'Not really. I was too young when he joined the war he didn't come back from.'

'We're more or less in the same boat then.'

'Yes, except that I heard about my father all the time,' Connie said. 'The memory of him was kept alive mainly by Granny. Mammy generally doesn't like talking about the past, but she'd often say things about my father. Granny said she loved him very much and it was hard for her to go on without him.'

Daniel didn't reply to this for Angela had come in with a box. 'I put the photograph in the box I kept all the letters in, because I used to write to your father, you see. Here it is.'

Daniel's hand shook as he took the photograph and he knew now how Mary and Angela had known who he was because it was like looking in the mirror, for he was so like the father he had never known.

'You say you used to write to my father?' he said to Angela in the end.

'Yes,' Angela said. 'Barry didn't mind me doing it. He said some of the chaps in his unit that got no post looked really sad when the letters were handed out. It connected you to

51

the people back at home and if no one wrote to them they might feel sort of forgotten.'

'I understand that perfectly well,' Daniel said. 'But you shouldn't have been writing to him. Or, at least, what I mean is you shouldn't have been the only one writing to him. My mother is his sister-in-law. Oh, I know there was that thing about him not contacting me, but as he was away fighting in a bloody world war, surely that should have changed everything.'

'Not in Betty, your adoptive mother's, book,' Angela said and she fought to keep any bitterness out of her voice, for she had thought Betty heartless. 'When Stan enlisted, he wrote and told Betty, but she never replied. And when we'd had no letters for weeks at the end we knew there was something wrong and eventually I got the telegram saying Barry had been killed in action, but there was no word of your father. I thought that, although the letters were sent here, he might have listed Betty as next of kin when he enlisted and so I wrote to her, telling her of the death of Barry and asking if she'd had any word from Stan. She must have replied by return and she made no mention of Barry at all and said Stan would never contact her as that was part of the deal they made and she would be obliged if I didn't write again.'

Daniel shook his head in bewilderment. 'You know, that is so callous,' he said. 'My father was the husband of the younger sister that she was supposed to adore and she passed me off as her child. She appears so hard-hearted. I have never seen that side of her, and though I don't doubt a word you say, you are describing a woman I don't really recognise.'

'Daniel, have you ever opposed your mother?' Angela asked.

Daniel shook his head. 'No, and if I had ever tried my father would have been very angry with me. That is, until now of course. When my last exams were over, my mother advised me to have a break for a while because I'd worked so hard. I wasn't that keen because I didn't know what I was going to do with myself. Those of my friends from uni who were not starting jobs immediately were going on proper holidays or camping somewhere. I knew my parents would never stand for me doing anything like that.'

'Maybe they have a holiday planned for all of you?'

Daniel shook his head. 'We never went on holidays. Don't know why, except for the fact that my father never seemed to have much free time. My mother used to say he was married to the bank. I imagine what my mother wanted was for me to sit with her and keep her company and the idea of doing that day after day filled me with horror. Of course, the letter from the solicitor chap changed all that. Tell me, did she know about the letter and money?'

Angela nodded. 'Stan wrote and told her,' she said. 'Mammy said it was too much of a shock to find out like this and she should tell you of Stan's existence at least. But that was another letter she didn't acknowledge and apparently told you nothing.'

'No, and another thing I must challenge her about,' Daniel said, getting to his feet.

'Go easy on her,' Angela said.

'Why d'you say that?' Daniel said.

Angela shrugged. 'She loves you very much. Maybe a little too much and that has made her act in ways that have not been sensible and sometimes downright hurtful, but she has never stopped loving you. Remember that when you are talking to her. Now I must try and rouse Mammy or she will never sleep tonight.'

'Can I come again?'

'Of course,' Angela said. 'Stan was always welcome here and so is his son.'

'Come and talk to my granny about days gone by,' Connie said as she let Daniel out of the door. 'She likes nothing better.'

'I will,' Daniel said with a smile for Connie and she watched him stride down the street till he reached Bristol Passage.

FOUR

They talked about Daniel often over the next few days and Angela wondered if he would return.

'Why?' Connie asked.

'Oh, you know,' Angela said vaguely. 'Maybe it would have been better for him not to know. I mean, you could see how it had upset him and his life had been going on fine and dandy till then.'

'I don't think it was,' Connie said. 'His aunt and uncle seemed to want to control everything he did. You heard him.'

'You're right,' Mary said. 'And if he had known about his father much sooner he wouldn't be so upset now. I said so at the time. How would it be if I told you nothing about your parents, Angela, and let you think you were our wee girl? How would you feel if you found out I had been lying all those years?'

'Granny's right,' Connie said. 'I would hate not knowing who my parents were.'

Connie's words caused a pang of guilt to slice through Angela's heart.

Connie had no idea of the huge shame that had lodged in Angela's heart when she'd been forced to sacrifice her helpless baby to a loveless life of drudgery for the good of everyone else. Even after all these years the self-reproach never completely left her.

She was wrong about Daniel, though, who came that very afternoon before Connie had returned home from school. She was so pleased with the gentle and patient way he had with her mother, who seemed delighted to see him. Sometimes Mary was very slow at conversation, but she never seemed to have a problem with Daniel. Mary had once explained that, though sometimes her mind was perfectly clear, other times it seemed to slip and she had trouble remembering what they had been talking about. It was different with Daniel though, because generally he wanted to know things about his father before that terrible war and her mind was usually crystal clear about events that had happened long before.

In addition, Angela could tell him about the Stan she knew, a great friend of her husband, Barry. She told him about the Christmas of 1913, which Stan had spent at their house.

'After a stupendous meal, as we couldn't go out as the weather was foul, he had us all singing carols. Remember that, Mammy?'

'Oh I do indeed,' Mary said. 'Your father had a good voice, Daniel, and your mother too. She was in the choir at the church and they both loved to sing. My lads spoke of it when they stayed there and when Kate was expecting you she used to sing you lullabies. She had a lovely singing voice. She told your father you might possibly remember the songs after you were born and know how much you were loved even before you actually arrived.'

Daniel's voice was husky as he said, 'I wish I had got to know her, that she hadn't died.'

'Oh so do I, Daniel,' Angela said earnestly. 'I had never heard your father's voice till that Christmas Day, because after your mother died, when I was too much of a child to notice such things, he never sang again. That day he began with "O Little Town of Bethlehem", which he said was her favourite carol.'

'I used to like singing too,' Daniel admitted. 'My mother used to hate to hear me singing so I never sang at home.'

'Why did she object?'

'I never could understand it,' Daniel said. 'I must have had some promise because the priest wanted me to be in the church choir and the music master at my grammar school choir, but my mother vetoed it both times. She said that she sent me to school to study not sing, and my father took me to one side and said it wasn't a very manly pursuit and I wasn't to keep on about it and risk upsetting my mother. But now I know the truth about my parents I think my mother didn't want me singing because it would have reminded her of how well they could sing and that I took after them. It would all be a reminder that she was keeping the truth from me – that they were hoodwinking me.'

'You could be right,' Angela said. 'Is that how you see it now, as them hoodwinking you?'

'Wouldn't you feel that way?' Daniel said. 'You were told all about your parents and your siblings. Though you lived with Mrs McClusky and her family, you knew who your real family had been. If your father had lived I'm sure you would know him – even if he couldn't look after you full time I'm sure he would have been a presence in your life.'

'You are right, Daniel,' Mary said. 'I often felt bad that Angela had neither parents nor even one of her siblings to survive. We took her into our hearts and loved her as much as we were able and I hope she never felt that lack, but I always felt that pang of regret on her behalf.'

'I never felt it, Mammy,' Angela said. 'You loved me totally and completely and I loved you in return. That's all a child needs.'

'Maybe it is,' Daniel said. 'But it must be a healthy love.'

'What d'you mean, healthy love?'

'My mother wanted to share me with no one,' Daniel said. 'Not even Roger very often, for she wanted me to love her intensely and only her.'

'What of Roger?' Angela asked. 'Did he love you too?'

'Yes, I think he did,' Daniel said after a short pause. 'He had trouble showing it, but many boys at school had distant fathers so that wasn't unusual. I never remember him putting his arms around me or holding me in his arms, even as a small child. The nearest he got to touching me was to give me a handshake. I was nervous of him when I was young because I thought I didn't come up to scratch as the son he wanted. I see why now – because I wasn't his son. At the time though, I was always trying to please him and failing.'

Despite all the advantages Daniel must have had growing up with the Swanages, Angela saw an unhappy, lonely boy. He had a mother who loved him so much she wanted to share him with no one, and Roger, who was probably aggrieved by his wife's preoccupation with the child and resented him. How much good it would have done the young, confused child if he had met up with his father who would have taken joy in his company. She thought of Stan and the sacrifice he had made to give his son a good and happy life, better than the one he thought he could give Daniel himself. Angela could see now it was wrong, but there was no point in this. Daniel's life had not been the bed of roses Stan had thought it would be, but she had to concede many had it far worse; in her mind's eye she saw the basket left on the workhouse steps.

She was glad to see Connie come in to lighten the atmosphere a little. And with her she had Maggie and Michael who she had met on the road coming home from school. It was hard to keep someone's appearance secret in the teeming, thin-walled, back-to-back houses, even you wanted to, so there had been great curiosity about Daniel, not least because his clothes were not the kind worn by most people in the area, even to Mass. He looked like some sort of official and, in the neighbours' opinion, officials arriving at a person's door usually meant trouble for those inside. Angela and Connie lost no time in telling their neighbours who Daniel was, for Angela agreed with her mother that there had been too much secrecy surrounding Daniel's whereabouts for too long.

The news spread like wildfire and those who remembered his birth, which had caused the death of his mother, and him being spirited away by the mother's sister, told the newer neighbours the tale. And most looked at the fine young man they had seen striding down Bell Barn Road going to or from the McCluskys' and thought it a shame that his true father's body must have been another left in a foreign field, because he hadn't returned from the war.

Michael was one of those who knew a lot of it. Living in the same road and being three years older than Angela anyway, he remembered the time better than she did. He said he'd like to see Daniel and maybe give an account of his father's bravery in the army.

'It might help,' said Maggie. 'It certainly helped Angela, knowing you were there at Barry's last moments.'

And so when Maggie, returning from shopping on Bristol Street that afternoon, saw Daniel at the McCluskys' door, she told Michael and the two decided to go down and say hello. Angela was delighted to see them and Daniel did appreciate Michael telling him what he knew of his father, the soldier, and that he must have done something special to earn his sergeant stripes.

'And the other chaps said he was an understanding sort of man. Sergeant stripes or not, he wasn't always bawling at the soldiers under his command. As in civvy street, he was known as a kind and understanding boss. He was just naturally considerate.'

'Thank you,' Daniel said. 'I find it really helpful that my father was well thought of.'

'Daniel, one reason your father went to war was because of you,' Angela said. 'He told me he wanted you to be proud of him.'

Daniel nodded. 'He put that in the letter,' he said. 'And I am immensely proud of him and the more I hear the more that pride deepens. I wish he hadn't died and yet, if he hadn't, I'd probably not be here, for I don't know how long my uncle and aunt intended to go on with the farce of not only bringing me up as their own natural son, but denying my father's existence.'

Michael looked a bit confused. He knew nothing about the aunt's ban on any contact between Daniel and his father, so they told him the tale, including Betty's ultimatum that, if Stan didn't agree to relinquish all rights to Daniel, she would refuse to look after him.

'He was too anxious not to agree,' Angela said. 'He had to work and would have had to find some sort of care for Daniel that he knew wouldn't be half as good as that Betty and Roger could provide.'

'I wish he had survived,' Daniel said wistfully and then asked Michael, 'Did you see how my father died?'

Michael shook his head. 'Sorry, I was out of it myself for some time after the shell that killed Barry exploded. We were all having a fag – Barry, another two mates and me. We knew we were destined for the front trench the following day – that's the one that leads the attack,' he explained to Daniel. 'If they hadn't managed to silence at least some of the guns and pick off any snipers beforehand, those going over the top first would soon be well aware of it. That's what happened at the Somme. Well, it was a bit nerve-wracking, however many times we'd done it, and we were working out some tactics. One of the chaps had got hold of a crude map and we were working out areas of cover to advance in. Barry suddenly gave a wave and said to us to hang on a minute, he'd seen someone he knew. I had my back to whoever it was and I did turn, but with the mist of the day and the billowing smoke from the guns it was hard to see who it was. Then one of the other chaps pointed out a clump of bushes on the map. It was hard to see how big it was from the rough map, but if we managed to get out of the trench without injury and slither under the wire, we decided to make for there and decide on our next move.

'I was concentrating on what my mate said and all around

us was noise. And there was the stink of cordite in the air and I didn't see or hear the shell till it was too late. I heard Barry give a frantic yell and only seconds later there was a massive explosion and I was knocked clean out.

'Days afterwards I came to to find I was minus a leg and my other two mates had copped it. People say Barry launched himself at this chap. No one seemed to know who it was, but I would imagine there was a state of confusion because I was told a barrage of shells followed that first one. One chap said that though it was obvious Barry was dead, the one he tried to save didn't look in great shape either so he might have died too. That was the war over for me.'

Angela, thinking of the pictures of the Somme she'd seen, could well imagine the scenario, with whining shells exploding all around the frightened soldiers as they desperately searched for cover to save themselves to fight another day. Daniel would probably have no idea of what battlegrounds were like – neither had she before the photographs from the Somme – but he turned to them all and said:

'I feel I've got to thank you all. I came here with some shadowy idea of a father who didn't care for me at all, a man who would leave me money when he was dead, but nothing of himself when he was alive. I am going away with a fuller picture than I ever imagined and, because of the photograph, I even know what he looked like. I now have a really full picture of the father I will never know.'

'Doesn't that make you sort of sad?' Connie asked.

'Maybe a little sad that I'll never get to see him,' Daniel admitted. 'But now at least I can think of him. I know he was a real flesh and blood person and he cared for me and he was my father.'

All were moved by Daniel's words spoken with such sincerity and Angela said, 'Daniel, I knew and loved your father dearly and I will say with absolute certainty that he would be so proud if he could know the man you have turned out to be.'

Daniel gave a wry smile and said, 'Don't know if you'll be so proud of me when I tell you that I'm starting in the bank on Monday.'

Disappointment flitted across Angela's eyes, for she thought Daniel needed to break free a little from the dominance of his aunt and uncle. But she betrayed none of it in her voice when she spoke. 'I thought you wanted to do something else?'

'I did . . . I do,' Daniel said, and then went on, 'To be honest, both Roger and Betty have been pretty foul to me since I said they should have told me the truth about my father. They made me feel really guilty when they said that that was all the thanks they got for bringing me up without a penny piece of support from my excuse for a father.'

'But they wouldn't accept anything!'

'I know, but they deny that now and my mother claimed he didn't even offer to give them anything. They financed everything, from the expensive uniform for the private school they sent me to in order for me to get to grammar school where the uniform was equally expensive. They cited the day-to-day expenses of bringing up a child, including Christmas and birthday presents – though they were never lavish – and the fact that they then financed me through university. Anyway, then my uncle said that the gravy train was coming to an end. I had to get a job and quick and pay my way in the world and pay them back for the money they have spent on me. He has a job set up for me at the bank and on Monday morning I am going into the city centre with him on the train. He said he will listen to "no nonsense" about anything I would rather do.'

'Golly,' Connie said. 'Why are they being so mean to you?'

'Because I am not doing what they want,' Daniel said. 'And because I am finding out more about the father they denied me, and they don't like it. They don't like me spending so much time here either, at least Betty doesn't.'

'What does she want you to do?'

'Basically, she wants me to keep her company day after boring day, and as I'm not prepared to do that, she'd rather have me at work under my uncle's watchful eye.'

'I can see the way they put it. You had no other alternative,' Maggie said.

'No,' said Daniel with a short dry laugh. 'The way my uncle went on though, I wouldn't be surprised if he wrote down every blessed thing I've ever been bought or caused him to pay in any way and presented me with a bill to be paid off out of my wages.'

'Doubt it will come to that,' Angela said. 'But, talking of money, what are you going to do with the money your father left you?'

'Oh, that's already sorted,' Daniel said. 'I took the solicitor's advice and saw the bank manager. I have opened an account and put it in there. Not the bank I will be working in but a new one altogether where my uncle is not known.'

'In a bank?' Connie cried and her voice came out like a squeak. 'Not a post office?'

'I don't know much about either,' Daniel said. 'Never had enough money to worry about where to put it so I did what the solicitor advised. That money in the end will signify my freedom. From what was said, there will be no financial help from my aunt and uncle, nor should I expect any, they said. They have paid for me to be well-educated and now it's up to me. I will save as much of my wages as I can and when I have enough I can say goodbye and at least live somewhere else, even if I have to continue working with my uncle for a while.'

'D'you think you will get to like it in the end?'

'Oh, I don't know,' Daniel said. 'I have the feeling it will bore me to tears. But jobs are not that easy to get, so I suppose I will stick at it till something better comes along at least.'

'Well, that's sensible.'

'I'm very sensible,' Daniel smiled. 'My friends would tease me about it. It was the way I was brought up, but they used to call me Doubtful Daniel. They would suggest something and I would often worry we might get into trouble if we did it.'

'Did you do it anyway?' Connie asked.

'Sometimes,' Daniel said and laughed, a low rumble of a laugh just like his father, and Angela laughed with him. As she did, she thought what a serious young man he was. She had never heard him laugh before.

'You can't be good all the time,' she said.

'Good,' said Connie. 'I'll remind you of that.'

'You watch out,' Angela told her daughter with mock severity. 'Or I'll clip your ears for you.'

'That'll be the day,' Mary said from her chair before the fire, for it was well known Angela had never laid her hand on her daughter. Mary began to laugh her wheezy laugh and it was so infectious that in minutes everyone was joining in.

Daniel was so grateful he had made contact with this warm and happy family, knowing there was another way to live to the way he had been brought up.

FIVE

They didn't see Daniel for a few weeks after this and Angela wondered if he would bother coming again.

'After all, he is nothing to us,' she said to Maggie, who had popped in one evening just after she had helped Mary to bed.

'Um, I suppose,' Maggie said. 'Where's Connie?'

'At Sarah Maguire's,' Angela said. 'They're as thick as thieves, the pair of them. They remind me a bit of me and you. Now the summer holidays have begun, I don't have to be so strict about bedtime, and anyway it's a fine light evening and Connie is only at the end of the street.'

'Oh, it will do her good,' Maggie said. 'Young people should be together. So, you think you've seen the last of Daniel then?'

'We could have,' Angela said. 'I mean, he's a nice young man, I'm not being nasty about him at all. It's just that he only made contact with us to learn more about his real father.'

'Your mother will miss him.'

'Aye, if she remembers him at all,' Angela said, a little sadly. 'Sometimes she looks at me a bit strangely. Funny thing is, though, she always knows Connie, though she does sometimes call her Angela. The thing is, it's not just her mind, she is almost bedbound now and you know she was always such an active person. Time hangs heavy on her and I suppose gives her too much time to think. Norah Doherty pops along to see her fairly often. She is a similar age but far more aware than Mammy.'

'That's life though, isn't it?' Maggie said. 'No one really knows how life is going to be for us as we age.'

Angela sighed. 'Aye, that's true enough.'

'You'll miss her when she's gone.'

'I know,' Angela said. 'But the fact is, I miss her now. The real Mary is hidden away somewhere and sometimes it barely surfaces. I used to talk to her about anything and everything and, though I love Connie, there are things I cannot discuss with a child – for that's all she is.'

Maggie nodded, for she could see that. 'You can load it on me if you like. I have broad shoulders.'

Angela smiled. 'I value your friendship, Maggie, and not just as a sounding board.'

'I know,' Maggie said. 'My mammy will pop in and see Mary if I ask her to. She thought a lot of her.'

'I know,' Angela said. 'But, as I said, the schools have broken up for the summer now, so Connie will be here most of the time if I ask her to and she is always very good with Mammy. She gets her talking about the old days, even before my time, when her and my real mother were girls growing up together and where they met their husbands and all. She's really interested in that sort of thing, and Mammy loves talking about her memories. It's strange that sometimes she is very vague and by dinnertime has trouble remembering what she had for breakfast, and yet you get her talking about the olden days and she has no trouble remembering everything.'

Maggie nodded. 'I've heard of that before in older people. Odd, isn't it?'

'Oh I'll say,' Angela said. 'But Connie encourages her anyway and doesn't seem to mind if she repeats herself and she never corrects her. Course, Connie loves her to bits and will be devastated when she is no longer with us.'

Maggie didn't say anything more. She had seen herself how frail Mary had become over the last months.

And Angela went on, 'At the moment Mammy is often quite silent or sleeping much of the time. I almost look forward to pulling pints at the pub. At least there is a bit of conversation there, even if it is pretty male-dominated.'

'Yeah, but what sort of conversation?' Maggie said. 'Men seem interested in only two things, football and sex.'

Angela laughed. 'We manage, though I am not a whit interested in football and put a veto on sex from the beginning. You would be surprised though how many men, hearing I was a widow, asked me if I was ever lonely at all. I know of course what that is a euphemism for and they got short shrift from me. I mean, I wouldn't mind, but most of these are married men. I know their wives and even if I was looking for another husband, and I'm not, I would not consider a married man.'

'Nor me,' Maggie said.

'Well, Michael might have something to say if you did.'

'Oh yes,' Maggie said and then added with a grin, 'And

then Michael's response would be nothing to the reaction of Father Brannigan if he got the merest hint of impropriety. God, he'd burst a gasket.'

'He would that,' Angela said and the two women laughed at the vision conjured up.

Despite the hilarity though, Angela had been shocked at first by the men who wanted to keep her company, stop her from feeling 'lonely'. Unbeknown to her, initially Paddy Larkin had watched carefully, ready to step in if ever the matter got out of hand. But he soon saw that Angela was able to refuse any liaison without causing offence, but in a firm enough voice that very few asked a second time, and so was able to relax slightly. The men appreciated the fact that Angela was a pleasant little body, always had a smile on her pretty face, with a good sense of humour so that she liked a joke as well as the next person. The fact that she wasn't sharing her favours with all and sundry marked her as a woman of principles, and the majority acknowledged that and treated her with respect so she was able to enjoy her job.

There was one particular man who seemed more keen on Angela than the others. His name was Eddie McIntyre, an Irishman who had spent time in America and who was now in Birmingham on business. He had become a regular in the pub and always made a beeline for her. He was full of confidence and funny stories. He made Angela laugh and forget about the cares of the day, but although she knew he was a bit sweet on her, she was careful not to give him any encouragement and refused his tips. She had no intention of getting a reputation, for once sullied it could never truly be wrung clean, she knew.

She did wonder though how long she would be able to work the long hours at night and leave her mother. Connie was good but only a child yet and Angela wasn't totally sure she realised just how sick Mary was.

However, Connie did; she was no fool. She thought Mary might like it if Daniel came to see them again, for her granny had enjoyed talking to him, but Daniel seemed to have gone back to his suffocating life in Sutton Coldfield. She was sorry about that in a way, and yet she had to admit he might find himself completely alone if he rejected the only parents he knew, because he seemed totally friendless. Connie couldn't understand it because he seemed nice enough and lovely with her granny.

But if Daniel wasn't going to come then he wasn't, and meanwhile she knew her granny was lonely. So, one morning, when her mother was out cleaning, she helped her granny on to the settee and manhandled her chair to the window where she could see out and watch the world go by.

'That will be better for you, Granny,' she said. 'Now the summer's here you won't need the warmth of the fire so much.'

It worked a treat, for as Mary waved at neighbours going past many would pop in and have a word. Some days she couldn't cope with much more than that, and on her vaguer days, if she wasn't always absolutely sure who everyone was, no one seemed to mind.

'God, this growing old is a bugger,' Norah said one morning, meeting Angela coming home from her cleaning job at the pub.

'But the alternative is worse,' Angela answered.

'That's true,' Norah agreed. 'And God knows we might all be the same some day.'

71

Angela knew that was all too true and she also knew 'the alternative' couldn't be put off for ever. She wondered how much Connie was aware of. But Connie knew her grandmother's life was ebbing away and knew also that her death would leave a big hole in her life because Mary had been a constant in her life since the day she'd been born.

There had been a time when Connie was younger when her mother had gone away. She had gone to Ireland and, though her grandmother loved talking about things past, she was always very vague about that time. Mary said Angela had had to go to Ireland and help a family out after the mother died, and yet she had previously told her that her mother had no relatives to take her in and so that was why she stayed with the McCluskys. And whoever the family had been that had called on her mother's help, her grandmother said she couldn't recall their name. Connie had missed her mother a great deal and been very glad her grandmother was there, a solid loving presence who soon would be no more.

The summer slipped by far too quickly. Angela could scarcely believe it was September and the schools were open again. Mary's chair was once more moved closer to the fire because those autumn days were windy ones and it was hard to keep the house draught-free. Despite the heat from the fire, Mary seemed constantly cold for, as the wind gusted down the road, it seeped through the ill-fitting windows and snaked under the door and along the floor, attacking the backs of Mary's legs like a cold flannel.

Angela, seeing how cold Mary was, brought down an extra cardigan and a blanket to wrap around her, knowing it was bound to get much colder still. She was glad she had the money to lay in enough coal and buy good food and plenty of it to help them all, and Mary in particular, cope with the drop in temperature. She had worried about leaving her mother on her own while she worked once Connie returned to school, but she needn't have worried for Mary was seldom alone as one of the neighbours would invariably pop in to see her. And at the weekend, when Angela worked the bar at the Swan in the evenings, Connie could stay up later because she hadn't school in the morning. Mary didn't keep late hours anyway and so the girl could easily help her grandmother to bed.

Angela knew how lucky she was. The house and area she lived in was not great but she was blessed with good, kind neighbours who cared for one another and a daughter and mother in a million. If Barry had returned from the war hale and hearty life would have been just perfect, but, as she reflected, few people achieve perfection in this life. She was content, only now she had met Stan's son, Daniel, she found herself wishing Stan had survived too. How proud he would have been of that young man, who, if he'd had the chance to know him, would have realised what a great father he would have been.

But there was nothing she could do about that, and besides, Daniel hadn't been near them since the early summer when they had put him straight about any misconceptions he'd had and told him the truth about his father. In the end he had returned home and taken a job in the bank Roger had secured for him that he definitely didn't want. Daniel was taking the line of least resistance for the sake of a quiet life, and yet she couldn't blame him. Betty and Roger had brought him up and made sure he had a good education, and he owed them something for that. But he couldn't spend the rest of his life being grateful for the good start they had given him, and she hoped he'd realise that eventually.

Soon, Angela had more to worry about than Daniel, for the winter had taken hold of the city by mid-November. The grey days were bone-chillingly cold and the houses so draughty and damp that it was hard to keep them adequately heated. Mary, not usually a complainer, seemed constantly cold and one day, coming in from work, Angela saw her mother's cheeks were glowing red. Though she still said she was cold, her skin was burning up.

'You have a fever,' Angela said. Her voice was calm and controlled but inside she was panicking. 'Bed is the best place for you. You must have my bed for now and I will take your place in the attic with Connie.'

'No need for such fuss.'

'I'm not fussing, Mammy, but being sensible,' Angela insisted. 'Now I'll just warm it up for you and bring down your things from the attic.'

Mary might have argued further but she was overtaken by a spasm of coughing and Angela crossed to the fire. It was almost out, even though Connie had filled a scuttle with coal before she had left for school. Usually Mary kept a good fire going but at that moment Angela was glad that she hadn't. She removed two firebricks with the tongs and wrapped them in a cloth she had ready, running up and slipping them between the sheets on her bed.

As she went up to the attic for Mary's things, Angela remembered for a moment the devastating Spanish flu that had rampaged through the whole world as the Great War came to an end. That epidemic had been indiscriminate and there was no cure – it depended on the individual's capacity to fight it – and at its height it affected a fifth of the world's population. It had raged on for two years and while some people died within days, when their lungs filled with fluid and they suffocated to death, others lingered on but still died just the same. By the time it had abated it had claimed fifty million lives, even more than the Great War, which had claimed sixteen million. Families were wiped out, many of the men who had survived a war of such magnitude lost their lives to the influenza and everyone had been fearful.

Many people had avoided crowds, shunning picture palaces and theatres, but children had had to go to school and Angela had sent Connie fearfully, knowing she wouldn't want to live if she were to lose her daughter. But she had come through unscathed and so had Angela and Mary. Angela was determined Connie wasn't going to catch anything from Mary now, and so she decided to adopt the strategies people had used before to try and combat the spread of the flu in 1918.

With her mother tucked up nice and warm in bed, Angela hung a sheet she'd soaked in disinfectant across the doorway. She vowed to wash her hands with carbolic soap and warm water whenever she dealt with Mary and would scald any plate, bowl, cup or cutlery she used.

A little later, after popping up to see Mary, who was lying in a fretful sleep, she went down to the presbytery and asked the priest to call. Then she went to see Paddy Larkin at the pub to tell him of her mother's collapse. Paddy was upset at the news for he thought a lot of Mary and so did Breda, and she told Angela not to worry about anything.

'If Maggie can take on all the cleaning, I'll give Paddy a hand in the pub at the weekend,' she said. 'Your place is with Mary now.'

Angela knew it was. Connie was home from school when the priest came, distressed to see her grandmother so ill. She watched her fighting for every breath and her anxious eyes met her mother's. They both thought that at any moment Mary would give up the struggle to breathe and slip away. The priest thought the same as he administered the Last Rites, though he didn't speak of it.

There was little Angela could do to ease Mary's symptoms, though a warmed flannel sprinkled with camphorated oil eased the pain in her chest a little. Mary didn't want Angela to call the doctor, for she claimed it was just a cold. Angela knew it was more serious than that and, when Mary refused to eat because it hurt so much to swallow, she said she was calling the doctor and that was the end of it.

The doctor confirmed that Mary had a severe chest infection and a quinsy in her throat. He fully approved of the precautions Angela was taking, for he said Mary's flu was very infectious. He prescribed a poultice for her to make up and lay on Mary's throat, as hot as she could stand, and he made up a bottle to help the cough that was further irritating her throat.

He could do little else. He knew the old lady was very ill and, with her heart weakened by the attack she had when she received the telegram telling her of the death of her son, he didn't think she had much of a chance of recovering from this. He didn't share this with Angela. He knew she was no fool and would know how seriously ill Mary was without having it spelt out for her.

Angela did know, and as the days unfolded she couldn't believe how Mary was hanging on. December wasn't very old when she fought off the debilitating fever, and the hacking cough that had once seemed to shake every bone in her body eased a little, as did her sore throat, so that she was able to swallow the broths Angela soon made ready for her. As the worst effects of the chest infection left her, strangely her mind seemed more lucid than it had been for many months and one day she said to Angela, 'You should be at work.'

'Work will keep,' Angela said. 'They're coping without me just now.'

'Maybe they will find they can cope without you permanently.'

Angela smiled. 'No,' she said. 'I have no fears on that score. They knew my place was with you when you were so ill. I am delighted to see you so much better. Sometimes I wished I could have breathed for you.'

Mary gave a wry smile. 'If I had thought of that, I might have wished you could too,' she said and then she added, 'Christmas is always a bad time for you, isn't it?'

'Of course it is.'

'Connie has noticed.'

'I can't help that,' Angela said.

'I told her it's because you still miss her daddy and you feel it more at Christmas,' Mary said.

'Well, you didn't tell a lie anyway,' Angela said. 'I do miss Barry. Every day I miss him, but I go on because I must, but what I did nine years ago, God, it eats away at me, Mammy. God may forgive me, but I will never forgive myself. I condemned my own child to misery and deprivation and it doesn't help that at the time there was no alternative and there still isn't. I sacrificed my own child, my baby, so that others wouldn't be hurt, and all I could give her was the locket that they probably won't let her keep. They might have even stolen it from her.'

77

Angela wasn't aware of when she began to cry. Mary hadn't the strength to put her arms around Angela as she wanted to and so she contented herself with patting her hand. And eventually Angela went on, 'I've never confessed, you know, Mammy. It was the worst thing I have ever done in my life and I could not bring myself to tell any priest. I asked God to punish me and He took Barry from me. When I saw you collapsed on the floor with the telegram in your hand I thought He had taken you too. Oh God, that would have been a heavy price to pay.'

'Oh my darling girl,' Mary said, her voice breaking with emotion. 'I don't know if God does things like that, but you really need to get absolution for your own sake.'

'Mammy, I can't,' Angela protested. 'Can you imagine what would happen if I did that? I know Father Brannigan can't tell anyone what I say in confession, but that won't stop him berating me, for he knows my voice. He will know the identity of the person the other side of that grille telling him of the dreadful, heinous thing I did and why, and that would be hard to bear. And what if someone overheard what I said in the confessional box, or heard him telling me off later and put two and two together? No, Mammy, I am not going down that road.'

'How about St Chad's? No one knows you there.'

Angela thought of the kindly looking priest that she knew people called Father John at St Chad's, the same man who had unknowingly protected her that dreadful Christmas Eve nine years before.

'I couldn't,' she said.

'Why not?' Mary demanded. 'That night, I know you took shelter there, but did he see you go into the church?'

Angela shook her head. 'I doubt it. I mean, he didn't seem to be in the main body of the church when I went in. I only saw him when the men from the house came looking for me. They admitted to him they hadn't seen me go in either, but they were checking everywhere because it was as if I had disappeared into thin air. Anyway, he sent them packing and if he had seen me come in in the agitated state I was in, I'm sure he would have spoken to me. I mean, the church wasn't empty as I told you, but it wasn't full like it is for Mass. There were only a handful of people there and, thinking about it, he probably knew most of them.'

'So why won't you go there? You said he looked kindly.'

'I have heard he's kind,' Angela said. 'But I might make him feel a bit of a fool, because I'd say he'd work out who I was, because I'll have to tell him everything if I want him to give me absolution. How could I tell a man, any man, never mind a priest, about that attack?'

'Angela, you cannot blame yourself,' Mary said. 'None of it was your fault.'

'D'you know, Mammy,' Angela said rather sadly. 'In the general scheme of things it hardly seems to matter whose fault it was.'

'God knows, and that's the truth,' Mary said.

'You know, when Barry died, I thought about enquiring after the child, or even bringing her here where she belongs to be brought up by her mother.'

'What stopped you?'

'Well it isn't done, is it?' Angela said. 'I mean, if you want a child or a baby, you go to an orphanage, but no one adopts a foundling from the workhouse. I've something to tell you, Mary. A few years ago, the pain and the anguish of not

79

knowing what happened to my little girl was so immense, I couldn't bear it. I was so wracked with the thought that she had died or was being cruelly treated, I was tearing my hair out with the worry of it all.'

'So what did you do?' asked Mary. She could see that Angela had a burden to unload and waited patiently for the woman she considered her daughter to speak.

'It was so bad that I went to the workhouse and asked about a young child who had been left there some years before. I pretended that I was making enquiries for a friend.'

'What did they tell you?' asked Mary, who couldn't believe that Angela had taken such a step. Though she realised that such a loving person as her daughter would leave no stone unturned once her heart was decided on such a course of action.

Angela's face took on a distressed aspect as she told Mary what had occurred.

'A hard-faced woman opened the door and wouldn't let me over the threshold. I tried to explain about the child and the locket but she refused to listen to me. Just said that once the children had come into the workhouse any family left had handed over control and they belonged to the workhouse now. Oh Mary, it was awful, she told me to forget about the child, it was no concern of my friend's now, and then slammed the door in my face. I felt sick, knowing that my child could be behind those walls. I'll never know what happened to her now – if she is safe, if she lived or died or if a friendly hand ever held hers when she was sad or lonely.'

Angela was in tears again now and Mary reached out to comfort her. 'She is in God's hands, Angela, and we must pray that He is her comfort as He must be ours.'

'Perhaps it is just as well as it would have opened a can of worms, wouldn't it? Eventually they would have tumbled to it that I was the child's mother and then everyone would know and the child's life could be blighted even further by the taint of sin. And how would Connie cope then, knowing the truth of it all?'

Mary didn't answer. She was now in tears too, knowing Connie would never be able to cope with such a distressing revelation. 'There is nothing to be done about it then,'

Angela nodded. 'That's the way of it. And my heart will break with each passing year as we approach Christmas. The pain never diminishes, because as the child grows she will know what she is and how alone she is in the world. She will likely experience no kind word or deed in the whole of her life and I should suffer for putting her through that.'

Mary's heart hurt also for she knew there were no words to say to ease Angela's conscience. A priest might but if she wouldn't go to see one then that avenue was closed too. She could no longer look on Angela's sorrowful eyes and her own were stinging with tiredness as she gave a sigh and lay back on the bed. Angela watched Mary's eyes flutter shut and she tucked her in and tiptoed from the room.

SIX

A few days later, Angela had returned to work. Mary insisted as she said Christmas was coming and they couldn't live on fresh air. Angela was glad to be going back and Paddy Larkin's wife in particular was delighted with Angela's return.

'They've all been asking for you and, to be honest, I wasn't sure we'd see you this side of Christmas. Is Mary much recovered?'

Angela shook her head. 'She's over the flu, which is a blessing, but she'll not recover much now I don't think. But she insisted I go back to work because she hates to think she is being a burden and Connie and I can manage her between us.'

'You have a good daughter there, Angela,' Breda said. 'She's a credit to you.'

'Thank you,' Angela said. 'I'd be grateful if you'd keep your ear to the ground for a single bed going begging. Mary won't stay in the bedroom, says there's no need and we have enough to do without fetching and carrying for her all day long. I can see her point, for the bedroom is cold and probably lonely. She insists on being downstairs during the day as she likes to be in the middle of things. But she does sleep a lot now, and she's hardly well rested in the chair.'

'I don't have to look far,' Breda said. 'I have one going spare myself. You can have it and welcome.'

'Oh, thank you.'

'No problem,' Breda said. 'As it's a dry day I'll get Paddy to bring it round later after closing time about half three. Any of his regulars will give him a hand, especially if they know what it's for.'

And so by four o'clock that same day Paddy and two of the customers carried in the bed. Angela already had firebricks heating up to be wrapped in flannel and laid on the mattress in case it should be damp, and she warmed the sheets and blankets at the fire before she would let Mary into the bed.

Mary would never have complained, but she was very glad to have the opportunity to lie down when she was tired during the day. She never found she had any kind of a refreshing sleep when she dropped off in the chair and she often woke with a crick in her neck. She said how grateful she was and continued, 'Now, Angela, I want you to go to your own bed each night. I don't want you sleeping in the chair next to me as you have done the last few nights. I will be as right as rain on my own.'

'We'll see.'

'Angela, I mean it. No one can sleep well in a chair.'

'And I said I'd see,' Angela said firmly. 'I'm having the doctor call to have a look at you and then we'll decide where I will sleep.'

She was concerned about her mother because, since the long conversation about the abandoned child, she had said virtually nothing of any consequence. Sometimes a day would pass and Mary wouldn't speak a word, or she would start a sentence and forget the end and look confused and bewildered. Or she would be overcome by tiredness and fall asleep in the middle of talking. The times when she was clear and lucid were getting fewer. Added to this, Angela could get her to eat only sparingly; tucking her into the bed earlier, she noticed that her mother had lost so much weight that the bones could be felt beneath the skin.

'Don't want the doctor,' Mary said mutinously. 'Can't do nothing for me.'

Angela knew her mother was probably right, but wanted assurance from the doctor that she was doing all she could and she said, 'Humour me, Mammy?'

Mary gave a brief nod and added, 'Now do something for me.'

'What?'

'See the priest in confession.'

'Mammy . . .'

'For my sake,' Mary cried. 'How can I die happy knowing you are carrying that huge load of guilt on your shoulders?'

Angela didn't insult Mary's intelligence by saying she wasn't going to die any time soon for she was very much afraid she well might. As for Mary herself, in her lucid moments, when her mind was clear and not all jumbled up, she knew she was dying and it was just a toss-up whether her mind or body would give up first. She didn't much mind, for she was often so weary and full of aches and pains and she didn't fear death. Maybe it would have been nice to have lasted a little longer to see Connie as a young woman, but she knew that wasn't going to happen and when she died she would see Matt again and her two beloved sons. She could almost look forward to that.

Neither mentioned their concerns and Mary said, 'Will you do this one thing for me?'

Angela swallowed the lump in her throat and said huskily, 'I'll see.'

Mary lay back on the pillows and said nothing more. Angela pulled the blankets round and saw Mary's eyelids flutter shut and she gave a sigh as she reached for her coat.

The doctor listened to Angela's concerns about Mary and agreed to see her, though he suspected he could do little for her because basically what she was suffering from was old age. To give him his due though, he gave her a thorough examination. He felt her limbs all over, asked her to put out her tongue and looked down her throat, then felt her neck, listened to her heartbeat, sounded her chest, checked her pulse and asked her plenty of questions about any aches and pains she might have and her general health. He was surprised she had survived the flu, for he hadn't been sure she would, but he knew it would make little difference for she was still a very sick woman.

Using the guise of washing his hands, he went to the cubby hole at the top of the cellar steps and Angela poured the warm water into the bowl she had ready.

'What d'you think, Doctor?' she said. She spoke softly, though Mary was out of earshot, for the bed was against the window on the other side of the room.

'Her heart is very tired,' the doctor said in the same soft tones. 'You were warned this day would come and you have looked after your mother well for her to last this long, but that last bout of flu has knocked her for six. Don't worry about her not eating much. Her stomach is distended and her throat is inflamed. She'll probably not feel like eating much and it isn't as if she's using a lot of energy. Just make sure she has plenty to drink.'

Angela nodded. 'I will, Doctor. D'you know how her illness will progress?'

'Her organs will gradually start closing down,' the doctor said. 'It will be very peaceful and pain-free, I will see to that, but you have to come to terms with the fact that you must say goodbye to your mother sooner rather than later.'

Tears filled Angela's eyes. It wasn't that she was surprised, but death was so final.

'H-How long has she got?'

'It's impossible to say exactly.'

'You must have some idea?'

The doctor gave a shrug. 'These things are very difficult to predict but it could even be before Christmas.'

Angela gasped. 'You are talking of weeks, just weeks,' she said.

The doctor gave a brief nod and Angela knew, whatever her mother said, she would be sleeping in the chair from now on.

'I'm sorry the news couldn't be better,' the doctor said.

'It's not your fault, Doctor,' Angela assured him. 'Death is one thing that comes to us all.'

After Angela had let the doctor out and her mother had dropped off to sleep again, she made a cup of tea and sat before the fire drinking it. She knew she had to go to confession for she couldn't deny Mary what she had pleaded with her to do, especially when all her life her mother had asked for so little. Angela knew for the sake of her immortal soul, not to mention her own peace of mind, she had to speak to a priest. She dismissed Father Brannigan straight away for he wasn't the sort of priest she couldn't imagine anyone confiding in; he was far too abrupt and judgemental. She didn't know really that the priest from St Chad's would be any better, but folk spoke well of him and at least he didn't know her. She decided to go to confession and tell him all, though it caused a blush to flood her cheeks just to think about it.

She told her mother of her intention when she woke. Mary said nothing but she smiled so Angela knew she was pleased, and that helped convince her she was doing the right thing.

Both St Catherine's and St Chad's priests heard confession on Thursday evening from seven o'clock so when, the following Thursday, Angela left the house for confession, only Mary knew which church she would be making for. It was a fair step and the evening was cold and icy. Sour freezing fog swirled in the cold air and Angela pulled her scarf higher to cover her mouth as she hurried through the night.

She was glad to reach the relative protection of the church and she slipped inside gratefully, dipping her hand into the holy water and making the sign of the cross as she did so. She had timed it well for the hour for confession was almost over, as she had intended, and only two old ladies were waiting. Angela genuflected before the altar and went into the pew behind them, knowing if anyone came after her she would let them go in first. She wanted no one outside the confessional box to overhear what she was eventually going to confess.

She knelt down, aware of her heart hammering in her breast

and the fact that the trembling of her body was not just due to the cold. She prayed more earnestly than usual and what she prayed for was the courage to go through with this and tell the priest everything. It was like laying her soul bare and she had no way of knowing how the priest would react, and she also knew she mustn't mention names or anything that the priest might use later to identify who she was.

The two old ladies obviously had few sins to confess and were in the confessional box for only a matter of minutes each. As no one else had entered the church, Angela was next to kneel on the pad in the dimly lit box and face the grille, knowing the priest on the other side would soon be listening intently.

'Bless me, Father, for I have sinned,' Angela said. 'It is a fortnight since my last confession.'

John Hennessy didn't recognise the voice. Having heard confession now for some years, he knew the voices of most of his parishioners. He was also aware of the nuances in voices, and knew the woman on the other side of the grille was nervous, and so he said reassuringly, 'Go on, my child.'

And Angela went on intoning the litany of things she had done wrong. In truth she wasn't a great sinner. She was honest and trustworthy, she used no profane language – as a child she'd known that if she used any bad words she would have had the legs smacked off her, at the very least – nor did she tell lies in the general way of things. Sometimes she would get a little impatient with Mary. She never said anything and tried hard not to show it, but the church said the thought was as bad as the deed and so she confessed to that and the lackadaisical attitude she had to her prayers, especially in the morning, and then she was silent.

The silence grew between them and eventually the priest asked, 'Is there anything else?'

Angela almost said there wasn't. It would be easy to accept absolution from the priest, do the penance he gave her and leave. But then she remembered Mary. She knew her mother wanted her to do this and feared she would never feel proper ease without confessing it. This might be the last thing she could ever do for the woman who had loved her so totally almost all her life, and so she gave a heartfelt sigh and said, 'Oh yes, Father, and it was one dreadful wicked thing I did too.'

'Go on,' said the priest.

Angela felt the slight chill in his voice and her heart sank but she continued, 'This goes back some time, Father, nine years in fact. You see, when my husband enlisted in 1915 we were left with little money to live on and we had a wee daughter and my mother-in-law also lived with us. One of us had to find work and that person had to be me, and so I took work in the munitions while my mother-in-law minded my child.'

The priest nodded. Many of the mothers in his parish had had to follow the same route during the Great War if their husbands were serving soldiers. It had always seemed monstrous to him that, despite the men putting their lives on the line for King and country, so little was paid to their dependants that the women also had to work in such dangerous places to be able to feed their children and themselves and pay the rent.

'Did this wicked thing happen in the munition works?' he asked, because he had heard that some of the people who worked in those industries were no better than they ought to be.

'Not exactly, but in a way,' Angela said in an effort to explain fully. She went on to say how, with such few men about, any women who wanted to were given the opportunity to learn to drive.

The priest was surprised at that. 'And did you take that opportunity?'

'I did,' Angela said. 'And I loved it too. I drove the small truck all over the city, but the firm had brought a man out of retirement to drive the big truck on longer trips. Then, one day, the older man had a heart attack and though he didn't die, the doctor said he was too ill to continue. There was at the time a great shell shortage and at that moment they had hundreds of shells piled high on the large truck that he had been due to drive to the docks that day. The boss said as I was the best and most experienced driver, and virtually the only one who could read maps, I must go in his stead.'

'My goodness,' the priest said. 'It is a great distance to the docks. Were you not nervous at all?'

'Oh yes, Father, as nervous as a kitten and scared,' Angela said with truth. 'But then I told myself my husband was probably scared when he had to face the enemy but he couldn't run away. And I knew how badly the shells were needed and with the older man out of action there was no one else to take them but me.'

'D'you know, you have surprised me,' the priest said. 'I shouldn't be, I suppose, for women are driving all sorts of vehicles these days, but I never imagined girls driving round trucks packed with explosives.'

'It's no more dangerous than making them, Father,' Angela maintained. 'There have been explosions in other places and girls killed and maimed. Before they let you go on to the factory floor, not only did you have to wear a boiler suit, a hat to cover all your hair and a mask and gloves, you also had to remove any metal you had on you. That included wedding rings and so I left my ring at home after that first day. Even hair grips had to come out because any metal could generate a spark.'

'I see that,' the priest said. 'I must say, the women of Britain were truly remarkable in that war.'

'Pity we weren't rewarded properly then, Father,' Angela wanted to say. She didn't, though she had been irritated that, despite all the agitation and campaigning by the suffragettes, and after women had been left to virtually run the country in the Great War, only women over the age of thirty who were homeowners had got the vote in 1918. But now wasn't the time to go into that. So she just said, 'Yes, Father.'

Time was getting on and Father John's stomach growled suddenly and he though longingly of the supper his sister, Eileen, would have ready for him at home. Eileen had been widowed early in the war but she was childless and had moved in to care for her brother when his previous house-keeper had left for more lucrative war work. Eileen's maternal instincts were brought to the fore looking after her younger brother, not least in shielding him from some of his zealous or needy parishioners. She actually had a good and generous heart, but thought some people didn't think the priest deserved a right to time off. She always said he was too kind for his own good and if he didn't watch out they would suck him dry.

The priest often thought his sister was probably right, but he did like to give people the benefit of the doubt and because of his profession was often pulled into other people's lives. And this young woman – for he could tell by her voice she wasn't old – had spoken of some terrible thing she had done. He really had to get to the bottom of what that was and, if she was truly sorry, dispense absolution, which he imagined was what she had come for.

So he said quite gently, 'I think there is something specific hanging heavy on your heart that you need to tell me about. You were on your way to the docks, I believe?'

'Yes,' Angela said and she told the priest of the long, hazardous journey. She'd been glad of the map the boss had drawn for her, which she'd had to refer to often to prevent getting lost. 'I was so relieved when I reached the docks and then found I was in a long queue, because many munition works had sent down any shells they had. Most of the drivers were young women like me, though there were a few much older men. When my truck was eventually unloaded, I looked for somewhere to eat before heading back. And after a feed of fish and chips I headed for home.

'I found it much harder going back, for all I had an empty truck then. There was far more traffic on the roads and I had to really concentrate, especially when true darkness fell and the journey seemed to take forever. I was feeling thoroughly worn out by the time I eventually I saw the lights of the yard. The boss had said he would wait for me, both to see I was all right and to secure the truck in the yard overnight. He wanted to call a taxi to take me home, but I knew it would cause a real stir in the street and so I refused. I offered him the change from the ten-shilling note he'd given me for my dinner, but he told me to keep it and I dropped the money into my coat pocket and left.

'I was nearly home,' Angela went on and the priest noted the change in her voice and knew she was no longer telling him her story, but living it. 'I was just yards away from safety when I was set upon by three drunken soldiers. They wouldn't believe I was a respectable, married woman because, as I said, I didn't wear my wedding ring to work. They thought because I was coming home alone at that time, I was a woman of the night, and the fact that I had money loose in my coat pocket seemed to prove it. Nothing I said made any difference. They said they wanted what I had been doing already that night, only they weren't going to pay for it. I fought them and they beat me up, nearly rendering me unconscious, and then they violated me.'

The priest was shocked and not at all surprised that Angela was upset at the telling. Gasping sobs seemed to be coming from deep within her and the priest said comfortingly, 'You have not committed a sin, my dear, it's the men who violated you did that. Did the police apprehend them?'

Angela took a grip on herself and said, 'I never told the police.'

'Why ever not?'

Angela told the priest that the families of those in the services had been warned not to worry fighting men about issues at home, especially as they would be unable to do anything about it.

'How would my husband have felt if he'd heard I had been raped and he hadn't been here to protect me?' Angela asked. 'I wouldn't tell him, of course, but if I told the police it would become common knowledge and I couldn't guarantee he wouldn't find out.'

'It seems monstrous that they got away scot free.'

'I know,' Angela said. 'But it gets worse from there.'

The priest wondered how it could get much worse, but he soon found out because Angela described the horror she felt when she realised that the violation had left her pregnant.

The priest heard the anguish and panic in her voice and he didn't wonder at it, because it was the very worst thing to happen to a woman and his heart felt heavy for her. She told the priest about the options they'd discussed. In the end they'd decided that the best thing was for her to hide away with a family member and, when the child was born, give her up to the Catholic orphanage for adoption.

'That was a very brave thing to do,' the priest said. 'In the circumstances you described to me, it was the only thing to do. And by doing this you have probably made a childless couple very happy and—'

'Father, the orphanage wouldn't take her,' Angela cried. She was now desperate that he hear it all, see how wicked she really was. 'They said that, since the war, applications for adoption had fallen off and they were full to bursting and could take no more babies or children.'

The priest nodded. He could well see how that might happen. 'So what did you do then?'

'What d'you think I did, Father?' Angela said. 'What choices does a woman have when she is having a child that cannot be her husband's? Could I bring her home and risk someone writing to my husband to say that not only had I been carrying on with another, I'd had the fancy man's bastard child? That would have ripped the heart from my dear husband and maybe he would have been too upset to take care and lost his life because of that. He died later anyway, but he died knowing I loved him and would be waiting for him at home with our legitimate daughter when the war drew to a close. And to be honest, I also feared the stigma, and not for myself alone. The open contempt that would have been shown to me would also have been the child's lot as she grew, and it would have impinged on my other daughter and my mother-in-law as well. Acknowledging all this, I took that tiny, vulnerable baby in a basket and left her on the workhouse steps and ran away.'

Angela was weeping but she carried on through the tears. 'There isn't one day, not even one hour in the day, when I don't think about that child and wish there had been any alternative to doing what I did. I am sick to the soul of me when I remember doing this, for you see I loved her, regardless of how she was conceived. She took away a sizeable slice of my heart and that was why I gave her the locket. To try and show her she was loved even though I was unable to take care of her. I tried to find her later, but the workhouse sent me away.'

She stopped then, wondering if she had said too much. She hadn't intended to mention the locket but Father John was barely aware she had stopped. He was remembering that Christmas Eve night many years ago when people had come from the workhouse looking for a girl or woman who had dumped a baby on the workhouse steps and disappeared. He remembered thinking at the time she must have been desperate to do such a thing. And she had been, for the woman the other side of that grille was the mother of that unfortunate child, and the child was conceived through a violent rape that she was an innocent party to. The perpetrators had gone unpunished mainly because of her husband who had been serving overseas.

As far as he could see, the woman was a victim as well as the child. He remembered that, when he'd next visited the workhouse to give the last rites to a dying man, he had asked if they had found the mother of the child left on Christmas Eve. They had not and had added that the baby had been clutching a silver locket in her hand.

'Oh,' the priest had said, surprised.

'Yes,' the governor, a Mr Benedict Masters, had said. 'It's not the usual thing foundlings are clutching when they arrive here, because it doesn't look tacky.'

'Where is it now?'

'In the safe in the office,' Mr Masters had said, 'I'll show you.'

He had led the way and a few moments later the priest was holding a beautiful silver locket in his hand.

'They are not allowed to own things from outside in the workhouse,' Mr Masters had explained. 'We provide the uniform and their clothes for church on Sunday and on arrival they are given a comb, a toothbrush and a hairbrush, which they must look after. Very few bring anything with them. In many cases the families have sold or pawned all they owned except the clothes on their back, which are usually in rags, to try and prevent ending up here. But if they have anything they will be given back those things when they leave us, which will probably be when this girl goes into service. I might add, the trustees were all for selling this locket to help pay for the child's keep as her mother had disappeared. I said it might be risky to do that because the locket looks as if it's worth something and we might be accused of theft.'

'Why did you bother to do that?'

'Oh I don't know, a moment of conscience, I suppose,' the man had said. 'I mean, this child has nothing. Somewhere there is a mother, maybe a family, but all that has gone now and she is alone in the world and I thought the locket might mean something. There was a reason she was given it. Anyway, I thought we shouldn't just dispose of it.'

The priest had been impressed by the morals of the manager of the workhouse, for he knew many who would have pocketed it.

'It's got something inside,' the manager had said. 'Open it.'

The priest had clicked open the locket to reveal the miniature of a very old photograph.

'A wedding, I would say,' Mr Masters had commented.

The priest had nodded. 'Yes, but why golden ringlets tied with red ribbon on the other side?'

Mr Masters had shrugged. 'Might be her mother's hair, I suppose. It isn't likely we will ever find out.'

'No,' the priest had agreed.

It was incredible that nine years later he was hearing the confession of the mother who had left that child on the steps and he heard her weeping quietly as he said:

'Please don't cry and hear what I am going to say. It doesn't matter how bad a crime is, God will forgive you if you are truly sorry, and in your case I think you were sinned against rather than a sinner yourself. You have been riven with guilt and sorrow ever since, so you will have God's forgiveness – so trouble yourself no more about that. Your penance will be a decade of the rosary and now make a good act of contrition. Wait in the church for me please. There is something I need to discuss with you. And I will join you as soon as I have said my prayers.'

'Yes, Father,' Angela said. 'Thank you, Father.'

However, when Angela stepped from the confessional she

made straight for the door and began to run along Whittall Street that dark and cold winter's night. She was glad of the fog that helped hide her as she ran under the spluttering street lamps because there was no way she was going to hang about for the priest to talk to her and maybe make waves and uncover the secret she had kept hidden successfully for years. Her heart did feel lighter though, and it was good to know that through the priest God had absolved her of blame, but she wanted no more of the priest than that.

By the time Father John came out of the confessional she was sitting in a tram on her way along Bristol Street.

Connie was surprised her mother had been so long and Angela excused herself by saying that she had met people in the church and chatted to this one and that.

'Must have had plenty of interest to say,' Connie said. 'Wonder you didn't stick to the floor. That church is always perishing.'

Angela's eyes met those of her mother, but she said nothing else to her daughter, thinking silence the wisest policy. She would tell her mother everything when they were alone and Connie began telling them both of something that had happened at school and nothing more was said about confession. Angela waited until she had gone to bed before she told her mother what had transpired. Mary was so relieved at what the priest had said; later, when Angela knelt by the bed to do the penance the priest had given her, Mary joined in too.

The priest's sister had plenty to say about her brother's tardiness, for the supper she had kept warming for him was almost ruined.

'I'm sorry,' he said, 'but I really couldn't help it. I heard the confession of a strange woman last thing. It was strange in that I've not heard her voice before and she had a long tale to tell and it took some time to hear it all.'

'I see,' said Eileen, knowing her brother would say no more. Whatever he'd been told was in the confessional and therefore secret. 'Well, eat your supper now and I hope it's not too dried up.'

'It's fine,' Father John said. Eileen was a good cook, and he enjoyed his food.

That night, though, he could have been eating cardboard and he'd hardly have noticed. His mind was full of the young woman's disturbing tale which he could share with nobody.

SEVEN

Though Angela's conscience felt a lot easier after her visit to the priest, she was so dispirited over what the doctor had told her about her mother she had no desire to decorate the house for Christmas.

Connie was aware just how ill her grandmother was and she said to Sarah, 'I think Mammy is wrong. Granny is going downhill fast. Mammy thinks I don't know, but I'm not a baby any more and I'm not stupid. I can see things for myself and I would like to make the house more cheerful for her. As well as that, Maggie and Michael are spending the day with us and they won't want to sit and eat Christmas dinner in a dull boring house at Christmas time.'

Sarah agreed with her, as did her mother, and the two girls set off the Saturday before Christmas to see what bargains they could find in the Market Hall in the Bullring.

'Where did you get so much money?' Sarah asked as they walked along Bristol Street and Connie showed her the two pound notes she had in a purse in her basket.

'Well, I didn't rob a bank,' Connie replied with a grin. 'I hoiked it out of my money box with a knife.'

'Yeah, but where did you get so much money to put in there in the first place?'

'Mainly from my uncles in America. They send me dollars every birthday and Christmas and Mammy takes them to the post office and changes them into pounds and pence and tells me to save them for a rainy day. Point is, this is meant as a surprise for Mammy so I couldn't ask her for money for garlands and things she knows nothing about. If I can I'd like to get some gloves for Mammy too – the pair she has are full of holes and she's darned them so often there's more darn than original glove now.'

'My mother's gloves are almost as bad,' Sarah said. 'But I'm a bit short of rich uncles in America. My sisters are very good and when they come to see us they nearly always slip me something, a thrupenny bit, or a tanner, but they can't afford more than that.'

'I know money's very scarce generally,' Connie said. 'I would be pleased to leave school as soon as possible and earn some money of my own and make life easier for Mammy financially. I really hope she gives up this notion of me getting my higher certificate.'

'Mammy says she doesn't know how she can afford to keep you at school.'

'Granny told me she saved a lot of money from when she was in munitions in the war,' Connie said. 'And there's something else, only you're not to tell a soul about this.'

'You know I won't,' Sarah said.

'Well, Mammy has some jewellery.'

'Jewellery?' Sarah repeated.

'Yeah. Granny said it was left to her by this old man who owned a shop and Mammy used to work for him before she married my father and afterwards for a bit too. Apparently he thought a lot of Mammy and when he died she found he had left her some of his mother's jewellery.'

'Where is it?'

'In the bank,' Connie said. 'The man left it in there for her and it's still there. Granny said Mammy intends selling most of it so she can fund me going to college.'

'Going to college?' Sarah repeated. 'Oh, get you. You'll be too big for your boots if you go to college.'

'I didn't say I wanted to go to any college,' Connie said. 'I'll talk to Mammy and make her see that. All her life she's been saving for me and my future. I'd rather she sold the jewellery and used that money and the money in the post office so that she can take life a bit easier and stop worrying about me so much. Anyway, we're here now so let's see what we can find to make the house a bit more Christmassy.'

There was plenty to choose from and Connie was delighted to find a little wooden set of the nativity that she knew would look a treat on the sideboard. Then there were deep green holly leaves sporting plenty of bright red berries woven into wreaths and tied up with red ribbon, as well as laurel garlands and paper streamers to decorate the room, and candy canes, glass trinkets, tinsel icicles and candles for the tree. And there was still enough left to buy her mother a beautiful pair of thick woollen gloves. They carried all the stuff to Sarah's house as her mother had agreed to keep it all in the bedroom till Christmas Eve. As Christmas Eve was a Saturday, Angela would be working that evening and they wanted to get the house decorated while she was away and Sarah was going to help her.

Barely had Angela left the house on Christmas Eve evening than Connie was bounding up the stairs to fetch the tree from the attic, just before Sarah arrived with bulging bags of decorations. Connie had told Mary what they were doing and she had no objection, though she dozed most of the time as the girls hung the holly wreaths in the window and the laurel garlands across the fireplace. They put paper streamers across the room and the nativity in pride of place on the sideboard.

The tree looked magnificent with all the new things Connie had bought arranged on it. They'd had other decorations too that they had put on the tree in previous years, but Connie discarded any that looked old and shabby. They put the candles in place at the end of the branches and placed the star on the top, then stood away from it to survey their handiwork.

'It looks grand,' Sarah said. 'I helped Mammy with ours a couple of days ago and it's not nearly so fine as this.'

'I will be happy if it puts a smile on Mammy's face,' Connie said. 'That's why I wanted it to look so nice.'

And in it that she succeeded, for Angela was delighted to see the place looking so ready for Christmas. It also made her feel a bit guilty, the fact that this would in all likelihood be Mary's last Christmas. It should have meant her wanting to make the place more festive, but instead Angela had let the misery she felt at the fairly imminent demise of her mother engulf everything, making it a poor Christmas for everyone.

She praised the new things Connie had bought, though she knew her daughter would have had to get money out of her money box because it was the only money she had. But she said nothing about that, not wanting to spoil the moment.

In the end it was a lovely Christmas. Maggie and Mike

103

arrived after Mass and Mary, with the considerable help of Angela and Maggie, got up and sat at the table on a chair padded with cushions. She didn't eat much of the delicious dinner and pudding, but had a smile on her face nearly all the time at the banter around the table and even joined in a time or two.

With Christmas and New Year out of the way, Angela, like everyone else, battled through the frozen days of January. As the temperatures dropped, biting, squally wind hurled itself around the house and chill gusts seeped under doors and rattled ill-fitting windows. Ice patterns formed inside the windows of the bedroom and attic and outside icicles dangled from window ledges and frost scrunched underfoot, made even slippier with the fresh snow falling constantly.

Angela was glad that she had made the decision to find her mother a spare bed so she could sleep downstairs and grateful that she could buy enough coal to keep at least one room comfortably warm. She was sleeping in the chair next to her mother every night now and Mary had given up protesting about it. Angela knew the schools would re-open soon and she would be back to worrying about Mary every time she had to leave her, but there was no help for it and the neighbours were very good at popping in.

Halfway through the month the doctor called and, after examining Mary, he increased the dosage of morphine.

'She will sleep more now,' he said. 'But it will give her more relief from pain.'

'Is she in pain?' Angela asked. 'She never said.'

'I'd say she's pretty uncomfortable,' the doctor said. 'Her face is quite drawn.'

It was, Angela realised, and she felt guilty she hadn't seen it for herself. She collected the medicine straight away, handing over the shillings that it cost, and gave it to Mary. She soon found the doctor was quite right, the new medicine made Mary sleepier. He had said she could go at any time and Angela would watch her slumbering for ages at first, her chest gently rising and falling as her life slipped further and further away. One day she knew her mother's heart would stop, her chest would be still and Mary would be no more, and that thought filled her with despondency.

It was towards the end of the month when Mary appeared restless in the bed. Angela only slept lightly now in the chair next to the bed and she was awake instantly. Mary was thrashing about slightly but her eyes remained closed and Angela wondered if she was in the throes of a nightmare. She searched for her hand and held it tight. The touch seemed to reassure her and Angela said gently, 'You're all right, Mammy. I'm right here beside you.'

Mary sighed and her hand tightened in Angela's for a brief second. Then her hand fell away, there was rattle in her throat and the room was suddenly very still. Mary had gone and already Angela was feeling lost without her.

In the days that followed, Angela knew she couldn't have coped so well without the neighbours' support, particularly that of Maggie and Mike, who helped her arrange the funeral and were constantly there for her and for Connie too. The girl was bitterly distressed at her grandmother's death. She would miss Mary a great deal. Although she had known how desperately ill she had been, and had sort of accepted the fact that she wouldn't recover, she still felt her loss keenly.

'It's because death is so final,' Angela tried to explain when Connie said how she was feeling. 'No one can really prepare for a loved one's death, even if it is expected. But she is gone now and we must go on through life without her.'

'It's hard, isn't it, Mammy?'

Angela nodded. 'It's the hardest thing in the world,' she said, and she gulped as tears ran down her face and she reached for her daughter and held her tight as she finished. 'This is the greatest pain you will ever feel,' she said. 'It's truly heart-breaking and we will have to do our best to comfort one another.'

Condolence letters with folded twenty-dollar bills inside came from Fin and Colm in New York. They had been kept abreast of Mary's illness from the beginning, and they also included Mass cards so that Masses could be said for the repose of Mary's soul. Angela put them on top of the coffin in front of the altar, along with the flowers from the neighbours.

The church was packed for Requiem Mass for Mary had been very well liked. Afterwards they walked behind the hearse to Key Hill Cemetery in Hockley where Mary would be buried next to her husband Matt. They stood around the grave Mary's coffin had been lowered into, listened to more prayers for her soul and then threw the clods of earth on top of the coffin, which Connie thought the hardest thing she had ever done.

Breda Larkin had felt so sorry for Angela for the loss of Mary. She knew she had loved her dearly and that it would be hard for Connie too. She hadn't known Mary that well herself but everyone said what a fine woman she was, so she offered to make up a spread for the guests after the funeral with her daughter's help. Angela was glad to take her up on the offer and when she looked at the laden table she was so grateful, for Breda had done them proud and given Mary the send-off she deserved.

'It's a great pity none of her sons were able to make it for the funeral,' Norah Doherty said to Angela.

'She wouldn't have expected them to, you know,' Angela said. 'She always said when a person goes to America it is like they are dead. Some don't even write much. Both Fin and Colm were always good about the letter writing, but she never expected to see either of them ever again.'

'I suppose but . . .'

'It would have been a great expense for them,' Angela said. 'And they have wives and families of their own now, and jobs, when not everyone does. Soup kitchens to feed the hungry and the homeless are operating in New York, so the lads told me, so maybe it isn't a good time to leave jobs. It isn't as if she'd know. In fact, if they'd come some time before she died, she was barely conscious a lot of the time and might have struggled to remember them.'

'Aye, I suppose you're right,' Norah said. 'Turning up for the funeral is only for the people left and that's you and Connie. I am sorry to the heart for you both.'

'Norah, I can't explain what the loss of Mammy means to me, because the depth of feeling is so great,' Angela said. 'It will take me some time to get over it and Fin and Colm popping over for the funeral and then returning after would hardly help at all.'

'No, I don't suppose it would,' Norah conceded. 'Anyway, you know where my door is if you want anything. Who's your Connie talking to over there?' she said with a jerk of her head to the other side of the room.

'Daniel,' Angela said in surprise, for she hadn't expected him to come and hadn't noticed him arrive. 'It's Stan Bishop's lad, though his name is Daniel Swanage now.'

'Oh yes, I remember Mary telling me,' Norah said.

'I'd best go and have a word as he has made the effort to come,' Angela said.

At that moment Daniel was saying to Connie, 'How old are you?'

'Fourteen in May,' Connie said.

'Oh, I'd have put you as older, sixteen or so.'

Connie laughed. 'Thanks. Do I look that haggard?'

'No, it's not to do with how you look,' Daniel said. 'It's how you are. I mean you are very mature for thirteen.'

Connie shrugged. 'Well, that's the age I am and it means I could leave school in the summer, like Sarah is going to. That is, if Mammy hadn't got this crackpot notion of my getting my higher School Certificate and going on to college or university.'

'I'm sure she is thinking of doing the best for you.'

Connie would have said more on the subject but she saw her mother approaching, so she fell silent as Angela reached them and said, 'How lovely to see you again, Daniel. Did you know it was Mary's funeral today or were you coming anyway?'

'He knew,' Connie put in. 'I wrote and told him in case he wanted to come.'

'I did,' Daniel said. 'I only wish now that I had known how ill Mrs McClusky was before she died.'

Angela shook her head. 'She'd hardly have known you, Daniel. The doctor increased her medication and so she slept most of the time and often seemed disorientated when she did wake. She sometimes struggled to remember my name, but strangely always knew Connie's.'

'I'm sure you will miss her sorely.'

Tears stung Angela's eyes at the sympathy in Daniel's voice and Connie gave a gasp as the enormity of her loss threatened to overwhelm her. She turned from her mother and Daniel and hurried away. Daniel would have called her back but Angela stopped him.

'Leave her be for now,' she said. 'Eventually we will help one another to cope, but she is still coming to terms with it herself just now.'

Daniel, though, was worried about the look of abject misery on Connie's face as she'd turned from them and when Angela went off to greet other mourners he went looking for her. After a few minutes' searching, he realised she was nowhere in the room or corridor and so went outside. He heard her before he saw her; she was hiding behind the dustbins and crying fit to break her heart and he was moved to pity for her.

She started when she heard him approach. He handed her his white pocket handkerchief and said, 'Don't feel embarrassed about crying. When a loved one dies you are bound to feel sad.'

He saw that she was shivering with cold and he stripped off his jacket and put it around her shoulders as he said, 'It's really too cold for you to be out here any longer though, particularly without a coat. Do you think you are ready to go back inside now?'

Connie wasn't at all sure if she was emotionally ready or not, but Daniel was right, the cold was intense. She gave a brief nod and they went back in side by side and stood in the corridor together. She wished the funeral was over and everyone would go and she could give way to the grief she felt churning inside her.

Watching her, Daniel realised he had never felt deep sorrow like that. True, his mother had died at his birth, but he hadn't really known of her existence till the solicitor's letter, which had also told him of his father's death. He had been angry with his aunt and uncle for not telling him the truth, and he regretted that he hadn't been able to get to know him. But he hadn't mourned the man he had never known. Daniel's feelings then were not remotely like the gut-wrenching sadness Connie was obviously experiencing, which seemed to be sucking the life out of her.

Connie had thought she could do this funeral. Though she had cried for days after her grandmother's death, she had thought she could cope with the funeral with dignity for her own sake, and to help her mother who she saw was behaving with iron control. She knew her mother had donned this façade like a second skin, because she had confided to Connie how bereft she was and she viewed the future as a bleak one without Mary in it.

That's exactly how Connie felt. Daniel heard the sigh and said, 'Are you all right?'

Connie took Daniel's jacket off and handed it back to him. She shook her head as she said, 'Not really. I don't think I will be all right for ages. I don't really understand myself because I didn't really feel that much sorrow when I heard my daddy had died. The news of it caused Granny to have a heart attack that weakened her heart ever after it and Mammy was distraught. She tried to keep it from me but I would often hear her crying at night, and in the day, she was sort of hollow for ages – you know, not a proper person.

'And she was always sad at Christmas and Granny would say that's when she mourned Daddy more because Christmas was a time when many people miss lost family members most. I felt guilty that I didn't miss Daddy more, but I can't really remember him; he went away when I was too young. Mammy has a picture of him by her bed and I used to pray for him at night and kiss the picture. And though I have never told Mammy, for I'm sure she would be upset, to me it was just a picture, not a real flesh and blood person.'

'You can't really blame yourself for that,' Daniel said. 'I didn't grieve for my father either.'

'You didn't know him at all.'

'I didn't know of his existence,' Daniel said. 'When my aunt and uncle were forced to tell me the truth because of the letter I had received, they said if I wanted to know anything more about my feckless father I should ask your mother and grandmother.'

'And so you arrived at our door,' Connie said. 'I was really glad you came. It's only right that you should want to know about your father.'

Daniel nodded. 'Yes,' he said. 'My aunt and uncle did me a grave disservice when they shut him out of my life. And though I have grown up calling them Mum and Dad, I no longer think of them that way and call them Aunt and Uncle. It upsets them, or at least upsets my aunt, but I feel that's the price she must pay for caring so little for me and my feelings that she denied me a father.'

Connie had always felt sorry for Daniel and, listening to him now, she knew she had been lucky to have had the constant love of her mother and grandmother all her life.

Had her father lived she was certain he would have loved her too because her mammy and granny always said he would.

'Where did you go?' Angela said, approaching them. 'Everyone is asking about you and I couldn't find you.'

'I . . . I just stopped outside for a bit.'

Angela understood a lot from the tear-trails on her daughter's face, the too bright shiny eyes and the hanky she still held in her balled fist. Her own eyes were full of sympathy as she said, 'I won't let it go on too long, I promise. But come away in now.'

So Connie and her mother accepted condolences from their friends and neighbours. There were a fair few people Connie didn't know that well, but in one capacity or another they had known Mary McClusky. All the people from down the yard came to pay their respects, including Nancy Webster, Norah Doherty and Mick, Michael and Maggie, and Sarah and her mother Maeve. Angela also made it her business to introduce Daniel and so he was able to meet people who had known his father. He noted all spoke highly of Stan and in fact of both of his parents.

'Did you mind people talking of your parents that way?' Connie asked.

'No, why should I have minded?' Daniel said. 'I liked it and though it doesn't change the situation one iota it sort of warms me inside. It makes them real people somehow.'

Connie knew exactly what he meant and she realised she liked Daniel very much, but thought after the funeral they'd probably not see him again.

Angela must have thought the same for when she bade him goodbye she said, 'Now don't become a stranger to us.

We all need friends in life and I'm sure your father would have liked me to be a friend of yours.'

'I felt I had no reason to come,' Daniel said. 'My aunt said I shouldn't impose.'

'Daniel, you are a man now and must cut the ties a bit with your aunt and uncle and make your own decisions in life,' Angela said. 'Have you spent any of the money your father left you?'

Daniel shook his head. 'I can't decide what to do about it.' Then he sighed and went on, 'In a way I feel like my life is in a state of flux at the moment.'

'You need friends at a time like this,' Angela said. 'If ever you feel you need to talk, remember my door is always open.'

'I will,' Daniel promised and shook both Angela and Connie warmly by the hand. They stood and watched him stride down the street till he turned and waved just before he turned in Bristol Passage.

Breda Larkin at the pub had told Angela not to hurry back to work, but Angela didn't want to stay at home. There was too much time to think there, and Connie could quite see that because she was looking forward to going back to school too. She thought it was best to get back to normal routine as soon as possible.

'It's you I worry about,' Angela said.

'Why?' Connie asked. 'What's there to worry about?'

'It's not the cleaning – you're at school then and it doesn't affect you. It's leaving you alone while I pull pints at the pub.'

'Mammy, I'm nearly fourteen, not a baby any more.'

'I know that, but Mary was always with you before.'

'Yes, but I was looking after her, not the other way round.'

'She was company for you though.'

'Mammy, she wasn't,' Connie protested. 'She slept a lot in the evening, even when you were home, you know she did. Anyway,' she went on, 'I wouldn't have had time to talk to her even if she had wanted great conversation – with all the homework I have to do now I don't have a lot of free time in the evenings.'

Angela knew Connie had a point; she was given extra homework, over and above what was set anyway to prepare her for matriculation. 'So what you are saying is you don't mind me working at the pub?'

'No.'

'Well, it's Thursday now. I could start tomorrow evening.'

'Do then.'

'What will people think though?'

'Who cares?'

'They may think it's too soon.'

'They may or they may not but either way it's not their business,' Connie said. 'Just because I am going back to school doesn't mean I won't miss and miss like mad the woman who has been a constant all my life who I loved dearly. I can't remember a time when I didn't love Granny with a passion and I also know she would approve of what we are doing. We should do what pleases us and what would please Granny. Other opinions don't really matter.'

Angela looked at her daughter with amazement, for she was absolutely right. This was the way forward for both of them.

EIGHT

Despite Connie's spirited words to her mother, she missed her grandmother dreadfully, every day she missed her. Though it was true that Mary had slept a lot in the days before her death, Connie had been used to the sound of her easy breathing and the crackling of the fire as the backdrop to her labouring over her homework. And sometimes she would wake and Connie would make them both a cup of tea and help her grandmother sit up so she could drink it. On the days when her mind was clear they would talk, not much for Mary had found conversations difficult, but she seemed to like Connie telling her about her school day. Other times, once the tea was drunk, Connie would help her lie down again and hold her hand until her eyelids fluttered shut again.

She had liked those special times she'd had with her grandmother. She felt it was her way of showing how much she cared to the woman who had showered her with love as far back as she could remember and it was hard to come to terms with the fact those times would never come again. Connie was glad though that she had never shared her thoughts with her mother because she knew she needed to work, for her own self-worth as well as for the money.

Connie was right: the job stopped Angela going under, giving her a reason to get up in the morning and keep going through the day. She loved pulling the pints and chattering to the Swan's regulars because she was achingly lonely without the woman she had always considered to be her mother. Sometimes the conversation was not that edifying but it was better than nothing. Paddy considered he had a star in Angela who managed to be on such friendly terms with the men without flirting and causing trouble with jealous wives. In the wake of Mary's death the customers were even more considerate towards Angela and many said how sorry they were, for they knew of the close and unique bond she always had with Mary and admired the fortitude she was showing.

She was also a great help to her daughter at this time. Connie had not really tasted grief before, but Angela could remember how she'd mourned her foster brothers Sean and Gerry when they'd drowned at sea on the *Titanic*.

It had been a terrible time for them all and Angela had been filled with grief and sadness, but deep down she'd known life had to go on. She coped with her own grief now by taking one day at a time and advised Connie to do the same.

'Don't think of her death,' she said. 'Think of the lovely things we did with her when she was alive. She is at peace now and I think she was ready to go, she was tired and looking forward to seeing Matt and her three sons again. Eventually, when you think of her, the pain will lessen. You will never forget her, but she will settle into a place in your heart.'

Connie found her mother's words very encouraging and

a fortnight after Mary's death she said to Angela, 'I had my granny for years. I wish it had been longer but no one can take away those years or my memories.'

'That's the spirit, Connie,' Angela said approvingly. 'My goodness me, your granny would have been so proud of you.'

Almost three weeks later Daniel called and was delighted and relieved to see that both Angela and Connie were recovering from the death of Mary so well. As it was a Thursday evening and Angela hadn't to rush out to work, she pressed Daniel to stay for a meal, not that he needed much pressing. And after the meal, with the dishes washed, Connie cleared the table and laid out her books to do her homework as she did every night.

'What have you got to do?' Daniel asked.

'English,' Connie said. 'I don't mind that, but then I've got Chemistry and Mathematics.' She made a face and said, 'The exercises are in the books but sometimes they might as well be written in double Dutch.'

Daniel laughed. 'I take it those are not your favourite subjects.'

'In a word, no,' said Connie with an answering grin. 'I don't really understand them. I know it all fine when the teacher discusses it with me before I leave. But by the time I come home and help Mammy with the dinner and do any errands and then eat tea and wash up, when I sit to do my homework everything the teacher said has gone out of my head.'

'Can I help? I'm good at Maths.'

'Are you?' Connie said disbelievingly. 'I didn't think anyone was good at Maths.'

'I'm a banker. I have to be good at Maths.'

'Well, that's one job I'll give a miss.'

'Sometimes it's not a matter of choice and beggars can't be choosers,' Daniel said. 'I mean, I'm not that happy being a banker. But a job's a job at the end of the day and, with the state the country is in, you stick with what you have. So in case you end up in a job when you have to add two and two, maybe you should try harder with the Maths.' He held out his hand and said, 'Let's have a look at the exercise.'

He scrutinised it for a moment or two and then said, 'I know what you must do here.'

He had drawn up a chair beside Connie as he spoke and the next minute their heads were together poring over the book as he explained to her what she must do. He explained it so well that it was suddenly crystal clear to her and she completed the exercise in double quick time, then tackled the Chemistry too, far more confident with Daniel by her side.

Angela thought him so kind to help Connie so freely. Truly he was Stan's son and she made tea before Connie did her English, which she excelled at and always got good marks for. But when Angela expressed her gratitude, he brushed it aside.

'You have done so much for me. It's the least I can do, giving Connie a hand, especially when it involves subjects I enjoy anyway.'

Connie gave a groan. 'Enjoy Maths and Chemistry!' she exclaimed. 'Seriously, Daniel, you want to get your head examined. Liking subjects like that isn't normal.'

They were all laughing but Angela chided her daughter. 'That's really not the right response when someone has been so helpful. "Thank you" would be much better.'

'I have said thank you and I will say it again as often as you like,' Connie protested. 'And I think Daniel knows how grateful I am. Don't you?' she said.

Daniel still had a grin on his face as he said, 'Yes, don't worry about it, Angela. I have the measure of Connie. And I enjoy coming because I somehow feel closer to my dad here. I can't mention his name at home.'

'Listen, Daniel,' Angela said. 'No one can make up those lost years for you. All I can do is encourage you to go out with your head held high for you are the son of a great man who loved you very much and would be so proud if he saw you today. And I hear what you say about employment, and we do have a massive slump at the moment, but you have a degree and so are better placed than many, I'd say. And if you really dislike banking, have you thought of teaching?'

'No, not really.'

'You're really good at explaining things,' Connie said. 'You even get thickos like me to understand in the end.'

'Are you fishing for compliments?' Daniel asked with a smile. 'Because you know you're no thicko.'

'No, I don't.'

'This is neither here nor there,' Angela said. 'I have heard you helping my Connie and I would say you'll make a fine teacher if you were interested in that kind of work.'

'I don't know,' Daniel said. 'In all honesty I never gave a thought to doing anything other than working in a bank. I always did what the people I thought of as my parents wanted and never really thought of having any sort of choice. If I do decide to go down another path it will not please my aunt and uncle.'

'Will that worry you?'

'No,' Daniel said after a moment's thought. 'Not any more, I shan't let it. I think teaching would be far more interesting than what I do now. Anyway, it won't hurt to make some enquiries.'

'Why would your aunt and uncle object to you doing something like that?' Connie asked. 'Sounds a very good job to me.'

'It is, and I should imagine rewarding,' Daniel said. 'But despite being at university, which gave me a glimpse into other people's lives and made me realise the way I'd been brought up was odd, I was still pretty much under their thumb. And so when my uncle arranged my interview with the bank that culminated in a job, I went along with what they wanted. Till the day I came here first I felt very alone. Meeting you and being so accepted and hearing the truth about my father has given me the courage to stand against them, certainly in this business of employment.'

And Daniel did just that and came the following week to tell them that, despite his degree, he had to do a further year at college.

'It's only fair, the way they explained it to us,' he told Angela and Connie. 'I mean, I know I have a degree but it's not much use if I cannot pass that knowledge on.'

'You have to me,' Connie said. 'I understand so much better now.'

'Yeah, but that's one-to-one, with someone I know quite well now,' Daniel said. 'I should say that it's a whole different experience standing in front of a classroom trying to teach children that same understanding. Particularly when many do not like Maths, have never liked Maths and would wish to be anywhere other than in that classroom listening to me droning on. I could really do with experience in learning to deal with all that.'

'I can quite see that,' Angela said. 'When do you start?'

'September,' Daniel said. 'And though I can go to a college fairly locally, I think I will have to leave my aunt and uncle's and find lodgings some other place weeks before then. They will hardly approve of my plans and I can't expect them to finance me further either.'

'Will you manage to go a year without money?'

'I might not be totally without money,' Daniel said. 'There are bursaries, but even without them I will be all right, thanks to my father. The money he left me I haven't touched except to add to it as soon as I began earning and I have until September to save more. I can't thank you two enough, because I don't know that I'd have ever thought of being a teacher if you hadn't put it in my head and now . . . well, I can't wait to start. I am really excited about it.'

'Surely you can tell your aunt and uncle how you feel,' Angela said. 'They do love you and if you love someone you want the best for them. I would hate to think your desire to be a teacher now, rather than a banker, should cause such a rift between you.'

'Angela, the rift began when I read the letter from my father and forced them to confess what they had done in keeping us apart,' Daniel said. 'It has widened since then and, if I'm honest, that's mainly my fault because I can't feel the same about them. I realised their love was conditional in that if I did what they wanted, toed the line and never deviated, then they would love me.'

Angela felt a lump form in her throat and felt it such a tragedy that Stan would never know the fine person her son had turned out. She admitted that had to be due to Betty and Roger in part, though in a way their conditional love and iron control had damaged him a little. Please God, he would now be able to rise above that.

Daniel came each week after that and he was such good company that Angela looked forward to him coming as much as Connie and he always helped her daughter with homework she was struggling with. Connie thought he'd make a fine teacher because he did explain things so very well and didn't make her feel stupid for not knowing or forgetting things he had already told her. He was like the big brother she never had.

He had been coming three weeks when, as they sat down to dinner, Angela said, 'Now Daniel, you're an intelligent man, you have helped Connie immensely and I'm very grateful. So maybe you can help me with a problem I have.'

Connie's eyes widened. 'You never said anything to me about any sort of problem.'

'I'm telling you now,' Angela said. 'It has only happened twice and the first time I thought it might be just a one-off.'

'What's only happened twice?'

'Someone's putting flowers on Mary's grave.'

'Well, didn't you tell me she was well thought of?' Daniel said. 'And it's obvious she was by the numbers who attended her funeral.'

Angela nodded. 'She was, that's true, but many here struggle to feed their families. I know no one who would have the spare money to buy flowers to decorate a grave. Even those not exactly poor have just about enough to manage. I don't know many with much slack. I mean, whoever it is has bought a vase and everything. They don't disturb anything I have there, they just add to it. It's very strange.

'All l can think is that it was someone from her past that I knew nothing about,' Angela continued. 'And that's odd too because I didn't think there was anyone she knew that I didn't. This is a really small community.'

'Does it matter who it is?' Daniel said. 'I mean, they obviously mean her no harm. Putting flowers on a grave is a nice thing to do.'

'I suppose it doesn't matter,' Angela said. 'It's just a bit intriguing and I would like to know who it is even if just to thank them. It's lovely to see fresh flowers there and the grave tidied up as if someone loved Mary as much as Connie and I did.'

'It will likely stop eventually and you'll probably never be any the wiser,' Daniel said and Angela sighed and said he was probably right.

Connie caught a bad cold just after this and Angela succumbed too. Both were laid very low and so it was almost three weeks before Angela felt well enough to take the walk to the cemetery. It was a Saturday morning, not a time when she had ever come before. She had a spring in her step for the bright yellow daffodils she had brought with her always cheered her. They were like the promise of spring not that far away, and even the day had a hint of warmth though it was still early in March. She was smiling as she pushed open the cemetery gates.

The smile died on her lips as she spotted the man kneeling by the grave arranging his posy of Christmas roses in the vase. She had no idea who he was, and yet there was something familiar about him.

123

'Excuse me,' she said and the man turned. The shock at seeing him was so great she dropped her flowers to the ground and she felt a sudden blackness envelop her. The man caught her as she sank to the ground and cradled her in his arms.

'Angela,' he called frantically. 'Angela, are you all right?'

Angela's eyes fluttered open and a frown developed between them as she tried to make sense of what her eyes were seeing that her mind refused to believe.

'Stan,' she said, her hesitant voice just above a whisper. 'Stan, is it really you?'

There was a deep sigh and the man said, 'Yes, it's me, Stan.'

Angela shook her head in bewilderment and Stan said, 'Will you be all right now? You gave me a right turn when you fainted like that.'

Angela struggled to her feet, saying as she did so, 'I'm fine but I don't know about giving you a turn! What about the one you gave me? You are supposed to be dead, for God's sake. Oh, Stan, I really don't understand any of this. Are you sure you aren't a ghost?'

Despite her confusion, Angela reached out for Stan and he wrapped his arms around her and she sighed in almost contentment. There was much for him to explain, but he was alive when many were dead and she guessed Daniel would be delighted at this turn of events.

Stan released Angela, gave another heartfelt sigh and said, 'I'm surprised you can even look at me.'

'What are you talking about? I'm so glad that you survived that blessed war,' Angela said. 'But I would like some explanation of where you have been all this time when I thought you were dead – everyone thought you were dead. But as for not being able to look at you . . . Stan, this is me, Angela. We were so close before that dreadful war.'

'That's what I mean.'

Angela shook her head slowly. 'Stan, you're not making sense. Shall we go home and you can tell me what this is all about?'

'No,' Stan said, 'not there. I'm not ready to meet people I once knew yet. It's you I need to speak with first. After I have told all to you, you might not want to see me again.'

'I doubt that,' Angela said and added, 'Oh Stan, you don't know how wonderful I feel that you are alive and Daniel . . . he will be just delighted.'

'Huh, my son in name only,' Stan said bitterly. 'He'd hardly want to know me. He never wanted to know me before.'

'A lot has changed since then, Stan,' Angela said. 'Your son is a fine young man and I would say he has need of you just now . . . We have so much we need to talk about.'

'You are right,' Stan said. 'Let's finish tidying up the grave and then can we walk together? I will probably find it easier to tell you everything that way.'

Angela nodded. 'Then we'll walk,' she said. 'I'm keen to get to the bottom of all this.'

She picked up the bunch of daffodils as she spoke, noting their bedraggled appearance after falling to the ground, but said nothing about it and helped Stan tend the grave in silence.

They were walking down the street before Angela said, 'I want to know, everyone will want to know, and most especially Daniel, why you didn't come back after the war, why you let everyone think you were dead? It was a cruel thing to do.'

'I would have to go back a little further than that,' Stan said. 'I know Barry didn't survive but do you know any details of how he died?'

'Only a little bit,' Angela said. 'Michael Malone was a school friend of his for years and he was with him the day it happened, along with a couple of other men. He told me that when they were on the field of battle, in all the confusion, Barry gave a shout and started to walk towards someone. Michael didn't see who it was because he had his back to Barry and when he turned around to see who he had hailed, the swirling smoke made it difficult to see anything. Anyway, his attention was taken then by the shell arcing above them and he could see Barry had seen it too. He gave a sort of scream and began running like mad towards the person he had called out to.

'Michael knew he wouldn't make it before the shell hit and began running the other way. He knew no more because he was caught in the blast himself and was out of it. Poor lad lost his leg, blown clean off it was, but both his other two mates were killed outright.'

'So you have no details of the man Barry tried to save?'

Angela shook her head and then added, 'I got a lovely letter from his commanding officer though and he said he was recommending him for a medal. Barry got the Military Medal for gallantry by giving his life to save another, but the letter didn't mention the man's name or even whether he had survived. Michael said there was a good chance he had died too and Barry had given his life in vain, but that happens in wartime. Anyway, there was no way of finding out because the shell that killed Barry and his two other mates wasn't just one stray shell but the start of a barrage that went on for some time. He was unconscious throughout, but he was told about it by others. There were many dead and injured brought in when the barrage was over, yet more casualties of war.'

Angela gave a slight shrug to try and hide the sense of loss she still felt at odd times when she allowed herself to think of what had happened to Barry. She willed her voice not to shake as she said to Stan, 'That's all I know of Barry's death.'

Stan didn't answer and Angela looked up at his face and saw the tears trickling down his cheeks. She linked her arm through his and felt the raw emotion running through his veins as she urged, 'Tell me, Stan. Something is tearing you apart. Nothing you can tell me can be this bad.'

Stan gave a groan and brushed the tears away almost impatiently. The words appeared to be forced out of him as he came to a stop, turned to look Angela full in the face and said in a voice husky with emotion, 'Barry didn't die in vain, Angela. I was the man he saved.'

Angela was so shocked she staggered. Stan steadied her.

'You?' she said.

Stan nodded and said, 'And I will fully understand if you never want to see me again.'

'Why ever would I feel that way?' Angela cried.

'Look, Angela,' Stan said. 'I didn't get through unscathed and was unconscious a long time – months. I had many operations to put my insides back together again and dig shrapnel out of my body. I was rambling and gibbering senselessly a lot of the time, but once I came round a bit and realised who had died to try and save me, I went right back to the beginning. I couldn't get over the fact that, because

127

of me, your husband – who I know you loved beyond measure – was dead. It was the very opposite of what I wanted. I'd told him this once upon a time, I told him he had everything to live for, while I had nothing, no wife, no child, no home, no one to mourn me if I didn't return.'

'What of us?' Angela said. 'I thought you cared about us?'

'It was because I cared I stayed away,' Stan said as they began to walk on again. 'I wasn't physically ready to leave hospital till the late autumn of 1919 and even then they were concerned by my mental state. I seemed unable to cope with people. Shell shock, they called it.'

'So you hid yourself away?'

'That's about the strength of it,' Stan said. 'Like an animal, crawling away to die or lick their wounds after a fight.'

What he didn't say, but what hit him clearly in the face now that he had seen Angela again, was how much he had been in love with her then and how much he still loved her now. It was another reason why he had stayed away, knowing it was wrong of him to love his best friend's wife in the way he did. The awful truth that Barry had died saving his own life made his shame a thousand times worse.

'But there was no need for it,' Angela said. 'I could never have resented you and neither could Mary. We both knew who was responsible for Barry's death and that was the German army, and them alone.'

'Didn't you ever wonder who it was he had tried to save?'

'Initially, but then I thought it wouldn't make a ha'p'orth of difference if I did know,' Angela said. 'I mean, it wouldn't bring him back, would it? I never dreamt it could be you because you had never met each other in all the years you were both at the Western Front. Barry saw you maybe a couple of times in the distance, like at the Somme. He often asked me if I had heard from you – I suppose to work out if you were alive or dead.'

'I suppose so,' Stan said. 'And you're right, our units were never near each other, but we had been transferred to give support for the Spring Offensive the Germans were planning. I heard Barry's name being mentioned because they were considering him for sergeant stripes so I asked where he was. I said he was a young cousin of mine, so they wouldn't think it odd me asking about him. When I heard they were in the neighbouring trenches to our section and he was due to lead the assault from the front trench the following morning, I decided to go and wish him luck. You know the rest.'

'Why was no one informed of the extent of your injuries?'

'As I said, I was unconscious for ages,' Stan said. 'No one knew who I was. My dog tag, which would have told them my name, serial number, brigade number and regiment, was God alone knows where, blown to kingdom come no doubt, and many who could have identified me had been killed. When I was alert enough to answer questions I also heard about the bravery of Barry and that he had sacrificed his life in an effort to save mine. That news caused me to sink into a deep depression. I knew then I couldn't load any more on you and Mary when you were already coping with the loss of Barry. I said there was no one to inform because my sister would hardly be interested, let alone concerned. I said I was alone in the world.'

'Only because you chose to be.'

'No, it wasn't really just through choice,' Stan said. 'You see, though my body healed slowly, my mind did not. I did think of my son but I knew he probably didn't know I existed.

My grip on sanity at the time was very tenuous and I was barely recovered from being a crazed lunatic.'

Angela smiled and Stan said, 'I'm not joking when I say I was out of control a lot of the time in the early days. I wasn't certain I had fully recovered and neither were the hospital. I couldn't risk trying to see Daniel because I certainly didn't want him to see me like that.'

Angela didn't say anything, but she knew Betty would have made mincemeat of him had he tried to see Daniel.

'And if I had risked it and he'd rejected me,' Stan went on, 'my mind might not have been strong enough to take that. I could have easily slipped back into the half world I'd once inhabited where injections followed by tablets kept me in a sort of stupor so I ceased to care about anything.'

Angela's heart contracted in sympathy for the way Stan had suffered, and not just physically. How hard it must have been to deal with it all alone. How friendless he must have felt, and yet she remembered Barry saying no one should make friends in wartime. He had lost a lot of comrades at the time and she could definitely see his point. But, she decided, she could at least put Stan right about Daniel.

'You're right about Daniel. It is just possible as a child he may have rejected you, because he had no idea of your existence until the solicitor contacted him when he passed twenty-one and hadn't claimed his inheritance. The letter you wrote pulled the wool from his eyes and, though he confronted his aunt and uncle, they refused to discuss it. Betty said some pretty hurtful things about you being weak and spineless, said her sister was too good for you and claimed you didn't want the bother of a son and had made no move to see him all the years of him growing up.'

Angela felt Stan start beside her and said, 'I know that was the very opposite of what happened, but she was hardly likely to tell the truth, was she?'

'I suppose not,' Stan agreed. 'So, has she been telling Daniel things like this all the time they were rearing him?'

Angela shook her head. 'No need to tell him anything at all. To all intents and purposes they were his parents. He knew nothing of you and didn't feel the lack of a father for he thought that was Roger. I didn't see the letter but when Daniel read it he was as disturbed as Mammy was. I prophesied he would be unless Betty had prepared him in some way, or at least told him of the existence of a father years before she was forced to. When Daniel confronted her, she threw those untrue allegations at him, but refused to discuss anything else. She told him if he needed to know more he should come and ask me, so one day he turned up at my door.'

'What's he like?' Stan asked. 'Over the years I've often wondered how he turned out.'

'He's very handsome and looks very much like a younger version of you. And he has your kindly nature because he is helping Connie with her Maths homework.'

'Good at Maths then, is he?'

'I'll say,' Angela said. 'He got a first at university. See, I want Connie to sit the School Certificate and go on to secondary education. The teacher is giving her extra home-work to prepare for it and one night Daniel offered to help her and now he comes every week, has a meal and so on, and gives Connie a hand. And the upshot of all this is that he's going to train as a teacher in September. It will just take him a year, he says.'

'So you know my son well then?'

'Fairly, I'd say,' Angela said. 'He is a fine son, one any man would be proud to own.'

'Well, I can claim no credit for the way he has turned out,' Stan growled out.

'I don't know,' Angela said. 'Daniel is a likeable young man and yet he has no friends. He is totally reliant on his parents for company. I sensed a loneliness in him when he first visited. He said we help bring him out of himself.'

'That doesn't surprise me in the slightest,' Stan said. 'I was more than lonely, I was sort of lost. Everyone had gone, I could scarcely remember my mother, and then my father died and poor Katherine lost her life giving birth to a son who was then spirited away from me. You saved me from turning bitter or depressed. You and Mary had a gift of making people feel part of the family. You both cared about me and that meant a lot.'

'Thank you, Stan,' Angela said. 'That's a lovely thing to say and that's why you put flowers on Mary's grave.'

Stan nodded. 'I didn't know straight away, not living close any more.'

'Who told you?'

'This old fellow in the pub, though he didn't tell me as such – he was just talking to his son. Apparently he lives by you normally, but he had been a bit ill. The son took him in to live with them till he was well enough to go home again and one evening when he was a bit better he took him for a pint in his local. I was there having a bite to eat and the man was saying what a shame it was that Mary McClusky had died, who he said was a lovely woman who would do a good turn for anyone and would be sorely missed. I interrupted and asked where she was buried. I wish things had been different and I had seen her before the end. Tending her grave was my way of saying I was sorry and also thanks for the welcome she always had for me.'

'The welcome's still there,' Angela said softly. They drew to a halt as they neared the town and she asked, 'Where are you living now?'

'I have lodgings in Aston.'

'We'll have to part here then, for I must make for Bristol Street,' Angela said, 'So what happens now, Stan?'

'I don't know,' Stan said.

'Well you can't just disappear again as if this morning never happened.'

He shrugged. 'Well I don't care what you say, it's hardly likely Daniel will want to see me.'

'Why not?' she demanded. 'Will you stop assuming you know how people feel about things! You were wrong about me and if I'm any judge of character at all, Daniel would love to meet you, especially if you were totally honest with him. He felt cheated as a child not knowing you at all. Handled right, you could have a great relationship with him as an adult. But you can't just walk into his life without him being prepared in any way.'

'So what do you suggest?'

Angela thought for a moment and then said, 'Daniel comes round for a meal every Thursday straight from work and after we've eaten, as I said, he helps Connie with her homework. Instead, this week I'll tell him how I met you here this morning and if you come about half seven he'll have had time to let the news sink in.'

'Can't I see him before Thursday?'

Angela shook her head. 'I think this is the best idea.

Anyway,' she added, 'what's the rush? You have waited years to see your son, so what's another three or four days?'

'I don't know,' Stan said. 'It's different somehow. This time it's really going to happen. I am going to see the son I gave away as a baby.'

'Yes,' Angela said. 'So it's got to be done properly.'

'All right,' Stan said. 'You obviously know my son better than I do and so we'll do this your way.'

He drew Angela into his arms again as he spoke and gave her a brief hug.

'Till Thursday then,' he said and Angela gave a wave in acknowledgement before they both went their separate ways.

NINE

Angela was deep in thought as she walked home that morning, wondering and worrying how Daniel would take the news that the father he had never known was alive after all. She'd like to think when he got over the shock of it he would at least be pleased and perhaps eager for the chance to get to know Stan. But how would Daniel view the years after the war when his father could have sought him out and yet did not? Would he see that as a sort of second betrayal?

Connie was surprised she had been so long away.

'Thought you'd got lost,' she said to her mother. 'I was just about to organise a search party.'

'I met someone,' Angela said. 'Just about the last person I expected to see this side of Paradise.'

Connie's eyes opened wider. 'Golly,' she said. 'Who was it?'

Angela had no hesitation telling her daughter. She was very fond of Daniel too, and might help in the telling, so she said, 'Stan Bishop, Daniel's father.'

'Daniel's father!' Connie repeated. 'I thought Daniel's father was dead?'

'I know,' Angela said. 'We all thought he was. I had a bit of a turn when I recognised him. Passed out completely and he caught me.'

'Mammy, I don't understand,' Connie said. 'Where was he and what has he been doing all this time?'

'It's a long story and the telling of it will take some time,' Angela said. 'We'll talk over a bite to eat for I am more than peckish.'

Later, as they ate, Angela explained, 'I think the main reason Stan didn't get in touch with us was because of guilt.'

'What was he guilty of?'

'Nothing and that's just the point,' Angela said. 'Many servicemen feel a measure of guilt that they have survived and left comrades and sometimes family members behind on the battlefield. In Stan's case it was worse because he was the man your father died to save.'

'Why wasn't this known before?'

Angela recounted to her daughter the story that Stan had told her, how Barry had saved his life on the battlefield and his struggles to regain his mental capacity.

'How could we have known? He wasn't discharged till the late autumn of 1919. Mentally he was still suffering and couldn't face us.'

'Cos he blames himself for Daddy's death?'

'Yes.'

'That's daft. How could he be responsible?' Connie cried. 'People die all the time in a war. Tell you what though, I wish he'd thought to let Daniel know he had survived the war. Daniel's been mourning a dead father when he was alive and well and living not that far away and he never even attempted to see him.'

'Betty would never have allowed them to meet,' Angela said. 'Stan said he was afraid of Daniel rejecting him like he had done once before. Though I doubt Daniel would have got that chance because Betty could, and I think would, have made trouble if Stan had tried to contact Daniel. She has the law on her side as Stan signed all rights to his son away. Anyway, Stan's anxious to meet his son and now Daniel's over twenty-one Betty has no jurisdiction over him.'

'So what's he going to do?'

'He's coming here about half seven on Thursday and before that you and I will have to prepare Daniel. I'm relying on you to help.'

'I will,' Connie promised. 'And I hope it goes all right for both of them.'

Angela was glad when Thursday arrived because every day since meeting Stan she had gone over what she should say to Daniel. She knew he was bound to be upset and have mixed emotions and she must be prepared for that. By tacit agreement, she and Connie had told no one else they both knew the first person who had to be told was Daniel. She longed to talk it through with Maggie, but was aware how things – especially shocking news like Stan reappearing when everyone thought him dead – could spread like wildfire in those narrow streets and possibly grow in the telling.

When Daniel arrived on Thursday he could tell Angela was stressed about something, but felt it wasn't his place to ask if something was bothering her. The meal was, as usual, delicious and as he ate they spoke of this and that as always, but he wasn't totally surprised when, as the meal came to an end, Angela said, 'Daniel, I have something very important to tell you.'

'Go on then,' Daniel said and, in an attempt to lighten the mood, smiled as he added, 'I'm all ears.'

Angela didn't smile back and even her mouth looked strained as she said, 'To tell you all, I need to go back to the Great War. You see, I found something out a few days ago that I have never known before.'

'What?'

'I found out that my husband died trying to save your father. He tried to throw himself over him when he saw the shell coming.'

Daniel's mouth dropped open and then he said, 'God, that must have been hard for you to hear. I bet you hated my father.'

'No, of course I didn't,' Angela said. 'My husband was killed by a German shell and the fact that Barry tried to save your father was probably an instinctive thing. Barry would have probably died anyway if he'd stayed where he was, just like Michael Malone's two fellow soldiers did. Michael himself lost his leg. One thing I am sure of is that your father is in no way responsible for my husband's death.'

'Maybe not,' Daniel conceded. 'Your husband more or less gave his life in vain though because my father died anyway.'

Connie gave a gasp and Daniel looked at her, puzzled. 'What did you do that for?'

Connie looked at her mother, who gave a brief nod, and she went on, 'Because your father didn't die.'

'What are you on about?' Daniel said incredulously.

'It's true,' Angela said. 'I found him just by accident at the cemetery the other day. He's the one been putting the flowers on Mary's grave.'

'Let me get this straight . . .' Daniel said. 'My father has been putting flowers on the grave of a woman who isn't even a relative and let me go on thinking he was dead.'

The hurt in Daniel's voice was almost palpable and Angela said, 'I know it's hard for you to understand this, but your father was very badly injured by the shell and it took a great deal of time to get him right physically. His mental state was unstable even when he left hospital, which wasn't until the late autumn of 1919. He felt he couldn't face us for he thought, as you did initially, that he was the cause of Barry's death and that I would hate him for it.'

'Yes, I see that, but surely he could have contacted me?'

'I believe he wasn't mentally strong enough to take rejection from you,' Angela said. 'He actually said that, but the fact is I am fairly certain Betty wouldn't have let you meet.'

'Does she know he survived?'

Angela shook her head.

'Aren't people informed in cases like this?'

'Usually,' Angela said. 'But with no wife and no dependants, it was easy for your father to slip through the cracks.'

'How long have you known he didn't die?'

'Only a few days,' Angela said. 'I met him at the cemetery, as I said, and he told me everything. I was very pleased to see him, but puzzled like you are, but when you look in his eyes as he talks you'll know he is damaged. Your father volunteered and so was in the war from the beginning and you would not be human if you were not affected by such brutality. He became a sergeant so he was in charge of young men and he had to order them over the top and watch them blown to bits or mutilated badly. Many men were affected like your father and they called it battle-weariness, shell

139

shock, but there was little help for sufferers. Remember that when you talk with your father.'

'When is that likely to be?'

'Soon,' Angela said, glancing over to the clock on the mantelpiece. 'I asked your father to call here tonight. I thought it might be better to meet here at first. He is anxious to meet you, that I do know.'

'He waited long enough.'

'Like I said, I doubt he could have been allowed to make contact much sooner,' Angela said.

Just at that moment there was a tentative knock on the door. Daniel got to his feet, aware of his heart thumping in his breast and his throat suddenly becoming extremely dry.

Angela opened the door. 'Come in, Stan.'

'Thank you.' Stan stepped over the threshold, noticing the girl who was the image of her mother. He realised she must be Connie, the child he used to build the towers of bricks for before the madness of the war began.

He smiled at her, but really he only had eyes for the fine strapping man before him, his son. He could have wept for the lost years they'd been forced apart. He wanted to wrap him in a bear hug, but sensed Daniel wouldn't welcome such intimacy from a perfect stranger. And that's who Stan was as far as Daniel was concerned – a stranger.

So he extended his hand and shook Daniel's warmly and said sincerely in a husky voice that shook slightly with emotion, 'Daniel, I am so pleased to meet you at last and I bitterly regret the years when I was unable to see you.'

Daniel said nothing for a moment or two. Angela worried that he was going to rebuff his father, but in fact Daniel's throat was so dry he wasn't sure if he could speak. He valiantly swallowed the lump that had appeared in his throat and replied, 'I regret those years too. We have much time to make up.'

'We have indeed,' Stan said.

'You are both welcome to stay here,' Angela said. 'Connie and I will be washing up in the kitchen so you will have the room to yourselves.'

'Thank you,' Stan said. 'But I talk a lot easier if I am on the move and I have much explaining to do to Daniel.'

'Funny enough, I feel the same way,' Daniel said and he lifted his coat from the back of the door as he spoke and said to Connie, 'Won't be able to help you tonight, I'm afraid.'

'It's all right,' Connie said. 'The teacher has given me mainly revision work and, as I've done it before, I know what to do.'

'So that's all right then?'

'Are you ready then?' Stan asked and Angela knew he was desperate to get his son to himself. And why not, she thought, he had waited long enough for it.

Stan turned at the door and said to Angela, 'Thank you for arranging all this and for looking after my boy.'

Angela waved his thanks away and, smiling nervously at her and Connie, Stan stepped into the street with Daniel beside him. When the door shut behind them it all felt rather flat. Angela had imagined them sitting around the fire discussing shared memories, building a picture for Daniel as well as maybe going some way towards healing Stan's traumatised mind. She told herself she was being unreasonable. Daniel was Stan's son who he had been kept away from for not a few weeks or months, but for the whole of his life. He knew not the slightest thing about him and they badly needed time together. He was not willing to share him yet – he had done that for twenty-one years – and so with a small sigh she began collecting up the plates.

She knew Connie felt as she had at first when, as she began helping her mother, she said, 'Well that's that then.'

'Yes.'

'That's the man you always championed,' Connie said. 'The one you said was forever welcome in your home, and who made such a fuss of me and he never spoke one word to me.'

'I know,' Angela said. 'And you know I doubt he even saw you. If you watched his eyes it was as if he was drinking in the sight of his son. Despite all we have told Daniel about his father, which was all true by the way, the two men are strangers. If they are ever to build any sort of relationship, which would be helpful to both of them, they need time to get to know one another. Don't begrudge them this time together. Daniel hasn't forgotten us, but just now he wants the company of his father denied to him all the years of his growing up.'

Connie knew every word her mother said was true and she suddenly felt immensely selfish.

Now that Daniel had been told about his father being alive when all thought him dead, others could be told. Daniel had been coming some weeks and was known. He had been introduced to many at Mary's funeral and, when the well-dressed man started visiting the McClusky house fairly regularly, those people told others who he was. However, his father's reappearance after all these years was stranger to fathom, though some, who like him had come through that savage bloody war, had some understanding of what he had been going through.

'It wasn't as if he had a loving family waiting for him,' Michael said. 'According to what you said, Angela, he thought he had killed Barry.' He held up his hand as Angela protested, 'I know you didn't feel that way, but he didn't know that and that meant he couldn't come here and see you as he did before the war. He couldn't watch you grieving for Barry when he felt responsible for his death.'

'I suppose, but there was Daniel.'

'Not in his life there wasn't,' Michael said. 'Let's face it, according to what Maggie told me, Daniel hasn't ever been in his life since the day his wife died giving birth to him. Anyway, how could he try to make contact with his son and keep the knowledge he was alive from you?'

Angela shook her head. 'He couldn't, not really,' she admitted. 'And he said he didn't think he could face me or Mary. The fact that he was alive and Barry wasn't was enough guilt for anyone to carry around, as many soldiers could identify with.'

'You're right there,' Michael said. 'In our company there was a chap called Bert who had joined up with his young brother, Bobby, a cocky young lad who thought going to war was going to be a great adventure. The whole family doted on him. He had five sisters and they all loved Bobby, the baby of the family, and his mother charged Bert to look after him.'

'He died, I presume?'

Michael nodded. 'He copped it less than a year after he joined up and Bert nearly got himself shot as a deserter.'

'Why?'

Michael sighed. 'When you go over the top you have to run and you mustn't stop for anything. They drum this into you and say that if even your brother falls before you then you must step over him and go on. When they said that, I could only be grateful I had no brother alongside me, because when all is said and done, blood is thicker than water.'

'Oh, I'll say it is,' Angela said with feeling. 'How callous.'

'War is callous,' Michael said. 'Anyway, I was in the second wave and Bert and Bobby had been in the first, and when I left the trench I came upon Bert bent over the prone figure of his brother crying and carrying on. The smoke had hidden him from view, but I knew when it cleared he could easily be shot for not obeying orders. They'd call it cowardice or desertion. Either way, not only would he lose his life, he would also be disgraced, and I could see he could do nothing for his brother. I had to half-drag him away and we took cover behind a bush for a few minutes till he was more himself. Any minute, as we advanced side by side, I expected him to be next because it was like he was in a daze and I knew his mind was back with his dead brother, not with fighting the enemy.'

'Ah.'

'You see how just the knowledge of Barry's death might have seriously affected Stan?' Michael said. 'War messes with your mind as well as your body, and once he knew the details of your husband's death he could easily feel responsible.'

Angela nodded. 'Yes, I see that.'

'What happened to Bert?' Maggie asked.

'Oh, he survived the war,' Michael said. 'Physically at least. He never forgave himself for . . . I don't know, allowing his brother to die, I suppose. I mean, I should say he knows that

144

there wasn't anything he could have done, but somehow the guilt remains. The tragedy is all the family blamed him too. He has a pretty awful life one way and another. He hasn't been able to get a full-time job since demob, like many more, but he is blamed for that too.'

'Terrible, isn't it?' Maggie said. 'I know it's hard to lose a child. My mam near went mad for a while when she lost our Syd.'

'What about mine when my eldest brother was killed in the war and then Mammy lost my two youngest sisters to Spanish flu?' Michael said. 'Dad said she was near beside herself with grief. And in a way Mammy lost them all because then she said she couldn't even try to stop my remaining brother and two older sisters hightailing it to America. I was still in hospital then and I missed it all, the death of my brother and sisters, their funerals and even the others sailing the Atlantic. Mammy said all she could offer them was death and they had to have the chance of a life. I think she thought she would always have me, that no one, not even Maggie that I had been sweet on for years, and writing to for ages, would want a man with just one leg.'

'Well you thought the same,' Maggie said.

Michael nodded. 'I know I did. You had to convince me otherwise.'

'I don't know why you thought I would feel differently about you.'

'I didn't want to hold you back,' Michael said. 'I suppose I wanted to give you the chance to marry someone able-bodied.'

'As I remember it,' Angela said, 'after that awful war there weren't many left that were able-bodied. Even those who escaped with all their limbs intact were often suffering from shell shock, or were battle-scarred in some way. Still, it must have been comforting for your parents to have one son left, particularly your mother.'

Michael nodded. 'It was odd for me though, coming back to an empty house. I mean, I was one of seven and my mother was like a shell at first, you know.'

'Oh, I know full well,' Angela said. 'Mary and Matt were just the same when news came through of the two younger sons drowning on the *Titanic* trying to join their brothers in America. Their bodies were there but the essence of them had gone somehow. If I'm honest, Matt never really got over it, but Mary did recover eventually.'

'Well, she had a marriage to arrange,' Maggie said. 'That's one of the reasons you married so young. It was a dreadful, terrible thing to have happened, but people do have to rise above it in the end.'

'Course they do,' Michael said. 'It helped Mammy to have me to fuss over. She would have wrapped me in cotton wool to start with if I'd let her.'

'You can't really blame her for that,' Maggie said. 'All those deaths and then three more emigrating is enough to turn anyone's brain. It's obvious she would want to keep you safe.'

'But I think people who died wouldn't expect us to mourn them for ever, or think that our lives have no purpose without them sharing it,' Angela said. 'That way we waste our lives too and we owe it to them to go on eventually, however painful it is to begin with. That's how I coped with the loss of Barry and more recently Mary.'

'I think that's a good strategy to have,' Maggie said. 'But you say Stan felt bad that Barry died in an attempt to save

146

him, but you didn't know that. If Stan had kept his mouth shut you would have been none the wiser.'

'Knowing Stan as I do, I don't think he could have kept quiet about something like that. My guess is that once he felt strong enough, he wanted to get some word out to Daniel in some way and told the bank manager something of the situation. So the bank wrote to Daniel and asked for instructions on what he wanted done with the money left him. Daniel knew nothing of any money and probably had no idea who his benefactor had been until he read the letter. He confronted Betty and Roger and demanded answers, but Betty countered that by blackening Stan's name and then told him if he wanted any more information he'd better contact me.'

'Good job he did what she said, in that instance at least,' Michael said. 'And now father and son are getting to know one another.'

'That's about the shape of it,' Angela agreed happily. 'And I'm thinking it might take them some time.'

TEN

Angela appreciated Stan's need to spend time with his son, knowing both had been hurt and damaged. She had expected either Daniel or Stan to pop around at the weekend; they must have known she would be curious as to how they were getting on. But the weekend passed with no sign of them. She did so hope and pray earnestly that they might get on together and forge a father–son relationship, so why did she feel so resentful and ignored?

Connie knew how her mother felt and didn't blame her for feeling that way. In fact, though she liked Daniel and was glad that his father hadn't died after all, she had no memory of Stan, this stranger her mother seemed to set such store by. She hadn't been there for Angela and Michael's discussion and so thought Stan a poor sort of father. And an ungrateful one too, for it was her mother who had brought these two people together and neither had bothered to come and thank her.

However, they both turned up on Thursday after work. But this time, Stan proposed buying fish and chips for them all and his suggestion made Connie's mouth water. Shop-bought fish and chips was a luxury they could seldom indulge in. As they were eating it later, Stan told Angela and Connie what had transpired after being reunited with Daniel.

'Betty had to be told first, we both thought,' he said. 'We owed her that. But not wishing to give her a heart attack, for I knew my reappearance would probably not be a welcome one, we thought it best if Daniel prepare the ground first, as it were, and for me to turn up later.'

'And what happened?'

It was Daniel answered. 'My aunt didn't believe me,' he said. 'Neither did my uncle. They both said if my father had managed to survive the war he would have come and seen me long before. So then I asked, if he had, would I have been told, let alone given the opportunity to meet him? I reminded my aunt of the agreement she insisted on that they would rear me only as long as he had no contact.

'My aunt had the grace to look uncomfortable. I told her that now I had spoken to my father I knew that for years he had lived not far from me and yet I had been unable to see him, or even know he existed because of the cruel rules she had set in place. Of course she tried to say it had been decided in a court of law, but, as I pointed out, the legal position was one thing, but morally she had behaved without any regard to my feelings at all. I said my father agreed that he would have found it extremely difficult to bring me up himself, but he had wanted to still be part of my life. But he had been afraid that if he'd insisted, my aunt and uncle would have ceased to care for me and left him in a real dilemma.

'I also told her that I would never get those years back, that she had robbed both me and my father of having any

149

sort of relationship for years. When he enlisted I could have written to him. He was badly injured at the end of the war but my aunt hadn't been informed because, knowing she wouldn't be interested, he had told the authorities there was no need to inform anyone, that he was alone in the world – because that was how it felt.'

'You did right,' Angela said. 'Your aunt surely did deal you a bad hand in life, for while you wanted for nothing materially, you were starved emotionally and her husband wasn't blameless.'

'Oh, my uncle was backing up everything she said, just as he always did, especially if it involved me,' Daniel said. 'Then my aunt said that as my father had apparently been so thick with you, he hadn't been alone in the world and that you'd probably been informed when he was so badly injured. I said you hadn't known, no one had, and she asked why, but I said that was my father's business. I really thought she didn't have the right to ask questions like that when she had washed her hands of him totally.'

'Did you explain to her how ill you had been?' Angela asked Stan.

Stan shook his head. 'Couldn't be bothered to,' he said. 'Betty wouldn't have been interested and, anyway, I didn't want to talk to her or Roger at all. I know now that when I signed the rights to my son over to Betty and Roger I wasn't in my right mind. I was still stunned by the sudden and tragic death of my dear wife. I believe she took advantage of that and the devil of it is that at the time I was grateful for Betty's intervention. But I bitterly regret it now.'

He looked across at his son as he spoke and Daniel said, 'It's all right, Dad. You told me how it was then and I know how forceful my aunt is, and my uncle is little better. When I went to university, friends could not believe the way I always did what my parents wanted, but it was the strict way I had been brought up. Strange though it sounds now, I didn't know that other people had more freedom than me.

'It had been hammered into me that I must never upset my mother and I translated that to mean doing everything she wanted me to do, even if I didn't want to. She would make me feel entirely inadequate and useless if I didn't do everything her way. It was her that was at fault, her and Roger together. They brought me up well in that I never wanted for anything, but I'm sure if I could have had you in my life too my life would have been altogether richer, even if I couldn't live with you all the time. But to not even tell me you existed was a wrong and cruel thing to do to both of us.'

'Well, she can do us no more harm,' Stan said. 'And we're making up for lost time.' He looked across at Angela and explained, 'I'm moving out of my lodgings and we are going to look for a place together, certainly while Daniel is going to the college.'

'Oh, you surprise me,' Angela said. 'But it's the ideal solution really.' She looked at Daniel and added, 'You did say that you would have to find somewhere else to live while you were training, because your aunt and uncle wouldn't approve of your teaching.'

'Yes,' Daniel said. 'And Dad might have found somewhere already.'

'Oh?'

'Yes,' Stan said. 'And you'll never guess where in a million years.'

'I haven't got that much time to spare,' Angela said with a smile. 'So you had better tell me.'

'The flat above George Maitland's shop where you used to work before the Great War,' Stan said.

Straight away the image of the shop flew into Angela's mind and kindly, generous George behind the counter. He and his wife, Matilda, had had no children of their own. People said he was never likely to have had any chance of any either, married as he was to that cold, stiff piece Matilda who was unable to truly love a kind man like George had been. But whether that was true or not, George would have loved children and had taken a paternal interest in Angela, who'd been only fourteen when she began to work full-time in the shop. He'd been sorry to lose her when she became pregnant with Connie. The first time she had called in so he could see the baby, he'd had tears in his eyes as he'd gazed at the child, and as she grew he always had a lollipop for her or a few sweets in a bag.

It was a shock to everyone when George, who had never complained of any sort of illness, suddenly keeled over and died just after Barry had enlisted. Nagged to death by Matilda and her equally vitriolic sister, Dorothy, who had moved in just months before, Angela believed. Matilda, who thought she had inherited everything, sold the lot and set about spending the large inheritance she had received in the will. Only she hadn't long to enjoy it because she'd suffered a stroke soon after. As beds in the hospitals were earmarked for injured servicemen, Dorothy had to look after her bedridden sister and few had had any sympathy for them.

Then, some months after George's death, Angela learnt of

the jewellery he had left her that had been his mother's. The manager of the bank said that some of the pieces were nice and probably worth something and that had pleased Angela. Despite the nest egg she had accrued from her wages working in the munitions factory, the jewellery assured Connie's future. When the time was right, the bank manager would sell the jewellery for her and invest it into an account and that would finance Connie's education.

'Who has the shop now?'

'Some nephew or other of George.'

'Oh?'

'Yes. You know how you thought his wife had sold it lock, stock and barrel?' Stan said.

'Yes.'

'Well, turned out she couldn't,' Stan said. 'The way the will was worded, the shop was to stay in her ownership until she died and then revert to this cousin they traced. He is the son of George's younger brother. He's called Harry and has spent all his life in America when his parents emigrated there when he was a small child. And, give him his due, he is trying hard with the place but he was telling me it was one hell of a mess when Matilda died and it reverted back to him. She must have been livid that George had worded the will in such a way that she'd been unable to sell the shop. Without that sale her inheritance wouldn't have been that much and the shop could not be sold during her lifetime. And she lingered for years – infirm though she was, she only died eighteen months ago.'

'Maybe she was so bad neither God or even Old Nick wanted her sooner,' Connie said and made everyone smile.

Though it was Angela, who knew just how vindictive and

heartless Matilda could be, who said, 'You could be right there, Connie.'

And thank God Matilda had never known about George's mother's jewellery that he had gifted to her, Angela thought. She said nothing to Stan about that though, for she hadn't told him about the jewellery. Although Angela wasn't aware that Mary had told her all about it, Connie knew, but she said nothing either.

Connie was in fact fascinated to hear all this, things her mother rarely spoke about, and Angela said with a smile to Stan, 'Oh, Stan, knowing Matilda as I did, she must have been spitting feathers not being able to sell the shop. George knew she had no interest in it.'

'Well, George certainly didn't think she did,' Stan said. 'According to Harry, he actually said so in the will.'

'So maybe he thought a nephew, even one he knew so little about, might have a greater love of it than his wife.'

'Maybe,' Stan said. 'But whichever way it was, she was angry not to get as much money as she expected and so she just barricaded it up and left it to rot. And it very nearly did. By the time this chap, Harry Maitland, took it on, it was so damp it was mouldy and in places rats had got in and gnawed away at the fittings inside and the mouldy food she left in there.'

'You seem to have got to know an awful lot about it.'

'Yeah, Harry was a talkative sort,' Stan agreed. 'He was telling me all this when he was showing me around and talking about what a terrible state the whole place had been in, left to go to wrack and ruin by Matilda. I couldn't help feeling that a lesser man than him and, if I'm honest, a poorer one, would have had the whole place pulled down and sold the land. Tell you, I was impressed when I saw the shop first after all these years because he has made it water-tight with a new roof and rendered walls. He has had the whole place fumigated and decorated, new counters and display cabinets erected. Honestly, Angela, you'd not know the place now and it's thriving.'

'I'll have to come for a look,' Angela said. 'I've not been near the place since that awful day when I found out George had died, I was feeling a little tearful then anyway. Barry had enlisted and I had gone into town to arrange for some of his wages to be diverted to me as I was getting so little in separation allowance. I called round for a few groceries before I made for home.'

'Yes, I remember you getting all your groceries there even after you left.'

'Why did you do that?' Daniel asked. 'There must have been plenty of nearer grocery stores because Maitland's would be a bit of a hike from your house. Did he give you special rates?'

'No, not exactly special rates,' Angela said. 'Though he would often pop in the odd thing not on the list. But I didn't get groceries from there because of that, but because George always played fair with his regular customers. See, people round here used to buy groceries week by week because they hadn't the money to buy any more.

'In fact, some were even worse off than that and would come in on Friday when their husbands got paid, pay any tick they had run up, buy food for the weekend and get their husbands' suits out of the pawn shop. Monday morning they would pawn the suits again and buy more food to last the week and, if they had more week than money left, they would run up tick in the shop. That is probably all alien to you, but that was the life many people lived, and still do. In the war, food was often in short supply, due to many food factories turning from food production to making weapons and so on. And so some toffs had the idea of having their carriage parked a few streets away and sending their drivers into grocery stores with a list. They had the money to clear the shelves of basic commodities and many shop-keepers allowed them to do this, despite knowing it was making life twice as hard for their regular customers trying to put a meal on the table for their families.

'At first Moorcroft's did that, so despite the fact it was literally on the doorstep, I boycotted their shop and went to George's, who was far too principled to do anything like that. By the time George had died, though, Moorcroft's had stopped selling to the toffs too. They would have seen their trade fall off, for many people did as I did and changed their grocer, and really people were spoilt for choice along Bristol Street. So Moorcroft's had to change their tune and look after their regulars better.'

Daniel could scarcely believe people were so poor they lived this way. Angela was watching his face and wondering what thoughts were tumbling about his head, but Stan was still thinking about George Maitland and the shop that he and Daniel would be living above.

'How did you find out what happened, to George I mean?' he asked Angela.

'A child from the street told me,' she replied. 'His wife verified it when I called to express my condolences. I needn't have bothered. She said it was what she had wanted to happen for years.'

Connie gave a gasp. 'What a thing to say! She must be a horrible person to say a thing like that.'

'Oh she was, Connie. You have no idea,' Angela said. 'Her sister Dorothy was living with her and one was as bad as the other as far as wickedness goes. I'm glad they got their comeuppance in the end when Matilda had the stroke and Dorothy had to look after her. If George hadn't written his will the way he had, that shop could have been bought by anybody now. Instead, George did his best to keep it in the family. I'm surprised that this Harry isn't living in the flat though.'

'No one could live in it in the state it's in now,' Stan said. 'His priority was to get the shop up and running so he stays in a B&B a couple of streets away. He has two rooms there and the landlady cooks all his meals, packs him sandwiches for his dinner, does his washing and ironing and cleans his rooms. He's perfectly happy being looked after.'

'What if he suddenly takes in his head to sell up and go back to America?'

'Well, you can't sell things like houses and businesses in five minutes, I shouldn't think,' Stan said. 'That would give us time to look around for something else. Anyway, we're only looking at this for the one year that Daniel is at college. After that he could be employed anywhere and might want to be off on his own anyway. But at the moment this will help his finances a bit, till he's earning properly.'

'It will be a help,' Daniel agreed. 'But though it's a solid enough flat, it needs redecorating everywhere and much of the furniture is broken and, well, the place is just such a mess. Couldn't really describe how bad it is. You should come for a look.'

'I'd like to,' Angela said. 'You want help moving stuff?'

Stan shook his head. 'Not a lot to move,' he said.

'Does this man Harry know the state of the place?'

Stan nodded. 'He knows. But after the state Matilda left the shop in he wasn't really surprised. He couldn't let the flat as it is now, but he said I can have it rent-free for as long as it takes for us to decorate and repair it throughout.'

'And the furniture?'

'He said all most of it is good for is making a pile of it in the yard and setting fire to.'

Angela shook her head. 'You know, it's hard for me to imagine this because Matilda used to be really house-proud when I was there. I used to come up every day for my dinner and I was always scared of spilling something on the sparkling white lace-edged tablecloths she always used. And the settee and chairs were immaculate, everything had to be just so – the cushions were even plumped in a certain way and the antimacassars and chair arm covers were snowy white. In fact, it was all so pristine I often thought it hardly a nice cosy home George could relax in after him being on his feet all the day.'

'No,' Stan agreed. 'A place can be *too* tidy.'

'Well, there's little danger our place will ever be too tidy, but I couldn't live in a pigsty either. If Betty will agree there are some things Daniel might want to bring.'

'Like what?'

'My desk, bookcases and my books of course,' Daniel said. 'And there's a nice cupboard that's got a load of my stuff in.'

'D'you really think she'll let you?' Connie asked.

Daniel shrugged. 'Your guess is as good as mine.'

'We're not going to argue about it whichever way it goes,' Stan said. 'If Betty won't let Daniel have his stuff we'll buy him what he needs. For now all the place is in great need of is a good turn-out and then a thorough clean.'

'I'll help you with that this weekend if you like,' Angela said. 'If you're certain you're taking it and have sorted it out with this Harry fellow and everything?'

'Oh, we're definitely taking it,' Stan said. 'I have to give a week's notice at my digs and I've booked a week from work too. I never have time off but I think I will need the time to get the flat so that we can live in it fairly comfortably. Daniel will come every evening after work to give a hand and then we'll in move in properly the following week. Everything to do with the tenancy of the flat is being finalised Friday evening.'

'That's my Saturday sorted out then,' Angela said.

'And mine,' Connie said. 'I'll help too.'

'It won't be the first time I have cleaned your house for you,' Angela said with a smile, remembering a time before the Great War when she had cleaned and polished Stan's home when he returned home after basic training in the army. That embarkation leave was short and precious and she had gone with her mother Mary to see him off at New Street Station. That had been the last time she'd seen him until she'd found him tending her mother's grave in the cemetery, and so she added with a wry smile, 'I'm sure you owe me.'

Stan looked straight into Angela's beautiful eyes and he said in sincere and honest tones, 'Oh Angela, I owe you more than you'll probably ever know. Cleaning my house, though I was immensely grateful, was just a very small part of it.'

Angela's stomach gave a flip at the look in Stan's eyes and

the sincere way he had spoken. Steady, she told herself firmly. This is Stan, your very good friend, and the only one he is concerned about building a relationship with just at the moment is his son, so it would be best if you didn't read more into it.

To break the moment she turned to Daniel and said, 'The house I cleaned was where your father used to live in the early years of his marriage, the house where you were born. Have you seen it?'

Daniel nodded. He didn't say that he had been as appalled by it as he had initially been by Angela's house. It would offend her and Connie to voice those thoughts, and make him sound snobby. It was just that the house he was born in was such a stark contrast to the one in which he'd been reared. He'd been raised in such a way that they had lived in a sort of bubble, so that he really hadn't known that people lived in those sorts of houses. And even though he'd had the chance to glimpse another life at university, he'd never been invited to anyone's family home while there. The rooms he had shared with peers had been quite spartan, but he could understand that as they had been student accommodation. It was hard for him to believe that people lived their whole lives in such places and brought families up there. His friends had mocked him for what they called his social ignorance and he supposed they had a point.

He knew his life would have been so different if he had stayed in the back-to-back house and been brought up by his father. Nevertheless, he doubted they would have been poverty-stricken, as many of their neighbours were. Even before the war, Stan had always been in work at a time when many had not been so fortunate. His father had told him he had worked at a place called a foundry and been made up to gaffer, and when he had enlisted in the Great War he had done so with the full approval of his boss who he had written to a time or two from the Front. After he'd been injured Stan had never written again so when the doctor deemed him to be as physically fit as they could get him he had called at the foundry. His boss had been delighted to find out that he had survived and found a job for him in the factory.

Stan had told Daniel this with some pride, but Daniel thought that the job in the foundry sounded horrendous. However, when he had expressed this, his father just shrugged.

'It was a job, a living, and far better than starving to death – and at that time that could have easily been the alternative. Believe me, even surviving that carnage was nothing short of a miracle.'

'I know that now,' Daniel admitted and then had added, 'I feel totally ignorant of a time when so many young men, like me now, marched off to war and so many, far too many, were killed in their thousands.'

Stan had given a grunt of agreement and then said, 'And something else to realise, Daniel, is when all the young fit men went off to war there were only the women left. They took on board all that heavy work that the men used to do, tough and laborious though it was.'

Remembering his father's words now, he said to Angela, 'Dad said women took on all the men's roles in the war.'

Angela nodded. 'They did.'

'I must say I was astonished at that.'

'Well, it was a necessity,' Angela said. 'There were just so few fit men around, so women made most of the weaponry used. They worked in steel mills and drop forges and they drove trucks and omnibuses, made tyres and shells and bullets and guns, aeroplanes . . . Oh, there was no end to the things women did and they still had to keep the country running at the same time. Others opened up their houses and put up the girls travelling the country looking for work, or ran nurseries to care for the babies so their mothers could work. Every man jack of us was needed and women everywhere seemed to be doing something for the war effort. Don't tell me such a devastating war didn't touch your life or that of your aunt and uncle at all?'

Daniel shook his head. 'War was never mentioned at home,' he said truthfully. 'And thinking about it now, they had a big and comfortable house and the bedrooms were large and we had one that was never used at all. Your talk about people opening up their houses to offer accommodation to these girls coming to Birmingham to work has made me think of that large and empty bedroom. Two, or possibly three, girls could have been easily housed there. Sutton Coldfield has little industry – though maybe through the war it was different – but even if that wasn't the case, the house was very near the train that ran straight into the city.'

'Yes, and passing many industrial areas on the way,' Stan said. 'Like Aston.'

'Oh, that was a real hub of activity in the war,' Angela said. 'So many factories were set up there making all manner of war-related things. And another thing, why wasn't your uncle called up? He wasn't that old, was he?'

Daniel shook his head and said with a slight smile, 'No. Though when I was a boy, I have to admit, I thought everyone over thirty was ancient. But now, thinking of it logically, he wasn't too old to be called up. Perhaps a doctor signed him off for medical reasons – he would have never discussed such things with me if so. Many of the boys I was at grammar school with had fathers at the Front, but that too was another thing never mentioned, never mind explained, and my aunt had never made any mention of war work she was doing either.'

'What about school?' Connie asked. 'I bet you talked about it there, especially as it was just a boys' school, wasn't it?'

'Yes, just boys,' Daniel answered. 'And though we spoke of it in the school yard, the school itself, the staff and all, made no big deal of it. Most of the teachers were old – the younger ones probably would have been called up – and so a stiff upper lip was the order of the day. Sometimes a boy would be sent for by the head and that was usually because a family member had been killed, or badly injured, but the rest of us had to work on regardless. And when the boy returned after a few days, or sometimes longer, no mention was made of any tragedy he have might suffered. We knew some boys had lost their fathers or a much loved brother, but there was little sympathy. It was quite the reverse, in fact, for if the boy showed any sign of still being upset, they would be told that there was no purpose in wallowing in self-pity and we must all face our lives with courage like our brave boys at the Front.'

Stan made a face at such lack of understanding and said, 'Sounds a little harsh. Believe me, when you lose someone dear to you, your head is all over the place. "Wallowing", as they chose to call it, is all you can do at the time, and I don't think young boys feel any less than an adult, for all their tender years.'

'I don't think they knew how to deal with any kind of

emotion,' Daniel said. 'Even when they read out the roll-call, as they did every Friday for all old boys lost in action, it was just a list of names for those of us who didn't have loved ones involved. And if I tried talking about it at home, asking questions and so on, I was shut up pretty sharpish. It wasn't suitable conversation for the table, or for anywhere else either.'

'So you lived through the biggest war the world has ever seen with colossal loss of life and none of it touched you,' Stan said angrily, quickly adding, 'I'm not blaming you, Daniel. You were and are a product of your upbringing and you were just a child anyway, only thirteen when the war ended, but it's as if you grew up in a bloody bubble.'

'I suppose I did,' Daniel agreed wistfully. 'Listening to you telling how it was then, I wish I had become more involved. I'd feel like I was doing my bit.'

'That's how nearly everyone felt that was left at home,' Angela said. 'Certainly all the women I worked with saw things that way.'

'What did you do in the war, Angela?' Daniel asked.

Stan answered for her. 'She made shells,' he said. 'She used to write to me and play down the dangers, though I read reports in any papers I managed to get hold of. She told me every piece of metal had to be removed, including hair grips and wedding rings, to prevent the possibility of a spark that could have caused an explosion.'

'God, how awful,' Daniel said, thinking of lovely Angela in danger like that. 'Weren't you ever scared?'

Angela thought before answering and then she said, 'If I'm honest I think if I really let myself dwell on what I was doing day after day I would have been terrified. I mean, as well as

164

removing all metal objects, we wore rubber boots, boiler suits, hats that had to cover every bit of hair, gloves and face masks.'

'Must be really dangerous if they were taking those kinds of precautions,' Daniel commented.

'It was dangerous work,' Angela admitted. 'No one ever tried to pretend otherwise. It was also hard work and shells were heavy. Empty, they weighed enough, but filled they seemed to weigh a ton. So the work wasn't easy and the hours were long, six to six Monday to Friday, six to twelve on Saturday and no day off other than Sunday.'

Connie, listening to her mother's words, remembered a time when her mother hadn't been there at all and had been gone for some months. She hadn't been at home, nor had she been at work either, and she said, 'You had time off once, Mammy. Lots of time.'

Stan, watching Angela's face, was surprised to see it flush as red as a tomato. His eyebrows rose in a query.

Angela muttered, 'Family crisis, I had to go over to Ireland to sort things out.'

Stan said nothing but he was surprised because he'd always understood Angela to have no family in Ireland or any other place. That was why the McCluskys had taken her in and reared her as their own. Surely any family would have claimed her when such a tragedy had engulfed her natural parents and siblings. Whatever the crisis was, it was clear that it had caused Angela acute embarrassment when Connie mentioned it.

However, even if he had been intending to comment, he hadn't a chance. Daniel had barely heard Connie's words, nor noticed his father's reaction, for he was still assimilating the hours Angela had been expected to work at hard physical labour and the harshness and apparent inconsiderateness of her employer not allowing her time off.

When he said this, however, Angela shook her head.

'There was a desperate shortage of shells and only us women to make them. Most of us had loved ones at the Front and knew they couldn't fight without the means to do so. We moaned amongst ourselves from time to time, but knew we had to get the job done. Mind you, to give my boss his due, he took on board what I said about the need to bid loved ones goodbye and the real dangers of coming back to work afterwards if your mind is distracted. And there was a lot more understanding as a result of that.'

ELEVEN

After the dishes had been washed and put away, Connie settled over her books at the cleared table and Angela, Stan and Daniel sat before the fire with a cup of tea and talked late into the night sharing their experiences. Angela retrieved a newspaper article from upstairs which recounted the terrible first day of the Battle of the Somme and the twenty thousand lives that had been lost on that day alone. Connie (who had lifted her head from her homework and was now listening in) and Daniel were almost stunned into silence. Daniel said he couldn't believe that something so terrible could have been allowed to happen.

Angela said, 'You must have heard about the Battle of the Somme before now?'

Daniel nodded. 'I know it was a really big battle. A lot of boys at school lost fathers, brothers, uncles. There were so many sent for throughout that summer they sort of had to tell us something.'

Angela nodded. 'The Battle of the Somme didn't centre on one day, though the greatest loss of life was on the first day.

It actually lingered on for almost five bloody months. The world knew more about these series of battles than any other because the Allies were so sure of victory they allowed the film crews and war correspondents with their cameras right into the battlefields for the first time.'

So Daniel read the account of the Battle of the Somme. The newspaper account explained that this was the first taste of battle for Britain's new volunteer armies, who had been persuaded to join up by patriotic posters showing Lord Kitchener himself summoning the men to arms.

Many 'pals battalions' went over the top that day; these battalions had been formed by men from the same town or village who had volunteered to serve together. The attack had been delayed by days due to torrential rain and so the battle started with a week-long artillery bombardment of the German lines on 1st July, with a total of more than 1.7 million shells being fired. It was anticipated that such a pounding would destroy the Germans in their trenches and rip through the barbed wire that had been placed in front.

'Now I understand the need for all those shells you were making,' Daniel said to Angela. 'One point seven million sounds like one hell of a lot of shells.'

'Yes,' Angela agreed. 'It is, of course, and that was only one battle. If ever I had any doubt that the work I was doing was vital and might make the difference to us winning the war or not, that told me more than anything.'

'And even that newspaper account doesn't tell the total appalling horror of that day,' Stan cried. 'And I am not surprised, for there are no words. I survived – God knows how when so many others didn't. Some men, who didn't even make it out the trench, were killed almost as soon as their heads were above the parapet. They would fall back with a cry and slide down the chalk wall to lie blood-stained and dying on the duckboards. Others were impaled on the wire and riddled with bullets, often with their innards hanging out. Countless dead and injured men filled the field as far as I could see, some with missing limbs, some half a head, some in pieces. Not all were dead, they screamed or sobbed in anguish and cried out for their mothers or sweethearts.'

Stan wiped tears from his eyes as he said, 'It was heartbreaking to cross that field and see the aftermath of man's inhumanity to man. In the initial surge it was every man for himself and you could stop to help none of them. No one could try to free those trapped on the wire, or put the men who were dying a slow and lingering death out of their misery, or tend those who had a chance of making it. If you did any of these things, or stopped advancing for any reason, you risked being shot.'

Daniel gasped. 'What an awful situation to be in. It's inhuman.'

'War is inhuman, Daniel,' Stan said. 'Never forget that.'

Angela suddenly glanced at the clock and exclaimed, 'Have you seen the time? We all have to get up in the morning and, Connie, you should have been in bed at least an hour ago.'

Connie could have claimed she hadn't finished her homework but she thought she'd get into more trouble if she tried that. She'd just have to explain to the teacher they'd had unexpected visitors and hope she didn't get too cross. Though even if she was, Connie decided, listening to her mother talking of times past and events in the war in a time she couldn't really remember were worth more than a teacher's bad humour. She bade goodnight to Stan and Daniel, kissed her mother and made her way to bed with no protest.

Stan and Daniel were getting into their outdoor coats when Stan said to Angela, 'Sorry if we overstayed our welcome.'

'You didn't,' Angela said. 'Don't be silly. It was good to remember and hear things from another's point of view. Michael seldom talks of his experiences either, and Maggie says he feels almost guilty that he was the only one to survive out of a group of mates, Barry included, that he had known all his life.'

'I can well understand that.'

'And I think it did Connie good to know how things were then. She used to plague me with questions when she was younger and I never could bear to relive times dead and gone and in the past. But the past shapes our future, I know that now, and it's also comforting to talk about what Connie would probably call "the olden days".'

Daniel laughed. 'A few years ago I would have called them the olden days as well, but whatever they're called it's good to know your history, where you come from.'

Angela's heart was pierced by pain and she gave a small gasp as she remembered the tiny mite she'd left on the workhouse steps, who would never know where she came from. Even her name would be one someone in there had given her and Angela knew there was not a thing she could do to help her.

'Angela, are you all right?' Stan cried, for he had heard the gasp and seen the blood drain from her face.

'It's nothing,' Angela said. In an attempt to change the subject, she asked, 'Now would about ten o'clock suit for

Connie and I to come round and clean the flat on Saturday morning?'

Stan wouldn't be deflected so easily. 'Ten's fine,' he said, 'but are you absolutely sure you are all right?'

'Yes,' Angela said slightly impatiently. 'Just a bit of sadness at stirring up memories, that's all.'

Stan might have probed further but Angela didn't give him the opportunity. She opened the door as a broad hint for them to leave and said, 'Now stop fussing, Stan, and be on your way and I'll see you on Saturday.'

Stan and Daniel had no option but to go, though Stan cast a worried look in Angela's direction as he passed. Angela shut the door behind both men with an imperceptible sigh, leaning against it and letting the tears trickle silently down her cheeks for the child she had abandoned.

TWELVE

The following Saturday morning Angela and Connie were almost ready to go. Each had a bag with cloths and various cleaning materials in, and a scarf to cover their hair, when suddenly the door opened (for no one locked doors in that area) and Maggie stepped in.

'You off out?' she asked.

Angela had a big smile on her face as she answered, 'Yes, and you will never guess where to, not in a million years.'

'I haven't got a million years to spare,' Maggie retorted. 'So you best tell me.'

'George Maitland's shop, or to be more precise, the flat above the shop that needs a darned good clean.'

To say Maggie was surprised would be an understatement. 'And why on earth are you cleaning it?'

And so Angela told Maggie how it had come about. 'It's been empty some time and it's in a bit of a state,' she said. 'And Stan didn't ask, I offered.'

'More fool you,' Maggie said. 'Won't be the first time you cleaned his place for him either.'

'I know,' Angela said. 'I reminded him of that, don't worry.'

'Won't it feel strange going in there again after all this time?'

'Maybe,' Angela admitted. 'But I am interested in meeting this Harry and seeing what he's done to the shop. Stan said he gutted the place, had to really by all accounts because of the state Matilda and her odious sister, Dorothy, left it in. Why don't you come and give us a hand?'

'I can't,' Maggie said. 'I actually called to tell you something pretty sad. Michael's father had a heart attack last night.'

'Oh God, is he all right?'

'Well he didn't die,' Maggie said. 'Not straight away anyway, but Michael went with his mother in the ambulance. One of their neighbours came banging on our door in the small hours and Michael got dressed and set off. I don't know what they told his mother – Michael said Hilda was beside herself and probably would have been incapable of understanding much said to her. They were probably relieved Michael was there. Anyway, the upshot of it was they don't think the old man will survive this, his heart is too weak.'

'Ah,' Angela said. 'And here's me going on about the shop.'

'Well, you weren't to know,' Maggie pointed out. 'And it is a shame, because Alf is a decent old soul.'

'I know you like him better than Michael's mother.'

Maggie grimaced and said, 'Hilda would be all right if she would stop fussing round Michael. She's like a mother hen and he doesn't like it, says it makes him feel about six.'

'Some mothers of sons are like that, they can't bear the thought that some woman is going to be more important in their son's life than them.'

Maggie shook her head. 'I think she can't get over the fact

173

that Michael losing his leg made no difference to the way I felt about him,' she said. 'And now, since he has had the artificial leg fitted, few would guess he is disabled at all apart from the limp he has.'

Maggie was right, Michael had made an amazing recovery. It hadn't all been plain sailing for there had been some chafing on his stump at first. The hospital had showed Maggie how to dress it with salve and muslin bandages before fitting the artificial leg, instructing him to make only short journeys using the leg to begin with. This had been the hardest part for Michael, who had been keen to get rid of the crutches. However, Maggie had been firm and now Michael could wear the leg all day with no discomfort except on days of intense heat. And, as Maggie said, days of intense heat in England were few and far between so that wasn't a problem either.

Hilda couldn't seem to see this improvement in her son though. The vision of him lying in a hospital bed after he returned from France pale and sick and missing a leg, and later hobbling round on crutches, was etched on her mind.

'Can't really blame Hilda,' Maggie said. 'I mean, she had a fine family once but she lost her eldest boy in the war and two young girls to Spanish flu and actively encouraged her next eldest son and two other girls to go to America. To lose so many children in such a relatively short space of time must have caused great heart-ache. Neighbours told me she cried for days. Alf was far more stoical and then when Michael came home sick and needing her she lavished all the attention on him. Understandable really.'

'Course it is and I don't think bottling things up helps either. Alf not letting himself openly grieve might have contributed to this heart attack.'

'Could well have done,' Maggie agreed. 'Anyway, I best be getting on.'

'We must too,' Angela said. Later, as they scurried towards Maitland's shop, she wondered if Alf died, or became too disabled to work, how much that would affect Michael and Maggie. Alf and Hilda ran a small guest-house in one of the big houses in Pershore Road and, despite it being a small concern, she doubted Hilda could cope with it on her own.

She didn't share her concerns with Connie, who was in any case more interested in the shop where her mammy had worked before she had been born. She wanted to see what sort of person had taken it on from George Maitland, the man who had thought so much of her mammy he had left her his mother's jewellery. Not that she could let on to her mother that she knew about that; her grandmother had told her in confidence.

Angela approached the store with a little trepidation but she needed have worried. This Harry obviously had a genuine interest in the shop, for it looked spruce and clean, large glass windows replaced the much smaller ones. The sign above the door that read 'Maitland's Store' in bright yellow letters was a great improvement on the old one.

She opened the door and a tinkly little tune rang out and Harry, who was serving a customer, looked up. The shop was full as it often was on Saturday, though there was no one Angela recognised. Nonetheless, she was rather mesmerised by the store. She had thought maybe she might feel a nostalgic tug, but she didn't. Harry had put his own stamp on it and it now bore no resemblance to the shop she had spent years serving in. She noted a far wider array of goods was on sale, much of it displayed on glass stands so that customers could help themselves. The tea was ready-weighed into quarters and the sugar into two-pound blue bags, but fruit and vegetables had to be weighed and there were still the assorted tubs of biscuits with see-through lids. The bacon cutter looked familiar and the cheese wire and the meat slicer, but the scales were new, as was the large shiny cash register beside the big gleaming counter.

Harry had been expecting Angela and Connie, so when he spotted them he knew straight away who they were.

'Excuse me,' he said to the woman he was serving. 'I will just be a moment but there is something I must deal with.'

The woman said nothing, but Angela noticed with a slight smile that all the women looked in her direction when Harry came from behind the counter with a smile of welcome on his face. She guessed they were trying to work out what Harry's business was with her.

'You must be the Angela that Stan speaks so highly of,' he said, pumping her hand up and down as he spoke.

Harry was about the same age as Stan, she noted, and though his hair was more grey than dark brown, it didn't make him appear old, it sort of suited him. He was quite a handsome man and his face was kindly and his grey eyes twinkled. He had an Irish accent but it was mixed with a little American, which was like something Angela and Connie had only heard about it and so different from the Birmingham accents all around them.

'And this must be Connie,' he said, turning to the young girl. 'Well, my my, aren't you like two peas in a pod?' And then he gave a wry smile and said, 'And I would guess you are fed up to the back teeth with people saying things like that.'

'Well, let's say it's been said more than once.'

Harry laughed. 'A very controlled response, my dear. Well, you are both more than welcome and I am grateful to you offering to help Stan like this but I think today might be more a throwing-out session than cleaning. Do you want me to take you up? Stan is already there.'

'No need to lead the way,' Angela said. 'I know it well enough and you have a shop full of people. I must say the shop is lovely.'

'You should have seen it when I first took it on,' Harry said. 'Somebody — and it's thought to be George's wife and her sister — made a right mess of the place, probably when they realised they couldn't sell it. And brace yourself for the flat above. It will be nothing like the place you remember, I'm sure. I think the best thing is to gut the place and start again as I did with the shop. Stan fully agrees with me.'

'Right,' said Angela. 'Best take a look then.'

Leaving Harry to attend to his customers, she opened the stair door at the back of the shop. They were only halfway up the stairs when Connie wrinkled her nose and said, 'Ugh! What's that smell?'

'Neglect,' Angela said. 'Neglect and damp.'

And minutes later when she opened the door to the flat, she was glad Harry had warned her because what she was looking at bore little resemblance to the flat she'd eaten her dinner in every day. It hadn't got into this repulsive state because of mere neglect, it had been vandalised pure and simple.

After greeting Stan, she said to him, 'No doubt this whole place needs a thorough clean and the damp will have to be dealt with eventually. But Harry said before all else there has to be a big clear-out and I'm inclined to agree with him.'

Stan nodded. 'We knew it needed work, but as Daniel said, that will make it more our own and we are having the first few months rent-free to decorate and do basic repairs.'

Angela thought it needed more than mere decorating, for the wallpaper was hanging from the wall in sheets and there were great gouges in the plaster. The paint wasn't just chipped and peeling off from the skirting board, but there were also great chunks of wood missing, which looked as if they had been chiselled out of it, and the door had deep gashes scored all down its length.

'Can you do all this yourself?' Angela asked.

'Most of it, I should say,' Stan said. 'Daniel can help me.'

'Yes, but it's not just a bit of paint and wallpaper though, is it?' Angela said. 'You'll have to virtually repair it all first, for Matilda and Dorothy did a real hatchet job – on this room at least. If fact, looking at the damage done to the skirting board, it wouldn't surprise me if they *had* attacked it with a hatchet. Those deep gashes could hardly have been done with a kitchen knife. As for Daniel's help, you might find he is not well versed at doing practical things like this,' she went on with a smile. 'He's a book learner.'

'You can be both,' Stan pointed out. 'He knows as well as I the work that has to be done to make this place habitable, and what he doesn't know I can teach him. Stand him in good stead when he has a place of his own anyway.'

'I suppose,' Angela said, looking round with a sigh. 'It's sad to see it looking so shabby when I remember how it once was,' she said to Connie. 'She was so house-proud, George's wife, and really took care of the furniture and now it's all either broken or chopped up.'

'I know,' Connie said. 'The table is totally ruined and the

dining chairs smashed to bits and yet you can see that they were lovely once.'

'There's the three-piece suite she set such store by, according to George,' Angela said. 'So much so that he was not allowed to sit on it. Look at it now, greasy and stained and lopsided because one of its legs has broken off and the cushions are split open. Nothing has escaped their savagery, not even the lovely sideboard.' She was sad to see the sideboard so destroyed for she had always loved looking at it. The wood had been perennially burnished to a glossy shine and a hint of lavender polish would often be wafting in the air as she'd entered the room. And behind the patterned glass doors had been glasses that sparkled and glittered in the light.

No one, not even George, had ever used those glasses, but they drank from thick everyday ones Matilda kept in the kitchen. Angela guessed those beautiful glasses only ever left their home in the sideboard when Matilda had taken them out to polish them to an even greater shine and then put them back. They were obviously to be looked at, not used. Now there were deep gouges in the sideboard, which was listing on three legs as one had been hacked off, and the glass on one of the doors was cracked and the door itself was hanging on one hinge.

And the rampage had obviously continued throughout the flat, for in the bedrooms mattresses had been slashed and ornaments, lamps and anything else they could crush underfoot were mangled. Wardrobes had deep gashes down them and the drawers were taken out and chopped up and curtains torn from the windows and ripped to shreds. Angela wondered if the flat had been broken into at some point – much of the damage seemed almost deliberate.

The mad rush was over in the shop and in the lull Harry joined them. Angela was still surveying the devastation where plates, cups and those thick glasses were smashed to smithereens and rancid food was ground into the ripped and sticky oil cloth.

'Tell you the truth,' Angela said. 'I never expected it to be this bad.'

'Well, that was partly my fault,' Harry said. 'The shop was in such a state and I knew I had to get that up and running to provide me with some money because I was running out of cash. So I have to admit I closed my eyes to the mess in the flat.'

'You wouldn't have had time to run the shop single-handed and do anything up here anyway,' Angela said. The shop bell tinged and she continued, 'You go down and we'll start moving the stuff. See how far on we are by dinnertime.'

'And I'll close the shop as usual and bring in some fish and chips,' Harry said. 'I know why you Brits go on so much about it. Couldn't understand it when I first came over but I'm a real fan now.'

As Harry went down the stairs Angela said to Stan, 'Where's Daniel when there's work to be done?'

'Packing his stuff up,' Stan said. 'Said he'd be here by the afternoon.'

'But where's he going to go?' Angela said. 'The flat will not be fit to live in for some time.'

'Oh, I know that,' Stan says. 'My landlady said he can stay with me for a week until we have the place in some sort of shape.'

'Come on,' Connie urged. 'We're wasting time just chatting.'

'Cheeky,' Angela said, but she knew her daughter had a

180

point and they all put their backs into clearing the flat as quickly as possible.

By the time Harry turned the 'Open' sign to 'Closed' and locked the door, they had collected a sizeable collection of battered and broken furniture and Harry was amazed at what they had achieved. Daniel had turned up by then and they stood in the yard and ate their fish and chips because there was nowhere to sit and indoors was little better. In fact, Angela considered it far worse because there was also a sour smell lingering in the air; though she had opened the windows to try and disperse it, it was still pretty strong.

'I don't think we'll get rid of it until everything is out of the flat and I get at it with the carbolic,' she said. 'Tell you the truth, till then I don't think it's healthy to eat anything in there.'

No one disagreed with this and as they ate Angela told them all about Michael Malone's father. 'Maggie said he was in a bad way and his wife was in bits.'

'Not to be wondered at, but even if he pulls through I would say this means a huge change for Maggie and Mike,' Stan said.

'I thought the very same,' Angela admitted. 'I can't really see any alternative than the two of them moving in with Michael's mother lock, stock and barrel but I will miss her if she moves to Pershore Road. I mean, it's not as if we live in each other's pockets, but I know she's there just up the road like she always has been since we were children together. She helped so much when I had the news about Barry and then when Mammy was so ill. I mean, we even worked in the shell factory together in the war.'

'True friendships like that will never die,' Harry said. 'Even if you don't see each other so often. And life changes all the time. Who knows what might happen in your life for it to change direction?'

'Oh, nothing much happens to me.'

'You can't say that,' Harry said. 'All you can say is nothing exciting or life-changing has happened yet. Who knows what might lie waiting just round the corner? Look at me. If you had told me last year that this year I would be in England and the owner of a shop I'd never have believed it.'

'I suppose,' Angela said. 'Anyway, I'm selfish just thinking of me. Maggie wouldn't choose to live there given the choice because she often finds her mother-in-law difficult.'

'Needs must,' Stan said.

Angela agreed with a sigh and went on, 'The same goes for me too. And just now, my needs are to get on with moving the rest of the stuff out of the flat because I have to be at work behind the bar at the Swan tonight.' And she added, wiping her fingers on the paper, 'After being at this all day I'll need a good wash and more decent clothes before I start pulling pints.'

They all set to work again. Harry helped them till two o'clock when he re-opened the shop and by the time Angela and Connie were ready to make for home, piles of broken and battered furniture filled the yard.

'What are you going to do with it all?' Angela asked Harry, who had taken advantage of another lull in the shop to see how they were doing. 'I know what you said about setting fire to it, but I don't think you could do that because there are houses all around you.'

'And there's probably a law against it,' Stan put in.

'Sure to be,' Harry said. 'What I need is some sort of place where they reclaim all the good wood and get rid of the dross. They have wood yards like that in the States and the other rubbish can be taken to a tip. There must be a tip about, but I wouldn't know where to start looking.'

'Where did all the old fittings for the shop go?' Angela asked.

Harry shrugged. 'The builders refitting the shop dealt with all that,' he said. 'I left them to it, to tell you the truth.'

'Well, they have to put the rubbish somewhere so there must be places like that,' Stan said. 'It's just not something you search out on a regular basis. I'll ask around. There's an Irish fellow in my lodgings and he runs a scrap metal business and seems to know everything and everybody. Poor fellow has done his back in so the doctor's put him off work for at least a week, and while he's not working he's not earning.'

'Aye, that's the rub,' Harry said as the shop bell tinkled.

Just before Angela followed him down to go home she said to Stan, 'I'm leaving all the cleaning materials that Connie and I brought here today and I'll have a word with Breda Larkin and see if she will do my lunchtime shift tomorrow. Then we can come straight up after Mass and give it all a good going-over.'

They walked home, talking of the state of the flat, but in actual fact it was Angela doing most of the talking and Connie just making non-committal replies. She was a bit annoyed with her mother arranging her whole weekend without asking her. She hadn't minded offering to give up her Saturday but she hoped she might see Sarah on Sunday. She knew that once Sarah started work at the hotel she wouldn't see much of her at all and she already felt they were drifting apart. She didn't say that though, but what she did say cut across what her mother was saying.

'Don't know if I'll be free tomorrow. I do have homework to do.'

'Well you have all this evening.'

'Doubt I'll get it all finished,' Connie said shortly. 'I'm given extra at the weekend.'

Angela glanced at her daughter as they turned into Bristol Passage and wondered if that were true or if she just didn't want to go back to the shop. She hadn't time to say anything about it because she saw Maggie going up Grant Street and called to her. Though Angela wanted to know the news from the hospital, time was of the essence if she was going to be able to grab a bite to eat before she had to be at work, so she gave Connie the key and told her to put the kettle on the fire while she had a word with Maggie.

Connie knew her mother would just be enquiring about Maggie's father-in-law, who she didn't know, and she contented herself with a wave and made her way home. Maggie told Angela Alf had died that morning just moments after she arrived.

'Oh I'm so sorry,' Angela said. 'I know you thought a great deal of him.'

Maggie nodded. 'I did, but he was an old man and the doctor said he'd never be right again, you know. And he would have hated to linger. Better he went like this, for him, I mean.'

'I suppose so.'

'For us it will mean massive changes,' Maggie said.

Angela nodded. 'Yes, I know that.'

'Look, have you time to come in for a cuppa?' Maggie said, but Angela shook her head regretfully.

184

'Can't, I'm working tonight.'

'Let's walk then,' Maggie said. 'I wouldn't like any eaves-droppers to overhear our conversation.'

'Why? What's up?' Angela said as the two women turned and began to walk up Grant Street.

'Big changes are afoot everywhere, it seems to me,' Maggie said. 'One of the nurses told me they are going to enlarge the infirmary because it isn't big enough. It is a teaching hospital and the only other one is Queen's and that's not large either. There are plans to build another hospital there where the workhouse is.'

'When?' Angela said urgently. 'Did she say?'

'I asked her that and she said when the sky falls in, which wasn't really that helpful,' Maggie said. 'I didn't want to appear too curious, you know, but I think the long and short of it is they haven't anywhere near the money needed. But it is going to happen some day in the future. I mean, in the paper it said they are closing workhouses all over the city, so the one in the town will probably be defunct too in the end. But by then,' she went on, lowering her voice, 'it's more than likely your child will be set on in service somewhere.'

Angela gave a sharp intake of breath and Maggie said gently, 'You knew that was the best she could hope for.'

Oh yes, Angela knew, but she thought of the unfairness of life. She had condemned her child to a life lacking in any sort of love or tenderness, and she was destined for a job where she would skivvy from morning till night, probably as a scullery maid, for that was the lowliest servant, while her sister had a dazzling future before her.

'It hurts me sometimes that I will never know what will happen to her,' Angela admitted. But she knew that any

185

attempt to make any sort of contact with the child would be thwarted, just as it had been when she had tried to see her at the workhouse some years before.

She sighed with the hopelessness of it all.

'Are you all right?' Maggie said in a low voice.

Angela shook her head. 'Sometimes I wonder if I will ever feel all right again. I go through the motions, that's all. And yet I have no right to be upset or care what happens to that child. I gave those rights away when I left a poor helpless baby on the workhouse steps.'

'You can't turn feelings off like that though,' Maggie said as the women turned back to walk down Grant Street.

'No, but I have no right to acknowledge them,' Angela said.

'Why don't you have the night off tonight?' Maggie said, looking at her friend's distressed face.

'Because I am not the sort of person to take time from work unless for a very good reason. Not going into work will not change the situation one bit, but give me more time to think. I'll see if Eddie McIntyre can take my mind off things. He's done it before. Even made me laugh a time or two.'

'Who's Eddie McIntyre when he's at home?'

'This Irish-American fellow,' Angela said. 'Here on business. Came from Donegal like we did and landed in Birmingham first and then went on to New York where he has been ever since. As my brothers are there I was interested in the place. He has a stock of tales to tell. You know I don't mind serving at the bar at all, but the conversation can be very dull and predictable at times. Eddie is a great distraction.'

'Oh yes?' Maggie said with a suggestive smile at Angela.

Angela lifted her eyes to heaven. 'Just because I mention a man's name you are convinced there's something going on.'

'I wish there was,' Maggie admitted. 'You are a free agent and I presume he's the same? You have been on your own quite long enough.'

'He is friendly, that's all, and it's my job to be friendly to all the men,' Angela retorted. 'And I am not looking for any more than that. Eddie is different in that he has seen and done things most people haven't. He has things to talk about other than football or the price of beer or moaning about their wife, kids and jobs. That's all you get from many of them.'

'You don't surprise me, Angela,' Maggie said. 'Don't they talk about sex as well? People say it's what most men think about most of the time.'

'Well I don't know what they think about,' Angela said. 'But if they tried any dirty talk around me they would get their ears boxed and well they know it. Oh God, look at the time,' she said. 'I must fly.'

'Are you sure you're all right?'

'Maggie, I'm as well as I ever have been,' Angela said. 'And if I don't get home soon Connie will come looking for me.'

Connie looked up from her books that she had spread on the table as her mother came in. Taking in Angela's red face and slightly agitated state, she said, 'You all right?'

'Fine,' Angela said. 'I spent too long with Maggie and had to run, that's all.'

'I'll say you spent too long,' Connie said. 'I made the tea but it will be stewed now and not worth drinking.'

'It'll do,' Angela said. 'Will you do me a piece of toast on the fire while I have a wash and change?'

'Course,' Connie said, but when her mother had sat down to eat it and was gulping at the stewed tea, she said, 'Well, how is he then?'

'Who?'

'Maggie's father-in-law,' Connie said. 'Isn't that what you wanted to speak to Maggie about?'

Angela had forgotten all about the old man and she said, 'Oh yes, of course. He died.'

'Golly, Maggie took a long time to tell you that.'

'Don't be cheeky, Connie. I'm entitled to talk to my friend for as long as I choose.'

'Don't think that was cheeky,' Connie said. 'And you haven't time to tell me off anyway unless you don't mind being late for work.'

It was Angela's pet hate to be late for anything and Connie knew that full well. She finished the tea but left half of the toast and then dashed down the road. She generally enjoyed her job and even more now that Eddie McIntyre was a regular.

THIRTEEN

By the following morning, Connie, who at first had been determined not to go with her mother to clean the flat, had changed her mind. She couldn't honestly claim that she had too much work for she had made a great stab at it the previous evening, and the rest she could easily finish off after her mother had gone to work that evening. Anyway, she thought morosely as she lay in bed staring at the damp and patchy attic ceiling, if she didn't go along with her mother, what was she going to do with herself all day? Sarah didn't seem to want to spend time with her any more, for all they'd once been together all the time. It had been usual for Connie to hightail it to her friend's house and they would spend the day together indoors or outdoors according to the weather. But they hadn't met up on Sundays for the last three weeks, and when they saw each other after Mass Sarah always had some excuse why they couldn't meet later that day. Connie was convinced they were excuses and not proper reasons.

She had to admit Sarah had changed really since just before the Easter holidays and could only presume that it was because she would soon be leaving school. In fact, if her fourteenth birthday had been before the schools broke up for the Easter holiday just two weeks away, her friend could have already left as she had a respectable job lined up. However, like Connie, her birthday was in May so she had to wait until they broke up for the summer.

Despite knowing that those were the rules, Sarah still felt a little hard done by, having to kick her heels for a few months more, just because of when she was born.

'It isn't as if I'm going to learn anything more,' she grumbled.

'What has that to do with anything?' Connie said. 'It's rules, that's all. You can't start school till you're five and can't leave till you're fourteen.'

Connie had initially thought Sarah would be as pleased as she was and that they would make the most of the limited time they had together, but her friend chafed at the delay to starting what she called her 'proper life'. To Connie, Sarah's withdrawal seemed as if she was putting aside the childish pursuits and friendships she had once enjoyed as she was preparing to join the adult world.

However, there was nothing Connie could do to counteract this, and she was bitterly hurt by Sarah's rejection of her. She said not a word to her mother and it bothered her that Angela hadn't seemed to notice her loneliness.

In fact, Angela had noticed and had a good idea where the problem lay. For the first time she doubted the decision she made for her daughter to matriculate and go on further if she had the brains. And if that included university, Angela wondered where she would figure in her daughter's new life as she moved into a new environment with new interests and friends. Connie was Angela's reason for living, but she worried that, by insisting on her continuing in further education, she might be in effect driving her away from her home and her working-class roots.

When she had planned out Connie's future with Barry it had seemed so simple, but she realised now it wasn't going to be simple or painless. The loss of friends was only the beginning and Angela was sad to see her daughter's true friendship with Sarah fraying at the edges. She was aware it would be wrenched wide open when Sarah joined her sisters at the hotel in just a few short months. She felt truly sorry for her daughter; she knew that if something had happened to part her so effectively from Maggie, she would have been desperately unhappy.

But then Barry's face swam before her face and his earnest wish to do the level best for his daughter. As he wasn't there to see his precious child grow up she had to do as he had wanted. She gave a sigh as she heaved herself out of bed to go to Mass before setting out for Maitland's and thought, really life was full of ups and downs and you just had to make the best of it.

Some time later Angela and Connie were staring with approval at the truck parked in the yard. Harry, Stan and Daniel had begun loading it up with the wrecked furniture and associated debris they had carried down to the yard the day before.

'You got the truck you thought you might be able to have a loan of and that's the biggest problem solved,' she said to Stan. 'So why the long faces?'

'We haven't anyone to drive it,' Stan said. 'I thought the

owner might be able to do just the one run to the dump, but it was no good. Even just driving the truck round here was too much for him. I had to near carry him back to the lodgings and help him into bed, his arthritis is so bad.'

'Can't any of you drive?' Angela asked. 'Didn't you pick up any driving skills in the army, Stan?'

Stan shook his head. 'There was never the opportunity.'

'What about you, Harry? I know Daniel has never learnt to drive but I can't believe you haven't.'

'Why is that so difficult for you to believe?'

'Because you are American and they have a reputation for doing things before we do in Britain and driving is becoming more common here.'

'Well you're right, I suppose,' Harry said. 'I can drive, my father insisted on it, said it was a good skill to have and that motor cars were the future.'

'I'd say he's right.'

'He probably is.'

'So if you can drive, what's to stop you driving the truck?'

'I wouldn't have the confidence,' Harry said. 'Tell you the truth, I hated driving and did as little as possible. I've never driven anything bigger than a car and we drive on the right side of the road in America. No, I haven't enough experience to get behind the wheel of something that big.'

'Isn't it like riding a bike?' Angela said. 'People say once you've learnt you never forget.'

'I don't know if that's true or not,' Harry said. 'But driving a truck laden down with stuff and driving on what, to me, is the wrong side of the road is not a safe way to test out that theory.'

'All right,' Angela said. 'I'll drive the truck.'

The three men looked at Angela and said in unison. 'You!!!'

'She can drive,' Connie put in. 'Mammy hardly ever tells me about the brave things she did in the war, but Granny told me about the driving. She went all over, she said.'

'Connie's right,' Angela said and looked across at Stan. 'Unlike you I was given the opportunity to learn to drive and I grasped it with both hands and drove all through the war. Unlike you, Harry, I have never driven a car, but I have driven any and all manner and sizes of trucks and to me driving on the left is normal.'

'No, I can't have this,' Harry said.

'I know that,' Angela said. 'So I can test my theory of never forgetting how to drive once I had learned.'

And then as the grey-faced disapproving men continued to shake their heads, Angela lost patience.

'Right, Connie and I will make a start on cleaning the rooms you have cleared as we arranged yesterday and you try and work out who else you are going to get to drive your truck.' And so saying, Angela turned on her heel and went back into the shop, Connie following her.

It didn't take long before Stan came to see her.

'I can't think of another way of moving the stuff, but it doesn't sit easy, you doing it. Harry's all for getting a firm in to do the lot.'

Angela shrugged. 'If you want, but it will cost some money to get someone in and a bit silly when you have the truck anyway. And if you decide not to use that fellow's truck someone will have to take it back so you can get another truck in.'

'Look Angela, just exactly how much driving did you do in the war?'

'Lots,' Angela said and went on, 'At first they used a retired driver for long-haul and I only did short runs. But then he had a heart attack and the doctor said he couldn't do it any more so I did most of it after that. I went to the docks and everything.'

'You did?'

'Yes, I did.'

'But it's a long time ago and there's more traffic on the roads now,' Stan said. 'Won't you be the slightest bit nervous?'

'Probably to start with,' Angela admitted. 'But I'm sure when I'm behind the wheel I will be all right, especially if I am given time to familiarise myself with the controls.'

In the end, grudgingly, the men agreed to let Angela deliver the stuff the following day.

'We'll need thick ropes and a large sheet of tarpaulin,' she said.

'We have those in the front of the truck.'

'Make sure it's all secured,' Angela said. 'You'd see the care I would take transporting shells. I had no desire to blow myself to kingdom come.'

'I should think not. I'm surprised Mary allowed you to do that,' commented Stan.

'She couldn't have stopped me,' Angela said. 'She knew how important it was to get those shells out. I wasn't the only girl who learnt to drive but I was the only one who seemed to enjoy it and, according to my boss, the only one who could read a map. Anyway, transporting the shells was no more dangerous than assembling them and it got me out of the stink and the noise and the choking sulphur dust that turned skin yellow and hair red, and that had to be a plus.

194

Anyway, though everyone took reasonable precautions, no one worried too much about staying safe because they had to do what they had to do.'

'We were told often that if it wasn't for the women in the munitions and such we wouldn't have any weapons to fight with,' Stan said admiringly. 'And they kept this country afloat in many other ways as well.'

'Well, I'm going to continue to work hard,' Angela said. 'So I'll get on with the cleaning because that's why we've come.'

Angela and Connie had broken the back of the cleaning by the time Angela clocked on for her shift behind the bar. The Larkins were very interested in the American who had bought George's shop and the renovations taking place.

'Funny that George never left the place to his wife,' Paddy said.

'You wouldn't think it odd if you'd met her,' Angela said, 'for a more spiteful and vitriolic woman never walked the earth – unless it was her odious sister, Dorothy, who was just as mean-spirited and spiteful.'

Angela usually never had a bad word to say about anyone and so Breda laughed. 'Angela, I wouldn't have believed I'd ever hear you use such words to describe people.'

Paddy wouldn't either but he said, 'Maybe Angela has reason. I mean Maitland's is a fair step from here but I heard about it when George died, some conversation about it over the bar counter. If it hadn't been for war talk taking precedence they'd probably still be at it.' He frowned a little as he thought and then went on, 'Casting my mind back, I remember some saying he was nagged to death.' And he swung his head round and, with a wink at Angela, fixed a meaningful look at his wife. 'See what nagging can do. Detrimental to a man's health, it is.'

'So is clouting said man with a rolling pin,' Breda said in mock outrage. 'And that might be the alternative. Tell you, Paddy, you get off light and don't get half the nagging you deserve.'

Angela laughed, knowing it was just play-acting between Paddy and Breda as she said, 'Many said George was nagged to death. It wouldn't surprise me as all the years I was there she never ever threw him a kind word. It must have been ten times worse for him when her sister moved in, thinking they owned the whole place. Dorothy went round forcing people to pay up their tick and few had the money to do that without hardship.'

'I know that well,' Paddy said. 'God, I'd have no customers if I didn't allow tick.'

'George knew that too,' Angela said. 'He was a kind and generous man and I was very fond of him and I know he was fond of me – not in any sort of wrong way, more paternal.'

'Well, of course he never had any children of his own.'

'Mary always said Matilda was the kind of wife that wouldn't be in the business of conceiving them. She said she'd seen it before – a very beautiful woman turning a man's head, promising him delights ahead, but he often finds she will not let him near her. I must say that seemed to describe Matilda Maitland to a tee. I think George always regretted not having children.'

Breda sighed. 'Aye, mine had my heart scalded many a time. What I wouldn't give to be able to turn the clock back and have the two lads sparring and fighting with one another and young Peg looking at her younger brothers with distaste from her lofty position as the eldest. God, life's hard sometimes.'

Angela saw the forsaken look flood Breda's face and turned away lest she be embarrassed. Breda and Paddy's youngest son, Billy, never came back from the war and Peggy was married and with a toddler son and expecting when her husband marched away. He'd been so badly injured in mind and body when he was returned to her that he would spend the rest of his life in a wheelchair and Peggy had to do everything for him.

'I tell myself I should be grateful our Colin survived, though it was always Billy who showed more interest in the pub. Colin's keeping it in the family in a way because he has a good job in Atkinson's Brewery and courting a lovely girl. You have to count your blessings, don't you?'

Angela nodded dumbly and Breda, as if changing the subject, asked her all about the owner of Maitland's. She told all she knew, saying he seemed a very pleasant man, but she said nothing about the idea of her driving the truck and the way it had all the men talking about how suitable it was.

Breda mentioned Maitland's to Eddie that evening, thinking he might be interested, being as the new owner Harry was American. But the only person he seemed interested in was Angela.

If fact, such was his interest in Angela that Breda mentioned it to Paddy much later that night as they got ready for bed.

'Now don't be looking for problems where there are none,' he said. 'They are both free agents and Angela is only a young woman yet. It isn't a crime to get another to warm your bed and satisfy needs she must still have, so good luck to them if they decide to make a go of it.'

Angela was unaware that she was the subject of speculation, though she knew that Eddie McIntyre always made a special effort to catch her attention. She didn't encourage him but didn't mind either, as he wasn't abusive or suggestive, but often funny and he made her smile.

'A beautiful woman like you should be out having fun and enjoying yourself,' he said to her one night.

Angela laughed and said that looks didn't pay the rent.

'A night out with me and you'll only be thinking of good times and laughter.' His eyes twinkled at her but Angela rebuffed him. Although she thought a night out would be a tonic, she had enough on her plate without people gossiping about her, she decided.

However, she wasn't thinking of Eddie McIntyre that Monday morning. Everything had been covered with the tarpaulin sheeting and roped up, but she checked it anyway, just as she had when driving for the munitions.

'Meet with your approval?' Stan said with an ironic grin on his face.

'Yes,' Angela snapped. 'And you can smile, but it's a driver's responsibility not to take a laden lorry into traffic that's not roped correctly or is unstable because if something falls off that's a hazard to other road users. Checking my loads myself is something I always did.'

'I'm sorry,' Stan said. 'I had no right to sneer.'

'Would you like to come with me?' Angela said. 'I might be glad of your help unloading when we get to the dump.'

Stan knew better than to betray any nervousness and said, 'Yes. I don't mind going along with you.'

And he swung himself into the cab beside Angela who was checking the controls.

Angela was more nervous than she would admit. Her hands were clammy and the roof of her mouth very dry, but she said nothing and Stan marvelled that she seemed as cool as a cucumber as she turned the key and the engine chugged into life.

It was a difficult manoeuvre to turn in the yard and going through the gate she knew would be a tight squeeze. Someone had got the truck in so she knew she could get it out, though still she drove cautiously and slowly down the small road. However, once out in the main street, negotiating her way through the traffic, her nerves left her.

'You so obviously like driving,' Stan observed.

'Oh I do,' Angela said. 'I mean, I always did but when I left the munitions I didn't think I'd ever get behind the wheel again. This is a sort of treat for me.'

Stan laughed. 'You are an amazing woman, Angela.'

Angela shook her head. 'No,' she said. 'There's nothing special about me.'

'Oh, I beg to differ. I bet there's not many women in our area who can drive. You'll have to teach me.'

'Ah, bit of a problem there,' Angela said. 'We'd need a car first. And then I might be no good teaching you how to drive a car. I've never driven one. I only learnt to drive trucks.' And then she added with an impish grin, 'So if you get hold of a spare one of those we can have a go if you like.'

Stan laughed but there was an ache in his heart for he realised he loved Angela more than he ever had done. However, she looked on him only as a friend and he valued that friendship too much to risk damaging it by saying words she wouldn't want to hear.

Angela was enjoying herself, relishing the freedom she

always felt when she was driving. She did wonder at Stan's silence, but didn't worry overmuch about it. As she'd imagined he would be, he was a great help in manhandling the stuff off the truck when they came to the dump.

'Thanks,' she said as they climbed back in the cab. 'I would have struggled with some of those things on my own.'

'They probably would have helped you more if I hadn't been here,' Stan said.

'Wouldn't take a bet on it,' Angela said. 'Did you see the look on their faces when they realised it was me driving the truck? Probably think if I can handle that, I can unload it too with no effort.'

'Well never mind, you had help and now I will go back to painting the walls,' Stan said.

'It's lovely and airy what you have done already,' Angela said. 'It's helped to lay that Matilda ghost for me.'

'Pleased to hear it,' Stan said as his lodgings came into view.

'Where does your mate park his truck?' she asked.

'Behind the paper mill,' Stan said, pointing to the other side of the road. 'He has an arrangement with the gaffer.'

'Right oh,' Angela said, and located the car park with ease.

'And I must say you are a first-rate driver,' Stan said as she parked, turned off the engine and jumped down from the cab.

Angela smiled as they began the short walk back to the shop. 'You were as nervous as a kitten,' she said to Stan.

'No I wasn't,' he denied stoutly and then, seeing the ironic look in Angela's eyes, added more honestly, 'Only to start with and I think I'd have been the same with anyone at the wheel because being driven round in trucks is not an everyday occurrence for me. My nerves were more to do with unfamiliarity than you being a woman.'

'I bet,' Angela said disbelievingly. 'Anyway, the job's done, rubbish disposed of and here we are back again. Time to roll up my sleeves and get another room scrubbed out and ready for you to decorate.'

Angela was at the flat most days that week, going down as soon as her cleaning job was finished at the pub and mainly giving guidance on furnishing and furniture needed. Stan and Harry thought her help particularly invaluable in the kitchen where she advised Harry on what range to buy, listing all the equipment needed in a functioning kitchen: the utensils, crockery, cutlery and pots and pans.

On Thursday she surveyed the place with pride. All the walls were painted and papered, there was fresh linoleum on the floors with rugs scattered here and there, and two easy chairs were before the range with a soft dark red rug set between the chairs. The dining table and chairs were much smaller and far less ostentatious than the one chosen by Matilda, but a lovely set just the same and it matched the dark wood sideboard and china cabinet.

While the new furniture was quite modest, it was more than many could afford, but Stan had saved carefully over the years and had a tidy nest egg which he broke into to furnish the flat. He was happy to do it to see Daniel settled and comfortable as he had not been able to help his son as he was growing up. In the bedrooms new beds rested on more fresh linoleum, with a fluffy blue rug beside each bed, and in each room was a corresponding wardrobe and chest of drawers.

Angela gave a sigh of satisfaction while she thought how easy it was to have a lovely home if you had the money to decorate and furnish it as you wanted, but what she said to Stan was, 'This will be a lovely home for you and Daniel to share. I can't tell you how pleased I am for you both.'

'I am just so grateful for your help.'

'Och!' Angela said with an impatient flick of her hand. 'What I did was nothing.'

'It was necessary,' Stan said. 'I don't think any of us hapless men knew the least thing about the furnishings needed for a house. Anyway, will we see you tomorrow?'

'No, not tomorrow,' Angela said. 'Michael's father is being buried tomorrow. I'm keeping Connie away from school, because although she didn't know the old man, she knows Maggie and Michael and that's all a funeral is about really, supporting those left.'

'Yeah, I think that too.'

'Anyway, tomorrow is the last day before they break up for the Easter holidays so she'll probably come home tonight with a mountain of work.'

'Don't keep her nose to the grindstone too much,' Stan warned. 'Give her time to meet her friends. She works hard.'

'Yes she does, but she's a bit short on friends at the minute.'

'Oh, you do surprise me.'

'She's like me,' Angela said. 'Although I got on well with most of my classmates, my one special friend was Maggie. Connie's is Sarah Maguire and she's leaving school in July and following her two older sisters to the Grand Hotel and so is cooling her friendship with Connie at the moment. When she starts there she will hardly ever see her, of course. I suppose it's for the best, but just at the moment Connie is at a bit of a loss. Sarah will be around a lot less this Easter holidays as well because she is going to help a woman her mother knows who runs a draper shop on Bristol Street. She was left a widow like me after the war and had savings enough to buy the shop when the war ended. She has run it with her daughter's help ever since. Now her daughter has to go into hospital and will be in for about a fortnight and she asked Maeve if Sarah could help her and Maeve agreed immediately.'

'How did the girl feel about that?'

'Oh, Sarah couldn't be more pleased,' Angela said. 'For, as her mother said, the money she will earn will be hers and they will use it to buy her some nice clothes that are not like the childish things she wore to school. She knew her mother would have struggled to find money for new clothes because Sarah has three brothers and a sister younger than her. Though her father is one of the lucky ones and in work, there is little slack in their house.'

'As is the case in many working-class homes,' Stan said a little grimly. 'It irks me to see the rich just get richer and the poor poorer still and those that are unable to find work often end up destitute. It's disgraceful to have people living on the streets, especially when they are often wearing greatcoats so you know they fought for King and country and were promised a land of milk and honey to return to. Your Barry and many more gave their lives and I often wonder for what?'

Angela had never seen Stan so fired up about anything and yet she couldn't blame him for she'd had similar thoughts herself. And then Stan said, 'I hear there's been an upsurge of destitute families turning up at the workhouse.'

Angela felt a lurch to her stomach at the mention of the

word. And Stan went on, 'I heard tell there was talk of closing some of them but, bad as they are, they are shelter of sorts. Dear God, I would hate anyone belonging to me to end up in one of these hellholes though. In fact, it wouldn't happen, for if I got wind of it I would get them out quick.'

And then he cried, 'Angela, are you all right?' for he'd seen the colour drain from her face. She swayed forward and he caught her before she reached the floor. Attempting to make light of it, he said, 'That's the second time I've caught you. You're making a habit of it.' He went on more seriously, 'But maybe it wouldn't hurt to have a doctor look you over, because, well, you don't look at all healthy to me.'

'I'm all right,' Angela protested, though she knew she was not. But what ailed her was not something a doctor could help her with because you can't put a bandage on a guilty heart and expect it to heal.

FOURTEEN

St Catherine's was packed for the Requiem Mass for Alf Malone. Maggie whispered to Angela as they sat in the church waiting for the Mass to begin that Michael had fought with his mother to be one of the pallbearers.

'Why didn't she want him to be?' Angela whispered back, mindful of Hilda sitting the other side of Maggie sobbing copiously and wiping her eyes with a large white handkerchief.

'Because of his leg, what else?' Maggie answered. 'Michael said if we have to live with his mother then we'll start as we mean to go on and he will refuse to be wrapped in cotton wool.'

Angela didn't blame him and later, when they carried the coffin into the church, she saw Maggie looking at her husband with pride. She felt a measure of it too and she hoped that the future wasn't going to be too hard for Maggie and Michael because she wouldn't think Hilda the easiest person in the world to share a home with.

Maggie was the first to agree with her as they gathered in

the back room at the Swan as usual after Requiem Mass and the visit to Key Hill Cemetery and they were able to talk at last.

'I don't think it will be too bad though and a good job as well, for we are stuck with her now, however we feel. We knew this day would come eventually with Michael being the only one left, but the house is big and that helps.'

Angela could see that that would be an advantage and she said, 'How many bedrooms has it?'

'Four,' said Maggie. 'And on the second floor is the attic where all the children slept when they were at home, one mattress for the girls and another for the boys. Michael said it was a squash, but it meant they could take in more lodgers so they never bothered complaining. There was no spare for wardrobes or chests though, and he said they had hooks on the wall and stackable packing crates for the rest.'

'So will you take one of the bedrooms now?'

'No, it will be better for Michael to have one of the rooms on the ground floor. His parents have always had one and the other was used as a sitting room. But now it will be changed to a bedroom. There's an area off the kitchen big enough for use as a sitting room, with a fire and all. Not that I imagine I will be doing much sitting. I would think Hilda will demand her pound of flesh and I'll be doing the lion's share of the work. Still, beggars can't be choosers. It will be difficult to do the weekend cleaning at the pub once we move out. Will you take it on?'

Angela nodded. 'Breda has already asked me and I agreed to fill in till they get someone else.'

'Be tough for you doing cleaning and working behind the bar,' Maggie pointed out.

'Yes but it's unlikely to be for too long,' Angela said. 'Meanwhile, you know what they say, hard work never killed anyone and that must be true or you and I would have popped our clogs years ago.'

'That's true enough,' Maggie said with a wry grin.

Easter was only a week away and Angela suggested that she and Connie make the most of the fine weather of the Easter holidays and go out together and see things they hadn't seen before or hadn't seen for some time. She proposed a visit to Sutton Park, or Cannon Hill and the Botanical Gardens, or even a walk along the towpath to look at the brightly coloured barges and maybe see one go through the lock, but Connie always refused, blaming the pressure of work.

It wasn't strictly speaking true. What Connie was finding was that what Daniel had said was right: if you have no friends and therefore no distractions you can get an awful lot of work done, and so she had finished many of her assignments set for the holidays. But for the first time she could remember she had begun to resent her mother, because if she hadn't had this bee in her bonnet about her matriculating she was sure she would still be friends with Sarah and getting ready to go on to work herself. Maybe Sarah's sisters could have found her a job in the hotel if they had known she was leaving too.

She saw years of study and further study ahead of her, and the more of that she did the more it would alienate her from the people in the area where she lived. Many of those at school already called her posh and said she thought she was better than everyone else. She didn't know why her mother hadn't realised that that would be the probable reaction of many. It hurt when they called her a snob and a show-off, yet her mother didn't even seem to care all that much, and Connie burned with the injustice of it.

The day before Good Friday, Angela said, 'You could have one day off, surely? We have lovely weather at the moment and also Maggie and Michael are moving to Pershore Road after Easter. Maggie will be giving notice at the pub and when that happens I will be busier than ever, for the time being at least.'

Connie shook her head. 'I'm busy now,' she said. 'Too busy and you can hardly complain as I am doing what you want, even if it isn't what I want.'

Her reaction hurt Angela and again she wondered if she was doing the right thing by Connie. Then Barry's face swam before her eyes. How could she let him down? Well she couldn't and that was that. Though it was upsetting and unsettling for Connie now, she was sure she would settle in the end and make other friends. All she needed was time.

On Easter Saturday Stan and Daniel arrived at the house with two beautiful eggs made of chocolate for Angela and Connie. The eggs were dark with chocolate piping and decorated with pink marzipan flowers. Angela had bought Connie a bar of chocolate, which she knew she would be appreciative of, for she got few treats like that. And, as she did every year, she had hard-boiled some eggs with onion skins in the water to turn them bright yellow so that Connie could decorate them and they could eat them for breakfast after Mass on Easter Sunday as they usually did. But neither she nor Connie had ever had eggs like the ones from Stan and Daniel. She knew they must have cost a lot and were almost too pretty to eat, but when she said that Stan roared with laughter.

'What will you do then, sit and look at them?'

'No,' Angela answered with a smile. 'But you know what I mean. Anyway, you arriving like this has saved me a journey because I was going to ask if you and Daniel would like to come and have dinner with us tomorrow? Paddy has given me the time off.'

'Well I'd love to come and I think I can speak for Dan too,' he said, glancing across at his son. 'What about it?'

'You bet,' Daniel said with enthusiasm and then went on, 'I mean, thank you very much, I'd love to come to dinner. I have already tasted and very much enjoyed your cooking.'

'Good, that's settled then,' Angela said. 'I must say, it will be nice to have dinner at dinnertime for once on Sunday. The one shift at the pub I do not like is the Sunday lunchtime one, but then beggars can't be choosers. Do you think Harry might like to come too?'

'He might give this one a miss,' Stan said. 'Seems Easter Sunday is his landlady's fiftieth birthday and the family are giving Flo a bit of a do. They've asked the lodgers and, as Harry said, Flo has been good to them.'

Stan was glad that Harry wasn't available and, though he had told the truth about his landlady's birthday, he knew he wouldn't mention the invitation to Harry, because he wanted Angela more or less to himself. In his opinion Harry was expressing far too much interest in her. The last thing he wanted was to have her whisked away to America before he had a chance to speak to her.

He was just waiting for Daniel to start on his new life at college before thinking of his own future, but he couldn't help but hope that future involved Angela for he had lost her once to Barry. He knew she had loved Barry heart, body

209

and soul, and might never love with such intensity again, but he would be grateful for any small bit she could feel for him. He had loved Angela McClusky for years and that had never diminished; if anything, his love burned brighter with every year that passed.

He thought no one was aware of his passion, but he was wrong because Daniel had seen the love light shining in his eyes whenever he gazed at Angela and thought himself unobserved. On Saturday evening as they finished their fish and chip supper he said to his father, 'Why don't you talk to Angela McClusky and tell her how you feel?'

Stan stared at Daniel as if he couldn't believe his ears. 'What?'

Daniel laughed. 'You heard exactly what I said, so why don't you?'

Stan was nonplussed and he began to splutter, 'Well I don't . . . I mean, she might . . . Don't want to put her on the spot . . .'

'Dad,' Daniel said. 'Has the fact you haven't said anything to her anything to do with me, like I might feel you are betraying my mother or something?'

'Would you feel that?'

'Of course not,' Daniel said. 'Look, Dad, I accept that you loved my mother very much, everyone speaks of the happy marriage you had. But to me, my mother is just someone people talk about and for years when I was growing up her name was never almost never mentioned. That didn't seem odd to me as to all intents and purposes I was Daniel Swanage, the son of Betty and Roger.'

'I know,' Stan said. 'And of course I don't expect you to grieve for the mother you never knew, but I thought you might feel a little betrayed. I mean, we've just found each other and it might seem I am looking for someone else.'

'You've hardly been actively looking,' Daniel said. 'Though you would be perfectly within your rights to do that if you wanted to. If you want my opinion, Angela McClusky is one of the nicest people I have ever met and she is popular, and small wonder. I mean, Harry likes her and think of those men she pulls pints for at the Swan. Any of those could have designs on her. I suppose what I'm saying is, if you hesitate to at the very least give her some indication of how you feel and sort of sound her out about her feelings towards you, someone might get in before you.'

'I never see her alone to have any sort of discussion with her.'

'Well, how about tomorrow? After Angela's dinner, which I'm sure will be sumptuous, I'll suggest Connie shows me round the area. She was telling me about the canals and the boatie people who live on the barges that they paint with elephants and castles and I'd like to see it. I never have. Connie hasn't been much. She said she was taken as a child, but as she grew she wasn't allowed near it.'

'In case she fell in, I suppose.'

'Might have been a bit of that too, but Connie thinks it was mainly so she wouldn't see the boys who go skinny dipping in the water. Mary told her decent little girls didn't hang around the canal, so I bet she'd like to see it now. It's hardly likely Angela will want to walk out anywhere, because she'll be working at the pub later, and so you'll have the place to yourselves for a bit. Don't waste it, Dad.'

Daniel's words of course only served to make Stan feel very nervous. He wasn't sure he was ready to lay his heart

211

bare to Angela, or whether she was ready to hear it. Daniel said he needed to know how Angela felt towards him, and that he had seen her look at him in a certain way, but Daniel wasn't really an expert in matters of the heart. And for as long as Stan didn't disclose his feelings to Angela, they could rub along the way they did now, developing at least a friendship, and he could allow himself to hope that one day there might be something deeper between them. This way he would know one way or the other how Angela felt about him.

Still, the day panned out exactly as Daniel imagined it would. Angela had managed to buy a chicken in the meat market at the Bullring and produced the most marvellous meal, and to follow she made treacle sponge with creamy custard.

'Ah, Angela, you are the most marvellous cook,' Daniel said, sitting back in his chair with a sigh of contentment. 'I imagine there is no one in the whole of the land who has eaten better than we have today.'

Angela laughed. 'Just a tiny bit of exaggeration there.'

'Not at all,' Stan said. 'Daniel spoke the truth and I agree with him.'

'Well thank you both,' Angela said.

'It was great, Mammy,' Connie said as she got to her feet and began to collect up the plates.

'Let me help,' Daniel said. 'It's the least I can do.'

And before Angela could jump up and say he was a guest and shouldn't be expected to do anything, or something similar, Connie said, 'I've no problem with that. I'll wash and you dry.'

'Oh no, Connie,' Angela said, getting to her feet.

'Oh yes, Angela,' Daniel said, pushing her back in the chair. 'I'm not totally helpless.'

'Why don't you sit down for once?' Connie said. 'Have a rest when you can. You'll be down the pub later pulling pints.'

Angela would never admit it in a thousand years but she was weary and so she didn't argue any more, but sank thankfully into a chair by the fire. Stan took the one opposite.

'I'll bring you some tea later,' Connie promised as she cleared the rest of the table.

In the scullery Daniel said, 'Is that how you feel too, like having a rest this afternoon?'

Connie shook her head. 'As far as I'm concerned, resting is for older bones than mine – or yours for that matter. What had you in mind?'

'Well, I've never seen any canals,' Daniel said. 'There were none that I knew of in Sutton Coldfield.'

'Oh, we'll have to remedy that then,' she said. 'I haven't been myself for some years and the day is at least dry, even if the sky is a little grey.'

'D'you think Stan and your mother would like to come with us?' Daniel said, feeling he had to ask, though he hoped they would refuse.

'Oh, I wouldn't want Mammy to go even if she fancied a walk out,' Connie said. 'She'll start work at seven tonight and be on her feet from then till almost midnight. And Stan won't go if Mammy doesn't. He'll stay and keep her company.'

And that's exactly what he did. With the washing-up done and everything put away, Connie made tea for Stan and Angela and took it in to them with a plate of biscuits from the tin, then set out with Daniel to show him the canal.

In the room where Angela and Stan had been talking of inconsequential things, a silence had grown between them. Angela sipped her tea before saying, 'Are you all right, Stan? You've been quite quiet today, as if you had something on your mind.'

'I'm sorry.'

'Oh, that's not a criticism,' Angela said. 'If it's anything it's concern. Have you got something playing on your mind?'

And Stan bottled out. Unable to ask Angela what she thought of him, he said the first thing that came into his head.

'It's not exactly playing on my mind, but I have wondered why you never wear the locket Mary gave you the day you married Barry.'

He was unprepared for Angela's reaction. Her mind went a total blank as she remembered pressing it into her baby's palm and she felt a pain in her heart that was so sharp she gasped. Tears trickled from her eyes as she heard Stan asking if she was all right, his voice sounding as if it came from a great distance away.

Seeing Angela upset was like a knife being twisted in Stan's heart. He dropped to his knees in front of her and wrapped his arms around her as he said consolingly, 'Don't cry, my darling. Please don't upset yourself so. I am sorry for causing you so much distress.'

Angela tried to pull herself together and remember what her mother had told Connie to explain the locket's disappearance. She been irritated that Mary had said anything about it at all, but it slipped out and Angela'd had to say something to cover. That was the trouble with raking up the past.

And now she would have to satisfy Stan with the same tale. Good, dear Stan, who was now holding her tight in his arms in a way that she could never remember being held by him, showing his feelings far better than the words he was hesitant to voice. Her heart sank. She had always loved Stan, not in the way she had loved Barry, but it had been a sincere love for all that. With Barry gone she could once have envisaged a fulfilled and happy life with him. However, she could never share a life with Stan without telling him about the brutal rape she had endured at the hands of three drunken soldiers, or the child resulting from that rape who she had abandoned.

She couldn't keep such a massive secret from the man who wanted to spend his life with her. Stan would know she was hiding something from him, he knew her too well, and it would put a blight on their wedding. But if she did tell him she knew she would see the contempt in his voice and disgust in his eyes, and she cared for his good opinion too much to risk that.

So she pulled herself from his arms, wiped her eyes with the backs of her hands and said, 'I'm sorry, Stan. I'm being silly.'

'What was it?' Stan asked, puzzled as he sat in the chair beside her and reached for her hand. 'You were very upset.'

'Yes, like I said, it was silly. I was just remembering, you know?'

'Is that why you don't wear the locket?' Stan asked. 'Painful memories?'

But Angela had recalled what Mary had told Connie and she said, 'Oh no, worse than that. I haven't got it any more. I lost it one day coming home from work. Didn't notice it had gone until I was home. I did look but had little hope of finding it in the blackout. It could have been lost anywhere on my journey from work.'

'Oh, I bet you were sad about that,' Stan said. 'Wasn't that the locket you were giving Connie on her wedding day?'

'The very same,' Angela said. For a moment or two she thought of telling Stan about the jewels George left her; one or two of those could be given to Connie in place of the locket. They wouldn't have the same significance, but at least Connie would have the photograph the miniature was taken from that stood on the sideboard next to the one of her father. But she didn't mention it to Stan because she thought the fewer people who knew about the jewels the better.

'I wouldn't have mentioned the loss of the locket to Connie at all, working on the assumption that what she never knew about she'd never miss. But my mother told her unintentionally – it just slipped out, she said,' Angela went on. 'Sometimes the memories, well, you know . . .'

'Even after so many years?' Stan said.

'Even then.'

Angela couldn't have put it plainer. She was telling Stan that she still loved Barry and the fact that he was dead seemed to make no odds to that love. All of a sudden, Stan realised he really did need to know what Angela thought of him. He needed to know whether he was wasting his time waiting for her to get over the one love of her life, knowing that even then she might not turn to him.

So, with a heavy heart, he said, 'Angela, I know you really and truly loved Barry with a love that only comes once in a lifetime, and I know too you have given him almost all of your heart. I would be grateful for a tiny piece of it if you could ever see your way to love me just a little. I love you and have done for years, my darling Angela. I never thought I would say those words to another after Kate, but I must, for I feel just as deeply for you.'

Angela was silent with her head bowed. Eventually she lifted her head and looked into Stan's eyes, which were filled with love for her, and her heart bled. Though she longed to take his hand and say she would be proud to be his wife, the vision of the tiny baby in the basket clutching the locket suddenly flitted across her mind and she gave a slight shudder.

Stan was slightly alarmed by the shadow that flitted over Angela's eyes and was staggered and bitterly hurt by her reaction. He could have sworn before now that Angela felt more for him than she obviously did, if baring his soul and declaring his love for her caused that blank look to flood her face. She had given a definite shudder as if in disgust.

His heart felt like a dead weight. While Angela felt bereft at the hurt confusion reflected in Stan's eyes, she was unable to speak, though she saw he was waiting for some explanation for her odd behaviour. Eventually she shook her head.

'No,' she said, louder and much sharper than she intended. But then she supposed it was better to be definite from the outset, so she said again with no softening of her tone, 'No, it's no good. I can offer you nothing.'

Stan couldn't understand what was happening. It was as if Angela had made a complete fool of him by pretending to feel more than she did. He had believed her to be true and honest, and so had opened his heart to her, and only then had she shown her true feelings. It was a cruel thing to do and he would have once said Angela hadn't a cruel bone in her body. He would have said he knew her well, very well, and he thought it just went to show that you never really knew someone's inner feelings.

Well, now something had been broken between them and Stan knew it would be a long time before he would think of Angela the same way again – if ever. After all, he had his pride, it was the only thing he had left. Angela was struggling to speak again but Stan could stand no more, his heart was filled with pain and he held up his hand.

'No need to say anything more,' he said. 'You've made it clear how you feel about me and I think it's best if I leave now.'

The eyes that Stan turned on her before he left glittered like splinters of ice. Once the door had closed behind him and she saw him pass the windows, the trickling tears became a torrent raining down her face as sobs shook her body and she cried as if her heart was broken. She knew Stan, the man she truly loved, would never forgive her because she had irrevocably hurt him beyond measure and she didn't know how she would be able to bear that.

Connie was finding that Daniel was a great person to talk to. He really listened to what a person had to say and was really keen on the canal. It was usually a hive of activity, but not on Sundays, a day of rest. It was pleasant to walk along the towpath on that lovely spring day watching the brightly painted boats bob in the slight breeze rippling the water and greeting other people doing the same thing.

'Have you ever seen a barge go through the locks?' Daniel asked Connie as they approached one.

She shook her head. 'As I said, I haven't been near the place for ages and I can't remember much from when I was younger. I've no idea how they work or even why they're there.'

'Well, they're there because the water levels are not the same in the canal and the locks lift or lower the level of the water.'

'How?' Connie asked. They had reached the lock now and she was looking with some disdain at the scummy, oil-slicked water. Before Daniel could answer her question, she said, 'Can you believe almost all boys in the area learnt to swim in there and lived to tell the tale?'

Daniel laughed. 'Most boys have little sense.'

'Bet you didn't do anything that daft.'

'Well, there was no canal nearby.'

'Wouldn't have done it anyway. You're far too sensible,' Connie said assuredly.

'Connie, I would never have been allowed to do anything like that,' Daniel said. 'And yet I probably would have wanted to as much as any other boy, I imagine.'

'Ugh, can't think why,' Connie said. 'You wouldn't see me sticking my big toe in there.'

'I admit I feel the same now,' Daniel said with a smile. 'Now about these locks . . .'

'Yes. How do they work?'

'They were built years ago and are in areas in the canals where the water levels vary considerably. They have to raise or lower the barge so that it can continue, and to do that they have to sail the barge into the lock chamber. That's it, I would think,' he said, pointing.

Connie went closer to the edge cautiously. The lock chamber was rectangular in shape, much narrower than the canal itself, with black sides that ran with water.

'It doesn't look like it's big enough for a barge, does it?' Connie said.

'It doesn't,' Daniel agreed. 'And yet it must be.'

'And there doesn't seem much water in there either.'

'No, not at the moment,' Daniel said. 'Like I said, the water there is adjustable and when the barge is low in the canal and needs to be higher, once it is in the lock chamber the gates behind it are closed. There are little trap doors in both gates and they are opened in the front gate so that the water rushes in. Then the barge rises up and, when it's the same level as the water in the canal the other side, the gate is opened and the barge goes on its way. Really, I think I would have to see it work a few times before I fully understood it.'

'Daniel,' Connie said as they stepped away from the canal. 'How do you know anything at all about the canal you said you'd never visited before?'

'I was interested so I looked it up,' he replied.

'Looked it up,' Connie repeated. 'Where did you find information like that?'

'Connie, I have a bookcase full of encyclopaedias that my aunt bought me for passing the eleven-plus. You can find out any information about just about anything in them.'

Connie's heart fell. 'We haven't got any books like that. We have a few at school, but they're too valuable to bring home.'

'Many of my friends at school were in the same boat,' Daniel said. 'And they used the library. Have you ever been?'

Connie shook her head and Daniel said, 'I hadn't either until I had finished at university and it is a marvellous place.'

'My teacher told me about it,' Connie said. 'She said that

I would have to get Mammy to sign the form, but then I could take two books out and keep them for a fortnight.'

'You can,' Daniel said. 'But there is more to the library than that. There is a reference section where you can find out about anything you would ever want to know. You can't take those books home, either because they are very expensive or because they are used by many other people, but you can make notes and there are facilities for that there. And there are reading rooms with all the papers you could ever want to read, many spread on the tables. The library in Birmingham leads to an art gallery too, so that when you want a break from books you can take a little look around there if you want to.'

'Sounds good,' Connie said. 'Bit grand for me though.'

'Course it isn't,' Daniel said. 'Can be a bit daunting at first, but you'll soon get the hang of it. Tell you what, what if we go together next Saturday and I'll show you the ropes?'

'Yeah,' Connie said. 'I'll certainly feel better with you there, but I'd like it even more if I didn't have to bother with all this and I could leave school in a few months' time with all the rest. It's a bit lonely at school now because even Sarah is strange with me. No one else is studying for their higher school certificate, just me, and all the others my age are gearing up to going out to work.'

'That might have happened to me too, but I passed the eleven-plus,' Daniel said. 'What will happen to you when you are sixteen?'

'Providing I get good marks when I take the School Certificate, I will be joining the sixth form at St Paul's, the grammar school for Catholic girls. It's not that far, I mean I can walk to it because it's only in Vernon Road and run by the Sisters of Charity. If I went to any other grammar school I would have to get permission from the priest.'

'My uncle and aunt had to do that so I could go to King Edward's in Aston,' Daniel said. 'I obviously hadn't enough marks to get into St Philip's, which was and still is the grammar school for Catholic boys.'

'Mmm, I know,' Connie said. 'And it's not far from the girls' school, so would have been a real hike for you every day.'

'That's what my aunt said, whereas the train took me direct to Aston Station and I could walk to the school from there.'

'Yes,' said Connie. 'Now do you mind if we talk about something else other than secondary education, which scares the life out of me if you want the truth.'

'Why don't you tell your mother how you feel?' Daniel said. 'Knowing your mother, I don't see her wanting to make you unhappy.'

'She doesn't see that she is making me unhappy,' Connie says. 'She sees it as giving me a chance of . . . a better future, I suppose.'

'What do you see it as?'

'Me slogging away at books when I could be working and making Mammy's life easier,' Connie said. 'And because she is insisting on me doing that, I am becoming alienated from all the neighbours and the children I grew up with, who already think I am getting above myself going on to matriculate.'

'Did your father feel the same way?'

'How would I know?' Connie said. 'Mammy said he did, but I only have her word for that. If he was here, maybe I could talk him round.' She shrugged and went on, 'I don't know because I don't know what sort of person he was, but Mammy said she made a promise to him that I would be well-educated if I had the brains and that's that as far as she is concerned. That's the point really – I can't argue with a dead hero that she made a promise to. The annoying thing is she told you to do what you wanted with your life and yet won't let me do the same thing.'

Daniel could see Connie's point of view and he felt a sudden flash of sympathy for her. 'I can see what you're saying but can't see any way round it really.'

'Nor me,' Connie said and gave a sigh as she added, 'S'pose I'll just have to get on with it. Anyway, I guess we should be getting back.'

'Yes,' said Daniel. 'That wind's getting up a bit now anyway.' And as they turned for home he added, 'I'll come back with you because my father might be still there.'

Connie shook her head. 'Don't know the time but Mammy's probably getting ready for work by now. She has to go in early because she had the lunchtime off.'

'You're right, she does work hard,' Daniel said. 'Do you think she'll ever marry again?'

He could see by Connie's face that such a thought had never occurred to her and so he wasn't surprised by her denial.

'She's still a young woman,' he said.

'She's not,' Connie said emphatically. 'She's over thirty.'

Daniel hid a smile, remembering that when he was Connie's age he'd thought someone who was turned thirty was old. Now he thought of thirty as still young.

'She wouldn't anyway,' Connie said with assurance. 'She loved my daddy too much.'

'My father loved my mother passionately,' Daniel said. 'Everyone says so, but I would be glad for him if he found someone new.'

'Well I wouldn't,' Connie declared. 'My mother doesn't need anyone else in her life. We have each other and that has always been enough.'

It certainly seemed that way, Daniel thought, when they reached the house a few minutes later. As Connie had said, Angela was in her bedroom getting ready but came down when she heard them arrive. She told Daniel his father had gone home as she had to change for work. Though she was perfectly polite, the words were stilted and there was a deadened look in her eyes and he knew from her manner that if his father had confessed his feelings to her it had not been well received. He castigated himself for urging him to do that; perhaps he should have left well alone and they could have continued as friends for years. Daniel knew it might be impossible to retrieve that friendship now.

He noted Connie seemed to see no difference in her mother, but then she didn't know what his father had intended to do when he and Angela were alone. None of it was her fault anyway, and so he arranged to meet her at the library the following Saturday at about eleven.

When the door closed behind Daniel, Angela said sharply to Connie, 'Why are you meeting Daniel Swanage again?'

'He . . . He's going to show me the library,' Connie said and went on to tell her mother of the books she could get out to read, and the reference section and reading rooms and art gallery. And then she asked, alerted by the frown on her mother's face, 'Mammy, is anything the matter?'

Angela sighed and said, 'I've had a row with Stan as a

matter of fact. Don't ask what it was about because it's a grown-up matter, but I think this will make things very difficult for all of us as he and I will have nothing to do with each other now. It will be awkward if you are friends with his son. However, as you knew nothing of this when you arranged things for this Saturday, perhaps it will be better if you don't speak of it. Daniel will know what has happened by the time you see each other next.'

Connie was totally confused – what could have happened between her mother and Stan who were such firm friends? She also thought it monstrously unfair that because her mother had a disagreement with Stan it would affect her friendship with Daniel. He'd always been very helpful to her and she thought of him as the big brother she'd never had, and knew she would miss him if the two families fell out properly. She wondered what the disagreement was about and whether it could be fixed. It was odd for she had never known her mother fall out with anyone before. In fact, the whole thing was very strange and she thought it sad that the happiness and pleasure she'd had that day had been wiped out by her mother's strange attitude. Connie decided that, whatever happened, she wouldn't fall out with Daniel and would keep their friendship to herself.

FIFTEEN

When Daniel arrived home that evening he found his father in a dreadful state. He listened almost open-mouthed with astonishment as Stan told him he had done as he had suggested and opened his heart to Angela, telling her how much she meant to him, and that she had shuddered at the very thought of anything between them and treated him with disdain. Daniel found it hard to believe that Angela could have been so heartless. It was not what he would have expected of her, though he didn't doubt the truth of his father's words, or the pain Angela had inflicted on him.

'You know, Daniel,' Stan said, 'this afternoon I witnessed the death of a dream I have carried dormant in my heart for years. When I regained consciousness in hospital and found that Barry had died in an attempt to save me, I wanted to die, certain Angela would hold me at least partially responsible. When, after years, we met again and I realised she harboured no grudge, I felt ecstatically relieved. Back then I really thought she had feelings for me and I truly loved her. I thought, as long as we took it slowly, in time she might feel the same as me and we could look forward to a wonderful life together. Now that can never be.'

There was a lump in Daniel's throat at his father's words and he felt a measure of guilt for encouraging Stan to tell Angela how he felt. He knew enough of his father now to know slow but sure was his approach to things and if he had left well alone they might well still be friends.

'Sorry,' he said. 'I obviously totally misread the whole situation and have made things far worse for you'

'Not your fault,' Stan said. 'I misread the situation myself. I thought she at least cared. She used to once upon a time, but things have definitely changed and it's not just that she doesn't like me any more. It's quite clear that she sees any relationship between us as abhorrent. I found that realisation hard to take, but it's always better to know.'

Daniel could only guess at how Angela's rejection had damaged his father, though he had some idea from his tortured face and manner. He felt dislike for Angela festering inside him and, although he knew it was totally unfair, that dislike extended to Connie too. He decided that, though he would meet her the following Saturday because he'd arranged to, that would be it. Connie had said that her mother needed no one else in her life, that they had each other, and they could stay that way as far as he was concerned.

The following Saturday Connie was nervous of meeting up with Daniel and might have cried off, but Angela said she mustn't do that as Daniel would be waiting for her.

'What is between Stan and I needn't affect you directly, though, as I said, it would be awkward if you were to continue to meet him. Just don't discuss it and you should be fine.'

As agreed, Connie and Daniel met outside the workhouse gates in Steelhouse Lane. They both felt a little constrained. Connie didn't know how much Daniel knew of the disagreement between their parents and Daniel felt no desire to talk to Connie as he once would have done, and so they walked up Colmore Row in silence.

Connie didn't mind; she didn't come to the town that much and when she did she usually made for the Bullring, so she looked about her with interest. There was a vibrant-looking place full of people called the Great Western Arcade on her left across the road, and not far from the gardens around St Philip's was the Protestant cathedral. The gardens looked very pretty, the borders ablaze with spring flowers, and garden paths intertwined between them, broken up here and there with benches for the weary. They passed by Snow Hill Station too and many banks and important-looking buildings. Towards the end of the road they passed the Grand Hotel where Sarah's two sisters were working, and then reached the steps of Chamberlain Square.

Daniel broke his silence to say, 'There's the library,' and he pointed.

Connie gasped because the building was magnificent, really magnificent. It was a beautifully sculpted stone edifice, as finely moulded as any church, and a tower rose into the air above the oaken studded front door with a large clock at the top of it.

Almost in a daze, she followed Daniel up the steps past the flowing fountain and through that quite formidable door, and once through it she stood and stared. She was standing in a white-tiled hall and looking up at the lofty ceilings and the sweeping oak staircase leading off to the left-hand side.

Daniel couldn't help but be amused at her awed silence as he led her into the lending library, which he said was the place to borrow the books. Connie was very impressed with the shining wooden counters and panels and shelves that gleamed with care and attention. The shelves were packed with books she couldn't wait to read. The librarian explained that she couldn't take books out that day, but she gave Connie the card for her mother to sign and told her on another visit she could take out two books and keep them for two weeks and after that they had to be returned. Connie could scarcely believe that she was allowed to take those beautiful books home with her and vowed she would look after them with great care.

She loved everything about the library, even the respectful, hushed silence. It seemed so right somehow that even her shoes sounded loud on the wooden floors. The reading rooms upstairs stunned her even more. The room had tables double-banked down the length of it, many spread with newspapers. She gasped at the beauty of the decorated pillars that supported the long room, which gave way to curved, elabor-ately embellished panels in the dome of the roof. The apex of the roof was made of glass so that spring sunlight spilled into the room in a myriad of colours. Connie gave a sigh of contentment.

That day there were only men in the reading room scrutinising the papers laid out on the tables with solemn faces, but there were more people in the reference library, where the bookshelves were arranged in squares to leave space for desks in the middle. Daniel pointed out the subjects in brass plaques above the various sections, which were then arranged in alphabetical order. He said there was a card for every book, filed in the drawers of the slatted wooden cabinets in each section so a person could see in a glance if the library stocked the book they might require. And Connie watched as people lifted these reference books and carried them to the desks and wrote things down in the notebooks they had brought with them, feeling a thrill of excitement as she imagined herself doing the self-same thing.

Once they left the library they went their separate ways by tacit agreement. Daniel didn't suggest delivering Connie home and Connie didn't invite him, knowing he wouldn't be welcome. And yet she felt sad when they said goodbye as if they never intended to meet again, and she didn't understand any of it.

By the time Connie returned to school she had joined the library officially, her mother having had no objection to filling in the form. Connie had proudly brought her first two books home, *The Phoenix and the Carpet* and *The Story of the Treasure Seekers*, and they had enchanted her. They were both written by a lady called E. Nesbit, and the librarian said she had written many more, so if Connie liked the book there would be a variety of others to choose from.

Connie was glad about that because she found she liked the books very much. In fact, she would have been lost without the library and often wished she had been introduced to it sooner. Once she returned to school she worked mainly alone, for the teacher had a class to teach as well as trying to get Connie through matriculation. So she was shown her lesson or exercise and then worked on her own to complete her tasks. This was much easier when she had the notes she had written up from the reference library on Saturday where she went every week to finish assignments set for the weekend.

At school she often worked through breaktime. It was preferable to standing alone in the yard, as if she had the plague, while groups of girls clustered together discussing the world of work they would soon be entering and how they were going to spend their wages, or at least spend the money they would be allowed to keep.

Now, provided the work was done, she could read. Those books would lift the friendless Connie from her back-to-back house in a grimy, grey street and she would join in the characters' adventures. She often found herself hating to finish because by the end she had become so involved in their lives. Angela was sorry Connie appeared so unpopular, but really the die was cast now, and she thanked God that the library seemed to be helping her daughter.

She wished she could find a similar distraction, something that would fill her mind and stop her remembering the devastation on Stan's face when he thought it was him baring his soul that had caused her to shudder. But she couldn't explain without telling him everything and she knew she couldn't do that, but she felt so wretched at the hurt she had inflicted on the man she was sure she loved. She slept badly but as soon as her eyes opened she felt melancholy descend on her, seeming to wrap itself around all the fibres of her being.

Oh, she longed to talk it over with Maggie, the only person she could talk things over with. But when she called to see her almost a month after Easter, Angela found her friend even more rushed off her feet than she'd thought she'd be, because just as soon as Maggie and Michael moved in permanently, Hilda had taken to her bed.

'Michael tries to see to his mother,' Maggie said to Angela. 'But there are certain things, personal things, he can't do – washing her and such. So I have to fit that in between cooking the four lodgers' breakfast, cleaning their rooms, washing the dishes, doing the shopping and cooking and clearing up after the evening meal. Then cleaning the rest of the house and doing the washing for the lodgers as well, and ironing the lot.'

Maggie had bags beneath her eyes and her face looked washed out and drained. She said she had barely time to blow her nose and often forgot to eat herself. Angela knew she couldn't load her problems on to her for she had enough of her own.

She knew work was the only thing that helped and ensured she would get some sleep each night, and so she called into the pub on her way home. She had taken on Maggie's weekend cleaning at the pub till they got someone else, telling them not to look for anyone else as she would take on her friend's duties permanently.

Breda was pleased because no one had applied that she thought suitable and trustworthy, but she did worry about the workload for Angela.

'It's a lot for you to take on,' she said.

'It's fine and hard work has never killed me yet,' she assured Breda.

'You'll not see much of Connie, at weekends especially.'

'I don't see much of her now,' Angela said. 'She spends most of Saturday in the reference library doing the work the teacher has set for the weekend and most of Sunday reading the library books she's got from the lending library. She'll hardly notice I'm not there.'

Angela spoke only half the truth, because though Connie found homework much easier when she had access to all the information, and the teacher was impressed by how much better and more confident she had become, she did miss her mother a great deal. As she didn't complain at all, Angela imagined all was well and that Connie wouldn't mind her mother taking on extra shifts at the pub, thinking she didn't miss her at all.

For her fourteenth birthday, Angela bought her a wrist-watch, Maggie sent her some pretty bangles with her card, and she had cards from America with dollars inside, but nothing came from anyone else. Connie told her mother not to set her heart on any sort of gathering because she thought no one would come.

Now and again she thought of Stan and Daniel. Though she and Daniel hadn't fallen out, they both felt loyalty to their respective parents and the subject was like a cloud over them so their relationship had cooled. She often thought it a particular pity that her mother had lost the friendship of Stan, a man she had known for years and who she had always spoken well of. Connie knew Angela wasn't happy about it either because she seldom smiled any more and never laughed. She wanted to urge her mother to at least try to make up the quarrel with Stan but was too nervous of her reaction to say anything.

The school closed for the summer and many of Connie's classmates got employment of one sort or another, including Sarah, who left Bell Barn Road with barely a backward glance and went to join her sisters at the Grand Hotel.

As for Connie, weeks stretched ahead of her. Although she had been given holiday assignments, she knew she would find it hard to fill those hours – in fact it would be virtually impossible without the library and that was where she went.

The librarians were used to her coming in every Saturday and always spoke to her. One librarian, called Miss Platt, was what Connie would describe as prim and proper. Her skirts were navy, black or grey and worn much longer than most ladies did, in fact almost touching the old-fashioned button boots on her feet. Her blouses were of muted pastel colours and fastened with a cameo brooch at the throat. She spoke in a very posh way, seeming to squeeze the words from between thin lips. Her sharp nose always seemed to be lifted, her grey eyes were like pieces of flint in her sallow skin and her grey hair was scraped so tightly back from her face it had caused her eyebrows to rise as if she were constantly surprised.

Inwardly she had no time for children, thinking them noisy and messy and nothing more than a distraction in a library. She knew if she had her way she'd ban them altogether, but as she couldn't do that she would go out of her way to make them feel tolerated rather than welcome.

Connie had sensed that from the beginning – she had met people like Miss Platt before – and initially she kept out of her way as much as possible, going with any queries or to have her books date-stamped to the younger and much prettier librarian Miss McGowan. She wore similar clothes to Miss Platt, but her skirts were much shorter and fuller, she had prettier shoes and her blouses were often open at the neck so the coloured beads she wore were visible. She had pretty hair, a mixture between blonde and brown, and though she too wore it tied back from her face, she allowed little curls to escape so they framed her face. She was a pleasant woman, a smile often lighting up her soft brown eyes, and she always had a kind word for Connie.

However, Connie's diligence while at the library, the respectful way she treated the books she borrowed and the regularity of her visits eventually wore down Miss Platt's opinion and she acknowledged with Miss McGowan that Connie wasn't that bad considering her age. So when she arrived that first day of the holidays and admitted she would probably be lonely through the summer, Miss Platt did not object when Miss McGowan said, if she was willing, she could come a couple of days in the week as well as her regular Saturday and give them a hand.

'There's always something to do in a library and we are usually busier in the summer,' she explained. 'We get a lot of children in and some do tend to throw the books about and it takes time often to put the library to rights after they've gone. And of course books are coming back in all the time and have to be replaced on the shelves.'

It was a dream job for Connie and she was more than willing. She told her mother about it excitably when they were sitting at their evening meal that night. Angela heard what Connie said, but she struggled to get enthusiastic about her about putting books away in a library. And she didn't know why the thought of working with this Miss McGowan she thought so much of should light up her face in a way Angela hadn't seen in ages. Pessimistic feelings crowded in on Angela. She acknowledged she was jealous that Connie was having a good time without her and tried to find the right words, saying how pleased she was for Connie. However, her falling-out with Stan, and the fact that she missed him, nagged away at her like a scab to be picked over. And all the while the deeper shame about her own child that she had left in the workhouse threatened to overwhelm her. Added to that, her levels of exhaustion meant she had little time for any respite.

Connie wasn't fooled by her mother's platitudes and she took her mother's lack of enthusiasm to be disinterest, deciding it would be a long time before she told her anything again.

Connie loved working at the library. There she felt valued and so had confided in Miss McGowan and Miss Platt about the coolness between her and her mother and the reasons why.

'She doesn't listen to me any more,' she said. 'I really think she cares more about the people at the pub that she works at than she does for me and she's unhappy most of the time.'

Miss Platt and Miss McGowan couldn't help with Connie's problems. They didn't know Angela and couldn't have interfered even if they had known her, but it helped Connie that they listened and she wished the holidays would go on and on.

Angela's inherent despondency had been noted at the pub and Breda and Paddy were at a loss to know what had caused her to lose her sparkle.

'When I ask her she says she's fine,' Breda complained. 'But I know she's anything but.'

'Eddie McIntyre was asking if she was ill,' Breda said. 'I said she wasn't, just a bit down, and it would do him no harm to ask her out a time or two.'

Paddy stared at her. 'You never told him that?'

'Yes I did and I don't know why you are so surprised,' Breda said. 'You were all for them getting together before and it was me had misgivings.'

'I don't know why I think that's not a good idea,' Paddy admitted. 'The man has done nothing to me, it's just a feeling. Yet there's something about him, he's a bit too sure of himself, and that laughter he's so ready with doesn't reach his eyes . . . And when he's had a few I've noticed that he has a quarrelsome temper on him. He's been on the verge of fist-icuffs more than once . . . Oh, I suppose I'm being silly and too protective of Angela.'

'I'll say you are,' Breda said. 'Not only is Angela a grown woman, she is also no fool and she has already refused Eddie once.'

'Has she, by God?' Paddy said.

'She has indeed, because the man told me himself,' Breda said. 'So maybe she felt the same doubts as you have about Eddie McIntyre. Personally, I think it a pity for he's about the only one can put even the ghost of a smile on her face. Still, that's her decision and if he has been rejected once he's hardly likely to try a second time.'

But Breda had underestimated Eddie, who was very attracted to Angela and frustrated that she wouldn't agree to walk out with him somewhere he might get her alone and show her some of the delights she must be missing. A young woman like her would have needs that he could guess hadn't been addressed in years, and handled right she would be ripe for the picking.

He pulled out all the stops to cheer her up because it was obvious she was depressed about something. He had no idea why, though he suspected it might be sexual frustration. A woman such as Angela might not ever recognise it as that, because he imagined she had been brought up thinking of sex as dirty and talking about it or even thinking about it sinful. But even if she wouldn't admit it, he imagined she must long for fulfilment, even if this sexual desire was buried deep.

Angela knew what the matter with her was: she ached with loneliness. She missed confiding in Maggie more than she thought possible, for she was the only one she could talk to totally freely. She had driven Stan away, as well as Daniel, who naturally enough sided with his father, and somehow she had also lost Connie. She felt her slipping away from her each day – their closeness was gone and that caused her extreme heartache.

Angela knew that the solution to her loneliness lay in her own hands, for if she went to Stan and apologised she was sure they could at least be friends. But she knew he would ask her why she reacted the way she did when he had spoken words of love and nothing but the truth would suffice. And the truth was the one thing she couldn't tell him.

As for Connie, maybe the slight animosity between them was something all mothers went through with their daughters of this age. Certainly the women in the street and those she served at the shop years ago had often complained their compliant younger girls disappeared once they had left school and began work. It was something she hadn't thought would happen between her and Connie though. She'd thought the love they shared was deep and strong enough to withstand anything, but she had to admit it had been hard-going of late.

Connie knew it had been her mother's choice to take up

extra hours at the pub, which meant there was little time for them to have their cosy evening chats with each other. By working all the hours God sent, Angela was saying, as far as Connie was concerned, that the drinkers at the pub and people who were barely more than strangers were more important than she was herself. So she certainly wasn't going to bend over backwards to make life easier for her mother. She knew Angela was hurt by this attitude, but she had found she didn't care like she should. The business with Stan was so out of character and to her mind Connie felt that her mother was making a rod for her own back with her attitude. With no explanation for why she had become so quarrelsome and introverted, Connie decided she had brought it upon herself.

The holidays came to an end and, with a heavy heart, Connie did her last day at the library.

Miss McGowan spoke to her before she left. 'I know that your mother would like you to go to university and you are totally against doing it,' she said. 'But I believe your mother has your best interests at heart, she just wants you to have a good job. Isn't that what most parents want for their children, Constance?'

Connie just nodded and Miss McGowan went on, 'I have been doing some research and if you get good marks in your Highers you would have a good chance of getting a job in a library. You certainly seem to like working with books.'

'Oh, I'd love that.'

'Well, I'd advise you to say nothing to your mother for now, see how you do in your exams first, but there are ways of moving up in the libraries if you wish to and that would please your mother. Meanwhile, you'll be able to continue working with the books you love and getting a wage for doing it as well. What do you say to the possibility? We'd put a good word in for you as you've been a great help to us in the time you've been here.'

'Oh, Miss McGowan,' Connie said, almost overcome by the librarian's thoughtfulness. 'Thank you so much.'

'It still means returning to school and nose to the grind-stone again.'

'I don't care so much about that now I have something to aim for.'

And it didn't matter and she returned to school in a more positive frame of mind. Miss McGowan advised her not to tell her mother but she had no intention of doing that. It wouldn't do any good, for her mother didn't seem to care about her any more and she was seldom at home these days anyway. If she had said this to Angela she would have to concede that she had a point for Breda had developed severe arthritis. She had coped with it through the warm summer weather and balmy September but October heralded its arrival with squally rain and gales and a plunge in temperature. Breda's arthritis flared up and the pain meant that she could no longer cope with the long hours behind the bar.

Angela volunteered for extra shifts in the evenings and lunchtimes and Paddy was only too glad of her extra help. It meant that Connie frequently returned to an empty house. She thought she would have welcomed company after her lonely days at school which left her feeling emotionally adrift. She often remembered with a little sadness the fun and laughter she had once shared with her mother and wondered, not for the first time, at her change in character.

* * *

It took Angela some time to realise that one of the perks of the extra shifts serving behind the bar was that she would see more of Eddie McIntyre for he was there every night. She'd come to rely on his company to lift her spirits and found herself disappointed if for some reason he didn't appear as usual each night.

He was handsome in his own way, though not like Barry had been. He was smaller with mousy brown hair but a twinkle in his hazel eyes that hinted of good times together. She often found herself smiling and laughing at his jokes and the way he had of saying things, and for a while her own troubles that had been a source of unhappiness began to be pushed to the back of her mind. She had dreaded the arrival of winter and the long, dark, dreary days which lowered her spirits at the best of times, and she began to wonder why she had refused him when he had asked her out, for it would have done her no harm.

Had she thought it wrong to go out with another man, especially when she liked Eddie well enough? She didn't know and Breda encouraged her.

'You're not marrying the man, just going out with him,' she maintained. 'You work hard and you deserve some time to enjoy yourself. You've heard that saying about all work and no play making Jack a dull boy. Well, it works for Jill just as well.'

'But Breda, I've refused him once already.'

'I know,' Breda said. 'And no man likes rejection and he will hardly ask again unless he thinks there's some chance of success this time. So you need to be extra nice and welcoming to him and then he might just try again.'

'And if he doesn't?'

'Then he doesn't,' Breda said with a shrug. 'And not much that can be done about that. But aren't you jumping the gun a bit here? Let's take one step at a time and the first thing you have to do is be nice to Eddie McIntyre.'

SIXTEEN

It was easy to be nice to Eddie because he was so easy-going and he soon recognised the extra warmth in Angela's voice when she spoke to him over the next few days. However, he was more cautious this time and waited until the bar had nearly emptied one night before approaching her as she was washing out glasses and asking if she would consider going for a walk with him the following day.

'Now Angela, I have asked you out before but you have refused me.' He had a challenge in his voice when he spoke and those eyes of his were dancing.

'Well I didn't really know you then.'

'Isn't that why people go out together initially, to get to know each other better?'

'I suppose, but you see, I'm not really looking for a new man.' Angela felt a pang in her heart as she remembered Stan and his earnest eyes as he declared his feelings for her. But she pushed them away; it was no use going over old heart-aches, that was done and dusted now.

Eddie smiled. 'Maybe you don't think you are, not

consciously, but I'd say you are missing something because you seem a little lost and unhappy a lot of the time now and you have never been like that before.'

Angela felt guilty when Eddie said that because she knew she had no right to bring her troubles to work. So when he said, 'How about it then, do you fancy the two of us taking a walk out together tomorrow?' she nodded her head and smiled coyly, feeling shy despite being a woman of the world.

'That's grand,' Eddie said. 'Then you can find out all about me and I can find out all about you.'

'Yes,' Angela said. But she knew there would be no way she would tell Eddie everything about her life for there were certain things best kept hidden. She didn't feel guilty keeping it from Eddie as she would Stan, so there was no earthly reason to tell Eddie of the rape she had endured or the child she had abandoned.

Unbeknown to her, Eddie was thinking similar thoughts, for he knew that he would be giving Angela only a very selective history of his life. He had far more of his past to hide than she had, but she was unaware of that. She told Connie that she might be a bit late the following night but didn't say why, knowing Connie would assume it was something to do with more work at the pub. Angela let her think that, for she had no desire to share anything about Eddie yet with her daughter.

Angela still did the lunchtime shift but Breda had given her the evening off so she left early and it was half past three when they set out walking side by side. Angela wondered if Eddie was as aware as she was of the curtains that twitched in the windows of many houses they passed down the street, or of the women standing chatting on their doorsteps craning their necks to see who Angela McClusky was stepping out with.

She decided to take no notice of them. She was harming no one and she was a free agent anyway and could please herself, but she said to Eddie, 'We'll be the subject of gossip in many homes today I think, judging by the interest we are generating.'

Eddie gave a shrug of his shoulders. 'If they're talking about us then they're leaving someone else alone. I have broad enough shoulders to take it because I believe people only take such a curiosity in other people's lives when they have nothing happening in their own, so I take no notice and advise you to do the same.'

'I intend to but we better get a step on because there's not that much light these late October days if you want to go all the way to Cannon Hill Park and back.'

'That's true enough,' Eddie said. 'But we needn't head for home as soon as the sun goes down. I thought we might go for a drink. The pubs should be open on our way back.'

'Oh,' said Angela. 'I know this sounds silly when I work in a pub, but I've never gone into one as a customer.'

Eddie was incredulous. 'Haven't you really? Well, we must remedy that.'

'Well, women don't, do they?' Angela said. 'I mean, how many women do I serve in the Swan?'

Eddie nodded. 'I take your point.'

'And I couldn't go in on my own, not even into the Swan. Only one sort of woman does that kind of thing.'

'It's perfectly respectable if a woman is with a man, particularly if the man is her husband or the fellow she's stepping out with.'

Angela frowned and said, 'Maybe things have changed now and I will have to take your word for that. But I do know that before the war when my husband was alive, no women, unless they were of ill-repute, frequented pubs, even with their husbands. Women could go into teashops or coffee houses, but not pubs. Not that Barry and I went to any place very often for there wasn't the money.'

'You loved your husband very much?'

It was a question and Angela answered emphatically, 'I did, but Barry was more, he was my soulmate and my big brother as well as a husband. Both Barry and then my daughter, Connie, were my reasons for living. And when Barry died it was like a piece of me had broken off, as if I was no longer whole and probably never would be again.'

Eddie was taken aback by Angela's words and he said, 'Very few people love with that intensity, so his death must have hit you especially hard.'

Angela nodded. 'It did,' she admitted. 'And his mother who lived with us had a heart attack when we got the telegram and she almost died too. She didn't die, but was frail ever after it. Mind you, we were both proud of Barry too because he won a medal for bravery for he died trying to save the life of another.'

'Did he succeed in saving the person?'

Angela gave a brief nod.

Eddie looked at Angela keenly. 'Did you blame the man your husband saved for his death?'

'Of course not,' Angela said candidly. 'We were at war so Barry's life hung in the balance on a pretty much daily basis anyway and I would say that throwing yourself over someone when you see a shell sailing in the air above you is a pretty instinctive thing to do. The point is, Barry didn't have to enlist at all.'

'Oh. How come?'

Angela explained that because Barry worked in a foundry, and they produced many war-related products, it meant he was in a reserved occupation. By now, they had reached the entrance to the park and, as Angela had said, the day was nearly over. It was becoming dusky already, with thick, grey clouds hanging ominously low and a keen wind sending ripples across the lake.

As they walked together, Eddie had taken her hand and she hadn't removed hers because it felt so nice. Now he dropped her hand and put his arm around her instead.

'What are you doing?' she asked in surprise.

'Cuddling you because you are cold,' Eddie said.

Angela couldn't deny it, for she was shivering. Her coat wasn't that warm and she felt a lot more comfortable with Eddie's arm around her so, though it was rather an intimate gesture, she said nothing more about it. She had no time to anyway because Eddie was asking, 'So why did your husband end up in the army then? What changed?'

'Oh, it was understandable in a way, their loved ones out in the thick of it in France and Belgium and Barry, a big, fine, strapping chap, as safe as houses at home,' Angela said with a slight hint of acrimony. 'But Barry was also beginning to feel guilty. Like most firms they had lost most of their male workforce when war was declared and their jobs had been taken by women. In the beginning Barry was needed to instruct the women on the use of the new machines they installed to make things for the war, but he had to admit they picked it up quicker than he had ever thought they would and soon he felt surplus to requirements.

'Meanwhile we were all getting snubbed by friends and neighbours we had known for years. It was hard to cope with at the time because it even happened at church, but the final straw for Barry was when he was sent the white feathers.'

'I'd heard of that sort of thing happening but didn't believe it really did,' Eddie said.

'Oh, it happened all right,' Angela said bitterly. 'There were three in the one envelope.'

'Do you know who sent it?'

Angela shook her head. 'It was pushed under the door but, as Barry said at the time, we would be spoilt for choice as to who sent it. It could have been anyone in the neighbourhood or anyone at the church or anyone else upset because Barry wasn't in uniform. Anyway, the feathers finally made his mind up to enlist. And when he told people that he was going to fight in the bloodied fields of France, joining with their loved ones in the carnage that had already claimed far too many young lives, all of a sudden he was a "fine fellow well met". Men who had crossed the road to avoid him were now falling over themselves to shake him by the hand and wish him God's speed – even the priest was at it. And so he marched away and I never saw him again.'

As they continued to walk through the park and round the lake in the deepening dusk, Angela told Eddie of the death of her parents and how the McCluskys had taken her in and raised her. She explained that Barry had always been her protector from as far back as she could remember. She told how two of her foster brothers had died on the *Titanic* trying to reach their two older brothers in New York and how that tragic event, plus the severe illness of her foster father, prompted her early marriage to Barry.

Eddie allowed himself a little smile, though he was careful not to let Angela see. He knew, despite her love for Barry, she was almost as sexually naïve as a child. She had fallen into marriage with Barry because he was there and probably to please everyone, but she had never been courted and desired, lusted after by a man. She had never been brought to the pinnacle of desire, the point where nothing matters but stilling the ache inside her, and he looked forward to that because he was determined to be the man to light her sexual fire.

But it got better still and he went on, 'So you have a daughter, what age is she?'

'Fourteen,' Angela said. 'She will be fifteen next May and still at school because I have put her down for matriculation, which she does when she's sixteen.'

'Bright girl then?'

'Bright enough I think.'

'And who does your daughter resemble?' Eddie asked. 'You or your husband?'

'Oh, people say she is the spit of me,' Angela said.

'Another beauty then,' Eddie said, and then with a short laugh added, 'Don't blush and don't try telling me you've gone through your whole life with no one telling you how beautiful you really are?'

Angela flushed, unable to answer. Barry had adored her, she knew that, but they had no need to speak of such things as they knew each other inside out. No one had ever complimented her or looked at her in the way Eddie was looking at her now.

'Angela, believe me when I tell you that you are gorgeous, exquisite, and you'll have to get used to me using endearments like those. I want to shower you with them.'

'Oh I hope not,' Angela said fervently. 'I would be so embarrassed.'

Eddie gave a throaty laugh and swung Angela into his arms, holding her tight. Though she tensed, he only kissed the top of her head.

'You darling girl, he said fondly. 'Now if we're going to take a dander around this park, we'd better get going before darkness overtakes us altogether.'

They walked on arm in arm and Angela felt her heart lighten and a tentative happiness which she had thought she might never feel again flow through her body.

Angela enjoyed her time at the park with Eddie, who made her feel so special in a way no one had done for a long time. On their way home from Cannon Hill Park, Eddie bought them both fish and chips. Angela didn't allow herself the pleasure of fish and chips often and she thought them delicious, and eating them from the paper with their fingers as they walked somehow felt deliciously daring. They had just wiped their hands on the paper and thrown them away in a bin when they came upon The Trees public house.

Eddie consulted his watch with the help of a street light and said to Angela, 'The pub's just open, I thought it would be by the time we were making our way back. So how about washing the fish and chips down with a couple of drinks?'

Angela hesitated. 'Ah no Eddie, I'd really rather not.'

'Come on,' Eddie said reassuringly. 'It's completely all right.

Times have changed and we will look as upright and sensible as it's possible to be.'

Angela shook her head. 'I'd be uncomfortable, Eddie.'

Eddie placed his hands on her shoulders and looked deep into her eyes. 'Would I ask you to do something wrong?'

'Um, I . . . I suppose not.'

'Definitely not,' Eddie said. 'Now link your arm through mine and we will go in together with our heads held high.'

Angela allowed herself to be led inside, although her insides fluttered with nerves and she kept her head lowered.

Once inside, despite feeling very uncomfortable, Angela peeped a look around but it wasn't that much different to the Swan. The bar was lit by hissing gas lights, though it was still very dim. The smoky grey windows let in very little light, as she knew from experience, and none at all once the sun had set. It was now dark outside and getting cold so the windows were misted up on the inside anyway.

The floor, she noticed, was made of wooden blocks, and wooden tables and leather studded chairs were scattered here and there. Before the gleaming polished bar was the almost obligatory brass pole and bar stools. Against the bar were the line of pumps, the optics at the back and on the shelves above were the pint glasses. Set into the wall was a fireplace, with a fire laid but not yet lit, and across the ample mantelshelf were many toby jugs.

It was all very familiar to Angela, as was the smell of the various drinks served and the blue fug of cigarette and cigar smoke that swirled in the air. Angela took in all this and also the fact that, despite Eddie's assurances about it being quite respectable if a woman was taken there by a man, she saw no other woman in there. But she told herself she was in a

251

similar establishment nearly every day and no one thought any the worse of her for it, and it wasn't as if she was going to drink anything alcoholic. However, despite the spirited words she told herself, she couldn't help feeling uncomfortable and Eddie caught the look and drew her closer and whispered in her ear.

'Hold your head up high, Angela. You are worth twenty of them and have a perfect right to be here. So sit yourself down and stop worrying about every blessed thing and tell me what you want to drink because my tongue's hanging out.'

Angela was a little nonplussed by this because, although she'd served behind a bar for years, she had rarely tasted alcohol and the smell in the pub had put her off seemingly for good.

'Lemonade, I suppose,' she said.

Eddie stared at her in amazement, for working in a pub as she did he had expected her to be a drinker. But he didn't want her to be satisfied with lemonade that night because in his experience women and girls were usually much more compliant with a drink or two inside them.

'Don't you want anything stronger?'

'Better not,' Angela said. 'It might go straight to my head as I'm not used to it. Anyway I don't like the smell of alcohol, never mind the taste. Lemonade will be fine.'

'Leave it to me,' Eddie said and the drink he brought to the table a little later was light red. She took it from him uncertainly and sniffed and it smelled nothing like anything she'd ever served either.

'What is it?'

'Port and lemon,' Eddie said. 'It's what all the ladies drink.'

'Is it?'

'Oh yes,' Eddie said with some authority. 'Have a sip. I think you'll like it.'

Angela loved the port and lemon and she thought nothing so deliciously purple could be that strong, especially as Eddie said ladies drank it.

'I've spent all the time we've been out talking about me,' Angela said. 'Now it's your turn, Eddie.'

Eddie, however, was rather sketchy about his life, which he said was very uninteresting. Angela knew that men didn't talk as much as women and she asked him instead about America and he painted a picture very like the one she'd imagined reading her brothers' letters.

'I'll tell you more when I get us both another drink,' Eddie said. 'Your glass is empty and I could do with another. Do you want the same again?'

Angela nodded her head eagerly. She liked it very much and this time when Eddie handed to her he said, 'Now listen Angela, you've got to take it a bit steady drinking alcohol or you'll be falling over. You can't knock it back like you do lemonade and it will affect you quicker because you're not used to it.'

'I know.'

'Do you feel all right?'

'I feel wonderful,' Angela said, for she did feel as light as air and without a care in the world. The worries she carried all the time wedged between her shoulder blades had shifted and she felt freer than she had for years.

'How did you end up in America?' she asked.

'Well, like you, we had to leave Ireland to save us all starving to death. Once in England my father found it hard getting any sort of regular work, but my mother had an elder sister, Minnie, who'd married a man called Sam Winters and gone with him to America years before. With the help of a rich benefactor, Uncle Sam had been able to open a business. However, they'd had no children and Minnie had died two years before and, knowing the dire straits we were in, he wrote for us to join him. My mother was so upset for she'd had to leave her parents and sister behind in Ireland knowing she would never see them again.

'I remember I was very ill with seasickness on the journey, and so was my mother, and we both felt pretty wretched. But the others, who avoided sea-sickness, caught cholera and by the time we arrived in New York, my father, two elder brothers and young sister were at the bottom of the ocean and there was just my mother and me. My mother looked after the house for my uncle and he sent me to a good school and made me work extremely hard. He was incredibly strict and if I misbehaved at home, or in school, or didn't get good enough grades for homework or in exams, he would whip me with a horse whip he kept in the study. Huh, I'll tell you I felt the sting of that whip a fair few times when I was growing up.'

'Did you hate him?'

Eddie shook his head. 'D'you know, I didn't. I sort of respected him and he said he would train me up to take over the business if I could show him that I was intelligent enough.'

'And were you?'

'Huh, I had to be,' Eddie said. 'I knew if I was to fail I would be out on my ear because he was that kind of man. He would have probably have kept my mother on because she could be of use to him keeping house and warming his bed, for we hadn't been there a couple of months before she had jumped into bed with him.'

'Ugh.'

'I didn't blame her,' Eddie said. 'She probably had little choice in it, but whether she did or not, she probably enjoyed it as much as he did. They always seemed on very fond terms and if they gave each other a bit of pleasure there was no problem as far as I was concerned.'

Angela thought there was a great problem with being so sexually free, but could hardly criticise Eddie's mother.

'What do your brothers do out there?' Eddie asked.

'They went into the car industry,' Angela said. 'No one could really understand it in Birmingham, for we didn't have that many petrol-driven vehicles at the time. But their sponsor said it would be big business before that long and so it's being proved, at least from what they say.'

'Yes,' Eddie said. 'England's been falling behind somewhat. Investment fell because of the war, but it has been building up steadily since then.'

'What d'you do then?'

'We deal with imports and exports,' Eddie said. 'For our manufacturing industry we need iron ore, steel and mineral oil which we get from Great Britain. In return we export wheat, tea, sugar, cotton and machine tools.'

'Oh, and when your business has been concluded will you return to America?'

'Don't know,' Eddie said. 'I have been going back and forward for a while now and Uncle Sam has been talking about setting up a base here in England. I'm here to drum up as much business as I can to see if it would be worth our while, so this trip anyway I might be here for some time. Would you like it if I was?'

'It really is none of my business.'

'That isn't what I asked you,' Eddie said, nudging her elbow and giving her a knowing look. 'If I was to stay we could see more of each other. Would you like that?'

In the early days when Angela first began working behind the bar she had got a lot of attention and been asked out by a fair few regulars. In the main, though, they had been married men, and not only that but neighbours, so their wives were known to her. So she had not only refused them but berated them too, though in a bantering kind of way, gently making fun of their suggestion so that few were offended by it. They were, after all, just chancing their arm, and were left in no doubt where Angela stood and what she meant, and very few asked again. But with Eddie it was different. True, he was a regular at the Swan now, but he had no wife or children and was quite exotic, coming as he did from the States.

She had never been asked such a question in such a way by anyone and she blushed as she found herself saying, 'Yes, I'd miss you very much if you were to go away and I would like to see more of you.'

Eddie saw the blush, which only made Angela look more gorgeous than ever and somehow naïve. He knew that she blushed through embarrassment for she would probably think it fast to tell a man how she really felt. Ladies didn't do that, certainly not at this stage in a relationship, and he guessed it was the unaccustomed alcohol that was loosening her tongue. That suited him but she was having no more: he wanted her malleable and compliant, not staggering about the place and throwing up all over him.

So he put his hand over hers, which caused her heart to hammer in her chest and her blush to deepen. She lifted her head and her eyes were held by the look in his and he said, 'You must know how I feel about you, Angela. I have longed for this moment. I thought it would have to stay in my imagination when you refused to come out with me.'

'I know,' Angela said in a low voice. 'I was silly.'

'So we'll do this again?' Eddie said as a question. 'I don't mean go to Cannon Hill Park every time of course. I mean, would you like to go out with me?'

And Angela heard herself saying, 'Oh Eddie, I'd love it. I'd just love it.'

Eddie lifted her hand and kissed it gently and the blush flooded back into Angela's face again. She was so excited for that had never happened before and she felt she might die with happiness.

'Drink up, darling,' Eddie said. 'Time to get you back home.'

Angela glanced on the clock on the wall and exclaimed, 'But it isn't quite half seven yet.'

But Eddie knew to leave a girl still wanting more and he said, 'It's better not to be too late. Your daughter . . .'

'Will not even miss me,' Angela finished for Eddie. 'I warned her I would be late and she is quite old enough to get a meal for herself and she will have her head in her books by now. She has mountains of homework.'

'Even so,' Eddie said. 'It's late enough for a first date and we don't have to go straight home, but I can't love you as I want in a pub.'

Angela gave a small gasp, but she withdrew her hand from Eddie's and drained the port and lemon as he'd asked her to. She felt it trickle down her throat and a warm glow seemed to envelop her. She had a broad grin on her face when she turned to Eddie, feeling suddenly grateful that he had been so kind to her and given her a really nice time. She tried to say this but her words were a little slurred, but Eddie brushed her words aside anyway.

'I enjoyed myself too, but there are ways of showing a man how grateful you are that are a thousand times better than words,' he said.

Angela didn't answer because she was having trouble standing up, her legs seemed to have a mind of their own. She was embarrassed, but Eddie knew what ailed her.

'Come on, you old lush,' he said good-naturedly and he hauled her up. She swayed slightly as he fastened her into her coat and tucked in her scarf around her, for he knew the night would be cold after the pub.

Eddie linked his arm through Angela's and she wasn't even aware of the looks of the other drinkers eyeing her and Eddie and shaking their heads. They made their way to the door, but when the night air hit Angela, she staggered and would have fallen to the ground if Eddie hadn't grabbed her.

A man going into the pub looked at Angela's vacant face and remarked, 'She should take more water with it.'

'Maybe,' Eddie agreed good-naturedly. 'She isn't used to it.'

'And she shouldn't get used to it,' the man said irritably. 'Alcohol isn't for the fairer sex. They should stick to tea and buns.'

Eddie turned away with a smile as the man went into the pub and thought of the cocktail-drinking women of America who populated the speakeasies springing up all over the place.

Speakeasies were the only places in the whole damn country where a person could have a drink of any sort, and even these were raided periodically for there was Prohibition in America and alcohol was banned in the whole country.

Such a law was hard to enforce, however, and it gave rise to a great deal of smuggling. Many police turned a blind eye to what was happening behind the closed doors of a speakeasy and women loved their colourful cocktails in their sugar-crusted crystal glasses and the cigarettes they smoked in their slender holders.

Fortunately, the exchange had gone over Angela's head and they began to make their way up Bristol Street, Eddie supporting Angela while she concentrated on putting one foot before the other. When they reached the warren of back-to-back houses, Eddie turned away from the main road and ducked down into the mean streets. When he came to an alleyway he judged far enough away from the main road, he turned down in the semi-privacy of the alley.

He had been affected by Angela's nearness to him on the journey home and had a throbbing ache in his groin, but knew he had to bide his time to win her over. He took her in his arms and she resisted and pulled back, thinking it was too short an acquaintanceship to be so familiar. But far from letting her go, Eddie held her tighter against him so that she felt the bulge in his trousers. She felt a little alarmed, although the fact that he was aroused excited her too. She thought any sexual desire had been turned off in her body, for it was many years since any man had touched her, but she remembered the way she had always felt when Barry had taken her in his arms and she had shivered in anticipation.

But then she reminded herself she had been married to

Barry, while Eddie shouldn't be taking such liberties. She knew she should rebuff him and yet, when his lips met hers, she gave herself up to the kiss, despite knowing in her heart of hearts that this was wrong. When he teased her mouth open and she felt his tongue slip between her lips, she couldn't stop the moan escaping from her any more than she could have stopped the sun from shining. She kissed him back with eagerness, feeling shafts of desire shoot through her body.

Eddie was surprised Angela had let him go so far on their first date. He had felt sure that she would be far more buttoned-up than that and could only assume it was the drink that had loosened her inhibitions. He wondered just how much Angela would let him do before she put the brakes on. She began to tremble, and he tore at the buttons of her coat in his haste to feel her breasts beneath his hands.

However, when he began to run his hands over her body, it stirred a memory in the recesses of Angela's mind. The very last time a man, several men, had laid hands on her in that way, and in the same sort of place, had been the start of her nightmare that culminated in her doing something so heinous to a helpless child.

All she knew was she couldn't let it happen again, and so when she began fighting Eddie with thrashing arms and screams to leave her alone she wasn't fighting him, but her abusers. However, he didn't know that and thought for a moment the unaccustomed drink had caused some sort of brainstorm.

Eventually he managed to capture the flailing arms and held them against her body with one hand, while the other covered her mouth lest someone hearing the screams might come and investigate who was being murdered. The one thing that Eddie hated more than anything was to be denied what he wanted and to be thwarted in his need of a woman and getting sex from her. He felt a hot anger rising in him, but his head was also working. He knew when he caught sight of Angela's panic-filled eyes in the light of the hissing gas lamp in the street there was more to her reaction than her merely objecting to a bit of slap and tickle, especially when he remembered her response to the kiss.

So, despite the kicks she continued to aim which had caught his shins more than once, he pushed his anger down and tried to speak gently.

'Angela, don't be afraid. It's me, Eddie, and I mean you no harm.'

Seeing that these words calmed her, he said the same words over and over again like a litany until suddenly Angela sagged against the bricks of the alleyway. Eddie took his hand from her mouth and she put her hands over her eyes. The tears came like a torrent that spilled from her eyes and dripped through her fingers while Eddie stood and waited for her to be calmer.

And when she was, he said, 'Angela . . .'

'I can't tell you,' she burst out. 'I can tell no one and it means I can never have a relationship with anyone.'

'Even me?'

'Anyone.'

'Oh Angela, no,' Eddie said. 'That's not right. You are a young woman yet and you have so much love to give.'

Angela shook her head so violently the whole alleyway swayed before her eyes and she said, 'Not physically.'

'Can you tell me why?'

Angela continued to shake her head vigorously. 'No, no. I can't tell anyone.'

Eddie had an idea what had happened to her, but if she wouldn't speak about it they were going to get nowhere so he said, 'Whatever happened you can't speak about, but what if I try and guess and ask questions and you just say yes or no?'

'No. No one must know.'

'You won't get over this bottling it up,' Eddie said. 'No details, no names, just some idea of what happened. All right?'

The tears had begun to trickle down Angela's cheeks again, but she gave a brief nod of the head.

'Were you attacked?' he asked.

Angela nodded and added through her tears, 'By three men.'

Eddie knew that the more information he got from her the better. It might come in handy in the future. 'Was it a bad attack? You know what I mean by that?'

'I understand and it was as bad as it can be.'

'Where did this happen?'

'Here.'

'Here?' Eddie said incredulously and then added, 'Or do you mean in an alleyway like this?'

Again there was a nod.

'Was it a long time ago?'

Again there was a nod and then Angela added, 'In the war and it was the last time anyone put their hands on me. Sorry, I can't get it out of my mind. You better find someone else who can love you properly.'

'No. I want you to get over this,' Eddie said. 'So I will

love you as I want to and but I will stop the minute you tell me to. Then we will see if we can get over this barrier that stops you fully enjoying a relationship.'

Angela stared at him. 'I can't ask this of you.'

'You're not asking, I'm offering.'

'Wouldn't you like to go out with someone less complicated?'

Angela saw Eddie's lips turn up in a smile as he said, 'No, I really like a challenge. Now come here,' he commanded her, 'and give me a kiss. Those at least you don't seem to mind.'

'Oh no, Eddie, I will kiss you any way any time,' Angela said, and as she melted into his arms and gave herself up to the kiss, waves of desire rose in her.

Eddie thought it wrong to push her after what she had told him and contented himself with tightening his arms around her, holding her so close she could feel his hard body against her own. She sighed for she felt protected and safe and happy and she hadn't felt that way for many a year.

SEVENTEEN

Angela did her best to appear sober and in total control of her emotions as she opened the front door. Connie was sitting at the table with all her books spread out. She looked up at Angela as she came in the room and removed her coat, and saw that her mother's clothes seemed all mussed up, there was alcohol on her breath and she had been crying.

'What's the matter?' Connie asked.

'Nothing. What do you mean?'

'You've been crying.'

'No, no, I have a bit of a cold.'

'Mammy,' Connie said sarcastically. 'I am no longer a baby. Your clothes are all over the place as well and you're drunk.'

'I am not drunk,' Angela maintained, annoyed that her tongue seemed twice the size it should have been and the words sounded thick and indistinct.

'Course you're not,' Connie said sarcastically. 'Stone cold sober you are. Anyway, what were you crying about?'

Angela was tempted to tell Connie it was none of her business but she knew that would only convince her she had something to hide. However, she couldn't tell her the truth, so she said, 'It's nothing. There was a man at the pub asked me to go to Cannon Hill Park with him as I had the evening off.'

'A man.'

'Yes Connie, a man,' Angela said. 'His name is Eddie McIntyre and he has been coming to the Swan for a wee while now. He's from America, here on business.'

Connie felt as if the world had shifted under her feet and the words seemed forced from her. 'You have no right to go out with men. What about Daddy?'

'Your father is dead, Connie, has been dead for years and I have not and am not now going out with men. Just one man, Eddie, and this evening for the first time.'

'And it's dark and has been dark for hours. You can't have been to a park in the dark.'

'I know. On the way home we went for a drink.'

'You went into a pub?' Connie said, appalled.

'Don't sound so shocked, ' Angela said. 'I seem to spend half my life in a pub.'

'Not as a customer.'

'Connie, it's not a crime to go into a pub,' Angela said. 'We had fish and chips and they made us thirsty with the salt and vinegar and all, and so Eddie suggested going into the pub we were passing on our way home for a drink.'

'So how did he make you cry?'

'He didn't make me as such,' Angela said. 'That was me being silly. We got talking about the war, and I told him how your daddy died. It was on the way home that I got to thinking of your daddy and shed a few tears thinking of what might have been.'

Angela felt ashamed at the lie she told her daughter but it was less shameful than the truth.

Connie looked at her mother and knew she wasn't being honest with her. She had shed more than a few tears, judging by the tear-trails on her face, and for that matter her cheeks were flushed as if she was embarrassed at the lies she was spouting. Connie could never ever remember her mother telling her any sort of untruth before and that was disturbing in itself. Connie would have said she knew her mother well, better than anyone, but the woman who that day had gone out to the park with a man for hours and then spent the early evening in a pub and arrived home unsteady on her feet, smelling of drink with the mark of tears on her flushed cheeks, bore no resemblance to the mother she had lived with for over fourteen years. She dearly wished she had Sarah to confide in, but she hadn't and so she kept it to herself.

Angela was more bothered with the events of the night than with Connie's disapproval. As she lay in bed that night, Angela told herself that if she wasn't able to put the memory of her violent rape by three drunken soldiers out of her mind then they would have won and succeeded in destroying the rest of her life. She knew she had to get a grip on herself.

Eddie had taken her out and they'd had a wonderful time together. He had bought her delicious fish and chips and then the drinks in the pub and she felt she owed him something for being so nice to her. On the walk home he had forced her to do nothing and her cheeks burned when she remembered how eagerly she had fallen into his arms. When he had kissed her she had kissed him back with a passion that matched his own, even though she was shaken to the core by her fast and forward behaviour.

But when he'd moved his hands over her body she'd been transported back to the alleyway: beaten, bruised and bleeding while one after another the soldiers thrust themselves inside her. She had fought against Eddie like a raging virago, lashing and kicking out – shouting and screaming loud enough to waken the dead.

She covered her face with her hands, crushed by the memories crowding into her brain of how badly she had behaved. Eddie had been very sweet about it, but he'd have had time to reflect now, and Angela faced the fact that he would probably never want to see her again. She was a little surprised at the lurch her stomach gave at that thought.

She couldn't wait to see him again and so Connie found her mother quite distracted when she came home from school that afternoon. She tried talking to her, telling her things about school that she'd always been interested in before, but Angela either didn't answer at all, or made non-committal murmurs. This continued even as they sat at the table and ate a meal together. It made Connie feel uncomfortable for it was obvious her mother's mind was elsewhere and it was quite a relief when Angela took herself off to work.

Even at the pub, Angela was like a cat on hot bricks until she saw Eddie come into the pub and cross the room to the bar in moments, smiling broadly. Breda smiled grimly to herself, for Eddie's actions showed he had enjoyed his time with Angela. She had asked Angela if she'd enjoyed herself but she just said it was all right.

'It was like getting blood out of a stone,' she said to Paddy later as they got ready for bed. 'And then when Eddie came in it was as if there was a light lit up inside her. And Eddie said he had had a marvellous time with Angela and would like to do it again, or something similar, as soon as she had another free day.'

'They seem to have something going between them right enough, but I'm not sure I like it too much. He is a worldly fellow and I think he has a temper on him besides,' Paddy said. 'I wonder how young Connie is coping with the news.'

'She might not know yet,' Breda said. 'If I was Angela I'd put it off as long as possible. It's been the two of them for so long she is more or less bound not to like Eddie McIntyre.'

'Aye,' Paddy said. 'And she'd never think, youngsters never do, that adults might have needs in the bedroom.'

Breda laughed. 'They think we're far too old for that sort of malarkey. And I'm thinking that Connie may well have to get used to it because I'd say they are getting very fond of one another.' And then she gave a sigh and went on, 'And although I think Angela has a right to a bit of happiness in her life, I'd hate Eddie to marry her and whisk her off to the States. And not just because I'll lose the best barmaid I've ever had.'

'Oh, that hadn't occurred to me,' Paddy said. 'D'you think that's likely?'

Breda shrugged. 'Don't know Eddie's long-term plans, but I'd say he could, he's a free agent,' she said. 'But I doubt that would be on Angela's agenda because she is fixed on the notion of letting Connie matriculate and that will all be up in the air if they move to America.'

'Aren't we jumping the gun a bit about this anyway?' Paddy said. 'They've only just met really.'

'Paddy,' Breda said. 'Eddie has been coming here for months and he has always made a beeline for Angela to serve him and they used to talk a great deal, usually about America.

Angela always said it was because her brothers were there, and I don't know if that's all there was in the beginning, for Angela at least. Eddie must have felt more for Angela more or less straight away though. Do you remember the way he was always asking questions about her when he came first and how his face brightened up when he learned she was a widow and not courting anyone so she was available? Must have been then he asked her out. Anyway, they might not hang about because they're not in the first flush of youth, are they?'

'Good God, woman, they're not drawing a pension.'

'I never said they were,' Breda said. 'Let's just wait and see.'

A little over a week later Angela knew she had to tell Connie how things were between her and Eddie before someone else did. However, Connie was no fool and knew something wasn't quite right and that it all stemmed from the night she'd told her she had been out with a man called Eddie McIntyre. Angela was seldom in in the evenings now and she knew her mother wasn't working at the pub every night of the week. It made Connie feel more alone and isolated than ever and it wasn't a total surprise when her mother told her she was getting 'very close' to Eddie McIntyre.

'I would like you to meet him,' Angela said to her daughter. 'I'm sure you'd like him when you got to know him.'

She didn't see Connie's stony face, and so was taken aback when she said in clipped tones, 'This man is your friend, he isn't mine and I don't want to meet him and haven't the least desire to get to know him better.'

Angela tried to remonstrate with Connie, but she got short

shrift. 'This is nothing to do with me,' she said, 'so you bring him here and I shall go out.'

'Why worry?' Eddie said when Angela related what Connie had said. 'I would have said she was almost bound to resent me. Before I came on the scene she was probably the focus of all your thoughts and attention so it would be very reasonable to be jealous, especially if she thought I was trying to take the place of her father.'

'What shall we do?' Angela cried. 'Maybe if you came and talked to her.'

'No,' Eddie said. 'I am the last person she will want to see just now. She will get over this in time and quicker if we make no fuss about it and carry on in our own sweet way.'

And the sweet way was very good indeed for, as October and the first half of November passed, Angela's need for Eddie grew with every passing day. She found if she drank enough she could push the memories of the attack to some dark recess in her mind, and Eddie didn't mind that, for the more drunk she was the more licence she allowed him. He kept his promise and never pushed her further than she wanted to go, but when he took her out to the music hall or the cinema and was so kind and gentle with her, she wanted to reward him, especially when they went for a few drinks on the way home.

The weather had grown colder now and so one day they spent the night drinking in a pub on Bristol Street and afterwards went to Eddie's lodging in Colmore Street. They had to creep past the landlady's room on the ground floor, for ladies weren't allowed in gentlemen's rooms. There the privacy they had meant that Angela allowed Eddie to touch areas of her body that even Barry never had, and he lifted her to heights of exhilaration she had never before experienced. She had always enjoyed sex with Barry, but her response had been tame in comparison to the lustful rapture she was feeling now with Eddie. After the birth of Connie, Barry's lovemaking had been more controlled, especially after he enlisted for he hadn't wanted to leave Angela with another mouth to feed.

However, there was nothing subdued or controlled about Eddie's lovemaking, for he was an experienced lover and liked to leave his women screaming for more. Angela couldn't believe she was the same person she had been just six months before, because not only was she allowing Eddie to do unmentionable things to her, she was helping him and wanting it as much as he was, though she never let him enter her. Angela drew the line there for she said that was very, very wrong and mustn't happen.

Eddie smiled to himself for he knew Angela was holding back from letting him take her fully with great difficulty. Eventually she would let him have what she wanted so much herself.

And so the next time she had a free night off they went to the pub and Eddie encouraged Angela to drink more than she ever had before. To please Eddie, for she always wanted to please Eddie, Angela drank the contents of every glass he bought her. He knew he would have to pretty much carry her to his lodgings, but he considered it worth it for he was determined that night to claim the prize she had so far hung on to. That night he intended to work her up to the point where in her drunken state she would be unable to help herself and he was sure she'd let him go as far as he wanted.

She was virtually unable to stand when Eddie decided they would make for his lodgings and, as he'd anticipated, he had to nearly carry her through the cold dark streets. He was glad his landlady was a little on the deaf side; he was sure if she wasn't she would have heard them on the stairs that night, for Angela was stumbling so badly and giggling about it while Eddie tried to haul her up the stairs as quickly as possible.

He laid her on the bed and she was too drunk to move, not even protesting when he started removing her clothing. His excitement mounted as he removed layer after layer and she helped him, tearing the clothes from her. He gazed at her spread out shamelessly in the bed and her body felt as if it was on fire.

'You're so beautiful,' he said huskily. 'So very beautiful.'

He began to strip and Angela sat up, though her head spun and she swayed slightly, and tore some buttons from his shirt in her haste to help him. When he was naked he stood beside the bed and she gasped for she was seeing the naked body of a man for the first time. She had never seen Barry unclothed and she saw Eddie's pulsating manhood and felt exhilaration flow through her so that she shuddered all over.

And then Eddie was on top of her, kissing her all over her body, her lips, her neck, her throat, her belly, till she could hardly breathe. He sucked at her breasts till they throbbed and Angela was writhing and moaning beneath him. Desire was almost consuming her and the ache between her legs was unbearable.

'Let me love you properly, Angela?' Eddie pleaded.

'Oh yes, please yes,' Angela cried.

And yet Eddie did not enter her. 'Are you sure you want this?'

'Want it?' Angela repeated. 'Almighty Christ I need it, quickly for I can't bear it.'

Eddie thrust his way inside her and Angela grasped his buttocks, and pulling her legs up, pushed him further and further in. Remembering the landlady, she bit on her lips to restrain the shouts of joy escaping from her and she rose in rapturous peaks of lust.

Eventually, much later, when the fires had died down a little in Angela, she lay back with a sigh of contentment. Eddie collapsed on top of her as she said, in a slurred voice, 'That is the best feeling I have ever had in all the world, the best, the very best.'

'Hear hear,' said Eddie. 'It's rare to find a woman who likes sex so much. But much though I'd like to sleep the night through cuddling you in my arms, and maybe have another sexy foray before you rise, we must get up and dress because it is after midnight and you must go home.'

Angela grumbled and complained, because she was filled with the drowsiness that often follows satisfying sex, and didn't want to leave the bed. Yet she knew that Eddie was right and she hauled herself up and began to pull her clothes on and then, with Eddie's arm around her lest she fall, they headed out. They kept away from the well-lit roads and eventually made it to the front door of Angela's house without incident.

'Watch how you go,' Eddie said. 'Especially on the stairs.'

Angela just smiled at him benignly and waved him away in the exaggerated manner of the very drunk. 'Don't fuss,' she said.

However, when she stepped in the house and no longer had the support of Eddie, she realised how unsteady she was.

Holding on to the furniture, she weaved her way to the stairs and fell in a heap at the bottom of them. With her head reeling, she knew she would never be able to climb the stairs in the usual way and so she ascended on her hands and knees. Once in the bedroom she pulled herself up, holding on to the dressing table. Her bed looked inviting and when she fell across it she closed her eyes and slept without removing anything.

She hadn't slept long though before the nausea woke her and she was sick in the pot beneath her bed. She longed to sleep but when she closed her eyes the room began to spin and then the urge to be sick would jerk her upright. That set the pattern for the night, for twice more she was violently sick in the pot.

Eventually, just before dawn, she dropped into an uneasy doze and when she woke a little later she felt as if she had stepped into the pit of hell. She was used to waking with a thick head if she had been out with Eddie the night before, but this was a throbbing pain so strong it was hard to raise her head from the pillow and her mouth was so dry she had trouble swallowing.

But, as she lay bracing herself to get up, the memories of the night before came flooding back. Parts of it were hazy but she remembered enough to know that she had behaved in a disgusting way. She felt bitterly ashamed of her behaviour. What had she been thinking of? She was little better than a harlot because there wasn't even any sort of understanding between them; Eddie had never hinted at marriage and yet she had allowed him to do things that only married couples do. But no, she thought, get it right. I didn't allow him, I encouraged him and helped him and wanted sex as much as he did.

She wondered if he had left her with a child. Well, if he had she only had herself to blame, there must be something radically wrong with her that caused her to behave in that shameless and immoral way.

She gasped with horror as she suddenly thought that the soldiers who attacked her that time must have sensed the wantonness in her. If that had been the case it had all been as much her fault as theirs. She couldn't bear the thought that the innocent baby left on the steps of the workhouse was the one who had suffered for her sins. She groaned in anguish, her head held in her hands at the thought of what she subjected that child to. Well that at least wouldn't happen again, because if she had been left carrying a child, she would rear it herself, however hard it was.

When she was eventually upright she felt incredibly nauseous and knew if she ate anything she would be as sick as a dog. In a way, that was just as well because she was going to be late for work as it was. She would have loved a cup of tea, but she hadn't the time to make it and drink it, and maybe that too was just as well for she gagged on the cup of water she did try to drink when she came back from emptying the pot in the lavatory. She managed only a few sips before she felt the bile beginning to gather in her mouth. She didn't try any more but left for work, hurrying as much as she was able to. She was on an early shift and slipped out of the house before Connie had risen for school. She was too ashamed to look her daughter in the face and hoped that she had not heard her banging and crashing through the house.

When she let herself into the side door of the pub she saw that as usual Breda wasn't down yet, but Paddy was there and looked up as she came in. It was an unusual occurrence for her not to be on time and so she said to Paddy, 'Sorry I'm late. I overslept.'

'Happens to us all now and again,' Paddy said and then he looked closer at Angela's face and saw the bags beneath her lacklustre eyes and the fact that they looked large in her white, drawn face. 'You all right? You look right peaky.'

'No, no, I'm fine,' Angela assured him. In truth she felt like death warmed up, her eyes burned and the pain in her head was so great she didn't know what to do with herself. But as that was totally her own fault she couldn't ask for sympathy or do anything other than carry out her job to the best of her ability.

But Paddy was concerned about Angela. She had worked there long enough for him to know when the girl wasn't right. But, he reasoned, it might be women's troubles so he went up and told Breda there was something the matter with Angela, for all she claimed there wasn't.

Breda gave a sigh and climbed stiffly out of bed and began to dress. 'Maybe she took a drop too much last night,' she said.

Once she would never have thought that of Angela, for the girl never drank a drop of anything – lemonade and only lemonade was her tipple. But that was before she began seeing Eddie. He was a heavy drinker, as were many men, but it seemed he had encouraged Angela because they had been seen imbibing rather freely in the Bell Barn Tavern further down Bell Barn Road during Angela's time off.

And Paddy had told her Eddie bought at least one port and lemon for her on the night she was working and had one waiting for her at the end of her shift. Breda had given a sniff of disapproval when she had heard this, for she didn't really approve of staff drinking behind the bar. However, her arthritis meant that she could spend little time there herself and really relied on Angela. Paddy too was prepared to turn a blind eye because he liked the odd tipple or two himself.

Paddy looked at Breda's disapproving face and said, 'Don't be too hard on her if she has overdone it a bit. It isn't as if she gets legless or owt.'

'Angela wouldn't need much though, would she?' Breda said. 'There's very little to her and she's not used to it.'

'Well, even if she was to take a drop too much, though I have never seen that myself, she's hurting no one. She's maybe just having a little fun in her life now that she has Connie nearly reared. Really, she's had precious little up to now and she was once as thick as thieves with that Stan and nothing came of that. Never sees hide nor hair of him now, nor that son of his.'

'That was odd,' Breda agreed. 'And after all Angela did for him as well. I suppose now he has his son back in his life he had no need for her company any more. Shabby way to treat someone if you ask me. And she was cut up about it because I asked about him one day and honest to God I thought she was going to burst into tears. I mean, that's one of the reasons I encouraged her to go out with Eddie. I could see he was keen on her and I thought it might cheer them both up. I never imagined for one moment that it would get as intense as it has.'

'Maybe they'll end up getting married.'

'I don't think so,' Breda said with a shake of her head. 'To me Eddie is more a love-them-and-leave-them kind of man.'

Recognising now that Eddie was the type that didn't want to commit to one woman and liked to play the field, Breda felt slightly guilty that she had encouraged Angela to go out with him. She had only intended it in a friendly way, to give her a lift, and she hadn't known then that Angela was going to fall for Eddie McIntyre hook, line and sinker the way it appeared she had done. What bothered her a bit was that she knew that some men encouraged girls they were keen on to drink, as even a respectable girl would often let a man do far more than she normally would if she had had more alcohol than was sensible. It was a known fact and she just hoped Angela was wise enough to keep her wits about her.

She hadn't interfered so far for she didn't think it was her place, but then Paddy had asked her to look at Angela. She saw straight away there was something very wrong with the woman and, being a publican's wife, she would have taken bets on the girl being badly hungover. She knew the time had come to have a wee talk. Angela was wiping the tables down when Breda walked into the bar, sat at one of the tables and asked Angela to join her.

'But I haven't finished, Breda.'

'The pub will have to make do with a lick and a promise today,' Breda said. 'You are more important.'

'Me?' Angela cried. 'There's nothing wrong with me.'

'Oh yes there is,' Breda said determinedly. 'You are sick and you look sick and the reason is because you had far too much to drink last night and you are now hungover. And this isn't the first time, but the first time I have seen you this bad.'

'I'm sorry.'

'There's no harm done yet,' Breda said. 'Tell me, does Eddie encourage you to drink?'

'I don't think so, Breda,' Angela said. 'The first day I went out with him I told him I didn't drink, that I didn't even like the smell, and he said he bet he could find something I liked.'

'And he bought you port and lemon.' Breda said. 'Because that's what you drink here.'

'Yes,' Angela said. 'And I loved it. It was Eddie told me to take it steady because I was drinking it down like I did lemonade. He said you had to treat alcohol with more respect.'

'Well he's right enough there,' Breda said. 'The thing with drink, Angela, is you sometimes do things that you might be embarrassed to do if you hadn't taken a drink, and the more you drink the bolder you can get. It could easily make you do things you bitterly regret the next morning.'

Angela lowered her head, but not before Breda had seen her cheeks aflame with shame, and she felt her heart drop to her boots. She was very fond of Angela and if that young woman had given herself to that charming, hand- some, but fly-by-night Eddie McIntyre, her life would be ruined, for she knew he would leave Angela even if she was in the family way with his child, without a backward glance.

But maybe it wasn't as bad as she feared. 'Angela,' she said. 'You haven't . . .?'

Angela lifted her sorrowful eyes and Breda watched tears brim over her eyelids and trail down her face as she gave a brief nod.

'This is where you tell me to leave because you don't want such a wicked person working for you. I gave myself to Eddie McIntyre freely last night when I drank far more than I ever have before and . . . well, I suppose Eddie did encourage me then in the pub, but I didn't resist or say no.'

'Why didn't you?'

'I wanted to please him,' Angela said simply and added, 'I always want to please him.'

'Does that mean what I think it means?'

Angela nodded her head. 'I was very drunk. Eddie had to nearly carry me back to his lodgings and . . . and, well, I don't seem to be able to say no to Eddie.'

'Do you love him, Angela?'

'I don't know,' Angela said. 'It's not the same that I felt for Barry. But I think about him all the time.'

'You know he isn't the marrying kind.'

Angela nodded her head. 'I sort of know that and somehow it doesn't matter. He has never said he loves me and there is no understanding between us and yet I let him . . . I would like to say he forced me because you might feel better about me, but he didn't force me, he didn't have to. Oh Breda,' Angela cried, covering her mouth with her hands so that the last words were hushed. 'I don't know what came over me but I wanted it as much as he did. How wicked is that?'

'Oh God, girl, none of us are saints,' Breda said. 'I'm not interested in how wicked you are. All I'm concerned with is that there are no consequences to your night of passion.'

'Oh, so am I,' Angela said fervently. She had more reason to wish that than Breda, for her employer never knew of the bundle left on the workhouse steps. If she hadn't been to blame for what had happened with Eddie, she would have pleaded with the Almighty not to let her suffer the same fate again, she would have begun a novena to the blessed Virgin, offered up a Mass. But how could she do any of these things when she had welcomed sex as much as Eddie had? She was as wicked as him and she didn't see why God would be interested in helping her. It felt a bit of a cheek to ask Him and expect Him to fix things.

Breda watched Angela's anguished face as her thoughts tumbled about in her mind. Though she wasn't privy to them, she guessed Angela would be blaming herself because she was that kind of girl and so she said, 'This isn't your fault, Angela. It was the drink you took made you act that way,'

Angela shook her head. 'Mary always said what's in a person sober comes out when they are drunk and I took the drink willingly. Eddie didn't hold my nose and pour it down my neck. There is no excuse for me, there's a definite flaw in my character. Are you sure you still want to employ me?'

Breda didn't answer that directly, but what she did say was, 'Angela, how long have I known you?'

'A long time, years.'

'Nearly all your life.' Breda said. 'Paddy and I had just become licensees of this pub when you arrived with the McCluskys when you were four. Our own children were young then and you all played in the street, you and Barry, the Dochertys, the Websters, the Maguires and all the others in the streets and yards around. And you all went off to school when you were old enough, you went to holy communion and confirmation with my daughter and Barry was an altar boy with my son. I know you and your whole family and I know you to be honest and respectable and if you were a wicked girl, I would say there would be some evidence of it before now.'

'Yes, but . . .'

'Hear me out, Angela,' Breda said. 'Believe me, what you

did with Eddie you did because you got so drunk that all your inhibitions flew out of the window and you behaved in a completely strange way. And though Eddie didn't force you to drink too much, he allowed you to, and I have no doubt he knew the reaction it would have on you, being totally unused to alcohol. So he was far more to blame than you.'

Angela couldn't tell Breda that at first she had welcomed the effect of the alcohol that blurred the edges of the attack, so that she was able to accept and even welcome Eddie's advances, for Breda knew nothing about the attack. Nor could she say that she hadn't just submitted to Eddie's desire for sex. She had given herself to him completely in total abandonment and she was bitterly ashamed. Without a wedding ring on her finger it couldn't be repeated, she knew that. Eddie wasn't the marrying kind and she had said as much to Breda, though she couldn't help hoping that now that she had given herself to him so completely he would feel some commitment towards her.

She didn't share this hope with Breda, and when she held her hands tight and looked into her eyes and said, 'This mustn't happen again, you do realise that?' Angela nodded her head.

'And it might be better for you not to drink anything if you are going to continue seeing Eddie.'

'I'd already decided that,' Angela said.

'Good girl,' said Breda. 'Now all we have to do is hope and pray there are no repercussions to last night . . .'

EIGHTEEN

Angela was working behind the bar when Eddie came in that night. She dampened down her initial feelings of excitement and Paddy crossed the bar in front of Angela and said to Eddie, 'What will you be having then?'

Eddie was a little puzzled, for normally Angela was left to serve him. His eyes met hers as Paddy was pulling his pint and she gave a slight shrug. Angela wasn't totally surprised though, because she knew Breda would have said something to Paddy to explain the long conversation they'd had earlier. She also knew Breda wouldn't have told him the whole truth of the situation for her sake, probably putting the onus on Eddie, saying he was bothering her or something.

Now Paddy, although he knew Angela was a grown woman and a free agent, was also aware that she was naïve in the ways of men, despite the fact she had been married and had a child. Barry had been as familiar to her as any blood brother before she married him. The marriage had been happy, no denying it, but she had looked at no man since. Most of the men she served were married and so she had straight away rebuffed any advances they might have made, never encouraging them in any way. Pleasant though she continued to be, she'd always made it clear the men were just customers to be served.

Then Eddie had arrived, an Irish man with a Yankee swagger, all charming and agreeable, with a host of tales to tell. And, most important of all, he was single – for Angela had established that from the beginning. Paddy suspected that there was more to what had gone on with Stan and that had made Angela vulnerable, but whatever had happened it obviously couldn't be mended and so eventually she'd taken up with Eddie. Whereas at first Paddy had not had any qualms about the two of them forming a friendship, a few months down the line he had reservations. He couldn't have explained them to anyone else, didn't understand them himself, but he had been a publican a long time and as a publican he soon got the measure of people. He knew while there might be nothing basically wrong with Eddie, he wasn't for Angela.

Eddie had encouraged her to drink alcohol when she never had before and, though Paddy recognised that she was an adult and doing nothing wrong, he knew a little alcohol would have soon gone to her head. He had been shocked when Breda told him what had ailed Angela that morning and that it had been Eddie who had encouraged her to drink, and had felt relieved when Breda went on to say that Angela had decided to stick to lemonade in future.

He fully approved of that and so made sure he, rather than Angela, served Eddie, thus effectively keeping them apart most of the evening. Angela at first was a bit irritated for she was a grown woman and, whatever Breda had told him, he still shouldn't treat her like a child. She knew what had happened between her and Eddie shouldn't happen again unless they were married, and she would have to speak to Eddie about that. But the previous night had not been Eddie's fault alone and so Paddy had no right to keep them apart in this way.

Eventually, seeing the landlord busy with another customer, Eddie sidled up to the bar.

'What will you have to drink?' he said, and even his voice caused the hair to stand out on the back of Angela's neck. When he put his hand over hers as he spoke, a tingle ran all the way up her arm. Eddie knew the effect he was having on Angela and, when their eyes met and he smiled at her suggestively, yearning shafts of desire so filled her being they caused her to tremble slightly . She had the urge to leap over the counter and kiss Eddie until she was breathless.

'What?' Angela said, for the intensity of emotions she was experiencing had driven everything else from her head.

'I asked you if you wanted a drink?' Eddie said. 'Port and lemon, is it?'

'No, just a lemonade, please.'

Paddy had heard what Eddie had said and moved towards them. 'Angela will have a lemonade,' he said.

Eddie ignored Paddy and said to Angela, 'Don't you want something a little stronger? You're a big girl now.'

'Lemonade she asked for and so lemonade it is,' Paddy said firmly and poured it out for Angela.

Eddie was affronted. 'She's not a child, Paddy, as I said. She should be able to decide for herself.'

'She did decide for herself and wanted lemonade,' Paddy insisted.

'No she didn't,' Eddie said. 'You decided for her.'

'Will you both stop talking about me as if I'm not here,' Angela said. 'And just at the moment I want lemonade and that's all there should be to it.'

Eddie said nothing further, but he was frustrated, because he wanted Angela compliant and willing for sex that night. He'd had a wire that day saying his uncle was ailing and he needed him back home pronto to see to things till he was back on his feet. He wanted something to remember Angela by and he knew she was capable of giving him that all right if he had her in the right mind, and that was usually when she had been drinking.

Angela seemed odd that night, and he put that down to the shame he knew she must have felt in the cold light of day, having been so wanton the night before. Even he had been surprised because, though he knew it was drink-fuelled, he'd seldom seen a girl as filled with lust as she had been. He was longing for closing time when he would have the opportunity to hold her close, kissing her and caressing her in the partial privacy of the alleyway to her house as they had done many times before. His limbs actually trembled at the anticipation of such delights awaiting him and so he was surprised that, when time was called, she said she didn't need anyone walking her home that night.

Eddie couldn't understand her, but Angela really didn't know if she was strong enough to resist Eddie and behave properly. She didn't know what was the matter with her because she had never felt this way for a man before – even, God forgive her, her own dear husband, Barry. Eddie was the first person she thought of when she opened her eyes in the morning and her excitement at seeing him mounted through the day.

If she was working, she waited on tenterhooks for him to appear. He always sat by the bar and if his hand brushed against Angela's she would feel a quiver run through her whole body. She often had to fight the urge to clasp his hand and lay it against her cheek, to kiss his fingers one by one. Then there was the more intense kissing and caressing they enjoyed in the alleyway to Angela's door as she made her way home after her shift.

Eddie was well aware how Angela felt about him and so he struggled to be civil and not betray his anger as he said, 'Are you sure, Angela? It's bitterly cold out there. I could at least keep you warm till you reach home.'

Warm? Angela felt as if she were on fire. Even his nearness was affecting her, and his voice. She longed for his touch and yet was afraid what she would do if he did put his hands on her body. She had to make him see that what had happened yesterday should not have happened and mustn't happen again. She felt a bit of a hypocrite because truthfully what she wanted was to repeat that wondrous experience, but she must resist that. Breda said it was the drink she'd had that caused her to forget herself, but she didn't know if that was true or not and so she said quite sharply, 'Thank you, Eddie, but that really won't be necessary tonight. I'm very tired.'

Paddy was confused. Eddie had always taken Angela home and he'd never seen any harm in it, but something had clearly happened between them. Though Breda had been unusually cagey about the details, it was obvious that that night at least Angela didn't want Eddie walking her home. And no reason she should put up with the nuisance of him if she didn't want to, so he said to Eddie, 'You heard the lady. Now you just sling your hook.'

Eddie had no option but to leave, but as he did so resentment fuelled the pulse in his head, which had started to beat incessantly. When that happened he knew he was liable to fly into a violent temper. Still, he knew better than to start on Paddy Larkin and with a dismissive wave to Angela he made for the door.

Before Paddy let Angela out a little while later, he cast his eyes up and down the street to see if Eddie was lurking about outside, but there was no sign of him. He turned to Angela with a smile and said, 'Coast's clear, lass.'

'Good,' Angela said fervently, 'I can't wait to put my head on my pillow.'

Paddy watched Angela's slight figure as she hurried through the night, illuminated now and then in the glow from the street lights. Eventually though, Paddy could see her no more and he shut and bolted the door. He thought it might be easier just to bar Eddie altogether, for all he was a good customer. On the other hand, he was well liked by many of the regulars so there were bound to be questions asked. In addition, many knew about the relationship that had developed between Angela and Eddie and they might draw their own conclusions. Then she could easily become the subject of gossip, even scandal, which was the very thing he was trying to avoid. No, he thought as he made his weary way to bed, he'd best leave things as they were and keep a weather eye on Angela.

Even as Angela hurried for her house, the cold of the night eating into her, she tried to be relieved Eddie hadn't waited for her. She was wondering what on earth was the matter with her that she felt disappointed Eddie hadn't waited. She had to admit he aroused feelings in her she hadn't known she had. She really had to be straight with him as soon as possible. She knew she had to be careful how to word things so that he wouldn't be hurt or disappointed, and she decided to give some thought to it in the morning when her head would be clearer.

Angela reached her own alleyway without incident and she sighed as she turned into it. But someone was there before her and suddenly her way was blocked. One arm encircled her and the other hand covered her mouth as a well-known voice said, 'Ssh, don't scream!'

Angela's eyes opened wide, though Eddie couldn't see that in the dimness of the alley, nor could he see them flashing in anger. But he heard the fury in her voice as she tore his hand from her mouth and snapped out, 'Eddie, what the hell are you playing at? I nearly had a heart attack.'

'Just waiting to see you,' Eddie said. 'Can't get near you in the pub with old man Larkin. Think he wants you for himself.'

'Paddy's not like that,' Angela said. 'He's just looking out for me. He reminds me in that way of George Maitland I used to work for when I was a girl. He was paternal too.'

'Paternal my arse,' Eddie spat out. 'Men like that are hoping to get their leg over, trust me.'

Angela opened her mouth to protest and Eddie broke in angrily, 'In the pub tonight he kept us apart good and proper and you didn't seem to mind. Thought you might have gone off me.' He lowered his voice to a husky whisper that made Angela feel weak at the knees. 'But then I knew you couldn't really have gone off me after what we shared last night.'

He drew her towards him as he spoke and opened her

coat so she could feel the bulge in his trousers. One hand sneaked up her jumper and cupped her breast as he went on, 'I'm sure Paddy and Breda would be shocked at your behaviour yesterday. Shall I tell them you couldn't seem to get enough sex yesterday? Begging for it, you were. You were utterly shameless and still are. Loving what I am doing to you and wanting me to do more.'

While Angela was still in semi-control she struggled to get out of Eddie's arms. But it was useless for Eddie just held her tighter.

'Oh yes,' he went on. 'People would love to hear how the prim and proper Angela McClusky is so filled with lust, she is little more than a tramp.'

'Eddie, please . . .'

'Oh, yes,' Eddie said threateningly. 'I could tell them all and destroy you and yours.'

Before she was able to reply Eddie's lips were on hers, his tongue snaking in and out of her mouth, and then he was kissing her throat and her neck and then her lips. Angela felt her body responding even while she burned with humiliation, for every word Eddie said was true. If he spoke of it he would be believed and her name and her daughter's would be dragged through the mud.

Despite this, her body was betraying her and when they eventually broke away she was panting. Angela had heard Paddy say that you needed to keep an eye on Eddie as he had a temper and that night she felt it emanating from him. But he had never been anything other than kind, gentle and supportive to her, so she thought it was his way of teasing her, of joking about what he could do, but with no intention of doing it.

'You're right, Eddie,' she said, 'I was shameless and I have been barely able to live with myself today when I remember what I did. You wouldn't tell anyone though, Eddie, sure you wouldn't.'

Eddie heard the tremor in Angela's voice and almost smelt her fear and smiled, but it was too dark for Angela to see that the smile never reached his eyes as he said, 'I might be persuaded not to if you were nice enough to me.'

Angela felt a tremor of unease run through her. She knew what Eddie meant and couldn't comply. She wasn't sure how he would react when she made that plain to him.

She was unaware of the fury coursing through Eddie that had been roused by Paddy Larkin's protectiveness. In the many dalliances he'd had with women, he was always the one who called the shots, not them. That was a lesson he would have enjoyed teaching Angela McClusky if he wasn't being called back to America as soon as he could arrange a passage.

All he wanted was her compliance. He wasn't asking much, for he knew she wanted sex as much as he did.

'And,' he said, 'I'd like a little kiss for a start.'

Angela hid the sigh as she went into Eddie's arms almost reluctantly, for his kisses caused strange yearnings in her body that Barry's kisses had never done. She felt guilty for comparing them, for Barry had been her one true love while Eddie . . . she didn't really know what she thought of Eddie. But while one part of her enjoyed his kisses and, if she was honest with herself, always wanted more, another part felt slightly alarmed by them and the power they seemed to have over her.

Almost as soon as their lips met Angela felt the familiar

tingling beginning in her body. When Eddie, holding her tight against him, prised her lips apart and thrust his tongue into her mouth, kissing her hungrily, carnal shafts of pure desire shot through her. Eddie felt it too and knew Angela was sinking, bending to his will.

And he was right. Angela was responding, she couldn't help herself, nor the moans that came unbidden that she tried to suppress. Then one of Eddie's hands was fondling her bare breast while the other was caressing between her legs. She was fully aroused and she moaned in the ecstasy of it. She felt she was drowning and she wanted to ignore the little voice of reason battering in her head because the need to have this man inside her was almost overwhelming.

Almost, but not totally. For an instant she saw again the cold dark night when she left her vulnerable baby on the workhouse steps. She knew that could never happen again and yet it took a superhuman effort to bring the kiss to a halt and push Eddie away from her. She stood before him, breathless with the desire that still flowed through her, her body aching to be touched, caressed, stroked and loved.

Eddie was so angry and frustrated he could barely speak. His manhood was as hard as a steel rod and the pulse began again to beat in his head and suddenly he wanted to destroy Angela. He had been just minutes from taking her and she wanted it as much as he did and showed it in every rapturous bone in her body.

'What the hell are you playing at?' he ground out.

'I'm . . . I'm sorry. I can't . . .'

'What d'you mean, you can't?' Eddie demanded. 'I have to go back to America in a few days and I want some beautiful memories to take with me.'

White-hot fury consumed him. All this time she had been teasing him, just like all women did, and now she thought he was going to take no for an answer. He grabbed her by the collar of her blouse and his other hand shot out and slapped her so hard across the face, her head snapped back and cracked against the rough wall. She gave a cry of alarm and pain and her hand flew to her face as hot scalding tears gushed from her eyes down her reddened cheek. She tasted blood in her mouth – the power of the slap was such she had bitten into her cheek.

Eddie had already started to move away from her as he barked out, 'You bloody stupid slut.'

Angela's head was reeling and for the first time she felt really scared of Eddie. She couldn't understand what she had done to make him so angry and wanted to ask him but her fear of him was so great her teeth began to chatter even as the tears continued to fall.

She remembered oh so vividly an assault like this years before and she recoiled as Eddie came nearer, folding her arms over her head in an effort to protect her face. He tore her hands away and Angela flinched, expecting another blow, but instead he spat out, 'You slack-mouthed whore.'

He knew the smack he had given her would probably remind her of that other assault and he spat out, 'No wonder you were raped, those soldiers knew that you wanted it really, because lust oozes out of you. Course it might not have been a rape at all. There would have been no need, for you would have opened your legs for free and taken joy in it. You're a dirty bitch and all the other street tramps are welcome to take you.'

He gave her an almighty push so that she fell back, her

head hitting the brick wall again with a crack. She crumpled in a heap on to the besmirched and grimy cobblestones.

Angela was stunned by the blow to her head, but she breathed a sigh of relief as her bleary eyes saw Eddie walk up the alleyway and out into the night without a backward glance. It was eerily silent as the sound of footsteps faded away and suddenly she wanted to be inside her own house and safe where no one could hurt her any more.

She scrambled to her feet and almost fell in the door, tripping over the step and ripping her lisle stockings and grazing both knees in her haste to be in. Once inside, with the door fastened and bolted behind her, she sat before the deadened fire despite the chill in the room and tried to make sense of what had just happened. Every bit of her ached. There was a throbbing pain in her head, a gnawing twinge in her neck where it had been wrenched back, her knees were bloodied, her cheek smarted and stung, and she was sobbing in fear, pain and confusion.

It was as the tears turned to dry, hiccupping sobs that she became aware of the intense cold and began to shiver. Groggily, she got to her feet and in the mirror above the fire she saw that, as well as her red swollen cheek, both eyes looked bleary and unfocussed. The one above her damaged cheek was particularly red and puffy. Her lip on that side was split open too and the blood from that and the blood and mucus seeping from one nostril mixed with the tears. Eddie had made one unholy mess of her face and she was at a loss to know how to repair the damage before the morning.

Eventually she decided to fill a bowl with water from the kettle and, with chattering teeth, dabbed gently at her face to at least clear up the smeared blood, then pulled off her ruined stockings and dabbed at her grazed knees. She was careful to be quiet so as not to wake Connie; if her daughter saw her now Angela had no idea how she would explain any of this to her.

She was longing to lie down somewhere warm and soft and she made for the stairs, cautiously stumbling across the room towards them as if she was indeed as drunk as a lord. She felt emotionally drained and not at all steady on her feet. She was also dazed by the bangs to her head and the stairs swayed in front of her eyes. She made the bedroom only by hauling herself up and leaning heavily on the banister. When she eventually got to her room, she lay down on the bed in her shift, because she couldn't face undressing, and sighed in relief.

The fact that Eddie, her sensual Eddie, who had taken her to heights of exquisite sexual pleasure she had never experienced before, had assaulted her just as the drunken soldiers had all those years ago kept reverberating in her head. She couldn't understand why he had changed from lover to abuser so quickly and where the anger had come from.

The soldiers had got away with the assault and Angela knew Eddie would probably get away with doing a similar thing too. If she revealed to anyone what had happened, it might be worse for all concerned. She knew Paddy would believe her and could easily feel so strongly about it that he might take Eddie to task and then he might be the one in trouble. She couldn't take that risk. Nor could she take the risk that Eddie would tell Paddy about what a sex-crazed harlot she was, filled with lust and wanton for sex. So she decided it was better to say nothing.

She slept fitfully that night and when she did eventually fall into a deeper sleep she was wakened by a nightmare of the attack by the three drunken soldiers. After the attack, and for some time afterwards, she'd had horrific and terrifying nightmares almost every night so that she was afraid of going to sleep. Over the years the bad dreams had eased considerably and eventually stopped altogether, but now they were back to the forefront of her mind again and she was afraid to let herself relax enough to go to sleep after that. She was almost glad when the night ended and she could get up, though she felt like a piece of chewed string and her movements were ponderous and slow and her eyes gritty with lack of sleep.

She thanked the Lord that she left for work before Connie got up for school. She knew she would have to use the face powder that she kept for high days and holidays very skilfully so that Paddy didn't ask any awkward questions. And she hoped Breda would do what she normally did and stay upstairs, because she doubted she could fool her with some tale about walking into a door.

As she made her way to work, she was glad too that it was very early and winter, so it was still cold and dark. Those few people she met, hurrying to work as she was, would not think it strange that she had her scarf pulled down to her eyes and another wrapped around her mouth. She greeted Paddy as she went in and set to work right away. He was always busy in the mornings and so he never really had a chance to see her face. Breda stayed upstairs and Angela left work thankful that Breda was taking the lunchtime shift and the first person she'd have to encounter would be Connie when she came home from school.

Powder could only do so much disguising and Connie stared at her as she came in from school and said directly, 'What happened to you?'

Angela had her story ready. 'I tripped up in the alleyway and hit my head on the side of the house as I went down.'

'Were you drunk?' Connie asked.

Angela was too stunned to reply for a moment or two and then she said quite stiffly, 'No, I was not drunk. What a thing to ask.'

Connie gazed at her mother dispassionately for a moment or two and then said, 'I think that's a very reasonable question because you have often come home drunk. I'm not the only one that has noticed either, because Maggie mentioned it to me.'

'When did you see Maggie?'

'Coming home from school yesterday,' Connie said. 'She was doing some shopping in Bristol Street.'

'You didn't mention it.'

'No,' Connie said. 'No, no, I didn't, because I was too embarrassed and ashamed of the things she asked me to say anything at all to tell you the truth. She told me that people have been gossiping about you, about the way you've been gallivanting around with that Eddie fella, but I couldn't bring myself to say it to you.'

Angela gave a sigh, knowing that Connie wasn't a child any more and could be fobbed off no longer. She deserved some explanation for her mother's behaviour.

'All right,' she said. 'Connie, you are old enough now to hear the truth about these last few months. Don't judge me too harshly because parents, mothers, make mistakes too, but I am sorry if that has affected you in any way.'

Connie listened to her mother as she explained that the attraction of Eddie in the first place had been the fact that he came from New York, the city two of her foster brothers had drowned trying to reach, and that he had entertaining stories to tell that often made her laugh.

'Everyone liked him and he liked me and he asked me out once and I said no. Then one day I thought, "Why not?" I was single and so was he and I was lonely.'

'Hope you're not implying this is my fault.'

'Of course not. I'm just telling it as it is,' Angela said. 'I told you before that we went for a walk in Cannon Hill Park and on the way back we went for a drink.'

Connie's eyes narrowed. 'And you know already that's not something a respectable woman would do,' she said incredulously. 'How many women do you serve in a week at the Swan, Mammy?'

'The Swan's different.'

'No it isn't,' Connie snapped. She didn't understand why her mother seemed not to realise that the worst thing a woman, especially a mother, could do was frequent a public house and drink. Any man, even a father, could drink and as much as he liked. Her granny used to tell her of Maggie's father who would often go along the road singing after a session at the Swan on a Friday and Saturday night and no one thought any the worse of him for that. Even if a man beat up his wife, no one interfered and the wife would usually put up with it, saying it was just how the drink took some men and that was that.

However, no women except the lowest of the low drank, never mind got drunk.

Connie faced her mother and said, 'You get drunk and

don't bother denying it. How could you have any respect for yourself when you behave like that?'

Angela flushed and thought if Connie knew the half of what she had got up to with Eddie when she was drunk her daughter would likely never speak to her again. Connie didn't know it, however, and thankfully there was little likelihood of her ever finding out. Angela felt a wave of shame hit her. How could she have been so blinded by Eddie and allowed herself to get so carried away? If only she and Stan had never fallen out, things could have been so different, but ever since then things had been just awful.

Angela saw contempt flood over Connie's face and, in an attempt to exonerate herself said, 'I know I shouldn't have been drinking at all but it wasn't that I drank loads. It was just that it affected me more because I wasn't used to it.'

'Yes, but that only works for the first time,' Connie said. 'Or maybe the second time. By then you must have known the effect it was having on you and you should have stopped, but I know you didn't do that because I was seldom asleep when you came home.'

'I'm sorry, Connie,' Angela said. 'Truthfully, I had two glasses of lemonade last night and that is all, honestly. And that's what I am going to stick to in future and Eddie McIntyre is going back to the States again soon anyway.'

Connie had never met Eddie McIntyre and had no interest in doing so. She didn't think he was a good influence on her mother and hoped he would stay in America for a very long time, though she didn't share that with her mother.

NINETEEN

Later that same evening Breda took one look at Angela taking off her coat and unwinding her scarf from around her face in the cloakroom at the back of the pub and grabbed her by the arm. She dragged her into the snug, which was fortunately empty.

'Who did this to you?' she demanded. 'Was it Eddie?'

Angela nodded dumbly and Breda winced.

'Oh you poor thing,' she said, and the sympathy in her voice caused the tears to stand out in Angela's eyes. 'What happened?'

Angela told Breda that Eddie had been waiting for her in the alleyway after Paddy had sent him packing earlier and that she didn't really know why he had been so cross with her. The aggression that had spiralled into violence began when she tried to stop him molesting her. She had tried to explain to him that the way she had behaved the previous evening had been shameful, and not the way she would behave normally. She had told him that it could only have come about because of the drink she had consumed.

Breda nodded. 'And?'

'He reacted badly. Really badly,' Angela said. 'Said he'd spread rumours about me.'

When Angela told her the type of thing Eddie had been threatening, Breda knew how fearful Angela must have been. Eddie was amusing and charming, a seemingly genial man and popular with all the regulars, and what he said about Angela would be believed. She had heard of men who had done this kind of thing before and Breda had always half-suspected that there was this nasty side to him. It was a vile thing to do and could destroy a woman totally; she'd known of women driven out of the area by enraged wives, worried about the temptation for their husbands. And all too often these women were not bad women at all – they might have made a mistake and gone further with a man than they intended, or possibly formed an unsavoury relationship, but that was sometimes all it took. If a man was determined to sully a woman's reputation this way there wasn't any way of counteracting it, and Angela would know that too.

'What was the payment Eddie demanded to keep his lips sealed?' Breda asked, though really she already knew the answer.

'Sex,' Angela said in a shame-filled voice.

'God,' Breda said fervently. 'Isn't he off back to America soon? Let's hope he stays there and hasn't left a little seed behind to deal with.'

'How would we deal with it?'

'Let's cross that bridge if and when we come to it,' Breda said. 'No man should get away with doing what he did to you,' she exclaimed. 'You and me will go to the police and . . .'

'No police, Breda,' Angela said. 'You know the list of lies Eddie would tell them and how plausible he is. He would be believed before I was. In their eyes I would be a brazen hussy and therefore getting no more than I deserved. Nothing would happen to Eddie, who might behave worse afterwards, and my reputation would be in tatters for he would spread that tale wide too.'

Breda didn't argue further with Angela for she knew she spoke the truth. It was sad and totally unfair, but that's how it was. What she did say was, 'Well all right, but you can't go behind the bar like that. There'll be talk and supposition and rumour and you can do without any of those. Take three days off – your face will be more or less back to normal by then, or near enough that you'll be able to disguise it with cosmetics.'

'What will you tell everyone?'

'That you are down with a bad cold,' Breda said. 'Now get yourself away before the pub starts to fill and go out through the side door because there's less likelihood of you being spotted.'

'All right,' Angela said, but before she closed the door behind her she said, 'I think it might be better not to tell Paddy. He might feel like teaching Eddie a lesson or something and then he'd be the one in trouble.'

Breda had every intention of telling Paddy, but she said to Angela, 'Don't fret yourself. Go home and rest. It's the best thing for you.'

Once out in the street though, Angela decided not to go straight home. Connie would not be expecting her and she thought she would call in on Maggie. She seldom had much free time and she knew Maggie too was a very busy person.

In fact, her friend had found she was busier than ever now since her mother-in-law had had a stroke and was bedridden.

When Maggie opened the door, Angela was glad but she looked around nervously. She knew she had to tell Maggie everything and didn't want to do that in front of Michael or indeed any of Maggie's lodgers. Maggie understood immediately.

'Let's go through to the kitchen for we have the place to ourselves at least for a wee while. The chaps are fed and watered and are probably in their rooms changing to go out, which they do most evenings, and Michael is in with his mother. She seemed particularly restless this evening. Sometimes he reads her snippets out of the paper but if he is in there a long time I have a peep in and often find him asleep in the chair with the paper discarded on the floor.'

She smiled fondly and then, as they'd reached the kitchen, opened the door to the side which led to a cloakroom and went on, 'Take off your coat and scarf or you'll not feel the benefit when you go out and the nights can be raw.'

Angela unwound the scarves almost covering her face and Maggie just stood and stared at her face, aghast.

'What happened to you?' she cried. 'Were you attacked again, you poor thing?'

'Not exactly.'

Maggie knew that this was the reason Angela had come, to tell her of some heinous thing that had befallen her. Taking her by the arm, she propelled her into the kitchen and sat her down at the table.

'Stay there and I'll put the kettle on.'

She disappeared into the scullery and came out minutes later with the teapot and cups on a tray.

'I . . . I don't want to put you out.'

'You're not,' Maggie assured her as she poured tea for them both. 'The evenings about this time are probably the best time to catch me having a minute to myself and of course I'm delighted to see you, though not looking like this.'

Angela said nothing and into the silence before it should become uncomfortable Maggie said, 'Your Connie's growing into a fine girl. She is surely a daughter to be proud of and the image of you. Did she mention I met her in Bristol Street the other evening?'

Angela nodded. 'Connie is not very friendly with me just now. She told me she met you tonight just before I left for work. But Breda wouldn't let me serve behind the bar with my battered face. She's given me three nights off. I'm supposed to have a heavy cold.'

'Did Connie tell you what we spoke about?'

'She did, yes.'

'And did what I said to Connie have any bearing on what has happened to you?'

'In a way,' Angela said.

And then it came out in a rush like a torrent: the whole sordid tale of her relationship with Eddie McIntyre. Angela had her head bowed, but her speech was rapid, as if she couldn't bear to hold it in any longer. She needed to share it with the only other person who knew what she had gone through already. Angela told the tale to the end and even as she recounted it, leaving nothing out, she burned with humiliation at how depraved it all sounded, especially as she had to admit that she had been a willing partner too.

'Now,' she said to Maggie, lifting her head as the tale

eventually drew to a close, 'aren't you shocked to the core? Don't you feel ashamed that you once called me a friend?'

Maggie reached across the table and grasped Angela's trembling hands.

'I didn't once call you a friend as if our friendship was at an end,' she said. 'I am still your friend and can't think of anything you could do to change that. What's more, I'm proud to be that friend.'

The flush on Angela's cheeks deepened as she pulled her hands free and said, 'You can't feel the same way about me after the things I have done.'

'Yeah, and things that you never would have consented to if you had been in your right mind,' Maggie said. 'Your problem is that you have had no experience with men.'

'How can you say that, Maggie? I grew up with five foster brothers and married one of them.'

'Yes, and they thought of you as their little sister and treated you as such, even Barry initially,' Maggie said. 'And when you agreed to marry Barry, did he excite your senses in any way?'

'Well, yes, because I loved him so, you see.'

'I know, but did he do anything to make those feelings stronger, touch you in any intimate way? Kiss you passionately or anything like that?'

Angela remembered in a flash how Eddie's kisses had made her feel, as if she had been transported to another plane where the rules and regulations she had lived her life by had ceased to matter, and she said to Maggie, 'Barry treated me with respect. He knew I was young and so he was gentle and kind and never asked me to do anything I might consider improper.'

And made you ripe for someone like this Eddie McIntyre, Maggie thought, but what she said to Angela was: 'Listen to me, people like Eddie McIntyre prey on naïve girls like you – and you are naïve, despite the fact you have been married and had a child. It's common for men like that to use alcohol to make a girl more malleable. God, it must have been like a gift for him when you told him you didn't drink, for he knew only a relatively small amount would affect you and he took advantage of that.'

'Breda sort of said that too,' Angela said. 'But I can't get Mammy's words out of my head.'

'What words were they?'

'She said that what's in a man sober comes out when he is drunk, so what if I really am that wanton hussy inside? And you know what tears me apart? Eddie actually said that those soldiers that attacked me recognised that lustful side of me and that is why they abused and raped me the way they did. He said they didn't have to rape me either – because lust oozes out of me, I would have done it for free and enjoyed it because I am sex-crazed.'

'Angela, you are not and you can't allow the man's hateful, cruel words that he threw at you to make you think this way.'

'Oh I can, do you see, because if it was somehow my fault I should have owned up to it and not have left a wee baby to pay the price.'

'Stop it, Angela,' Maggie said quite sharply for she saw Angela's wide, panicky eyes and heard the shrill note in her voice and knew hysteria wasn't far away. 'I have known you since we were both five and went through school together. When war began and Barry was enlisted, we worked side by side in the munitions factory. I know you better than any Eddie McIntyre and I'll tell you what I think. You were probably lonely, for there was that rift between Stan and Daniel that seems unbridgeable. Connie is probably working too hard to be any company for you and you probably missed me just being up the road for, busy as I am, I missed you a great deal. And you were maybe flattered by this man's attention because he was well-liked and entertaining.

'So you were attracted to him and that's not a crime, but McIntyre used that attraction to encourage you to drink and that made you act in a way you never would have done if you had been sober. Whatever Mary said, there are no carnal desires buried deep inside you, though it is normal to yearn after a man. I still do after Michael now and it was hard sometimes to put the brakes on when we were courting and I wanted him just as much as he wanted me, but we were both in agreement to leave it till the marriage bed. So I know how powerful sexual attraction is. If your defences are down because of the amount you have drunk and the man is not helping you to resist, but instead exciting you to heights of passion you possibly had never reached before, oh Angela it would be almost impossible to stop when you are in the throes of it.'

Angela stared at her friend. She had described so accurately how powerless and out of control she'd felt, consumed by an insatiable passion that demanded some sort of release. 'That's just how it was.'

'Did you ever let him take you completely?' Maggie asked.

Angela nodded.

'I hope to God there are no repercussions to this,' Maggie said. 'That man took advantage of you.'

'No, Maggie, he didn't,' Angela said. 'I would like to say that he did, even that he forced me, and then you wouldn't think the worst of me, but I have to admit I was as mad for it as he was. I could no more have stopped him entering me then than I could have stopped the sun from shining.'

And because that would be the last thing a sober Angela would allow herself to do with anyone, Maggie said quietly, 'And the next day?'

Angela gave a shudder. 'Oh God, the next day I was so hungover I thought I would die,' she said. 'But after I told Eddie I couldn't do that sort of thing any more, he threatened to spout rumours about me.

'And I wouldn't be able to deny them with any conviction because he would be more or less right. I was mortified with shame because, no matter how drunk I had been, those memories were stark and clear. And this is the terrifying thing, Maggie: though I know what I did was terribly wrong, it was the most truly wondrous experience I have ever had. And that's why I think I am rotten, wantonness is running all through me.'

'It's not a sin to enjoy sex,' Maggie said. 'Ideally it's supposed to be like that. Well, very pleasurable anyway. Did you and Barry . . .'

'I loved sex with Barry, don't think I didn't,' Angela said. 'But we called it "making love" and there is a difference. That's what we did – showed the love we shared and gave pleasure to each other and it felt good, quite beautiful, but nothing like the sex I had with Eddie. And I'll tell you something, Maggie, if Eddie has made me pregnant it will be my fault as well as his and I will rear the child and put up with the shame. The hardest thing in the world is giving birth to a child and not being able to rear it.'

'Remember why you did that?' Maggie said. 'It was to prevent Barry hearing that you had given birth to a bastard child. I know Barry died anyway but he died loving you with all his heart. What if the words on a letter from some old busybody telling Barry of your unfaithfulness caused his death through despair, carelessness?'

'I know,' Angela said. She thought of the three spinsters who she was fairly certain had sent Barry the three white feathers that had prompted him to go down almost immediately to the recruitment office and sign his name on the dotted line. They were just the sort of people who would think it their bounden Christian duty to inform Barry of his wife's infidelity. Even if she'd attempted to tell them of the attack on her, they were the sort to never let the truth get in the way of a good gossipy, scandal-ridden story.

'Then I had Mary to think about,' Angela said. 'And little Connie and the job I needed. Oh, they were all good reasons, and there was nothing else I could have done, but I will never totally forgive myself, even though I did go to the workhouse later and they sent me away.'

'I know,' Maggie said. 'I never thought I would be the one advising you to do that dreadful thing. I feel a measure of guilt as well. Anyway, when Hilda had her stroke in the summer I went into the hospital with her. I was talking to one of the nurses and she was telling me what will be happening to the workhouse, and very soon too.'

'What's that?'

'You know they've enlarged the infirmary as it isn't big enough to house all the patients? They had plans to build a new hospital on the site and empty the workhouse and I said to you not to worry because it would take them ages to have enough money to build.'

Angela nodded again and Maggie continued, 'They must have thought the same way about the cost and thought it would be quicker and cheaper to enlarge this one at present used as a workhouse.'

'So what will happen to the inmates of the workhouse?'

'The nurse wasn't absolutely sure but said adults would probably be sent to other workhouses around the city some-where and the children housed in orphanages.'

Angela felt as if the bottom had dropped out of her world and she wondered why the news had affected her so much. It wasn't as if she ever had contact with the daughter she had abandoned, but it had been some comfort to know where she was.

She'd often had a vague notion of maybe being able to help her one day. In her heart of hearts she knew it was pure fantasy – she hadn't an idea of the child, not what she was called, what she looked like, what sort of personality and character she had. And then in the middle of this fantasy would appear the three leering faces of the brutal, drunken soldiers who beat her up soundly before violating her. Was it possible this child brought up without a mother's love and gentling influence could have any traits of the man who had fathered her?

'Are you all right?' Maggie almost whispered. She was so fearful for her friend, for she had watched the thoughts tumble around her head, her face twisted in anguish at the memories she knew never left her.

Angela shook her head. 'Sometimes I wonder if I will ever

feel all right again. I go through the motions, that's all. Did the nurse know when these alterations were going to take place?'

'Only vaguely,' Maggie said. 'It was supposed to be the autumn but it's been put back to the New Year because of finding places for the inmates before work can start. But I thought the news might upset you.'

'It did, and yet I have no right to be upset or care what happened to that child at all. I gave those rights away when I left a poor helpless baby on the workhouse steps.'

'You can't turn feelings off like that though,' Maggie said.

'No, but I have no right to acknowledge them,' Angela said and gave a sudden sob that took her by surprise. Maggie held her tight and let her cry because it was all she could do for her.

She left Maggie's when she had recovered herself a bit, though she felt emotionally battered and the pain was far worse from that than from any physical injuries inflicted by Eddie McIntyre.

Breda called to see her the next morning just before it was time to open the pub. She had a smile on her face as she stepped into the room and without any preamble she said to Angela, 'McIntyre's has gone back to the States by all accounts. Neither of us have to worry about him one minute longer.'

'Are you sure?' she asked Breda.

Angela couldn't understand why she felt regret that she would never see him again mixed with the relief. She did hope she was truly done with him though and he had not made her pregnant. But time would tell and there was no

311

point worrying about it until she knew one way or the other.

Breda nodded grimly. 'I'm sure all right. So draw a line under Eddie McIntyre, put the madness he seemed to induce in you down to experience, and let's hope and bloody pray we will be allowed to do that.'

TWENTY

Angela was glad to go back to work, though it took her a few days to stop looking up each time the door opened to see if it was Eddie. Then one evening in mid-November a stranger walked up to the bar.

'Hallo, Angela.'

Angela's head shot round at the American drawl with the definite New York accent.

'Harry,' she cried. 'What are you doing here?'

Harry smiled. 'I'm here for a pint of your warm beer and looking for you,' he said with a smile.

'Why?' Angela said as she pulled the pint and passed it across the bar counter.

Before Harry could answer, Paddy approached. After the incident with Eddie McIntyre, her boss was even more protective of Angela than ever. Angela introduced him with a brief explanation as to who he was and Paddy saw immediately that, though Harry too was American like Eddie McIntyre, he was a far more suitable man for Angela to be friends with. Angela could see Paddy was impressed with Harry's manners and the way he called him 'Sir' as he shook him by the hand, but she was astounded when he said, 'It's quiet enough tonight, so why don't you take your friend into the snug and have a proper chat.'

'Are you sure, Paddy?'

'Quite sure,' Paddy said and added with a grim smile, 'Now get yourself away before I change my mind.'

'You must have a drink,' Harry said.

'Just a lemonade,' Angela said with a look at Paddy. Harry didn't urge her to have something stronger but bought the lemonade and carried the glass and his pint into the small room to the side of the pub.

'The snug is a good name for this place,' Harry said, looking round.

'Yes, it's not that well used,' Angela admitted, sitting down at one of the leather-topped tables. Harry sat beside her as she said, 'Now tell me why you came looking for me. Did . . . did Stan send you?'

'No,' Harry said. 'I came to ask you something which I should have asked you a long while ago, but I didn't know how things stood with you and Stan. I knew there had been some sort of disagreement but disagreements can be fixed all the time.'

'This one can't,' Angela said in a clipped tone.

'So I understand,' Harry said. 'That's why I'm here . . .'

Still Angela waited, her eyes puzzled and a look of expectancy on her face. It was obvious that Harry was nervous. He licked his lips and cleared his throat twice and Angela took pity on him.

'Come on, Harry, out with it, whatever it is. I don't bite.'

'No, and the thing is I'm going back to the States. My

father's heart is not too good,' Harry said. 'Mom wants me home to see to things to take the heat off him. I intend to get there for Thanksgiving.'

'When's that?'

'The fourth Thursday in the month of November. So this month it's the twenty-fourth.'

'So soon,' Angela said. 'What are you doing with the shop, selling it?'

Harry shook his head. 'Stan's taking it on. Now Daniel is settled at college and will be earning before too long, Stan has used his gratuity from the army and savings from his wages to date to buy a partnership.'

'Does Stan know anything about running a shop?'

'He's been helping me out on Saturdays for a while now,' Harry said.

'Yes, Harry, but there's quite a difference from helping out to running the whole show.'

'I know,' Harry said. 'And as soon as this was on the cards I took Stan out and about to meet the suppliers and such, showed him how to order, tot up the books and all. Daniel said he'll give him a hand with the book work.'

'But Stan has a job.'

'Not any more, he hasn't,' Harry said. 'Gave it up a fortnight ago and has been working with me hand and glove since. Foundry work is for a young man. It was getting too much for him.'

'Has he been ill?'

'Not ill,' Harry assured her. 'Just tired, not that he'd admit it, but he likes shop work anyway.'

'I'm really glad it has all worked out for you both,' Angela said. 'But where do I come into all this?'

'Well the thing is . . . I know that this must seem like it's come out of the blue, but I wondered . . . Angela, would you like to come with me – back home to America?'

'What?' Angela cried, for it was the very last thing she had thought Harry would say. 'Me go to America?'

'I mean you no harm, Angela,' Harry said. 'I would make arrangements for you to stay with my parents. They would love to meet you.'

'They don't know me.'

'They know of you,' Harry said. 'Years ago, George used to write to my father about you working in the shop – his "little ray of sunshine", he called you – and when I met you years later I understood why. I wrote to my parents all about you and my mother was astounded when I told her about you driving a large truck full of shells through the busy, traffic-filled Birmingham roads through the war, and then more recently about you driving a truck full of debris and junk from the flat above the shop. She said she'd love to meet such an intrepid woman.'

'Oh, I think she would be sorely disappointed if she met me,' Angela said. 'I hardly think of myself as anything special, let alone intrepid.'

'No one could be disappointed when they met you,' Harry declared stoutly. And then very tentatively he took hold of one of Angela's hands and said earnestly, 'I am very fond of you, Angela.'

'I am fond of you, Harry.'

'Could you be more than fond?' Harry said. 'I don't want to press you, but I think I love you.'

'Dear Harry, I don't think of you that way.'

'Well, could you start thinking of me that way?'

316

'Harry, you are a good and honest man,' Angela said. 'And you deserve someone to love you as much as you love them. Sadly that person can't be me.'

'How about just coming over for a holiday then?' Harry said desperately. 'We can get to know each other a little better. There would be no promises I'd expect from you, but it could be the chance of a new life for you and Connie.'

Suddenly the idea of a new life and a fresh start felt like the answer to all her problems. She could re-establish herself as a respectable widow with a daughter.

But then she wasn't sure Connie would want to go to America and she really had to start considering Connie, for she knew she had ignored and side-lined her when Eddie had been on the scene. She was cool enough with her as it was and she knew it was time to try and build bridges with the daughter she loved so much. Anyway, she remembered that the mad period when she behaved like a little trollop with Eddie McIntyre might have results and she couldn't load that on to Harry.

Harry was anxiously awaiting her reply and she smiled at him. He was a lovely man, and in a way his innate kindness and consideration for others reminded her of Barry, and so she was gentle when she said, 'It is a lovely offer you've made, Harry, but . . .'

'Just give it a try, please?' Harry pleaded. 'You could meet up with your brothers.'

'My brothers are just names on a page to me now,' Angela said. 'It's sad, but they have lived their lives away from me and they have families of their own. They'd hardly want a sister they'd barely remember turning up out of the blue and muddying the waters.'

Harry was disappointed, so disappointed that Angela saw tears lurking behind his eyelashes, and they softened her heart because she hated to upset people. But she knew whatever Harry said, if she did go with him to the States, it would make it worse when she returned home again and he would be more disheartened than ever. It was such a long way to go on a whim.

'I'm truly sorry, Harry,' she said. 'But you may thank me when you arrive in America and meet the girl of your dreams.'

'Too late,' Harry said huskily. 'I've already met her and lost my heart.'

'Oh Harry, I'm sorry.'

Harry drained his pint and took a deep breath. 'If you can't say yes then I wonder if you could do me another favour?'

Angela didn't know what he was going to ask but said anyway, 'Anything, if I can.'

'I know you and Stan have had your differences, but would you be able to look in on him every now and again and see that he's doing all right? You know that shop like the back of your hand, and that experience might prove invaluable to Stan. I know you two have had your differences of late, about which I was truly sorry to hear because I know how much Stan has missed your friendship, but I thought you'd want to know that I was leaving. Stan could do with your help over the next few months.'

Angela didn't know what to say. 'That might be tricky . . . but I'll give it some thought.'

'Goodbye, Angela. I hope we'll see each other again,' said Harry.

'So do I.' And Angela shook his hand as he left.

Angela sat for a moment and did feel bad about both

Harry and what he had said about foundry work being too heavy for Stan. It was a cause for a little concern and she had a hankering to pop into the shop and see for herself how he looked, and to make sure he was all right with the running of the shop. But she didn't because she didn't know that Stan wouldn't order her out of the shop, still nursing his heartache. Best leave him well alone, she thought.

Stan was in fact very busy once Harry had left, and a little lonely too, for he had liked him very much and he had been good company. Harry hadn't told Stan about his hankering after Angela and so Stan put Harry's melancholy down to his regret about leaving for he knew he hadn't wanted to go. Harry was happy to let Stan think that and actually he did feel a pang when he looked around the shop that last morning. He knew his father would be pleased that he had turned old Uncle George's shop around.

'This isn't goodbye, Stan,' Harry had said as he got in the taxi. 'It's just so long. I will be back to see how you're getting on and you write if you have any problems.'

'I will,' Stan had promised. 'Go on now and don't worry about me. Hope your father is as well as can be expected.'

'My mother would have wired me if there had been any change,' Harry said. 'And once I'm home I'll make sure he takes things easier. Won't be easy though. He can be a stubborn old cuss when he wants to be.'

'You'll have to work your charm.'

'Hmph, might have to find it first,' Harry had said and Stan gave a throaty chuckle as Harry shut the door of the taxi and it sped off to New Street, the first leg of his journey to Southampton.

TWENTY-ONE

November gave way to December and, as it did, Angela felt the familiar unhappiness settling on her heart about the child she had left behind in the workhouse. Maggie seemed to think it was good news that her daughter would be moved to an orphanage in the New Year, but Angela hadn't any great hopes that an orphanage would be a whole lot better than the workhouse and it was very hard for her to not even know where in the city the child might be living. Still, there was nothing she could do about any of it and, as Christmas was approaching, she would have to pretend happiness and excitement for Connie's sake. Relations with her eldest daughter had improved somewhat, but the closeness between them had been damaged. Angela knew that was entirely her fault and so she had to fix it.

However, her youngest daughter wasn't in any orphanage or workhouse. Angela had not been the only one dismayed at the council's decision to empty the workhouse and extend the General Hospital, for Father John was upset too. Though he agreed the city's poor needed better and more medical facilities, after hearing the confession of the woman who'd come to his church that day, the orphan Chrissie Foley had preyed on his mind and he had plans concerning the child. After the woman had come to his confessional box, he'd made discreet enquiries about the child left on the steps of the workhouse. Benedict Masters, the governor of the workhouse, told him that, while the children in his care were not encouraged to consider themselves as special or in any way different to other children, Chrissie Foley was indeed a naturally kind and helpful child and was no trouble, unlike some of the others who kicked out at the dreadful restrictions placed upon them. The meals they ate were plain and tasteless at best, they were allowed no play or enjoyment, just sewing or mending tasks when they were not at their lessons. Father John knew that things were better for orphans than they had been when he was a young man, and workhouses would soon be a thing of the past completely, but there were still some like this one that took in the poor, the infirm and the destitute as well as poor mites who had no one, like Chrissie.

He'd intended to talk to his sister about having the girl to live with them when she was twelve and ready for outside work, but he couldn't wait for that now.

So, one evening in early December after a delicious evening meal, Father John told Eileen he wanted to talk to her. Without any preamble, he went straight into his plans for bringing the foundling Chrissie Foley to live with them.

Eileen was astounded. It was so unexpected. 'And what d'you think she would do here?' she asked.

'I thought you could perhaps train her up to be a lady's maid or something.'

Eileen laughed at her brother. 'Of course I couldn't,' she said. 'I don't know the slightest thing about being a lady's maid.'

'Well then, could you have her in the kitchen with you?' John asked. 'You could teach her to cook maybe, then you could take life a bit easier.'

Eileen fastened her eagle eyes on her brother as she snapped out, 'John, I am not in my dotage yet.'

'I didn't suggest you were,' John said.

'Why does this child mean so much to you?'

'You know why,' the priest said. 'I spoke to her mother in confession and so the child should at least be reared as a Catholic as she had a Catholic mother. But that apart, this child will have no one. She has a mother, but one who can't acknowledge her, so she will grow up all her life without knowing a mother's love. She might have a family who will never know of her existence.'

'John, surely she isn't the only child like that.'

'Maybe not,' Father John acknowledged. 'But because of her mother's confession I sort of feel I know this child. I know from what she said that she was no willing party to what happened to her – and yes, before you say anything, I know that that is not a completely rare occurrence either. The point is, I might have been very like Chrissie when our mother died just after I was born, but you were there to care for me and love me and always support me.'

There were tears in Eileen's eyes, for she had indeed tended for her baby brother. There had been no one else, just a rake of older brothers who were more of a hindrance than a help and a father so destroyed with grief he had turned to the bottle and was drink-sodden more often than not. John would have had a poor rearing if she hadn't stepped in.

'I've always appreciated what you did for me,' John said. 'Because of you, I was given a chance to do what I wanted in life. I wanted to do the same for Chrissie, redress the balance a little, but perhaps I am asking too much of you ...'

'How old is the child?' Eileen asked.

'Almost eleven,' Father John answered. 'I've had this in mind for some time, but I wanted to wait until she was twelve. But now, with the closure of the workhouse, by the time Chrissie is twelve she could be anywhere in the city and hard to even trace.'

'Oh, I can see that,' Eileen said. 'If she is coming, it will have to be now, but will they allow you to remove a child just like that?'

'She is in the care of the workhouse to all intents and purposes, but they will want to send her out into the world in a few years to earn her own keep. Perhaps they'd send her to one of the mills or to work in service,' Father John said. 'Even if they really want rid of her because that would mean one less to worry about, they would probably need to ascertain that she was coming to a respectable home and that I have no intention of syphoning her off to the white slave trade.'

'John, really!'

Father John grinned. 'I'm sure you can be a hard taskmaster but not that bad ... maybe! Well, I think Benedict Masters, the governor, can vouch for the fact I won't be into any of that sort of thing. I have got to know the man very well over the years, tending to the Catholics in there, and he is a reasonable man, though he can do nothing to ease the grim interior or the austere life of drudgery many of the inmates are subjected to. He said a few years ago he went to the trustees cap in hand to ask for the allowance for food to be increased, at least for the children, but he was refused. And he said it wouldn't have been so bad but the trustees seem remarkably well fed. Every one of them is plump and portly and when they have a trustees' dinner they are veritable banquets, very lavish, with the very best of food or drink. Yet they wouldn't increase the food bill one brass farthing. He was very frustrated about it, but stays on because he thinks they are better treated with him there rather than somebody more corrupt.'

'I would be concerned too,' Eileen said. 'Any time you spot a workhouse child they look half starved. The first thing I shall have to do with this Chrissie Foley is feed her up, I imagine.'

'Feed her up,' Father John repeated. 'You mean . . .?'

'I mean we'll have the girl here if it means so much to you,' said Eileen. 'And I would see about it as soon as possible, or they might ship her out regardless.'

'I will go early tomorrow,' Father John promised.

So early the next morning, the priest sat on the other side of the desk from the workhouse governor and told him he wished to offer a home to Chrissie Foley. Benedict Masters' mouth dropped open in surprise for he had never had a request like that in his life before. Eventually he recovered himself and said, 'Why would you want to do that?'

'Without betraying my vows, I can only tell you Chrissie's mother came to me in confession two years ago and admitted abandoning Chrissie Foley, who was conceived because of a violent attack made upon her.'

'Did you recognise the voice of this woman?'

The priest shook his head. 'And that means she wasn't one

of my parishioners and the child should have been brought up a Catholic. She tried to leave her in a Catholic orphanage, but they couldn't take any more. She said normally they had plenty of childless couples ready and willing to adopt a child, but due to the war and the men being away – and some women being widowed, I suppose – adoptions had dropped right off. They were full to bursting with children they couldn't place already and could take no more.'

'And you have no idea who this woman was?'

'None,' the priest said. 'I asked her to stay but when I left the confessional she had fled.'

'But even if you did speak to the mother, you are not responsible for her child.'

'I know, but wanting to do something for this child is linked to my past. I could have ended up in a similar position when my mother died when I was born if it hadn't been for my sister Eileen. Surely it is for us to emulate God's grace and do what we can for the needy.'

'And is your sister in favour of this?'

'She is, yes.'

'You do realise this would not be countenanced, a man alone taking a young girl into his home, even if the man was a priest, unless your sister was there in residence too?'

'I understand that perfectly,' Father John said.

'As it is, well, I will put it to the trustees but I can't foresee any problem.'

'Should we ask the child?'

'No need,' Benedict Masters said. 'You are offering her an opportunity to better herself and that is something few found-lings are given. How she feels about it is irrelevant.'

Father John would have preferred to see the child and

explain things to her, but he was unable to do that. So the first she knew about it was when Mr Masters told her that she would be leaving the following day to live with the priest.

She knew the priest – that is, she knew what he looked like, but had no idea what he was like as a person or what it would be like to live with him. In her young life she had met few kind people, but many nasty, cruel ones, and she trembled in fear that Father John might be the same.

The priest had an interview with the trustees about his application. On Masters' instruction, he said not a word about confession or any contact with the mother. He just said his sister wasn't as young as she was and if she had a young girl from the workhouse she would be sent to school and learn to keep house and cook and so on, so that she would be ready for a life in service when the time came. Mr Masters recommended the girl Chrissie Foley, as she had no family whatsoever.

The trustees thought it an admirable arrangement. Father John was well-liked and respected and they fully approved of him being the young foundling's guardian.

'But the Welfare Department need to speak with your sister,' the senior trustee said. 'Stuff and nonsense of course, but there you are. They need to see if your sister is agreeable and the set-up in the house, where the girl will sleep and all.'

Therefore Eileen was expecting the visit and had no trouble showing them the bedroom she had ready for the child. She could see they were impressed.

'And what will her duties be?' one of them asked.

'Schoolwork,' Eileen said sharply. 'Chrissie's not quite eleven years old so she still has three years of school.'

'I understood you needed her help in the house,' one of

326

the female trustees said and Eileen remembered that's what her brother had told them.

'I have arthritis,' she said truthfully enough. 'It's not too bad yet but will worsen with time and one day I might be immensely grateful for a young girl's help. By then hopefully she'll know how to do most household tasks because we'll do them together and she will learn from me. But she will not be expected to work long, exhausting hours, or do anything that might affect her schoolwork. I will teach her at home at first as I want to fill any gaps in her education so that she will not be that far behind when she does go to school.'

The two female trustees nodded, because they knew if children could write their name and reckon up to ten or twenty, that was considered more than adequate for a child from the workhouse.

And yet one added with a slight sniff, 'Very commendable I'm sure, but it wouldn't do to give this girl ideas above her station.'

Eileen was suddenly furious, but she swallowed her anger, knowing it wouldn't help her case to allow them to annoy her.

One of the others said, 'Well, I don't know about you, but I think that young girl is very lucky coming here to live in this comfortable house with people who care what happens to her.'

Eileen let out the breath she hadn't been aware she was holding as another said, 'May I say, I respect both you and your brother offering this foundling a second chance. We will certainly approve your application and our report to the trustees will definitely be positive.'

'Thank you,' Eileen said fervently.

Two days later Father John received a stamped official letter approving their application to be a guardian of a foundling child of no known parentage, known as Christine Foley. The letter instructed him to make arrangements with the workhouse for the child's removal.

'Like she was some sort of parcel,' Father John complained.

Eileen shrugged. 'It's just how they word official documents,' she said. 'But what the words say is more important than the way it is phrased.'

Father John said nothing more, knowing his sister was right. Only a couple of days later he went to bring Chrissie to her new home. She was in the reception area and Father John glimpsed her through the window. She was dressed in a threadbare coat that was much too small for her, boots that had seen better days and no socks.

He followed Masters to the small annexe of the office. One wall was lined with shelves and, sat alone on one of the shelves, was a cardboard suitcase.

'Her other clothes are in here,' Mr Masters said, pulling the case out, and Father John hoped heartily they were better ones than those she had on. 'The Sunday clothes the children wear for church have not been included, nor the uniform they wear in here. She would hardly want them anyway as they would mark her out as a workhouse waif. I should think she would want to do all in her power to forget she was ever in this place.'

'I would in her shoes,' the priest said in agreement. 'Where are her other things?'

'Well, she hasn't much more,' Benedict Masters said. 'It all went into the case. She has her toothbrush, hairbrush and hand mirror, which all the inmates have. Oh, and a birth certificate of sorts. I hadn't her mother or her father's name, nor even her actual date of birth, but she had to be registered in some way and I just gave the day she was left at the workhouse.'

'I understand,' Father John said. 'Now, I just need the locket that you showed me before.'

For a split second Masters' face was blank and then he said, 'Goodness me, of course, the locket. I keep that in a strong box in the safe in the office. Just a minute.'

Father John waited with no sense of unease and then Masters came in holding a metal box in his hands.

'It's gone,' he said to Father John. 'It's disappeared. I kept it in this box and it's empty.'

Father John was furious. 'You're lying to me,' he cried. 'You've sold it like the trustees wanted you to initially!'

'No, no,' Masters said. 'I swear to you I know nothing about this disappearance. The trustees would have forgotten all about wanting to sell it now. I had almost forgotten it was there myself.'

'Someone evidently hadn't,' Father John said. His voice shook with anger and sadness as he went on, 'It was all she had – no parents, no family, just a silver locket given to her by her mother. It was to show she loved her although she couldn't care for her. That's what she told me in confession. Do you see what a boost that would give to this poor destitute child?'

'Father John, I am heart-sore about it myself,' Masters said. 'And I will try my damnedest – beg your pardon, Father – to get to the bottom of this. All I am grateful for is that we didn't ever mention it to her so she knows nothing about it.'

329

Father John knew though and felt dispirited about the whole thing and wasn't at all sure he trusted Benedict Masters. The governor understood how the priest felt and, though he had nothing to do with the theft of it, he felt responsible because he didn't always lock the safe when he left the room. Just lately a number of things had gone missing as well – a silver snuff box, a rather nice cigarette case, a pendant and ring had disappeared from the rooms belonging to various members of staff – though as yet he hadn't informed the police. But it was true what he had told the priest: he had almost forgotten about the locket and, as the other missing items had disappeared from the staffroom, he hadn't thought to check the locket was safe. He would have to get to the bottom of the thefts and stop ignoring them.

Father John's despondency lifted slightly when he entered the reception room and saw the child properly for the first time. This was no time to think of himself, for the young girl was so frightened and nervous, it was seeping through the pores of her skin, and he felt his stomach lurch in sympathy.

He had also never seen a child so still or so quiet. With bright blue and intelligent eyes, she was sitting so far back in the chair in her ill-fitting clothes that her legs didn't reach the floor. They too were still and her hands were folded demurely in her lap, and she didn't utter a sound or move a muscle, just as she hadn't when he had glimpsed her through the window. Chrissie could have told the priest that was how you survived life in a workhouse – by making yourself as small and quiet as possible, as if you were invisible. You never spoke unless asked a question and then you answered as briefly as possible. You learned to sit as still as a mouse for long periods, but be ready to leap into action the moment you were asked to do something.

Father John's heart was smote with pity for this child and he wondered if she looked like her mother. He put out his hand and said, 'Let's go home, Chrissie', but she made no move towards him. She couldn't ever remember holding someone's hand.

Then Mr Masters said, 'Go on, Chrissie. You will be living with Father John now', and she knew the die was cast, her future was decided.

So she gave a little imperceptible sigh as she wriggled off the seat and took Father John's hand. He picked up the case and they walked out of the workhouse together.

TWENTY-TWO

Eileen tried to hide her shock when she first saw Chrissie as she stepped into the hall. The child was very small considering she was almost eleven, and she was thin, as all the children from the workhouse appeared to be. Her cheeks were slightly sunken in her wan little face and her deep blue eyes showed the anxiety she was filled with. It was hard to know what colour her straggly hair was as it seemed matted to her head.

And if that wasn't enough, she also wore a coat and boots in the worst condition that Eileen had ever seen. As they entered the hallway, Father John dropped the child's hand and said, 'Take off your coat now, Chrissie, and I'll hang it up.'

Chrissie obediently removed it and Eileen saw the girl's dress was in a worse condition than the coat – thin and washed-out – and the threadbare cardigan would do nothing to keep her warm. Her heart constricted with pity and her eyes met John's above the child's head, registering her horror and shock.

'There's more clothes there,' John said, indicating the suitcase he had placed on the floor.

Eileen gave a small sigh of relief, hoping there were more suitable garments in the case, and said as she picked it up, 'Come on, Chrissie, and I'll show you where you are to sleep tonight.'

Chrissie followed her up the stairs, which were lined with patterned lino, and into a small room that was so beautiful Chrissie gasped.

There was similar lino on the bedroom floor and there was also a fluffy blue rug beside the most comfortable bed Chrissie had ever seen. It was covered with a beautiful pink coverlet that Eileen later told her was called a counterpane. All her life so far she had only ever been given a sheet and a blanket to cover her as she lay in her hard bed in the bleak, cold dormitory alongside all the other children.

Her head was reeling with the thought this whole room now belonged to her, because the bed was not the only amazing thing in the room. The room had what Eileen later told her was a wardrobe, something else she called a dressing table, as well as a chest of drawers. Though even if Chrissie had known the names of these items at the time, she wouldn't have known what they were used for.

When Eileen opened it up, she found that all that was in the case, apart from the bag containing a toothbrush, hairbrush and mirror, was a dress identical to the one Chrissie was wearing, one pair of knickers and a raggy old thing she supposed she used as a nightdress.

Eileen already knew the first thing she was going to do was to replenish Chrissie's clothes and she had enough money to do it. Then she was going to draw the child a good bath.

When her husband had died in the early years of the Great

War, it had been just about the same time the housekeeper-cum-cook had left her brother's employ to take better-paid work in the munitions. After that, with so many war-related and therefore lucrative opportunities opening up for women, Father John had trouble engaging someone else.

It had seemed sensible for Eileen to move in and look after her much-loved brother and he insisted on paying her as he would anyone else. Eileen had a widow's pension and no children to provide for and did not need the wages John paid her. Never having been a big spender, she had opened a post office account and had a tidy sum in there now.

She looked at the thin, undersized ragamuffin gazing around the room with a rapt expression on her face and she had a sudden desire to see what she would look like with more flesh on her bones and better clothes. She couldn't think of a better way to spend her money than buying Chrissie some good warm clothes and boots and a topcoat that fitted.

They would be taking a dander to the Bullring, but not until they'd eaten, for all it was only eleven o'clock. Eileen had made a sustaining broth and would like Chrissie to have that inside her before she went out into the cold of the day in such inadequate clothes.

Chrissie had noticed the picture on the wall of Jesus on the cross. She knew about the cross because she had heard about it at Sunday school, but there wasn't usually a man fastened to it and she didn't think she liked it very much.

Eileen followed her gaze. 'That's Jesus Christ,' she said.

Chrissie nodded for she knew about him.

'He's the son of God,' Eileen went on. 'Did you know that?'

Chrissie nodded and said in her timid little voice, 'He died for our sins.'

She hadn't understood the phrase when she had first heard it and still didn't understand it now. She had been so afraid of being punished at the workhouse she had gone out of her way to do nothing that might be deemed even slightly naughty. At the workhouse, they often talked about souls being as black as coal and full of sin – well, some people's might be like that right enough, but she imagined hers was pretty good really. Maybe not spotlessly white, but certainly a light grey.

Eileen wondered what Chrissie was thinking about so hard and she said, 'Do you know who I am?'

Again Chrissie nodded. 'Mr Masters said you're Father John's sister.'

Eileen smiled. 'That's right, I look after him and I'm going to look after you as well now.'

'Oh!' said Chrissie, because that was a novel experience – for her to be 'looked after'.

'Will you like that?'

Chrissie lifted her head and regarded the woman in front of her. Though she was still incredibly nervous, she thought Eileen looked all right.

'Um,' she said. 'I suppose.'

'And you can call me Auntie Eileen. Can you do that?'

Chrissie nodded her head and Eileen went on, 'Shortly we're going to the Bullring and I am going to buy you some warm clothes.'

Chrissie's eyes lit up. Warm sounded good for she was often cold.

'Are you really?' she asked, hardly able to believe it.

'I am really,' Eileen assured her. 'But before that we are going to eat. Are you hungry?'

Chrissie couldn't remember a time when she wasn't hungry.

A gnawing emptiness was always there and the thin porridge she'd had for breakfast that morning had not gone even near to filling her stomach. When she'd arrived she had nearly passed out with the nourishing smell coming from the kitchen. The only time she had smelled things like that in the workhouse was when the trustees had one of their famous dinners.

So she rewarded Eileen with a big smile and said, 'I am really, really hungry.'

'Come on then,' Eileen said, catching up Chrissie's hand.

When they reached the kitchen, Eileen set up a flurry of activity setting out bowls and spoons and cutting bread.

Chrissie's head swam at the aroma of the broth simmering on the range in the kitchen. There was a solid-looking scrubbed table in the kitchen but she thought it highly unlikely she would be asked to eat with these fine people.

But when she asked where she was going to eat, Eileen laughed before saying, 'With us of course.' She crossed the room and held Chrissie's hands between her own. 'You're part of the family now.'

Chrissie started, because she had never been part of a family before. She looked down at Eileen's hands holding hers. She made no move to remove her hands as she struggled to control herself, feeling tears prickle her eyes. She dared not let them fall though, because the workhouse didn't approve of tears. There a child could get punished for doing a lot of it and she didn't know if the woman she was to call Auntie Eileen felt the same way.

Eileen wondered at Chrissie's stillness and lack of response. She had surprised herself by saying the girl was family, and knew it wasn't what she'd envisaged when she'd agreed to take in the foundling John seemed to see himself as semi-responsible for. But when they had turned up that morning and she had seen him holding the scrawny child's hand, she had realised the girl was scared witless and her heart had been touched. The child needed love as much as she needed food and Eileen had seen her face when she said the words, and known it was right that Chrissie be part of their family now.

She released her hands and said to Chrissie, 'Now you go and find Father John, wherever he is, and tell him there's food on the table. You'll probably find him in the church.'

A few minutes later Chrissie was sitting at the table perfectly still as Eileen ladled delicious food into the bowl before her.

'Oh lovely,' Father John said, coming into the room and rubbing his hands. 'Eileen does a very tasty broth, very tasty indeed. Just the thing to stick to a body's ribs in this weather.'

Chrissie swung her head round to look out of the window. She shivered to see the day was so intensely cold that the frost from the night before still covered the yard.

Father John took his place beside Chrissie and said, 'Are you hungry, Chrissie?'

'Of course she is,' Eileen said. Chrissie was glad she answered on her behalf since she was concentrating on the bread Eileen had put on the table. She didn't want just one slice, she wanted slice after slice to cram into her mouth like a starving animal and eat and eat till she could eat no more. That was an experience she had never had and she used to fantasise about doing just that, like many of the workhouse inmates. But she knew she couldn't shock Father John and Aunt Eileen with such a display of bad manners and iron resolve ensured her hands stayed meekly folded on her lap as Father John said, 'Well, Eileen always maintains the best thing a person can ever bring to a table is a good appetite, isn't that right, Eileen?'

'It is,' Eileen agreed. 'And now, John, if you would like to say grace we can start.'

Chrissie was used to saying grace before a meal, and though she hadn't heard the prayer Father John used before, she was just glad he didn't linger over it. She waited for Eileen or Father John to give her permission to eat. And her head swam and mouth watered but she didn't move a muscle.

At first, neither Father John or Eileen were aware that Chrissie hadn't even touched her spoon. Eileen was surprised when she did notice for she had been expecting Chrissie to attack her meal with gusto.

'Chrissie, what is it?' Eileen asked. 'You haven't touched your meal.'

Father John, who knew more of the rules of the workhouse, said, 'You're waiting for permission to start, aren't you?'

Chrissie turned grateful eyes towards him and nodded her head.

'Well Chrissie, you have it and welcome,' Father John said. 'You are no longer at the workhouse and their rules don't apply here. Once we have said grace you can eat straight away and as much as you want. So pick up your spoon and dig in.'

Even years later, after she was grown, she would never forget that first meal in the priest's house: that first delicious spoonful, followed by another and another, the gravy dripping down her throat and sopped up by the crusty bread.

Father John and Eileen watched Chrissie in slight amusement. She didn't talk to them because talking hadn't been allowed in the workhouse, so it was not strange to her. If

Father John or Eileen asked her a question, her replies were brief and to the point, though she answered respectfully enough. Chrissie didn't want to be distracted from eating what she wanted to eat without censure for the first time in her life.

She ate and ate till she could eat no more and then she sat back with a small sigh of contentment. Her stomach felt as tight as a drum. Many times she had imagined what it would feel like to have a full stomach and it felt even better than she had imagined. But she remembered who had made the delicious meal and she turned to Eileen and said, 'In all my life I have never tasted anything so delicious. Thank you so much.'

'You are very welcome,' Eileen said. 'Let me tell you, it is a pleasure to cook for someone so appreciative. Now, there is little light these days in winter and now we have fed the inner man, as it were, we will have to clothe the outer one.'

Eileen saw her puzzled eyes and knew Chrissie hadn't understood what she was talking about.

'I mean,' she explained, 'that when we have washed up these things we will make our way to the Rag Market in the Bullring to buy you some new and warmer clothes.'

Chrissie was as excited to be going to the Bullring as she was at the prospect of getting new things to wear. She had never been. The only time she ever left the workhouse was to go in a crocodile to St Philip's Cathedral, which was no distance away in Colmore Row. There she had listened to a man droning on and looked forward to the time when she would be syphoned off to Sunday school, which was usually better and often included a Bible story and sometimes colouring pictures.

Many had looked down on them in the congregation, even the Sunday school teacher, but that was so commonplace that it had hardly registered with Chrissie. What had registered was the life outside the workhouse. They had passed shops on their way to St Philip's, all closed because it was Sunday, but she could imagine them bustling and full of life. They had passed a station called Snow Hill and what she would have given to have had a peep in there at the trains.

There were virtually no visitors to the workhouse. She heard from other inmate children that when the parents eventually arrived there, the families were split up. Mothers, fathers and children were separated and the parents expected to work to provide for their offspring. They didn't see each other again until they left at fourteen. Some had relatives outside the workhouse but they didn't come to visit. It wasn't encouraged and, as one girl said:

'Altogether there are six of us kids in here and we have a gran, but she's had to give up her place and move with my auntie because she couldn't pay the rent. My auntie also has a husband and four kids of her own and money's always tight. But, if they came to see us, they might think that we expected them to get us out of here and they haven't the money to do that. Tell you what though, I can't wait till I'm fourteen and leave this place and see life beyond these walls. I'll be in service and people say the hours are long, but I shan't mind that if I get wages. At least in my time off I can do as I please and might even get to visit the Bullring that the warders are always talking about.'

If the warders were in a good mood they would tell the envious older girls what they did on their time off. The one place Chrissie longed to go to was theBullring, for the warders always made it sound like a magical place.

And she supposed it was, but she had been so used to walking with her head lowered she had only tantalising glimpses of it that first day. There were many things she would have liked to have asked Eileen too, but questions had not been encouraged at the workhouse. Holding Chrissie's hand as they made their way through the throngs, Eileen was aware of the excitement running through her and yet she was quiet and almost still.

Eileen told her brother about her strange reaction that night after Chrissie had gone to bed.

'She was clearly fascinated and yet she said nothing. I didn't want to linger till I got her some warmer clothes, for she was chilled to the bone, and I didn't want her to take a cold for I'd say she would have little resistance. But she gave me no indication she wanted to do that anyway and most times walked with her head down as we made straight for the Rag Market.'

Eileen went on to explain that when they had reached it, however, Chrissie had thought it a strange place for some goods were displayed on trestle tables while others were laid out on blankets on the floor. Eileen told her the Rag Market was where the bargains were to be had, and that there were second-hand stalls too which sold good-quality clothes relatively cheaply.

'Was she pleased at any rate with the things you bought her?' her brother asked.

'John, she was speechless,' Eileen said. 'I mean, she isn't loud anyway, but her eyes shone with happiness and I saw that before she lowered them to the floor again.'

'Well, you spent a tidy sum on her.'

'It was just lying in the bank doing nothing,' Eileen said. 'And it's added to every week. Anyway, I didn't buy anything she didn't need: just undergarments; winceyette nightdresses; three winter-weight dresses for everyday and one better one for Sunday; two thick cardigans; three pair of thick black stockings; a pair of leather boots and a thick winter coat. And all bought at a fraction of the price they would have been in the shops. The woman was kind enough to let Chrissie step behind the curtain and dress in the new clothes right away. Once she was much more warmly clad we went back out into the Bullring again and with my encouragement she looked around the stalls.'

'I did notice that she came back smarter than she went.'

'I'll say,' Eileen said with a laugh. 'What was really nice for her was that, as darkness began to fall, some of the stall-holders lit the gas flares and she was ecstatic about that.'

Chrissie could hardly believe the wonderful things that were happening to her. Later that same day, after a meal Eileen called a Lancashire hotpot, she was given a bath. They had never had proper baths of their own in the workhouse; sometimes they'd had to share baths with each other and the water was usually cold. The children avoided them if they could but when there was a lice infestation they couldn't and it would be followed by kerosene being soaked into their hair . . . But this was a bath like she had never experienced before. Eileen rinsed warm and fragrant suds through her hair and the hot water made her feel sleepy and cosy.

'Chrissie's enjoyment in such simple things is making me look at things I've taken for granted in a different light entirely,' Eileen said to John later. 'I mean, she went into raptures about the warm bath. And by gum she needed that bath. I had no idea the dirt was so ingrained. As for her hair, that's almost a different colour, and now it's brushed and the tangles teased out, it's very fair and quite pretty. In fact she's quite a fetching child.'

The fetching child at that time was wondering whether she had died and gone to heaven. Her skin tingled from the bath and her hair was so soft she couldn't stop running her fingers through it. Added to that, she was given yet more delicious food before dressing in one of the warm winceyette nightdresses and being tucked into the softest and comfiest bed she had ever slept in. There were blankets galore over her, all covered by the counterpane, so she knew she would never be cold in that bed whatever the weather outside, and she drifted into a deep and dreamless sleep.

Downstairs later, John was telling his sister about the missing locket, which still irked him. Eileen was outraged that anyone would take something from a child that had so little anyway.

'Yes,' Father John said. 'It's not the monetary value of the locket, though it might be worth something, but it might mean the world to Chrissie because it would show her that her mother loved her. Benedict Masters said it was pressed into her palm and her fingers had closed over it like a fist.'

Eileen asked, 'How much do you trust this Benedict Masters?'

'Before the locket went missing I would have said implicitly,' Father John said. 'Now I'm not so sure. I mean, even if he wasn't involved in the theft of the locket directly, according to him it disappeared from a metal box that was in the safe in his office and he failed to safeguard it.'

'Ah well, it's lost and gone for ever and thank the Lord she wasn't told of its existence,' Eileen said. 'What she never had she'll never miss, as they say.'

'Yes,' Father John said with a sigh. 'I'll go and see Masters in a couple of weeks, just before Christmas, but I don't hold out any great hopes he will have good news for me. Once the Christmas holidays are over they will be starting on the renovations so really if Masters has no news that's the last chance gone.'

It turned out that Benedict Masters had news, but nothing really that benefitted Chrissie. Mortified that he hadn't taken proper care of the locket, he had talked to those members of staff who'd reported things stolen from their rooms and called the police. Masters had had doubts about the honesty of a male warder but never had anything concrete to sack him for. When, as part of the investigation, the police searched the man's room, a number of items were found, including some items that hadn't even been reported missing, but there was no sign of a locket.

'When the police took the man away I searched that room myself,' Masters told the priest. 'I turned it upside down, sure that if he had taken all those items he had taken the locket as well, but . . .'

'He hadn't?'

'He may well have taken it, but he denies it and we can't prove otherwise.'

'Thank you, Benedict,' Father John said. 'It's really only what I expected.'

'Sorry I couldn't do more,' Masters said. 'How's young Chrissie Foley shaping up?'

'Oh Benedict, you wouldn't know the girl,' Father John

enthused. 'Eileen is very good with her and becoming fonder of her as each day passes. She has a pension of her own because her husband was killed in the early years of the Great War. I pay her a wage too, not nearly enough, but the only figure she would accept and that reluctantly. Anyway, she took Chrissie to the Bullring and kitted her out with warmer clothes and she looks a treat and she's filling out. Mind, she would do for she has an appetite like a hunter.'

'Oh, you know what I felt about the food they got here,' Masters said. 'It always falls short of adequate, no matter how much I badger and berate the guardians to improve things. They prefer to line their own pockets.'

'Well, she was thin when she came, almost gaunt if I'm honest, and though Eileen was upset about it, she looked at it as a bit of a challenge to feed her up and she is an exceedingly good cook. Mind you, we had to encourage the child to have more if she wanted.'

'Children are not encouraged to ask for seconds in the workhouse, for there are none.'

'And it wasn't only not asking for seconds,' Father John said. 'She was initially scared to put a foot wrong in case she got into trouble. Once she inadvertently knocked a cup off the table and she couldn't stop saying how sorry she was. She shook from head to toe. It was pitiful and when we said it had been an accident and it was all right, her relief was palpable. Apparently she thought she was going to be beaten. Anyway, that was two weeks ago and now she is transformed. She is best of friends with Eileen and they have decorated the whole house and church for Christmas. And as well as this, she has helped Eileen ice the Christmas cake, stirred the pudding and made mince pies on her own – under Eileen's directions of course.'

'Is she not going to school?'

'Not yet,' Father John said. 'It was so late in the term there was little point when she arrived and, as Eileen said, she needed more meat on her bones before she faced the rigours of school. Anyway she would probably be very far behind the others for Eileen says she can barely read, though she's far from stupid. Eileen was a teacher before her marriage and she wants to work with Chrissie and get her at least reading more confidently and better with her numbers so that she is not so far behind the others when she does begin school.'

'Does she need that level of education for the type of work she will be aiming for?'

'You're deciding her future when she's still a child,' Father John said. 'Chrissie's future is a little brighter now because she will not be coming from a workhouse but from a private home. That might make a difference to the employment open to her. Anyway, Eileen says education is never wasted and helps to open doors.'

'All right,' Masters said. 'Point taken.'

'Now I must be off,' Father John said. 'Eileen is having a little birthday tea for Chrissie because she's eleven today and I promised I would be there.'

No one had ever made a fuss of Chrissie's birthday before and she was fizzing with excitement. Eileen had secretly made a sponge cake for it and, as well as the sandwiches, there were also little iced biscuits and scones and something very delicious called jelly and custard.

And if that wasn't enough, Eileen had bought her a pair of

nice warm slippers and a book. Chrissie looked at the book with slight alarm and hoped Eileen wouldn't expect her to read it. It hadn't even got any pictures in it to give her a clue what it was about. But Eileen had caught the look and, having expected such a reaction, said, 'As well as poor teaching, I would hazard a guess that one of the reasons you don't read well is because you couldn't see the purpose of it. Am I right?'

'I suppose,' said Chrissie. 'Though maybe it's because I'm just stupid. That's what they used to say at the workhouse.'

'Chrissie, I used to be a teacher so know what I'm talking about and I am telling you now you are far from stupid,' Eileen said. 'What books did you have to read in the workhouse?'

'A few picture books and the Bible.'

'Well, there is of course nothing wrong with the Bible,' Eileen said. 'But it isn't easy to read and understand and I think the thing to do is show you the magic that can be between the pages of a book. This book is called *The Secret Garden* and I could read a chapter to you every night and let the words paint pictures in your head. Would you like that?'

Though she had preferred some warders to others, Chrissie had never felt love for another human being before. But since settling in the priest's house, every time she thought of Eileen, she felt a warm glow in her heart. She didn't know if that was love, she just knew she would jump through hoops to please her, and so she said, 'Yes, that would be lovely.'

Eileen smiled in satisfaction, knowing that once Chrissie realised what pleasure she could have from books, she would want to learn to read them for herself. Children learnt much better if they wanted to do something.

'We'll start this evening,' she said. 'And then after Christmas I'll enrol you in the library. We can take two books out and keep them for a fortnight, so think of the pleasure we have ahead.'

TWENTY THREE

Angela's heart would have been easier if she could have seen her youngest child that Christmas morning. Eileen had bought Chrissie mittens, a scarf and bonnet in muted pastel colours that looked a treat with her winter coat and she was as warm as toast as she walked to Mass.

'Don't say Chrissie is from the workhouse,' Eileen had said to John the previous evening.

'Why?'

'Because it will be easier for her to make friends and fit in better if people don't know she is from the workhouse. Many make assumptions about children from that place and surely that slur hasn't got to follow her all the days of her life.'

'So who should I say she is?'

'Could you say she's your ward?'

'Wouldn't people think it odd she hasn't been seen before now?' Father John said. 'Anyway, it's not true and I am a priest. I can't go round telling lies.'

'Course you can if it's going to help someone else,' Eileen

said. 'Do you think your God would prefer you to tell the truth when because of that truth a child will suffer for something that's not their fault?'

'Eileen—'

'I'm just saying, the God I worship wouldn't want me to do that.'

Father John laughed. 'You can't possibly say what God wants,' he said. 'I have to do what is right.'

'Right for who?' Eileen demanded. 'Right for you and your conscience or right for an innocent child? You know the life she'll have if everyone knows she comes from the workhouse.'

Father John remembered telling Masters that Chrissie might have a better chance of employment as she was living no longer at the workhouse, but reflected that wouldn't be the case if everyone knew about it anyway.

'Look,' Eileen went on. 'I will say she's the orphaned daughter of a very dear friend of mine. You just have to nod, if you are so concerned about a sin on your soul.'

'What about *your* soul?'

'I'll take a chance on mine,' Eileen said. 'I'm telling a lie in a good cause and that makes a difference.'

When Chrissie was told what Eileen intended, she was pleased. She had no desire to tell everyone she had been brought up in the workhouse, because she knew people would judge her and she'd already had her share of that.

'It's only a little lie,' Eileen said. 'Because you don't have any contact with your mother and father you may as well be an orphan. You don't mind telling people that?'

'No, I'd much prefer it to the truth,' Chrissie said.

And so she became Chrissie Foley, the orphaned daughter

of Eileen's best friend, and was afforded respect because she lived with the priest and his sister.

Connie was glad they had been invited to Maggie's for dinner and that Breda had given Angela the whole day to celebrate with her. Maggie's house was beautifully decorated and there was a tree with a twinkly star on the top, festooned with glass balls which shimmered in the light from the candles.

'Oh, how pretty it all is,' Connie exclaimed, following her mother in. They had presents for them all: warm slippers for Maggie, whisky and socks for Michael and a pretty bed jacket for Hilda.

The Christmas dinner was marvellous but Maggie waved away their thanks and praise.

'Don't be embarrassing me,' she said. 'I'm used to cooking for many people now. It becomes like second nature and Christmas is the absolutely right time to get together with family and friends.'

Angela smiled. 'Well, I think I can speak for Connie as well when I say that we really appreciate it.'

Connie nodded in agreement and Maggie smiled at her. Connie loved Maggie and always had, and Angela hadn't been the only one to miss her when she'd moved to Pershore Road. Angela knew there was a bond between them and throughout that Christmas Day in Maggie's house she'd been impressed with the easy way Maggie had with Connie. She thought it a tragedy that she'd had no children of her own because she was so much better with Connie than she was.

Connie thought so too. Maggie seemed really interested in her, listening to what she was saying, and she understood her passion for books. That day, Angela was learning things that Connie had never discussed with her, like the names of the librarians she had made such friends of, and the great job she'd had through the holidays in the library that she hoped to repeat.

Maggie asked about school and there again Connie said the reference library was a mine of information.

'It's so much easier to work in the quiet,' she told Maggie enthusiastically. 'The librarians always give me a hand if I need it, especially the younger one, Miss McGowan. She's really good at finding just the books I need for whatever it is I'm studying. She's really lovely and ever so helpful.'

Angela had a sudden and unexpected pang of jealousy strike her heart to hear her daughter speak so warmly about a librarian. And she felt guilt too, because she was the one who'd urged Connie to go for matriculation and so she should have been the one to support and encourage her. She had let her down and the first chance she got she would try to put things right between them.

After such a delicious dinner and sumptuous pudding, no one seemed inclined to move at first and they sat around the table talking of other Christmases they remembered from when they were children. Angela spoke again of the last Christmas before the world went mad, before the men enlisted.

'Yes,' Maggie said. 'And then the men were gone and you and I were making shells together, Angela, and somehow the world was never the same again.'

'No,' Michael agreed, getting to his feet. 'Anyway, as this washing-up won't do itself, shall we get on with it? And then I must see to Mammy because she's been very restless today.'

Maggie groaned but could see Michael's point and began

piling the plates up. They all helped with the washing-up and, when the kitchen was tidy once more, Michael went off to his mother's room with a cup of tea and a mince pie. Hilda had not been well enough to have Christmas dinner with them and had eaten hers in bed. Maggie poured tea for Angela, Connie and herself and they sat around the table. Maggie also put down a plate of mince pies but they were all too full to think of eating one.

'Oh, I forgot to tell you, Connie,' Angela said. 'Harry came to see me in the pub a few weeks ago.'

'What did he do that for?' Connie asked.

Angela knew better than to say Harry had asked her to go to America with him. According to her daughter, she had been married to her father and that should be enough for her. She could and should live like a vestal virgin all the days of her life. So she said instead, 'He came to say goodbye as he was going back to the States. Sent his regards to you too.'

'That was nice of him,' 'Connie said. 'Was it always on the cards that he'd go back?'

'Eventually he would have done, I suppose,' Angela said. 'Though I must admit he seemed fairly settled in England. I suppose he might have been here far longer, but his father became ill and the doctor said he had to take things easier so his mother sent for Harry to take over the business.'

'What a pity when he had done so much in the shop and everything.'

'Oh, he's not giving the shop up,' Angela said.

'Who's taking it on then?'

'You'll never guess,' Angela said.

'No. Who?'

'Stan.'

353

'Stan!' Connie exclaimed. 'Does he know anything about running a shop?'

'Well, I'd say more than he did anyway,' Angela said. 'Harry seems quite happy. Apparently he has been helping him on Saturdays for some time as Daniel is out and about with the friends he has made at college then.'

'I am glad of that, anyway,' Connie said. 'I mean about Daniel, because he was never encouraged to make friends, was he, when he was being brought up by his aunt and uncle?'

'No. His aunt in particular wanted to almost possess him body and soul. If he had no friends he was reliant on his aunt and uncle for company.'

'Yes, but that's not really healthy, is it?' Maggie said.

'No, course it wasn't,' Angela agreed.

'The point is, he thought it was a normal way to go on,' Connie said. 'And because he never had friends, never went to their houses and none came to his house, to him it was normal. It was only when he was at uni that he realised how restricted his life was, but all those years of being more or less isolated from his peers, except when they were in lessons at school, affected him.'

'How d'you mean?'

'Well, he always seemed a bit lonely to me,' Connie said. 'I recognised that straight away, because I have often felt that way myself and know how soul-destroying it is.'

There was a silence after Connie's words and to cover this Connie said to her mother, 'Anyway, Stan helping Harry out on Saturdays isn't the same as single-handedly running a shop.'

'Yes, but you see, Harry said Stan was finding the foundry

work harder for him as he grew older,' Angela said. 'And so Harry made him a partner and he has been showing him the ropes for a month or more. Balancing the books flummoxed him a bit, but Daniel said he'll help him there.'

'Oh yes, and I bet when Daniel has shown him how to do it and explained it to him, Stan will be able to do it himself,' Connie said. 'Daniel will make a great teacher because he really is the only person who could explain things I was finding difficult. He was so good at it that they suddenly became crystal clear and I could see immediately where I was going wrong.'

'Didn't he used to help you with your homework?' Maggie said.

Connie nodded. 'Yes, and it was him who told me about the library and showed me how to use the reference side of it. It was a good job, because we never see him or Stan any more because of some stupid falling-out between Mammy and Stan that really should have been sorted out ages ago.'

'Connie, you have no right to . . .' Angela began.

Connie noted her mother's crimson cheeks, which she knew signified how cross she was, but for once she didn't care.

'No right to what, Mammy? No right to an opinion? I think I have.'

'It's rude. You are being rude.'

'Why is it rude to say what I think?' Connie demanded. 'And I'm right as well. If I had fallen out with a friend I had had since the year dot, you'd want to know the ins and outs of it and advise me to make friends again.' There was a slight pause and then Connie added, 'At least, that's what you would have done once, when you noticed I was there and cared what I did.'

355

Angela gave a gasp, but her face flushed, for she knew Connie had a valid point. However, she didn't think this was the time or place to talk of such things, so she said quite sharply, 'That will do. I think you have said quite enough. I think this is an appalling way to behave on Christmas Day and in someone else's house.'

Connie acknowledged that and she turned to Maggie and said, 'I'm sorry, Maggie. That was wrong of me.'

'It's all right,' Maggie said, for though she'd heard Connie's angry words, she also heard the bewildered unhappiness behind it. She knew Connie was trying to reach out to her mother to show she was still important to her. She hoped Angela realised what she was trying to say. 'No harm done.'

As Angela and Connie returned home that crisp and cold Christmas evening, Connie braced herself for the scolding she was expecting from her mother, but it never came. When Angela thought about what Connie had said, she realised all her daughter had done was speak the truth as she saw it and she wasn't far wrong either. Angela had to admit that when she'd been seeing Eddie McIntyre she'd thought of little else but him. Everyone else was way down the list – even Connie.

Angela knew that she was cross only because Connie had spoken in front of Maggie. Her daughter's actual words had been truthful enough and had also showed Angela how hurt Connie had been by her seeming indifference.

She was right, for Connie was still wary and disappointed in her mother. She had always thought her strong and true, someone who would hold to what was right, no matter what. To see her change so completely, presumably because of the influence of one man, unsettled her. Previously, she had known where she stood and her mother had instilled in her a strong moral code to live her life by. When Angela had thrown her own moral code into the air, Connie had felt the solid ground beneath her feet shift.

Now this Eddie McIntyre had disappeared back to the America he'd come from, her mother had reverted to the mother she always had been. And yet Connie couldn't entirely relax, because what was going through her mind was the thought that Eddie could return at any time. Or what if her mother met another man intent on leading her astray as this Eddie McIntyre seemed to have been and she was unable to stand against him as well?

Connie wished she could ask her mother these questions but she couldn't and so she fretted about it all the time, so much so she felt as if there was a chasm separating them.

Angela didn't know exactly how Connie felt but she knew enough to know she was desperately unhappy. She knew things had to change and it was time to build bridges with her daughter.

Later, after Angela and Connie had left, Maggie told Michael a little of the disagreement Connie had had with her mother and went on to say, 'I think Connie was confused and unhappy about Angela's behaviour with McIntyre. I mean, she said as much the day I met her on Bristol Street, remember I told you about it?'

Michael nodded. 'I bet she was as pleased and relieved as you were when you found out McIntyre had gone back to America.'

Maggie nodded her head and said fervently, 'Not half. The point is, Michael, I have known Angela all my life and the things I was hearing about her . . . Well, it was like she was a different person. I think she was in the grip of a wild infatuation with the man. I know it happens.'

'And you think Angela is that stupid?'

'She has been my friend for years,' Maggie said with spirit. 'But when she told me she had stopped thinking of Barry as a brother and started thinking of him as a lover just before they married, I don't think that was necessarily true.'

'You mean she didn't love Barry?'

'Oh, she loved him all right,' Maggie said. 'But somewhere the lines between brother and lover merged. Though she said sex between them was enjoyable, she also said it was more making love together rather than just sex. She also said Barry had to be very careful even after marriage, because when the war began he didn't want to leave Angela with another mouth to feed.'

'Ah,' Michael said. 'That would mean he would have to pull back when the . . . You know what I mean . . . ahem, before it was properly over. God, that's damned hard to do when you're coming to the climax, which is the best bit for a man.'

'It would be hard for Angela too, I'd say,' Maggie said. 'She would constantly feel dissatisfied and frustrated but probably have had no idea why she felt like that. And that was the only experience of sex she ever had – and she didn't have it for that long either. But she must have buried any latent sexual desires deep in her heart, for never did she put a foot wrong all the years I have known her.'

'And then along came McIntyre.'

'Basically yes,' Maggie said. 'She was attracted to him from the beginning but she denied it. She told me he was funny and charming and made her laugh and her eyes would sparkle when she spoke his name.'

'So why did she agree to go out with him in the end?'

Maggie shrugged. 'Maybe she eventually acknowledged the fascination she had for this man and went out with him like a lamb to the slaughter.'

'Aren't you being a little dramatic?'

'I don't think so,' Maggie said. 'McIntyre was an experienced and oversexed gigolo. To him, Angela would have been like a blank page, almost an untried virgin. On that first date he would have known by her own account how naïve and artless she was. He would also have known Angela would soon be like putty in his hands. I think he set out to seduce her. Then he attacked and threatened her when she didn't continue to comply.'

'It's a good thing that McIntyre took himself back to America where he belongs,' Michael said. 'Or I might have got a couple of chaps together to encourage him to go. I have no time for a man who raises his hand to a woman.'

'Very glad to hear it,' Maggie said with an impish grin. 'For if you thought any differently I'd have to take up boxing lessons.'

On Boxing Day, Angela told Breda she could no longer do the cleaning in the pub. With her pension and the cash she earned working behind the bar, they had plenty of money to live on. Giving up the cleaning meant she could eat breakfast with Connie every day.

Breda could quite understand why Angela wanted more time at home and thought she was right, for Connie's sake as well as her own.

'Who shall I get to replace you though?' she said.

'Well, I have been giving that some thought,' said Angela. 'My first choice was Nancy Webster, but she told me when I asked her that she is going to look after Jennifer's baby when she goes back to work in the New Year. Her man has been out of work six years now and they desperately need Jennifer's money. So then I asked Maeve Maguire and she was more than willing if you are agreeable.'

Breda smiled, for she knew Maeve to be a respectable and honest woman who had raised polite and well-mannered children. She would suit very well, especially as Angela offered to stay on for a while to show Maeve the ropes.

It was Connie's reaction that brought tears to Angela's eyes though. When she told her daughter that she would no longer be cleaning in the pub so that they could have breakfast together every day, the girl threw her arms around her mother.

'Oh Mammy, I am so glad,' she said. 'I have missed you so much.'

TWENTY-FOUR

Hilda Malone lost her grip on life towards the end of January 1928 and the funeral was held soon after. St Catherine's was packed with neighbours, friends and the few relations she had left, and both Angela and Connie attended the little 'do'.

The following morning Angela was sick in the pot and when she came back from emptying the contents into the lavatory Connie had the kettle on and was cooking the porridge.

She turned as her mother came in the side door. 'What was all that about?'

Angela shrugged. 'Could be anything.'

'You didn't drink too much?'

'Connie, you were by my side most of the time,' Angela said. 'I drank nothing, if you are talking of alcohol. I had two glasses of lemonade and a cup of tea and that was all I had.'

'Well, it couldn't have been anything you ate or I would be sick too, for we ate a lot of the same food.'

'Don't worry about it. It's easy to pick up these odd bugs.'

What she said reassured Connie, but Angela was concerned that it was no bug, however much she wished it was, for the sickness more or less confirmed the fact that she was pregnant with Eddie McIntyre's child. When she went into the bar at ten thirty that morning Breda was there too, which was unusual. It was half an hour before the doors opened and, as Angela was removing the towels and sorting out the glasses, she said to her, 'God girl, you look a bit peaky. You all right?'

'I'm fine.'

'You sure?'

Angela sighed. 'You may as well know. It's not something I can keep secret for long anyway. I was sick this morning and my monthlies were due the end of November and I've seen nothing.'

'Ah almighty Christ!' Breda exclaimed. 'That scandalous bastard has filled your belly and left you high and dry. I said a novena that there would be no repercussions from that mad period you and Eddie McIntyre enjoyed together and the novena was no bloody use either.'

'It was my fault as well.'

'Yes, but it's you alone who will carry the stigma and suffer name-calling, and Connie too most likely. And the child will be known as a bastard all the years of its life.'

'I know,' Angela said in a voice little above a whisper.

'I know someone who can get rid of it for you.'

Angela gasped. 'I can't do that, Breda. It would be murder.'

'Course it wouldn't be.'

'Yes, it would be,' Angela said firmly. 'Look, I wish this hadn't happened and I don't want this child, but I will do my level best to ensure it never feels unwanted. I cannot murder it because it's inconvenient.'

'All right then,' Breda said. 'How are you going to square this with young Connie?'

Angela's sigh this time was heartfelt, for that was the one thing she worried about constantly, the thing that jerked her awake through the night and caused panic attacks in the day when she envisaged telling her. Since Christmas, they had been making tentative moves to retrieve the closeness they once had. It was early days and Connie was still not totally sure if she could rely on her mother any more. Angela was aware of this and understood it. She knew there was no way she could tell her daughter, not quite fifteen, that she was having the bastard child of Eddie McIntyre in such a way that she would understand any part of.

She risked losing her daughter's love, trust and respect, and yet she couldn't bring herself to destroy the life inside her. She remembered Mary warning her about trying to abort a child when Angela had been pregnant with the child she had left on the workhouse steps. She'd said some abortionists knew bugger all and others were dirty devils that could leave a woman with an infection which meant they could never conceive again. And she had gone on to tell her that she had seen the results of some of their handiwork, like the young lass who had bled to death because she was 'too scared of going to prison to summon an ambulance'.

Furthermore, there was always a risk that the child would be damaged and how could Angela live with herself then? No, for better or worse, she would have this child and if she lost her daughter through it then that's the price she must pay. It was a harsh punishment but she needed to suffer for being so sinful.

* * *

Each day, Angela wondered if it would be as well to tell Connie so she would have time to get used to it, or if it was better to let her tumble to it herself. She didn't know if she was doing right or not, but she couldn't bring herself to speak of it until she had to. She didn't yet look pregnant so day followed day with Connie ignorant of the Sword of Damocles that would shortly spear her heart . . . Angela just couldn't bring herself to tell her daughter, and although the months passed by, with loose clothes she was able to hide the truth from the world for a bit longer.

She couldn't help but think that being with child was some sign from God, that she must pay the price for her sin with Eddie. She couldn't shake off the need to confess but couldn't face Father Brannigan, the local priest at her church. He would know her voice and would no doubt never let her forget it. She thought about the kind priest who had heard her confession at St Chad's and felt herself drawn to the church.

The following Friday, she found herself at the back of St Chad's watching the men and women come and go from the confessional and wondered if she had the courage to come forward. She sat there for a while and, as the church crowds thinned out, she knew that she would soon miss her chance. Father John was just about to leave the confession box, thinking that he was finished for the day, and so was surprised when a young woman entered the cubicle.

'Can I help you, my child?' He could feel from his long years of experience that this was a soul needing God's forgiveness, not just one of the congregation who came out of a sense of duty and only confessed to swearing and haranguing their husbands or scolding their wives.

'Bless me, Father, for I have sinned.'

When Angela spoke, the priest looked at her curiously through the grille, for he felt that he recognised her voice. He realised it was the very same woman who had come to the church after abandoning Chrissie and then come back years later to confess her sin.

The priest made the sign of the cross and waited patiently for her to speak.

'Father, I am ashamed to say that I am with child but have no husband.'

'I know you, my child, you have come to confess with me before and told me of the child that you left at the gates of the workhouse. How has this happened to you again, were you attacked once more?'

The priest had such a kindly voice, so full of compassion, that Angela felt even more shame and started to weep.

'Come, tell me what has happened and remember that God loves sinners more than those who are not.'

Angela spilled out the story of what had happened with Eddie. 'Father, it was my lust that has got me to this terrible situation.'

'Yes, you are human and to sin is part of that condition, but from what you tell me this man was the greater sinner. He led you astray, though you willingly followed, but I can see that you are truly sorry.'

'I know that I must have this child and bear the shame. I know I should have done that also before with the child that I left at the workhouse.'

'God moves in mysterious ways, my child, and we have no way of knowing why He sends us the tests or the trials that He does, but we must try to do the right thing. You should bring the child up in the ways of God and pray for His forgiveness. His grace will guide you. But I must tell you that I have news of the workhouse child that you left on the steps. The child's name is Chrissie and she is no longer kept at that awful institution.'

Angela could scarce believe this news and said through her tears, 'I don't understand. What has happened to her? Is she in any danger?'

'No, my child, far from it. She lives with my sister and myself and is happy and safe with us. I made enquiries after you came before and when the workhouse was to be closed we took her in. She is thriving now.'

Angela felt an overpowering relief flood through her. Thank God her child was now safe and so close too, maybe just in the rectory attached to the church. If she wanted she could just stand up and walk over there and see her, hold her in her arms again like she had longed to.

'Oh Father, how can I ever thank you? My little girl is safe now and it's all because of your help.'

'My child, I should love to speak with you properly, perhaps after confession we could talk . . .'

But Angela knew that she must leave, her shame at being pregnant again out of wedlock was too great, and she stood up, saying, 'Bless you, Father, and thank you. Please tell my daughter I love her dearly.'

She ran as fast as she could away from the church, almost as if she had the devil at her heels. She made it home to her back-to-back and fell in the door, overwhelmed with the news she had just heard and full of emotion.

As she tried to catch her breath, Angela suddenly felt a pain in her lower belly and felt the need to dash to the lavatory. There she saw scarlet blood was seeping from her and staining her stockings.

For a moment she didn't know what to do, then she hurried up the yard, packed herself with a towel and clean underclothes and made her way to the Swan. She went inside and told Paddy she needed to see Breda as a matter of urgency.

Breda came down wrapped in a dressing gown, rheumy-eyed and tousle-headed from sleep, but she knew Angela well enough to know that she wouldn't have woken her up unless it was of crucial importance.

'What is it?' she said.

'I'm bleeding,' Angela said. 'I mean lots.'

'Oh Christ,' Breda said. 'Look, go back home, put on plenty of water to boil and sort out all your towels. I'll throw some clothes on and be round in a jiffy.'

Though as she dressed, Breda couldn't help feeling that, if Angela was to miscarry this child, it might be the best solution all round.

Angela said to Breda, 'I'm losing it, aren't I?'

Breda nodded her head. 'I very much think you are.'

'I don't care,' Angela declared. 'I'm glad.' But tears glistened behind her eyes as she went on, 'Now you know the true extent of my wickedness – being glad at the death of a baby.'

'This isn't your fault and I know you don't mean that,' Breda said. 'You did nothing to hasten the birth and I've heard the doctor say that if a woman miscarries often the child is damaged in some way.'

'That would be a comfort in a way to know that,' Angela said and then as a contraction took hold of her she grabbed Breda's sleeve. 'You won't leave me?'

'Only to tell Paddy he must manage on his own,' Breda

said. 'It won't hurt him and Monday is one of our quiet days anyway.'

So Breda left to do that and returned again and the two women waited hours and hours until eventually Angela got the urge to push. The tiny life that had ebbed away inside her was so small that even when it slipped out of her it wasn't the unbearable ache she had felt with her previous two pregnancies.

'It was a boy,' Breda said, wrapping it in a towel and letting Angela see too. There didn't look to be anything wrong with it but she knew you could never guess at what was happening inside the little body. He looked beautiful and perfect and quite dead and Angela stroked the downy hair on the little child's head, knowing she would have loved this child like her other children. The tears spilled freely from her.

'Sad, isn't it?'

'It is,' Breda agreed. 'But in this instance maybe all to the good. Now we must tidy this room before Connie sees it.'

'Oh God, yes.'

'It's all right, I have a plan,' Breda said. 'I'll take the bloodied towels to my house and put them in my boiler in the cellar. Wouldn't do for all the people in the brew house to see them.'

'No indeed. And the child?'

'Let us deal with that too,' Breda said. 'The child was stillborn so there will be no funeral or grave or anything. We will dispose of the body if that's all right with you.'

Angela swallowed deeply, for she thought it a very clinical way to deal with the body of a child that had once been a living being inside her. But she had to think of practicalities and so she nodded her head. 'Yes please.'

Breda gave Angela a few days off work and Connie went to bide at the Swan because she was told her mother had a fever that was infectious. By the time Angela was fully on her feet again, any lingering sadness about losing the baby was replaced by relief and she was back to her own self. Sometimes she thought of all the things that had befallen her and was heartily glad to draw a firm line under everything and make peace with her daughter again.

By the summer Chrissie could read very well; true to her word, Eileen had introduced her to the library. Chrissie could hardly believe there were so many books in the whole wide world as there were in that library, and the thought of being able to take those wonderful books home for two whole weeks sent frissons of excitement shooting through her. At first, she couldn't read well enough to follow the books she chose, but because she wanted to read on when Eileen finished a chapter she made great strides forward and Eileen knew the girl was far from stupid.

There were sometimes many children in the library, but Chrissie noticed one in particular. She was always alone; no adult, no cluster of friends surrounded her as she perused the shelves quite seriously. She had beautiful golden ringlets, which were always tied up with a ribbon, and once, seeing Chrissie watching her with such intensity, she flashed her a smile and Chrissie saw her eyes were a brilliant blue. That night, as they ate dinner, she told Eileen and Father John about her, saying she was the most beautiful girl she had ever seen and that her golden ringlets were tied back with a red ribbon.

Father John remembered the lost locket had ringlets tied

up with a red ribbon and felt an icy finger run down his spine as he said, 'How old is the girl?'

Chrissie wrinkled her nose as she thought and eventually said, 'Older than me. The sort of age when she should have left school.'

'Maybe she has.'

Chrissie shook her head. 'No, I overheard her talking to the librarians. She's very friendly with them. Seems she's at St Paul's.'

'Must be a clever girl then, for that is the only Roman Catholic girls' grammar school in the city,' Father John said. 'And, talking of Catholicism, it might be as well to get you baptised before you start school in September. I have explained the faith to you and I suppose you do want to become Catholic, don't you?'

Chrissie didn't care what religion she was, she'd have been happy with no religion at all, but she looked from Father John to Eileen and knew her becoming a Catholic was important to both of them. They had been so kind to her that if they'd asked her to dance on red-hot coals she would have considered it, and this was such a small thing to ask and so she said, 'Yes, Father John, I'd love to become a Catholic.'

Father John gave a sigh of relief. 'People would think living with a priest would be odd if you weren't a Catholic,' he said to Chrissie. 'And, quite apart from anything else, your mother was a Catholic.'

Chrissie was suddenly so very still she could hear the tick of the clock on the mantelpiece. Her eyes widened as she stared at the priest and into the strained silence Chrissie asked tentatively, 'Father John, do you know my mother?'

'No, my dear,' Father John said. 'I really wish I did.'

'But you said . . .'

'What your mother told me was in confession. You remember I told you I cannot repeat anything people tell me in confession.'

Chrissie nodded.

'I surmised that your mother was a Catholic as she sought absolution from God for a terrible crime she thought she had committed, but she wasn't one of my parishioners or I'd have recognised the voice.'

'What crime did she commit?'

Father John shook his head. 'That I cannot tell you, my dear. But I will say your mother said she loved you very much but was unable to care for you.'

'Why not?'

'You know John can't tell you that,' Eileen chided gently. 'He has already told you why. Now we really need to discuss your baptism, for that is the first step.'

So Chrissie was christened into the Catholic church so that she could be confirmed by the bishop the following spring along with boys and girls of similar age. It all seemed very strange to her. Aunt Eileen was what was called a godmother and Peter, one of Father John's brothers, a godfather. She had to stand by a bowl in the church Father John called a font and put her head back and he poured water all over her head.

Afterwards, Eileen made a little fancy tea for them all and Peter joined them but no one else because it was a bit of a secret thing. Chrissie didn't mind that, for she didn't know anyone she'd have liked to invite, but she did wonder why Auntie Eileen had insisted on secrecy and asked her to explain.

'As I was brought up Catholic,' Eileen said, 'if you had been the daughter of my best friend, the likelihood would be that so was she. In that case you would have already have been christened a Catholic when you were just a baby.'

'It's quite monstrous to have to go through such subterfuge,' Peter said. 'But necessary, I know. Many people seem to have such contempt for children from the workhouse, even though it's not their fault they ended up there. Incidentally, I applaud what you are doing and must say I think Chrissie a splendid girl.'

Chrissie blushed immediately, but she liked Peter. He was very like Father John in his mannerisms and his looks, only he wasn't a priest.

'My mother was a Catholic,' she said. 'So Father John said I had to be brought up a Catholic as well.'

'That's what the church says, all right,' Peter said to Chrissie and then he turned to Father John and said, 'I didn't know you knew the mother?'

'I don't,' Father John said. 'But she came to see me in confession and that fact alone would have pointed to her being a Catholic. The confession she made confirmed it.'

'But you have no idea who she is?'

Father John shook his head. 'None, except she is not from this parish for if she was I would have recognised her voice. I did ask her to wait but when I came out of the confessional there was no sign of her.' He looked across to Chrissie and said, 'I'm sorry, Chrissie.'

'It's all right,' Chrissie said. 'It wasn't your fault. It would be lovely if I could find my mother, but if I can't I would rather be here than anywhere else in the world.'

And Eileen was not the only one to lower her head so that Chrissie would not see the tears in her eyes.

Confession was a worry for Chrissie and she asked Eileen for advice.

'You confess what you have done wrong to the priest,' Eileen explained. 'He gives you a penance, prayers to say, and that's all there is to it.'

Chrissie, however, couldn't think of anything she was doing wrong. She had been so grateful at being taken from the workhouse and housed with these lovely, lovely people that she tried very hard not to put a foot wrong.

'It might have been easier to go to confession if I had still been in the workhouse,' she told Eileen.

'How's that?'

'Some warders were always telling us how wicked we were,' Chrissie said. 'Sometimes it started as soon as you raised your head from the flat, uncomfortable pillows, and it would go on through the day, though often I didn't know what I'd done to make them say that.'

'That is just silly,' Eileen said dismissively. 'You're not wicked. Let me see, do you always remember your morning and evening prayers?'

Chrissie coloured. 'The evening ones are always easier to remember,' she admitted.

'There you are then, that's one sin to confess.'

'Oh, I've thought of another,' Chrissie said. 'When I say I'm the orphaned daughter of your friend, or you say it and I agree, that's a lie, isn't it?'

'Well yes, I suppose it is, but could you imagine what

would happen if we let it be known that you were some little workhouse waif?'

Chrissie nodded. 'They would look down on me so I am glad we are telling a lie. Is it wrong to be glad you are telling a lie?'

Eileen smiled. 'Probably but not very.'

'Still, another one to add to the list and tell Father John.'

'I suppose so.'

However, Chrissie found the hardest thing about confession was telling someone she knew well and thought so much of all she had done wrong.

'He can tell no one,' Eileen said reassuringly. 'He can speak of nothing you tell him in confession.'

'I know,' Chrissie said. 'But it is his good opinion I care about before anyone else's really.'

'Chrissie, Father John will think no worse of you because of what you tell him.'

Chrissie wrinkled her nose. 'Maybe not now, but what if I was to do something really bad?'

'Like what?'

'Like, um . . . oh, I don't know, steal something perhaps.'

Eileen laughed, but gently. 'But you wouldn't steal anything anyway,' she said. 'You know that's wrong and wouldn't need Father John to tell you that. Remember, we are all given a conscience and free will. If you are tempted to do something you know is wrong, that is your conscience at work. If you ignore the conscience and go ahead anyway, you can do that because that's your free will.'

'And then you have to confess it to Father John?'

'Well yes, because if you don't the sin stays on your soul.'

Chrissie put her head on one side and a shy smile played

around her mouth as she said, 'You know, taking it all round, I think it's far better for me to stay on the straight and narrow.'

Eileen burst out laughing and blessed the young girl's blossoming personality.

Chrissie knew, however uncomfortable she felt about confession, she had to go through with it. Her soul had to be clean before she could take communion and it had already been noted that she didn't ever go to the rails at Mass on Sunday morning. Those who had the temerity to ask Eileen why had been told that the girl had been traumatised by the death of her family, but that she was now coming to terms with it. Many accepted that, for the child hadn't been to school either, and most said they were glad that she was eventually getting over it.

Before she went to confession for the first time, Eileen had given Chrissie a little red book. It was a catechism, the beliefs of the Catholic Church, and all children learnt it, so Eileen and Chrissie read a little bit of it every night. Chrissie tried to commit it to memory, beginning with the basic questions.

'Who made you?' Eileen would ask and Chrissie would answer, 'God made me.'

'Why did God make you?'

'God made me to know Him, love Him and serve Him in this world and be happy with Him forever in the next.'

And so on and Father John would test her at breakfast the following day. She picked up the catechism as quickly as she had reading and writing. She was also soon learning arithmetic, partly because she was bright and partly because she was desperate to please her new guardians, particularly Eileen, who she had begun to love deeply.

The first time she followed Eileen out of the pew to kneel at the rails of the altar to receive communion she was incredibly nervous, even though Father John and Eileen had gone over it the night before and she had seen many do it at Mass every Sunday. She watched what Eileen, who was beside her, did and put out her tongue and received the host, which melted away on her tongue as she returned to the pew. Father John had told her that it was not bread, that during the Mass it changed into the body of Christ. That made her feel a little bit sick but she didn't share that feeling, knowing even he might not understand. But still, she thought, if that's what they want me to do every Sunday – forego my breakfast so that I can take part in communion – then that's what I'll do.

In Father Branningan's parish, Angela and Connie sat together in silent prayer after taking communion. Angela's body was recovering from the miscarriage and she was starting to feel like her old self again. All of the business with Eddie and the aftermath was starting to feel like a bad dream. She often thought back to Father John's words about never knowing God's will and took comfort in them. Whatever she had done – and she truly felt ashamed and wanted to be forgiven – she knew in her heart that to have that poor baby boy had not been in God's plan for her. She hoped now that she could forget about these events and that she would never have to see Eddie McIntyre again.

Connie felt that she had got her real mother back again in the last few weeks. She was loving and kind and asked about her daughter's studies. Maybe they really could get back to where they had been before. As they left the church,

Connie thought it was a good moment to tell her mother about something that had happened recently.

'I ran into Daniel at the Bullring the other day.'

Angela was not too surprised – on a weekend the whole of the city seemed to come out – but she was surprised that Daniel would be out at the busy market with the fishwives and the city's hoi polloi.

'What was he doing there?' she asked.

'He said that it was Stan's birthday and he was going to get him a present from Woolworths.'

'Did he say how Stan was getting on in the shop?' Angela asked.

'He said it was going well, but that Stan was still learning the ropes. He said that he could do with someone who knew about how everything worked to help him out still as there was so much to learn.'

'Are you going to see Daniel again?'

Connie thought it was funny that her mother had asked that and that her attitude seemed to have mellowed.

'Well, now you ask, we did like seeing each other again and he asked me out for a walk on Sunday. I accepted.'

Angela thought about this. Connie and Daniel had been friends and it didn't now seem right that her falling-out with Stan should stand in the way of her daughter's own life. She was growing up and had to make her own decisions.

'Well, I think that's a good idea. He's a nice young man and going places.'

Connie smiled to herself – yes, this definitely seemed like the mother she knew and loved.

'Don't you think it's time to put your disagreement with

Stan aside, whatever it is? It can't really have been so bad after all this time?'

Angela didn't answer, for she wasn't sure herself. She had missed Stan so much, and knew that all the problems she'd had were a result of not having such a steady man in her life. But could they be friends again?

TWENTY-FIVE

In the early summer Eileen decided to take Chrissie into the Bullring to buy her some lighter clothes. It was their second visit; the first was when Chrissie was still fresh from the workhouse and not at all sure of Eileen. She had kept her head lowered most of the time and, thrilled though she was with the clothes, she had found it difficult to say anything and was glad that Eileen seemed to understand.

This visit to the Bullring was very different and, as they descended the incline, she said to Eileen (who always encouraged her to ask questions as she said that's how a person learnt), 'Who's he?'

She pointed to a statue of Nelson, standing on a plinth with metal railings around him, the whole thing ringed by flower sellers.

'Nelson,' Eileen said. 'He was a famous and very brave sea captain and so he is honoured with a statue.' And she added, 'When we pass by, sniff the air and it will be fragrant with the aroma of the beautiful flowers.'

Chrissie did just as Eileen suggested and thought she was

right – the smell was just magnificent. But neither had money to waste on flowers and so they wandered down the cobbled incline with barrows piled high with produce of every kind lining the road.

Opposite the barrows was a shop called Woolworths, which, Eileen told her, sold everything for sixpence or less. An old lady was standing outside and her strident voice rose above the clamorous chatter of the customers and the raucous calls of the costers shouting out their wares. She was selling carrier bags and determined to let everyone know about it as she cried out incessantly, 'Carrier bags. Handy carrier bags.'

'Been there years,' Eileen said in explanation to Chrissie. 'She's blind and every day, bar Sunday, her family bring her here and she sells the carrier bags.'

'D'you think she minds?'

Eileen shook her head. 'Doesn't appear to. I should imagine she is looked after by her family and this is her way of making a contribution. The alternative if her family couldn't afford to keep her would probably be the workhouse.'

'Oh, I'd sell the carrier bags and gladly,' Chrissie said so fervently that Eileen smiled.

But then Chrissie's attention was taken by the shop next door to Woolworths. It was called 'Hobbies' and Chrissie gazed at the wooden models of the planes, cars and ships of all shapes and sizes.

Eileen told her: 'People can buy kits inside to make the models themselves and lucky young boys might find one in their stocking at Christmas time.'

Chrissie was enchanted by the man selling mechanical spinning tops from his barrow. Seeing her interest, he wound one up and set it spinning.

'On the table, on the chairs, the little devils go everywhere,' he chanted. 'Only a tanner.'

Chrissie had clapped her hands with pleasure at the sight of the brightly coloured tops weaving all over the table, but she had to shake her head.

'They are lovely, but I have no money.' Eileen said nothing, but silently decided one of them could easily find its way into Chrissie's stocking at Christmas.

'Now we are crossing the market to the Rag Market at the side of the church,' Eileen said. Chrissie nodded and she went on, 'Watch out for the trams. Some of them come hurtling round in front of St Martin's like the very devil and there might be a fair few dray horses pulling wagons as well.'

Accordingly, Chrissie took care as they approached the church. It was beautiful, built of light-coloured bricks with stained-glass windows set in ornate frames and an enormous steeple pointing heavenwards. There were iron railings surrounding it, though these were mainly hidden behind trees, and here and there were more flower sellers.

They soon reached the Rag Market and after Eileen had bought Chrissie some summer-weight clothes – dresses and skirts and blouses and cardigans – Chrissie was so overcome with gratitude she could again barely speak. Eileen understood when she saw tears standing out in Chrissie's eyes. To give the girl time to compose herself, and also distract her a little, she led the way to the Market Hall, for, as she remarked as they left the clothes stall, 'We didn't take time to see it last time we were here.'

The Market Hall was a very imposing building built in the Gothic style with large arched windows either side of the stone steps. But Chrissie barely saw the grandeur of it once she saw the men on the steps. All of them were shabbily and inadequately dressed, though some had threadbare long coats that Eileen explained were the greatcoats given to soldiers. Their boots were well cobbled and they had greasy caps rammed on their heads, hiding most of their grey faces, and all of them had trays around their necks selling razor blades and shoelaces and matchsticks.

Eileen watched Chrissie covertly but she said nothing till they were inside the hall itself where the noise was tremendous. Eileen had thought she might have been impressed by the building itself, knowing she would have seen nothing like it for the ceilings were lofty and criss-crossed with beams and poles led down from the beams to hold up the roof. High arched windows lined one side with smaller arched windows at the ends, spilling summer sunshine into the Market Hall and lighting up the stalls of every description that lay before them.

However, all this was lost on Chrissie, who turned to Eileen and asked her who the men were and why they had been on the steps. When Eileen explained that they were old soldiers who had no work, and that many had not had a job since being demobbed from the army, she felt sadness envelop her. She couldn't tell Eileen why the sight upset her so much, for Eileen and Father John didn't like her mentioning the workhouse, but she had seen men in there with deadened eyes and grey, pinched faces like the men on the steps.

Eileen might not have understood why Chrissie had been so affected by the old lags, but she knew she was truly miserable. The first place she led her to was Pimm's pet stall and, when they reached it, Chrissie's mood lifted immediately and she stared at the animals, enthralled. She'd never even come near an animal of any description. The canaries twittered around them in their cages and Chrissie was enchanted, then knelt down to look into the large boxes on the floor. One held mewling kittens that she stroked gently and in the other one boisterous puppies tumbled over one another in their eagerness to get to Chrissie and she laughed when they nipped her fingers playfully. She saw fish swimming serenely around in large tanks and cuddly baby rabbits and guinea pigs in cages. She was allowed to cuddle some of the smaller creatures and they left the pet shop reluctantly to find the cacophony of noise outside had decreased a little.

There was an air of expectancy in the air and Eileen said, 'They must be waiting for the clock to strike.' She indicated the clock on the wall edging towards ten o'clock. It was a beautiful device made of wood and very intricately carved. Suddenly Chrissie watched fascinated as three knights and a lady emerged to strike a bell ten times, causing a tantalising tune to play before the hours were struck.

'Oh, isn't it just lovely?' Chrissie breathed.

'It is,' Eileen agreed. 'And a pity the man who made it wasn't paid in full for it.'

'Oh, surely that's wrong?'

'Of course it's wrong but it happens. The clock was in an arcade in Dale End then. The man was supposed to put a curse on it – not,' Eileen warned, 'that you and I believe in such things, but people say that's why the arcade failed to thrive and now it's here.'

All in all, Eileen judged the trip to the Bullring a success, but she knew Chrissie could still be marked out as different for she had seen and done nothing outside of her workhouse walls for eleven years. Therefore she set about taking Chrissie out and about. They went to Calthorpe Park and Cannon Hill, and one day took a train to Sutton Park, and they visited museums and places of history around Birmingham and even visited the cinema a couple of times. Chrissie had been astounded by Eileen's generosity of spirit and she felt her mind extending with the kind of education that she wouldn't find in books.

Not that the library wasn't still important to them both and, all through that long summer, whenever Chrissie went to the library, the girl with the golden curls was there. She was usually not choosing books herself but replacing books on shelves and Chrissie had even seen her behind the counter stamping the books to go out. She was far too shy to talk to her though and, as if the girl knew this, one day she smiled at the younger girl and said, 'Hello. My name's Connie. What's yours?'

Chrissie was so awed at this beautiful girl talking to her that she was almost struck dumb. Fortunately, she recovered herself enough to answer and tell the older girl her name and to say what pretty hair she had. Connie said she had inherited both the colour and the waves from her mother and she added, 'Your hair is a lovely dark brown and very shiny. Maybe you take after your mother too.'

For a split second, Chrissie almost told this girl the truth about her parentage, but she stopped herself in time, sticking instead to the story Eileen had thought up to explain her appearance at the presbytery.

Connie was intrigued. 'Growing up with a priest,' she said incredulously. 'Never heard of that before. Is it interesting or is it grim? Is he very strict?'

Chrissie's laugh was almost too loud for the hushed library

and she went on in a whisper, 'Father John is soft and, if it wasn't for his sister, Eileen, he would allow himself to be walked over and never have a minute to himself. She can be strict about that sometimes, but she is kindness itself to me.'

'I'm glad about that at least,' Connie said.

'Not as glad as I am,' Chrissie said and the two girls smiled at one another.

The summer eventually drew to a close and in September Connie began at St Paul's grammar school where she would stay two years to do her Highers. There, for the first time, she met girls who worked as hard as she did. She was no longer thought an oddity or called a 'swot', and so she was much happier at school.

At the same time, Chrissie began at St Catherine for her last two years of basic schoolwork. Although the school was told the truth of where Chrissie had come from, they agreed that no one else needed to be informed, and Chrissie fitted into school seamlessly. Many had seen Chrissie at Mass and were intrigued because she lived in the priest's house, and because Eileen had taught her well she didn't find the school-work unnecessarily arduous.

As the days folded one into another, she looked forward to her twelfth birthday just before Christmas and the birthday tea Eileen had planned for her.

'Maybe next year you can have a few pals to share your birthday with you,' Eileen said.

'Maybe,' Chrissie said, for she was making friends, which was a novel experience for her. Her innate shyness had prevented her from inviting anyone this year as she'd been afraid no one would come.

One night, Chrissie was in bed and Eileen was saying goodnight when the knock came to the door. This wasn't an unusual occurrence, for there always seemed to be someone in need of a priest somewhere and so Father John opened the door with a slight sigh and was surprised to see Benedict Masters outside.

'Come in, come in,' he said.

'I will,' Masters said. 'And I think I can safely say that you will be very glad to see me before you are much older.' As Father John ushered him into the living room he pulled a small box from his pocket and placed it in his hand. 'Open it.'

Father John opened it with fingers that shook and there, nestling on a bed of cotton wool, was the lost locket. Eileen heard her brother's gasp of surprise and entered the room as Father John lifted the locket from the box and held it dangling from his fingers.

'Is that the locket you told me about?' she asked.

'The very same,' said Father John. 'Praise be to God.'

His eyes stung and a lump formed in his throat. He was overcome with happiness that the locket had turned up.

'I'll tell you how I came upon it,' Benedict Masters said. 'First of all, as I lost my job when the workhouse closed, I am employed at the hospital as an administrator – which means general dogsbody. Anyway, when the workhouse was cleared out, although all the inmates' beds went for scrap, I retained some of the staff beds – those in good condition – and had them stored in the cellar. I did wonder if it was a waste of time because they had all special hospital beds on the wards.

'And then this year they built an annexe for those patients

386

who were recovering but not yet fit to go home. They were talking about buying beds for this annexe so they could transfer the patients there and free up the hospital beds for the more seriously sick and suddenly I remembered the mattresses in the cellar. The hospital said they were more than suitable. We'd just begun carrying the mattresses up to the annexe when I noticed a slit in one of them and put it aside to dispose of it. But then I noticed inside the slit was a small folded piece of paper and I pulled it out and it was a pawn ticket.'

'A pawn ticket?'

'Yes,' Masters said. 'Not that I thought it had anything to do with the locket, but the address of the pawn shop was on the ticket. It was a dingy little place in Needless Alley and there was the locket. I couldn't have been more delighted and lost no time in redeeming it.'

'Nothing is missing at any rate,' Father John said, opening it. 'Look Eileen, there's the photograph of some long-ago wedding one side and those blonde ringlets tied with a red ribbon in the other.'

'Chrissie will be delighted to have this,' Eileen said. 'It's a beautiful piece of jewellery anyway, but what is inside must be something to do with the family she came from. Oh thank you, Mr Masters, this will mean so much to one young girl.'

And so it proved. The following morning, as they sat eating breakfast, Father John said, 'Chrissie, what do you know about the day you arrived at the workhouse?'

Chrissie was surprised at the question because both Father John and Aunt Eileen had said she must wipe her years at the workhouse from her mind as if they didn't exist. She hadn't been able to do that fully, but she knew they wouldn't want to hear that so she never mentioned it to them. Now she said, 'Someone left me on the workhouse steps and I was called Christine, because it was nearly Christmas, and Foley because that was the name of the warder who found me.'

'It was your mother who left you there,' Father John said. 'But it wasn't her fault. Without betraying the things she admitted to me in confession, I can say no more, apart from telling you she gave you the most precious item she owned to show you how much you were loved, and how sorry she was that she was unable to care for you herself.'

Perplexed, Chrissie asked, 'What did she give me?'

Father John withdrew the box from his pocket and took out the locket.

'This,' he said. 'You were holding it in your hand when you were found.'

Chrissie stared at the locket, awestruck. She withdrew it from the velvet box and dangled it from her fingers, overcome that she was holding something that her mother had given to her. Even if she was never able to trace her, the locket would always remind her that out there somewhere was a mother who loved her.

'You weren't allowed personal possessions in the workhouse,' Father John said. He didn't wish to go into the business of someone stealing it and pawning it, and just said, 'When the workhouse closed down it was mislaid and Mr Masters found it and brought it round yesterday.'

'Open it,' Eileen suggested.

Until then, Chrissie hadn't been aware it opened, and she gave a cry of surprise as she did so. The golden ringlets reminded her of the girl in the library, but the picture at any rate took all her attention.

'It's a wedding at a guess,' Eileen said.

Chrissie looked at the dour faces and the odd clothes and said, 'My parents, do you think?'

'Grandparents more likely.'

'Oh,' Chrissie breathed. 'Somewhere, I may have a whole proper family.'

The emotion in Chrissie's voice and the wistful look in her eyes caused Eileen's own eyes to water and to cover herself she said to Chrissie, 'Shall we put it in the box now to keep it safe?'

'Oh no,' Chrissie said. 'I want to wear it near to my heart always.'

Eileen didn't argue with the child, she just fastened the locket around her neck. Chrissie smiled, touching it with her fingertips and thinking about the mother who loved her enough to leave her this keepsake.

Angela stood outside George Maitland's old shop and marvelled at how bright and neat it looked from the outside. All the bad years when Matilda and her sister had left it to wrack and ruin were just a distant memory and Harry, and now Stan, were doing her old boss proud.

Through the glass windows Angela could see Stan serving customers inside. In his pristine white overalls he looked a little different and with a few more grey hairs too. She patted herself down, wondering what he would make of her now and hoping that the time that had passed had allowed some of his feelings to soften towards her.

She didn't know if she could ever tell him the truth about Chrissie and the child at the workhouse, but she was determined to make amends, to be the friend to him that he had been to her, for herself and for Barry. She could see now that she had let all the emotions over her workhouse child cloud everything else. But now that Chrissie was safe and cared for, she could see more clearly.

Angela pushed a stray hair out of her eyes and, holding her head high, stepped inside Stan's shop . . .

If you liked this book, why not dip into another one of Anne Bennett's fantastic stories?

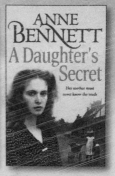

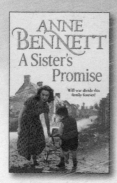
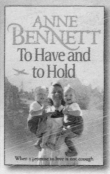
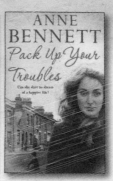

'The beauty of Anne's books is that they are about normal people and are sewn through with human emotions which affect us all'

Birmingham Post